BUTTERFLY
KISSES

Detective Damien Drake

Book 1

Patrick Logan

I only ask to be free.

The butterflies are free.

-Charles Dickens

Prologue

THE MAN WIPED SWEAT from his brow and then hooked two fingers between his tie and throat and yanked it loose. Heart racing, he stumbled into the alley, heading toward the single light that cast a jaundiced glow over a metal door roughly halfway down the narrow passage.

He hurried towards the door, no longer attempting to avoid the puddles that threatened to soak his custom alligator loafers.

A delicate splash, like a marble being dropped into a swimming pool, sounded from somewhere behind him and he whipped his head around. Squinting, trying to force his eyes to focus, he scanned the alley.

Where are you? What do you want from me?

Remaining completely still, the man waited. When the sound didn't recur, and he didn't detect so much as a flicker of movement in the shadows, he turned his attention back to the door.

His searching hand confirmed what he already suspected: the door had no exterior handle.

There was no way to open it from the alley.

The man swore, then, as much as he was opposed to the idea of being seen here, in this place, this alley, he realized that he had no other choice.

Not with *him* coming.

With a deep breath, he made a fist and pounded against the door.

"Hey! Anyone in there! *Hey!*" he shouted. "Hey! Open up! Please!"

The man's voice was strangely tight, almost unrecognizable to even himself.

With the hand not pounding on the door, he reached into his suit jacket pocket and pulled out his cell phone, hoping that it had recharged while lying dormant.

Just enough to turn on, to make a single call.

"Hey! Anybody in there?"

His heart fluttered in his chest when rubbing his thumb over the button near the bottom failed to illuminate the screen. He swore again and slipped the dead phone back into his pocket. Desperation reaching a fever pitch, knowing that the man couldn't be far behind, he used both hands to pound on the door now all the while shouting for someone to open up, to open the *goddamn door*.

Something fluttered beside his ear, and the man yanked his head away, a scream caught in his throat. He swatted about his head madly with a free hand, his heart jackhammering in his chest so hard that he thought it might burst from his ribcage and thrum across the concrete alley like a gnat on a steel drum.

"No," he moaned, trying to evade the flying insect that seemed to have taken a keen interest in him. "It can't be."

The insect banked hard to avoid his palm, and the light reflected off its wings.

"Please. That was so long ago," the man whimpered, *"Please."*

The yellow light above the door reflected off the insect's wings and for a brief moment, he thought that it *was* a Monarch butterfly, with beautiful orange wings segmented by smooth black lines.

It can't be—it's too early for butterflies... it—it can't be.

But then the flying insect drifted upward toward the light, and he realized that it wasn't a butterfly. It was just a generic moth, drawn, much like he had been, to the only light in the alley.

And yet this realization did nothing to slow his racing heart.

On the verge of hyperventilating, he pounded on the door again.

Monarch or not, he knew that this wasn't over.

Not yet.

"Please, someone—"

And then, unbelievably, the door *did* open, if only a crack.

"Shifty, that you? Whatchu doin' out der at 3 AM? Whatchu—" a woman's scratchy voice demanded.

The man didn't hesitate.

He thrust his manicured fingers into the two-inch gap between the door and frame and gripped it tightly. The woman immediately tried to pull the door closed again.

"You ain't Shifty," she said, a tremor in her voice. The door was crushing his fingers now, but he didn't care.

Nothing in this world would make him let go now.

The sound of footfalls in puddles in the alley behind him forced the man into action. Gripping the door tightly, ignoring the pain as the metal bit into his knuckles, he pulled with all his might.

At first, the woman in the dark interior of what he thought might have been a crack den, resisted, but she was no match for his strength, for his determination.

After all, she didn't know what was chasing him.

The woman cried out. She had been trying so hard to keep the door closed that when it was finally swung wide, she went with it, her rail-thin body thrown into the alley.

The man saw her emaciated arms peppered with red track marks, her damp, mangy hair, and sunken eyes as she flew by him.

"You ain't Shifty!" she cried, as she pulled herself to her feet in an action that was all knees and elbows. "You ain't Shifty!"

The man ignored her and stepped inside the pitch-black building. As he did, the toe of one of his loafers clipped something lying on the floor. The object skittered across the surface, which seemed uncharacteristically soft, like sand or dirt. It made a *whoop whoop whoop* sound as it receded into the darkness before it struck something hard and exploded into what could only be breaking glass.

Where are the lights? Where are the lights? His mind screamed. *Where the hell are the lights?*

He ran his hands along the wall, ignoring the rough texture that scratched his palms.

"You ain't Shifty!" the woman screamed from the alley, her voice even more shrill now.

That's good; keep yelling, wake others.

"Shifty gonna come back and he gonna—"

Her words came to an abrupt halt, and without looking back, the man stumbled deeper into the building, frantically rubbing the walls now, desperate for a light switch that didn't seem to exist.

Sweat dripped down his forehead and stung his eyes.

Just when he was about to give up hope, his fingers struck something jutting from the wall.

Yes! His mind screamed.

He flicked the switch up.

Nothing happened.

He flicked it down.

Still nothing.

Close to tears now, he flicked the switch up and down repeatedly, as if trying to manually prime a building whose only electricity seem to feed the sickly yellow bulb in the alley.

"Please," he moaned. "It was—"

But a gloved hand slipped around his nose and mouth from behind, cutting off his sentence just as it had done to the crackhead in the alley.

He screamed, but the sound was muffled by thick leather. His own hands grabbed for the glove, tore at it, trying to peel it from his face.

But the grip was just too strong.

Something sharp pricked him in the side of the neck, just above the collar of his dress shirt. And then... nothing.

Time seemed to slow, and he thought that the hand on his face was loosening.

Hope crept into him like a virus. Hope that he might just make it out of here after all. That the man would let him go, forgive him his sins, his transgressions, like a compassionate priest or chaplain.

But then he felt a deep burning sensation in his throat and lungs, a burning that flooded his system with such intensity that it dropped him to his knees.

From there, the man was lowered gently to the ground, before being flipped onto his back. This deep into the building, the darkness was all-encompassing, but the man in the alligator loafers thought he saw something in the blackness nonetheless.

A butterfly.

A beautiful Monarch butterfly spreading its wings and ascending toward the heavens.

And then it, like the man in the suit, was gone.

PART I - Caterpillar

Chapter 1

A GUNSHOT SHOCKED NYPD Detective Damien Drake from his slumber. His hand immediately slid between his jacket and shirt, his fingers searching for the gun buried in the holster beneath his armpit.

He blinked once, twice, then moved his hand away from the butt of his gun. Breathing heavily, he worked his fingers into the pocket of his worn sport coat, and squeezed the small, glass bottle between thumb and forefinger.

As he teased the miniature bottle of Johnny Walker Red Label out, he tried to stretch his legs, pushing his feet into the floor of the car between the gas and brake. He groaned, then closed his eyes for a moment.

He had heard a gunshot, but it hadn't come from outside.

It had been in his head.

As had been the face of his partner, Clay Cuthbert, his eyes wide, moist.

His pale cheeks hollow with the tangible wrench of terror.

Drake heard another sound now, but unlike the gunshot, this one was real: the unmistakable *clink* of metal tabs breaking as he unscrewed the cap on the miniature.

When he opened his eyes again, he was surprised that the sun had decided that today it would finally shake free of its frosty shroud. For March in New York City, this was no less than a formidable feat.

As Drake brought the bottle to his lips and took a sizable gulp, he observed the squat brick building with the circular drive outside his window, his eyes skipping along the fence that cordoned off a small park.

I must have been out for three hours, he thought, unwilling to confirm or deny this by expending the effort to look at his worn Timex.

He supposed he could have looked at the digital clock embedded in the dashboard, but he had never bothered to set the damn thing. For twelve years he had owned the creme-colored Crown Victoria, and yet in none of that time had he bothered to fiddle with the damn thing. Unlike the sun, some things just weren't worth the effort or frustration.

He grunted and took another sip. Aware that the interior of his car reeked of stale sweat and staler alcohol, he cracked the window an inch, relishing the familiarity of smog-tinged air.

The sound of a bell ringing cut through the miasma that filled the Crown Vic. This time, Drake stopped his hand before it made it to the butt of his gun.

Cut it out. Get control of yourself.

As if to prove to himself that he was indeed in control, he finished the miniature, screwed the cap back on, and tossed it to the floor of the passenger seat. When it clanged against several other bottles, he cringed, expecting to hear the sound of glass breaking. But after several more clinks, it eventually settled, and he relaxed his shoulders.

The damn things were usually made of plastic, anyway.

The muscles in his upper back had tightened, and the fact that he had slept in his car more nights than a bed since his suspension had started had done nothing in terms of making him more accustomed to the conditions.

Isn't the body supposed to adapt? Get used to shitty thoughts, shittier accommodations?

A gaggle of children, ranging by Drake's estimation to be anywhere between five and fifteen years of age, flooded out of the side door of the school as if the building itself was regurgitating them. Their high-pitched squeals of glee, jubilant cries, and amorphous grunts filtered up to him through the crack in his window, and he instantly regretted opening it. And yet he made no move to close it.

Instead, he watched their smooth faces, most lineless even in smile, his gaze following them across a paved area with basketball hoops that hadn't seen an actual net for longer than most had been alive.

The younger kids—Drake only identified them as such as they seemed to have not yet gained the insight of self-awareness, their eyes locking in on a play structure without first darting to their friends for approval—went mostly to the swings and slides, while the older kids moved toward the giant field at the back of the school. The field was bordered by chipped white soccer goalposts, but during all the days Drake had parked outside Hockley Middle and High School, he had never actually seen anyone playing soccer.

Or basketball, for that matter.

As the kids spread out and their incessant drone became more diffuse, Drake found himself staring at three boys with spiked hair and backpacks adorned with chrome spikes and patches from bands that he didn't recognize. They shuffled instead of walked, their heavy boots barely rising off first the paved basketball area then the newly shorn grass field. The teenager on the left, who was two or three inches taller than the others and sported long blond hair that nearly reached his shoulders, leered at a much younger girl in a miniskirt.

The boy said something, and while Drake was too far to pick out the exact words, and an experienced lip reader he was not, the toothy expression on the kid's face said enough.

The girl responded sharply, and her grimace allowed an exchange to play out in Drake's mind.

The boy stopped smiling and the trio tucked behind the school, their backs pressing up against the wall.

What are they doing?

But when the blond boy, eyes darting again, reached into his backpack, Drake felt a sudden pang in his chest.

Columbine was a long time removed, and now most everyone in NYC expected the next attack to come from a dark-skinned man speaking Arabic, Drake still felt on edge.

Without thinking, his hand snaked over to the door handle, and he gripped the warm metal tightly, ready to pounce.

He let go when the boy pulled out a worn pack of Marlboro's and furtively held it out to his friends.

What the hell is wrong with you? Get a grip!

Drake took a deep breath and looked away from the wannabe punk rockers smoking cigarettes, his eyes drifting back to the front of the school.

And that's when he saw her. At first, he tried not to overreact—*it's not her, just like the cigarettes weren't miniature pipe bombs*—but as he stared more intently, he realized that it *could* be her. Her back was to him, a pink backpack slung over one shoulder, her long, straight, brown hair descending halfway down her back. She was wearing tight dark jeans and a pair of worn Converse sneakers. A white blouse clung to her thin shoulders.

It's her.

Drake swallowed hard and grabbed the door handle again, although this time he wasn't trying to strangle the metal.

Instead, he pulled gently, and the door opened. Warm air rushing against his face, which he only now realized was covered in a thin layer of sweat.

As Drake stepped out of his Crown Vic, another car pulled up beside the girl and the window slowly lowered. She turned and must have recognized the person inside, as she walked over to the car and leaned on the half-open window.

Now in profile, Drake knew it was her. He recognized that nose, straight but thin, and the long eyelashes, full lips.

Drake closed his car door and started toward her, wondering who this person in the car was.

The girl suddenly threw her head back and laughed, her long hair quivering like a cape.

Squinting hard, knowing that he shouldn't be here, that he was overreacting, he peered through the rearview window of the Mercedes.

It was a man, he concluded. And judging by the way the shadow of his hair was thinning, it was an older man at that.

No, this isn't right.

Drake realized that his hands were balled into fists, and he slowly forced them open.

It's nothing. A teacher, maybe. A friend's father. Don't overreact, Drake. Don't lose it again.

But when the girl reached for the door and started to open it, all rational thought fled him.

She's going to get in the car and never be seen again!

He broke into a jog.

"Suze!" he yelled. "Suze, don't get in the car!"

But either the shouts from the kids playing in the playground or the music that he could now hear coming from the car window were too loud and the girl didn't hear him.

He picked up his pace as she started to lower herself into the car seat.

You're never going to see her again. Never. Kidnapped. Raped. Murdered. And it will all be your fault.

"Suze!" he yelled. "Suzan, *don't get in the car!*"

The girl turned, and when their eyes met, the smile slid off her pretty face.

Hatred burned in those dark hazel eyes.

Even before she raised her hand and flipped him the bird, he realized what was going to happen. She started to close the door, and he could see her lips moving.

Go, let's go, she was saying to the driver, who had turned his head around in response to his shouts.

Drake could see what was happening, and there was only one way he figured he could stop it.

If Suzan left in that car, she would be gone forever. For some reason, he was sure of this.

Damien Drake reached into the holster under his left armpit and pulled out his pistol.

"*Get away from the car, Suze! Get the hell away!*"

Chapter 2

"NOW, SUZE. DON'T EVEN think about it," Drake said. Even though he was speaking to the girl with the backpack, he wasn't aiming the gun at her. Instead, the barrel was focused squarely on the shadow of the man's head in the rearview window.

"What the hell are you doing?" she snapped back, her thin eyebrows knitting together. Her face had turned a deep shade of scarlet. "Put the damn gun away!"

Drake shook his head.

"Not until you get away from the car," he repeated.

The driver side door suddenly flew open and a thin man hauled himself out of the Mercedes.

"What is going—" he began but stopped when his eyes fell on the gun in Drake's hand. Unlike Suzan, any color that he might have had in his narrow face drained away.

Without so much as uttering a word, he immediately tried to slide back into the driver seat.

Drake didn't let him.

"Get out!" he shouted.

The man's eyes darted from Drake's face to the gun, and back again giving the detective just enough time to think *don't do it* before the man leaped into his car.

Drake swore and rushed at him, lowering the gun to his hip.

Thankfully the window was open, and Drake grabbed the opening before the man could put the car into drive.

"Get out of the car, now," he hissed. For a split second, Drake thought that the man—who he now saw was in his mid-forties, sharply dressed in a maroon V-neck and a pale gray sport coat—was going to put the car into drive anyway.

But when he raised the gun again, not quite putting it in the window, but just raising it high enough that the sun glinted off the silver barrel, the man withdrew his right hand from the gear shift and held it up with his left.

Drake opened the door and then twisted his fingers into the collar of the man's sport coat.

"Get out," he grumbled. This time he helped the man complete the request by yanking him from the vehicle.

"I don't know who you are, but I'm gonna call the fucking cops," the man said. At that moment, he must have realized that others were around them now, standing a respectable distance from Drake and his gun.

Anywhere else, they might have run screaming or thrown themselves to the ground and covered the backs of their heads with trembling hands.

But this was NYC; they didn't run when they saw a gun. Instead, they watched.

And their presence seemed to imbue the man with courage.

"Call the police! Someone call the police on this psycho!"

"Shut up," Drake spat. His fingers still gripping the collar of a very expensive feeling sport coat, Drake spun the man around and shoved him gruffly up against the car. Then he leaned in close, smelling his own whiskey-tinged breath even before he spoke. "You think you can come here in broad daylight and kidnap a teenager? You think you can—"

"Someone call the police!" the man yelled. Drake pulled back then shoved again. The man's nose bounced off the hood of the car and he groaned. Yet despite his obvious pain, he never stopped yelling. "Call the police! Help! Help! Call the cops!"

Drake grit his teeth.

"You better—"

"He *is* the police!" Suzan suddenly shouted. "He is the *fucking* police!"

And with this, the man with the now bloodied nose clammed up.

"Yeah, that's right," Drake said, tugging the gold shield off his belt and flashing it in front of the man's face as he looked over his shoulder. "You think in broad daylight you can drive around in your fancy car, wearing your fancy suit and lure young girls into your car? In front of a *cop?* You cocky—"

Someone grabbed his arm, and Drake roughly shrugged the hand off. When the voice that cried out was young and female, he turned.

Suzan was standing a foot behind him, tears spilling down her cheeks as she massaged her palm.

"He's not a pervert," she said quietly.

Drake's grip on the man's jacket loosened.

"Suze, sweetie, you don't know that. He may seem nice, and I don't know what he offered you to get into his car, but men like this… I *know* men like this. All they want is—"

Drake bit his tongue.

The girl was already terrified, and nothing could be gained by making inferences to other crimes that her father had gone to great lengths to protect her from.

She was shaking her head, and as he watched her hands went to her face, cradling her soft features.

In the distance, Drake thought he heard a police siren. And then he was outside of himself, watching the scene play out before him not as the orchestrator, but as one of the bold spectators.

What the hell am I doing?

Drake's hands fell to his sides, and the man on the car managed to flip around, only he was no longer clean-shaven, with neatly, if thin, cropped hair and gold spectacles framing his narrow face.

Instead, *this* man had a thick brown beard and dark eyes. Eyes that were welling with tears.

It was Clay Cuthbert's face, his partner's face, moments before he died.

"Wha—" Drake croaked as he stumbled backward. If it hadn't been for Suzan standing behind him, he might have fallen on his ass.

"He's not a creep," Suze said angrily. "He's my fucking psychiatrist!"

Drake shook his head and turned to look at her.

"Your *what?*"

"My psychiatrist!" she screamed. And then, completely unexpectedly, Suze slapped him across the chest with both hands.

"Suze—"

"Don't fucking *Suze* me! Only my dad calls me that!" she slapped him again, and Drake moved away. "You fucking ruined everything! *Everything!* Why don't you just leave me alone?"

Drake was shocked to the point of silence.

Psychiatrist? Why was a seventeen-year-old girl seeing a psychiatrist?

But he already knew the answer; after Clay had been killed, the use of a psychiatrist had not only been offered to all members of NYPD Homicide but had been encouraged.

And this offer had been extended to their families, of course.

Suzan's face was a mess, the tears streaming down her face spreading what little makeup she wore in streams like melted crayons.

"You ruined everything!"

Drake swallowed hard and slipped the gun back into the holster under his armpit.

"I'm sorry," he said quietly, holding back tears of his own. Now it was his turn to look around. Children stared at him from between the bars of the fence, the black metal framing their faces as if they were being held in a pediatric prison. Teachers stood gape-mouthed, clipboards clutched to their chests so tightly that a small breeze might cause the particle board to snap.

Parents were frozen half-in and half-out of cars that cost at least five times as much as his own.

What the fuck are you doing, Drake? What are you doing?

"I—I—I'm sorry," he stammered. He pulled his detective shield out again, this time holding it up for everyone to see. "NYPD—this is all just... just a terrible misunderstanding. Please, there is no danger here. Go back to your... to your classes."

Drake was saying the words loud enough for every bystander to hear, but they were only meant for one person: the terrified girl standing with her hands at her sides, her long hair now draped in front of her face.

"I'm sorry."

And then he turned and hurried back to his car.

"You got blood on my shirt!" the psychiatrist called after him. "I'm sending you the dry-cleaning bill, asshole!"

Drake's own face was burning now, and his ears felt as if they were on fire. He knew that everyone was staring at him, but Drake's only focus was on his rusty Crown Vic.

His hands were shaking, and when he was finally within the safe confines of his vehicle he reached into his pocket for another miniature. And he would have pulled it out too, right there with everyone watching, when time unexpectedly burped forward and the sound of kids resuming their games as if nothing had happened reminded him of where he was.

Clutching the bottle inside his pocket, he used his other hand to slip the car into drive and sped off, trying his best not to look at anyone, Suzan Cuthbert included.

Chapter 3

DRAKE WIPED THE WHISKEY from his lips with the back of his hand and was about to reach for another when the radio on the passenger seat suddenly squawked.

"Detective Drake?"

It had been six months since his radio had come alive with all the clarity of an AM station in the Lincoln Tunnel. The first month, he had checked the batteries nearly every day, making sure that they were still good, hoping that he would hear his name being called.

The second month, he had kept it close to his side.

By the third month, he had begun to loathe the thing, and now, sixth months after his partner's murder, it held all the appeal of a rotten banana.

"Drake?" the staticky voice chirped again.

Drake cleared his throat and grabbed the radio. No matter what had happened, he still had a job to do.

"Drake here," he said, surprised at how calm and even his voice sounded.

"A body was found in an abandoned warehouse in Clinton Hill this morning."

What, no welcome back, Drake? No, we missed you, Damien?

His brow furrowed and his brain immediately started to formulate a scenario based only on those four words: *abandoned warehouse, Clinton Hill.*

"Where in the Hill?"

"Luther Avenue."

And with that, his narrative was nearly complete.

"Junkie? Tweeker?"

There was a short pause.

"No. Well-dressed man, expensive shoes."

The narrative dissolved.

Expensive shoes?

"Is it—"

"Just get there, Drake."

The radio clicked, and Drake pushed his lips together, surprised by the dispatcher's curtness. He debated pushing the button and asking more questions, but the abrupt tone and end to the conversation changed his mind.

Drake suddenly wished that he had more whiskey left, but the only bottle remaining in his car was Listerine. He filled his mouth, swished, spat, and then started his car.

Twenty minutes later, he arrived at his first crime scene in six months.

There were more squad cars than Drake expected, even if the victim had been wearing "expensive shoes". Clinton Hill was no stranger to its share of homicides, but most were drug-related, usually involving local residents.

The last time he had been in the neighborhood, he had been investigating a small-time meth pusher who had been murdered by repeated blows to his head with a towel rack of all things.

Three staggered police cars blocked the entrance to a narrow alley, and Drake had already been forced to weave between two others to gain access to the adjoining street.

Drake parked next to one of the squad cars, briefly smelled his breath and then stepped out into the sun.

He had taken maybe three steps before a man in uniform approached. He opened his mouth to say something, but Drake held up his shield before he got a word out.

"Detective Drake," he said, lips pressed together tightly. "Homicide."

The uniform was a dark black man with a bristly mustache and light-colored eyes as if he was wearing tinted contacts. As a policeman for a decade, and a homicide detective for four years, Drake thought he knew most, if not all, of the beat cops in NYC. Not *everyone*, surely, there were over thirty-thousand of New York's Finest on payroll, but someone like this, a man in his mid-to-late forties, in this neighborhood, he should have definitely come across in the past.

But while he was a stranger to Drake, the way the uniform looked at him, as if Drake had uttered a blaspheme in church, suggested some recognition on his part.

Drake made a face.

"And? The body?"

Dark lids slid over gray eyes in a slow blink.

"Sorry, come with me please, Detective."

The lean black man, who hadn't offered his name in return, briskly walked toward the alley. Several of the other officers that they passed stared at them, and it was all Drake could do not to stare back, to ask them what the hell they were looking at.

His first thought was that Suzan's psychiatrist had called him in, or worse, placed a complaint. But given his history, he knew that the strangely silent radio now clipped to his hip would have crackled like the Fourth of July if that were the case.

You're imagining things just like back at the school, he scolded himself.

They had nearly reached the yellow police tape with the ubiquitous *CRIME SCENE DO NOT CROSS* written on it, when a young woman, not much older than Suzan herself, came toward him. She was short, maybe five-four, with dark brown hair tucked neatly behind her ears. Her eyes, which were locked on him, were a brilliant green color, but aside from them and a slight blush to her cheeks, her face was otherwise devoid of color.

A reporter? Some broad straight out of NYU trying to boost her blog ratings? How did she get past the uniforms?

Drake reached out and put a hand on the officer's shoulder in front of him.

"Hey, what's she doing here? She a reporter? I—" *hate reporters,* he was about to say, when the man shrugged him off awkwardly and continued forward.

Before he could speak again, the woman, for despite her short stature and smallish features he now saw was in her mid-thirties, lifted the yellow tape and tilted her head as an invitation for him to duck under.

"Homicide Detective Damien Drake," he said curtly. The woman nodded and again gestured for him to pass under the tape.

This time he obliged.

When he was on the other side, she turned and started down what he now saw was an alley that extended for maybe a hundred and fifty yards.

He reached out again but pulled his hand back at the last second.

"Umm, and you are?" he said, trying not to sound like a complete asshole.

She craned her neck around, and he was surprised that she was holding a hand out to him.

"Chase Adams."

Drake hesitated, his eyes darting to her hand, before coming back to her face.

"Yeah, but who are you?"

A hint of a smile crossed her lips.

"Homicide."

Drake raised an eyebrow, then quickly lowered it when he realized that his reaction was not only expected but desired, as well.

"I'm your new partner."

Chapter 4

DRAKE SCRATCHED AT THE beard that was starting to grow on his face, the length of which surprised him.

"Yeah, I don't know about that."

Chase squinted up at him, her manicured eyebrows knitting.

"You don't know about that? Well, here's what *I* know: there's a dead body here," she sighed, as if this whole interaction was an incredible bore. "If this is going to be a problem, take it up with Sergeant Rhodes."

And with that, she spun on her flats and started down the alley. Drake watched her go for a moment, trying to catch his bearings.

Partner? No one told me about a partner—shit, nobody told me about anything. *Just, "take six months off, get cleared by the head shrink, then come back".*

That was it.

Not, *hey we are going to team you up with some rookie homicide detective, a replacement for your partner. Shit, he's been dead for a half year now, isn't that long enough? Aren't you over him yet?*

He cleared his throat, and then wished that he still had another sip of Johnny to get him through what was already turning out to be a bumble fuck of a day.

With a shake of his head, he hurried after Detective Adams.

"Wait up," he said, but she didn't slow. It was only when he made it up next to her did she start speaking, only she didn't look at him this time.

"White male, mid- to late-thirties," she said, her voice flat, even. "Naked from the waist up, hands bound behind his back."

Drake's brow furrowed.

"Shirtless? What about the shoes?"

Chase hesitated, but only for a moment.

"Ah, dispatch," she said with an air of understanding. "Yeah, dress shirt, suit jacket. Laid out nicely on a chair. Was still wearing his shoes; looks like they're made of snake or alligator skin. Expensive."

Drake nodded. Clearly, robbery was not the motive.

"Cause of death?"

Chase shook her head.

"Unknown."

As they walked, Drake was keenly observing his surroundings, trying to piece together what had happened. The alley was narrow, devoid of street lights. A place to be avoided by a man wearing six or eight hundred-dollar shoes. Clinton Hill was known for its junkies and the occasional prostitute, but mostly the former.

Alligator shoes was a new one for him.

"Is the medical examiner on the way?"

Chase nodded.

"A senior medical examiner by the name of… Dr. Beckett Campbell? Yeah, I think that's it. You know him?"

Something happened to Drake's face then, something so foreign that at first, he thought he was stricken by some sort of palsy. But after a moment, he realized what it was: a hint of a smile.

Beckett was young, with bleach-blond hair and tattoos covering both arms, which Drake suspected extended to his back and chest too, although he hadn't had the opportunity to confirm.

Beckett Campbell was pretty much the antithesis of Drake himself, but maybe that's why he appreciated the man as he did. That, and Beckett had a way of speaking that made Drake feel like he had been to medical school, and not a fucking idiot who squeaked through high school by the thinnest of margins. In fact, it was probably this attitude and approach that had made Beckett so amenable to both his peers and to homicide, which had, in turn, more than likely contributed to his rapid rise to Senior Medical Examiner.

"Yeah, I know him. Good guy. Better doctor."

Drake allowed his eyes to drift as he spoke. The alley was long and narrow, flanked on one side by a chain-link fence, and a row of buildings on the other. There were doors marking the building, all of them handleless and flush with the brick wall, mostly as a deterrent to burglars, although Drake hadn't an idea what a potential robber would hope to steal here.

All the doors looked the same, except for the red one that he didn't need his detective skills to know that they were headed towards. That one was covered by yellow crime scene tape.

"Who discovered the body?" he asked, eyes drifting to the windows that started ten or more feet up, all of which were covered with bars.

"A junkie—Rachel Adams, no relation."

Drake waited for her to continue, but when she offered nothing else, he prodded. It was like pulling teeth.

He shook his head and resolved himself to starting over.

"Look, Chase, I think—"

Chase suddenly stopped and turned to look at him. He expected coldness based on the abruptness of the maneuver, but was surprised by the solemn, almost sad expression on what he now conceded wasn't just a face, but a *pretty* face.

"Damien—"

"Please, just call me Drake."

She raised an eyebrow as if to say, *oh, so now we're chummy*, but then the look vanished.

"Okay, Drake. I just want to let you know that I'm not here to replace Clay. I heard that you guys were close, and I'm sorry to hear about what happened to him. I know…" her eyes became vacant for a moment, then she shook her head briefly. "I just want to solve this crime, and move on to the next, you know?"

Drake nodded and then surprised himself by holding out his hand. She looked at it, and he instantly recognized the expression.

It was the same one that he had given Chase when she had offered her hand to shake. But unlike him, she grabbed his and pumped it twice.

Her hand was soft and strangely cool to the touch despite the sun beating down on them. Drake went to pull his hand away, but she held firm and then drew him closer. The act, as well as the strength in her small frame, surprised him.

"And don't drink next time you come to my crime scene, alright?"

Drake's eyes bulged slightly, and he looked away, feeling his ears go hot again. Chase released her grip and a smile returned to her face.

Then she turned and continued down the alley, and Drake followed.

Chapter 5

"SO, THE TWEEKER RACHEL called it in?"

Chase nodded, lifting the police tape across the red door and gesturing for Drake to enter. He hesitated.

"After you."

Another eyebrow raise, but Chase made no move to enter. Drake shrugged.

Chivalry really is dead.

He crossed the threshold first.

"Yes," Chase answered, following him inside. "She's down at the station now giving an official statement. Said that last night around three AM, she was awoken by someone pounding on the back door, yelling to open up."

Drake's shoes crunched on the ground and he looked down. It appeared as if someone had laid a thick layer of sand across what he thought might be concrete.

"And she did?"

Chase nodded.

"She opened the door, then says that our vic pushed by her and went inside. Said he looked scared, eyes red, like he had been crying, maybe. Could have just been the rain though."

Drake remembered the drying puddles in the alley outside.

"And then what?"

"Rachel says someone bopped her over the head, and she was knocked out cold. Woke up in the alley a few hours later, came inside and found the body."

Drake cocked his head.

"She said that the man knocked at three and she was out cold for an hour or two… so why are we only getting here at—" he checked his Timex, "eleven-thirty?"

"She says she was scared, didn't know what to do."

"You believe that?"

"Rachel Adams is well known to the police—the uniform that took her to the station had arrested her twice himself: once for possession of crystal, the other for soliciting. The way I figure it, is that she needed to clean up some of her product before calling it in."

Drake thought about this for a moment.

"Which would explain why she opened the door at three am instead of calling the uniforms right away. Probably expecting a custy or a delivery. She mention that she was waiting for someone? Her pimp? A dealer?"

Chase reached over to a small box on the floor and pulled out blue shoe covers. After putting them over top of her flats, she offered a pair to Drake. He took them and slid them over his worn loafers.

"That's what I was thinking. But no pimp. Uniforms say that she just turned tricks on her own in order to score— wasn't a regular thing. A dealer makes more sense."

Drake bit his lip.

"Did you ID the vic?"

Chase shook her head.

"No wallet."

"Hmm. Give the station a call, get them to question her about a wallet. If she was turning tricks to score some dope, I wouldn't put it by her to steal a dead man's wallet."

Chase stared at him for a moment, and Drake looked back, confusion washing over him. When her eyes darted to the radio on his belt, he realized why.

"Sorry," he grumbled. "It's just that Clay was always the one to call things in. We can talk to her directly when we get back to the station."

Chase reached for her radio and unclicked it.

"That's alright, I'll let them know to hold her until we come in."

While she made the call, Drake looked around.

They were in what appeared to be some sort of warehouse. One of the officers had set up a bright light in the corner, which cast the entire space in an artificial glow with hard shadows.

He guessed the main room was eighteen to twenty feet long, but only about ten feet wide. The sand on the ground was disturbed in many places, and he saw long, flat depressions at regular intervals.

It was a crack den, he was sure of it; the deep indents were from people sleeping on the floor. Toward the back half of the room was a white plastic sheet that ran floor to ceiling, behind which he could make out the bright halos of other lights.

There were several used condoms on the floor and a smashed bong by one wall, all of which had yellow tags with numbers on them placed beside each item. There were two uniforms inside the warehouse, and perhaps more behind the plastic curtain based on the shadows he noted within; one was busy taking pictures of the paraphernalia, while the other had his nose buried in his cell phone.

He kicked at the sand with his covered shoe. Then he turned to Chase, who had since reclipped her radio to her hip.

"Not going to find any usable footprints here," he said. "What's with the sand?"

Chase started to walk toward the plastic curtain.

"Junkies lay it down," she paused. "You ever see someone deep in a k-hole?"

Drake shook his head. He was familiar with the concept: essentially, if you injected enough Ketamine, your brain would completely disconnect from your body and you were lost in a sort of void.

The k-hole.

"Well, sometimes if you go deep enough, you can shit or piss yourself and not even know it."

Drake screwed up his face, and then leaned down and adjusted the boot coverings so that they covered his entire loafers.

"So, this is like some sort of kitty litter for crack addicts?"

"Something like that."

When Drake continued to look at her, she raised a hand defensively.

"What can I say? Worked as a Narc in Seattle for seven years."

Again, Drake was taken aback by this comment.

Seven years? She can't be older than... what? Thirty-three? Thirty-five at most?

Chase looked away, clearly uncomfortable now.

"Anyways, there's something else you are going to want to see."

Drake had a feeling that this was coming.

"The reason why our vic was shirtless?"

Chase smiled.

"Bingo," she replied, then pulled back the curtain, revealing the crime scene.

Chapter 6

THE MAN LAY FACE down, his arms and legs bound behind his back by a single length of rope. There was a worn chair off to one side, and on it were laid a shirt and suit jacket, both of which looked to be draped with care as if to avoid wrinkles.

The man's back was bare, and on it was a crude, almost child-like image of a butterfly painted in a dark brown substance. The body of the butterfly, a simple, sausage-like shape with two projections near the top, ran nearly the length of the man's spine, and the wings, two 'B' shapes, one backward, extended to his shoulder blades.

"A butterfly," Drake muttered unintentionally. This, he had not been expecting.

"A butterfly," Chase repeated. "Can't confirm it yet, but it appears to be drawn in blood."

As Drake processed this information, he moved closer to the body. The uniformed police officer stepped aside to allow him access.

The blood, if that was indeed what it was, didn't appear to have come from the man's back. In fact, aside from the drawing, his flesh appeared unmarked.

Drake moved closer still, stepping near the man's head and crouching on his haunches.

The vic's eyes were open, and what he suspected were hazel irises had turned a slight milky color in death. He was clean-shaven, and his hair had recently been cut—short, professional.

His pale lips were open slightly.

"He was placed here after he was already dead," he stated matter-of-factly.

Chase appeared beside him.

"How can you tell?"

Drake reached into his breast pocket and pulled out a pen, and then used it to indicate the area around the victim's mouth.

"See here? The sand is the same height as the rest of the area around the body. If he had still been breathing, his breath would have blown it away."

Drake squinted hard. In moving his pen around, he noticed what looked like a small amount of dirt at the corner of the man's mouth, which didn't fit with his otherwise manicured appearance. He got the impression that this was the type of man who would be mortified if caught with a piece of spinach lodged between two perfectly white teeth.

He moved the pen toward the man's face.

"It looks like —"

But the sound of the curtain being drawn back gave him pause.

"Tsk, tsk, tsk, Drake, my man. You should know better than to touch the body before a doctor is in the house."

Drake turned to see Beckett moving toward him, his shock of hair spiked high atop his head. He was grinning, showing off a winning smile.

Drake stood.

"You're not a *real* doctor."

The man shrugged.

"That's right, I only play one on TV," he turned to Chase next. "And who's this?"

Chase extended her hand.

"Chase Adams, Homicide."

He shook her hand, a short and perfunctory process, unlike his own experience, then turned to the body on the ground.

"Beckett Campbell, at your service."

He whistled loudly.

"Butterfly, huh?"

In one fluid motion, he pulled a set of purple lab gloves from the pocket of his leather jacket—*how many doctors wear leather jackets,* Drake wondered—and slipped them on.

"I think there's something in his mouth, dirt maybe," Drake offered.

Beckett held up a finger.

"In time, my friend. In time."

He straddled the victim's body, and then closed his eyes as if in some sort of trance.

Chase moved forward.

"We think the vic died—"

Beckett sucked in a deep breath and waved his arms dramatically.

"Silence while I do my work."

Drake rolled his eyes, and Chase looked over at him. He shrugged and turned back to the charade.

Beckett squatted over the man, looking as if he was going to sit on his back, and then gently prodded his ribs with two fingers. Apparently satisfied, he moved his hands upward, ending at the base of the man's neck. After cradling his head briefly, Beckett stood straight, and then stepped over the body, moving toward where Drake had been moments ago.

Before he crouched, he turned to Chase, still beaming.

"I was only kidding. You can talk as much as you want."

Chase said nothing, and her face gave away less, and Beckett shrugged.

"No external injuries as far as I can tell," Drake offered.

Beckett gestured toward a small black bag that he had set down after entering the curtain. Drake fetched it for him and then the coroner withdrew what looked like a scalpel missing the blade.

"No, no external injuries. Except, of course, the injection site near his neck."

Drake grimaced.

"The what?"

"The injection site. Small pinprick on the left side of his neck. Little red dot, you know?"

Drake, incredulous, walked over to that side and hunched down low.

As he did, Beckett asked Chase for an evidence container.

And there it was, something so small that Drake couldn't really blame himself for having overlooked it. A tiny red dot on the man's otherwise flawless skin.

"Area still looks a little puffy," Beckett continued. "Must have been some pretty serious inflammation to have lasted for… what? Eight hours since he died?"

Chase confirmed the timeline.

"Damn, I'm good," Beckett muttered. "Oh, and there's also this."

Drake moved to the other side of the body again and watched as Beckett eased the metal device into the man's mouth and used it to push his lips to one side like a dentist attempting to clean his molars.

And that's when Drake saw it: a flicker of movement, a dark shape wriggling toward the back of the victim's teeth.

Drake felt his stomach lurch, and now regretted the second bottle of whiskey.

And the third.

"Jesus," he muttered.

"No, not him, I'm afraid," Beckett replied. "Unless Our Lord and Savior was reincarnated as a caterpillar."

As the dark form wriggled completely out of the man's mouth, Drake looked away. His eyes fell on Chase, and he was glad to see that he wasn't the only one who was feeling queasy.

Beckett brought the plastic specimen container close to the victim's face, and then put his tool in front of the caterpillar. The insect crawled on top of it, which Beckett used to put it in the specimen container. After screwing the lid closed, he put it in a clear plastic bag and held it out to Drake.

"Looks like your killer has a thing for butterflies," Beckett said, hooking a chin toward the corpse. "But I guess you knew that already, didn't you?"

Chapter 7

"**HERE'S WHAT WE KNOW,**" Drake said to the half-dozen detectives standing in the conference room before him. "A man in his mid-thirties, dead via some sort of injection—tox report should be back this afternoon or tomorrow morning at the latest. Our victim appears affluent, but without ID."

He saw several eyebrows rise.

"His body was found in an abandoned warehouse on Luther Street in Clinton Hill. But he was a non-drug user, so far as we can tell. Again, tox will clear that up. This was no opportunist crime; this was cold and calculated. I want to know why this man was in Clinton Hill if anyone in the local bar scene saw him around that night. Right now, it's just an informal question and answer situation. We will be meeting every morning at 8 am until the case is solved."

Someone groaned at this, and Drake pushed his lips together tightly.

Some things apparently never changed.

"And based on the presumed status of the victim, we want to keep the media out of this for as long as possible. As soon as they catch wind of this, they are going to be all over it. Mark my words on that."

Drake paused for a moment, surveying the faces of men and women in the room. He knew all of them, of course, as they had all been here before... before the *incident*. But the faces of these people, ones that he had known for decades in some cases, seemed different to him.

Only, it wasn't their *faces*, *per se*, but the way they looked at him. He saw something that he never thought he would in their cold eyes, their flat expressionless mouths: disdain.

Disdain and anger.

He swallowed hard.

"I'm sure you've all heard about the butterfly; I can confirm that there was a butterfly drawn in blood on the vic's back. When canvassing Clinton Hill, keep your eyes and ears open for anything that might be related to insects—butterflies in particular."

He looked over at Chase and hoped that she got his mental message to keep the presence of the caterpillar to themselves for now. They had discussed this issue after speaking to Beckett again, who had since confirmed that the caterpillar in question was a Monarch, and it had been up in the air as to whether or not they should mention it to the other detectives. Chase was all for it, but Drake had his reservations. They had decided to play it by ear, and now, seeing what seemed to be the faces of strangers staring back at him, he had gone with his initial instinct.

They would find out, but not right now. He couldn't chance this information being leaked to the media. He had a sinking feeling in his guts that some of the detectives that he had once called friends, but now looked at him with distaste, might let it leak just to get back at him for what had happened.

After all, they may have been his friends once, but Drake had no doubts that when it came down to it, they had much preferred the smile and calm demeanor of Clay Cuthbert to his brashness and straightforward nature.

"Chase will now go into more detail about the witness, a junkie named Rachel Adams, no relation, and her account of what happened. If there are any questions, I'll—"

The glass door to the conference room opened, and Drake was surprised to see Sergeant Rhodes's small eyes buried behind round spectacles peer in.

"Chase will be heading the investigation," he said curtly, his gaze locking on Drake.

Disdain, distaste, and something else... something more visceral.

"If you have any questions, direct them to her."

There were several murmurs, and Drake felt his face start to redden.

"Drake, my office," Rhodes finished before grimacing and allowing the door to close.

Drake's ears felt like they were on fire again.

He had known that coming back would be somewhat of a transition, that he might have to regain the trust of some of his colleagues, but he hadn't known that their scorn had run this deep. And Sergeant Tom Rhodes had quashed all of his efforts with an ill-timed interruption.

Drake cleared his throat and fought the urge to curse out loud.

Get a grip, he admonished himself, recalling the episode with Suzan's psychiatrist.

What a fucking day this was becoming, and it wasn't even dinner yet.

He cleared his throat and raised his chin.

"Right, all questions to Chase," he said without looking over at her. "And remember, no media leaks. Keep in mind that there is a dead man here—he's a victim and despite eight-hundred-dollar alligator loafers, he demands the same respect as anyone from your family."

As soon as the words were out of his mouth, he regretted his choice.

Family. We—NYPD Detectives—had been a family once.

Clay had been family. As had Suzan.

Then Drake started to move toward the door as Chase started to recount the story that he had heard Rachel Adams recount a half-dozen times already.

He had to snake his way between the detectives to exit the conference room; no one moved out of the way to allow him to pass.

Chapter 8

"TO SAY YOU'RE ON thin ice is like saying a polar bear is just a large albino kitty," Sergeant Rhodes said.

Drake screwed up his face, no longer able to keep his emotions from bubbling to the surface. His relationship with Sergeant Rhodes had always been strained, what with the man more concerned with his reputation and ambitions, which, if the rumors were true, extended even beyond just the NYPD. But Drake, a no-nonsense man who solved more homicides than just about anyone else in the department, was also an asset, and he knew it. And aspiring men likes Rhodes needed someone like Drake. So long as he kept the media out of their affairs, Rhodes didn't even seem to bat an eyelash when Drake stretched the rules. After all, Drake wasn't like that fat idiot Steven Britt who had six convictions overturned for punching suspects in the face. And, besides, when things had deteriorated between them, Drake always had Clay to step in.

He *had* Clay; as in past tense.

The sergeant leaned forward, his elbows planting on his desk like spindly roots, his long, thin fingers interlacing.

"You're back for one reason, Drake: Internal Affairs said there was no way to get rid of you," he nodded to a manila folder sitting in the center of the large oak desk. "You remember what I said? I said, think carefully before your psych exam? You remember that?"

Drake simply stared at the man, watching his Adam's apple slide up and down in his throat with obscene fascination.

The truth was, everything immediately following Clay's murder was a blur, a dirty smudge of reality obscured by copious amounts of whiskey and even more sleepless nights. And yet Drake thought he did remember Rhodes saying something along these lines. Only at the time, he had considered it a kind of, *get well soon and come back to us,* statement.

Only now did Drake realized how very wrong he was.

The two men stared at each other for what seemed like an eternity drawn out like sugar taffy.

Drake was afraid to answer; afraid because he thought that the only response that he could manage was one of fury.

Is he forgetting that Clay was my *partner? My best friend?*

The faces of his fellow detectives came to mind then, the way they had looked at him first in the alley behind Luther Street and then in the conference room moments ago.

They can't all blame me for what happened to Clay, can they? He shuddered.

Why wouldn't they? A small voice inside his head chimed in. *After all, don't you blame yourself, Drake? Why wouldn't they?*

Eventually, Rhodes broke the silence.

"Chase will be heading the Clinton Hill investigation — she'll be reporting directly to me. You'll tag along and give her any and all support she needs to solve the murder. But that's it. That's the extent of your involvement. I want you to be a silent partner on this one; keep your interactions with suspects and witnesses to a minimum, and for Christ's sake Drake, you are not to speak to the media in any capacity. Do you understand?"

Drake swallowed hard and nodded.

"Good," Rhodes leaned forward and pointed directly at the center of his chest. "You slip up once, *just* once, and you'll be lucky if your next assignment is giving out parking tickets in

Long Island, I don't care what IA has to say. Do you understand?"

This time Drake didn't offer anything as a response; no head nod, not so much as a blink.

He was suddenly struck with the idea that Chase taking over the case the day he returned to work was no accident, no coincidence. This was part of a bigger strategy, one that Rhodes was at the heart of, one that was designed to get Drake as far away from 62nd precinct as possible.

Parking tickets in Long Island...

Rhodes wasn't being facetious; that was exactly where he wanted Drake. After what had happened to Clay and the subsequent New York Times exposé about the Skeleton King, Drake had burnished Brooklyn Homicide and the 62nd precinct with a nasty, swollen black eye.

And this type of thing just didn't jive with Sergeant Rhodes and his damn aspirations.

Drake suddenly wished that this morning when he had thrown the man in the V-neck and sport coat against the hood of his BMW that it had been Rhodes's razor-thin nose that had been bloodied.

Thoughts of earlier in the day also brought back echoes of Suzan's words.

You ruined everything!

Drake bowed his head and started to stand, aware that Rhodes was still staring at him, but no longer caring.

He half-expected the man to stop him on his way to the door, to utter another not-so-veiled threat. But Rhodes didn't, and Drake left the Sergeant's office with his head still hung low.

***

Chase was waiting outside the Sergeant's office when Drake stepped into the hallway. She had something between a grimace and a look of solemnity etched on her pretty face. Drake nodded an acknowledgment and she sidled up beside him as he made his way toward his office.

"You alright?" she asked quietly, cognizant of peering eyes and perked ears.

"Fine," he grumbled.

"You know that—"

Drake silenced her by holding up a hand. The fact was, he *knew that*—he knew what she was going to say. Young as Detective Adams was, she seemed very much in tune with what was going on around him and the station. And for some reason, she didn't let it faze her.

He liked that.

"I'm fine. I'm just here to solve a murder." When her eyes softened, Drake's did as well. "But I appreciate it," he said.

This time it was her turn to nod.

They made their way down the hall, both aware that nearly everyone they passed was staring at them, but this seemed to bother Chase even less than Drake.

He liked that about her, too.

"So, what now?" Chase asked.

Drake smiled.

"You're the boss, you tell me."

She made a playful *hmph* sound, realizing at once that he was making a joke.

"You hear back from Beckett?" she asked after they had made it to his office door. One of the slots still read *DAMIEN DRAKE, HOMICIDE,* but while his name had always been on top and Clay's beneath it, Clay's had since been removed and Damien's was now on the bottom. The top slot was empty.

He wondered if this too had been part of Rhodes plan.

"No, not yet," he said, reaching for the handle. He paused and turned to face her. "Hey, let me ask you something… you wouldn't happen to have a cell phone charger, would you?"

She squinted.

"What kind?"

Drake slid a hand into his pocket and fingered the phone within.

"Step inside, there's something I need to show you," he said, this time holding the door for her.

Chapter 9

"YOU TOOK THE MAN'S phone?" Chase asked, her tone matching the shocked expression on her face.

Drake held the cell phone out to her as if to say, *yep, and here it is.* But Chase was having none of it and interlaced her fingers behind her back.

"Drake, why the hell did you take the vic's cell phone? Drake, you're... the way the others look at you..." she sighed, trying to collect herself. "I think you know how the others feel about you. This is too risky; you need to get the phone into evidence, pronto."

Drake frowned and he shook his head.

"How they *feel* about me? I could care less how the others *feel* about me, or whether they stare at me until their eyes dry out and fall out of their faces, or if they want me gone. Besides, Rhodes basically told me he's going to do everything in his power to get me fired, so who cares about all that noise? I certainly don't. All I care about is getting this case solved before I go."

Saying the actual words made the feelings Drake harbored more real, and it was a surprisingly cathartic experience.

The feeling was short-lived, however.

"So, let me get this straight," Chase began, eyebrow raised. "Instead of doing everything by the book to make sure you *don't* get fired, you go ahead and abandon all the rules... you break the chain of custody so that evidence might not be admissible in court later on? You sure it isn't *you* who wants to be fired?"

Her final comment struck a chord with him, and Drake mulled this over for several seconds, first considering what had happened that morning with Suzan, then the events of this afternoon with Sergeant Rhodes.

But then his mind flicked to Clay lying on his back, a bullet in his chest, coughing up blood.

The vest... why weren't you wearing your vest, Clay? Shit, I was wearing mine...

Realizing that he was taking too long to answer, he shook his head briefly.

"Chain of custody isn't broken, Chase—the phone just hasn't been admitted yet," he moved the cell phone even closer to her, but she took a step backward as if he was holding out a broken vial containing Ebola.

"Why'd you take it then?"

Drake smiled. Apparently, Chase didn't know *everything* about being a detective in NYC yet.

"Maybe things are different in Seattle, but here, in NYC? Once this phone goes into evidence, good luck getting it back out again. First, you need to get a judge to issue a subpoena, and as you've already pointed out, I'm none too popular around here. Jump through that hoop, and then you need to somehow open the phone. Good fucking luck with that. Apple's privacy laws are tighter than North Korea's. You're going to need to get a second subpoena to get them to unlock it. That could take months. A year, even. Then what? By then our guy is already worm food."

Drake cringed at the last comment, wishing that he had chosen his words more carefully.

While Chase and the other uniforms in the Luther Street warehouse had been watching Beckett tease the Monarch caterpillar from the vic's mouth, he had slipped a hand into the dead man's suit coat and had put it in his own pocket. Despite his previous diatribe, he wished that even half of much forethought had gone into the act. The truth was, he just did it, hoping that his ingrained detective skills hadn't led him astray.

He thought that Beckett might have seen him take the phone, but he was maybe the one man that Drake could still count on, as both a colleague and possibly a friend.

Chase's frown suddenly transitioned into something different, an expression that he had seen before and already started to recognize despite their short time together.

She had made the same face moments before they had "started-over"; she was torn between two options, two frames of mind.

It was a place Drake had been many times during his career. Detective Adams was sandwiched between following the rules and solving a case.

"Promise me something," she said at last.

"What?"

Chase reached out with surprising quickness and snatched the phone from his hand.

"That when your ship goes down in flames, you give me enough time to abandon ship. That seem fair?"

Drake smiled wryly.

"Ay, ay, Captain. Or do you prefer *boss*?"

Chase frowned and turned her attention to the cell phone. She turned it over, running her fingers over the Apple emblem on the back.

"Tell me something... how'd you plan to unlock the phone once it's charged?"

Now it was Drake's turn to show his displeasure on his face.

"Unlock it? What do you mean, *unlock it*?"

Chase raised her eyes to look at him.

"Seriously?"

"What?"

She shook her head disapprovingly.

"You really are a dinosaur, aren't you?" she pulled her own cell phone out of her pocket, and Drake recognized that it was nearly identical to the one he had taken from the vic.

Charger? Check.

She swiped the screen and showed it to him. He saw what appeared to be a grid of numbers.

"Everyone locks their phone these days," she said simply. "You need a four-digit code to get in."

Drake's heart sunk.

"Well, how many combinations can there be?"

"Lemme see: ten numbers, zero to nine, four digits... oh, what is *ten thousand*, Alex."

Drake's eyes bulged.

"Ten thousand?"

Chase nodded.

"Ten thousand."

Drake grunted.

"Really."

"For real."

"Then you get your wish: I'm going to drop it into evidence after all," he said, reaching for the phone.

But Chase pulled it back and he looked up at her, confusion washing over him.

This woman was messing with his head.

And now she was smiling.

"What now?"

"There are ten thousand combinations and we're never going to guess it. I don't even think the phone will let you do something like 1-2-3-4 anymore, or just the same number four times."

Drake frowned.

"Yeah, I get it; fine. Then why are you smiling?"

"Well, because you can either put in the code or… this is an iPhone 7."

He shrugged.

"So?"

"So, you can also open it with a fingerprint."

He suddenly realized what she was getting at and was beginning to think that maybe she was going to be a helpful partner after all. Chase was no replacement for Clay, no one was, but that didn't mean she didn't have a few tricks up her sleeve.

And now he was smiling. Drake opened his mouth to say something when his own phone started to ring in his pocket, a loud, obnoxious *bleep bleep bleep*.

He reached into his pocket and pulled out a Nokia phone.

"Drake," he said and then listened. Thirty seconds later, he added, "Yep, good. We're on our way."

Then he tucked the phone back into his pocket and smirked at the confused expression on Chase's face.

Without saying anything, he started toward the door.

"Let's go," he said at last.

Chase blocked his path.

"You going to tell me who was on the phone, Zach Morris? Was it your pal AC Slater calling from nineteen-ninety-four?"

Drake had no idea who she was referring to but answered anyway.

"That, Chase, was our man with the fingerprint; that was Beckett Campbell, and he wants us to visit him in the morgue. That okay by you, boss?"

Chapter 10

"HYPERCYTOKINEMIA," BECKETT SAID AS he pointed at the swollen red area on the vic's neck.

"Hyper *what?*" Drake asked, staring stupidly at the ME. Usually, Beckett spoke like a human, but in the six months that had passed since they'd seen each other, the man seemed to have reverted to the inane medical lingo that only a select few could even pretend to understand.

But then Drake realized that the doctor wasn't even looking at him, but at *her.*

He's trying to impress her, he realized with a hint of a smile.

"Look, Beckett, you're going to need to translate," he indicated himself and Chase, "neither of us graduated *cum laude* from—"

"Cytokine storm," Chase interrupted as she moved next to Beckett to inspect the wound herself.

"A *what?* Jesus, do either of you guys speak English? And you," he said to Chase, "In all of your twelve years of life, did you happen to go to med school during your seven years as a narc in Seattle? Moonlight as a pathologist, did you?"

Chase laughed, but instead of answering, she lowered her head and observed the vic more closely.

"No, no med school, I'm afraid. But there was this case once at a clinical trial facility where seven people died from what was supposed to be some simple test for a generic version of a headache medicine."

"Ok, great, so Dr. Quinn, care to explain what happened here?"

It was Beckett who answered, his voice again transitioning to a professional air that was foreign to Drake.

Oh, he's laying it on thick now.

"Basically, an uncontrolled allergic reaction—a positive feedback loop of cytokines—*err*, immune molecules that causes the body to produce massive inflammation. In this case, our vic's lungs swelled so much that he couldn't breathe."

Drake remembered the lack of disruption in the sand around the man's mouth when he had laid face down in the crack den. At the time, he had thought that he was dead before he hit the ground, but now he couldn't be so sure.

"So, what caused it?"

Beckett pointed at the swelling on the man's neck which Chase continued to inspect as if she expected words to rise out of the man's skin, perhaps revealing the killer's name.

Or even the victim's.

"Injection—still running tests, but it looks like it was a concentrated insect slurry. And," now he pointed at the bloody butterfly on his back, "given the killer's choice of artwork and our furry friend we found in his mouth, if I were a betting man, I'd put my money on a butterfly."

Drake was still listening, but he had lowered the man's volume inside his head after he had said the words *insect slurry.*

A shudder ran through him.

"So, this man was, what? Killed by injecting a butterfly—" he couldn't bring himself to say the word *slurry,* "—parts? Then the killer drew a butterfly in blood on his back. Wait, *is* it blood?"

Drake half expected Beckett to spout another medical term that he didn't understand but was pleasantly surprised when he simply nodded.

"Yes, but not the vic's."

Drake processed this for a moment.

"So, he has a butterfly drawn in someone else's blood on his back. What about the caterpillar?"

"Put in there post-mortem. So far as I can tell, it didn't really do anything. Just hung out there until we arrived. Oh, and one more thing, the blood on his back? It's from a female."

"Oi," Drake said without thinking. His face flushed slightly when Chase looked at him with a curious expression. "A woman?"

"A woman," Beckett confirmed.

New narratives started playing out in his mind. In his experience, this type of crime was rarely committed by a woman.

A scorned lover, perhaps?

But then why the whole charade, why was the man running from her in the alley?

It certainly didn't feel or even look like some sort of demented crime of passion.

He shared his opinions with Chase and Beckett.

"Definitely not," Chase agreed when he was finished. She turned to Beckett. "Did you send blood samples to the lab for DNA analysis?"

Beckett confirmed that he had.

"They are backlogged to shit, though. Could be months, and even then we'll only get something if the person's blood is in the system. Seems like a longshot. I mean, someone who goes about making a butterfly slurry and carries around Monarch caterpillars doesn't seem like they would make a dumb enough mistake to leave their DNA at the scene, do they?"

"Great, another detective," Drake grumbled with a hint of sarcasm.

Beckett held up his hands.

"Just trying to help, Columbo. Just trying to help."

"Speaking of which," Drake said, moving forward. "I was hoping that our vic might be able to do just that—well, maybe not lend a hand so much as a finger."

Beckett squinted at him and looked about to answer when Chase produced the cell phone from her pocket. Beckett turned to her.

"The vic's?"

She nodded.

"We just need to charge the thing first," Drake said.

Chase smiled and pressed the button near the bottom of the screen. It lit up, showing the same number pattern that she had shown him on her cell back in his office.

"Already did," she said.

"What? How?"

"Charged it in the car."

Drake held up his hands as if to say *where the hell was I?*

Beckett took the phone in a gloved hand and then pulled one of the victim's arms off the table. Without saying a word, he extended the man's index finger, rubbed it briefly, then placed it on the button. A second later, Drake saw the screen change.

Behind a background of icons, he saw an image of their vic, smiling, his arms wrapped around a pretty blond woman and a white-haired boy.

Chase suddenly drew a sharp intake of breath, and Beckett looked like he might be sick.

"What? What is it? Do you know this guy?" Drake asked.

Chase nodded and he saw her jaw clench.

"Yes," she said in an airy whisper. "And you should, too."

Chapter 11

"THOMAS ALEXANDER SMITH," CHASE said softly, spinning the newspaper around for him to see. "I didn't recognize him when he was lying on the ground, and at the morgue, I was too busy looking at his swollen neck. But on his phone..." she let her sentence trail off and Drake turned his attention to the article from the finance section of the New York Times.

At the top of the half-page article was a photograph of their vic, smiling with perfect teeth, a comically large pair of scissors in his hands poised to cut a ribbon. Flanking him were two well-dressed men that looked important enough for Drake to know them, although he didn't.

Thomas Smith cuts the ceremonial ribbon at the inauguration of the NYC Library that now bears his family name.

Drake swallowed hard, and as he continued to read, he said.

"Yeah, so you know when I said that the press was going to have a field day? Well, fuck, they're not going to have a field day, they're going to go on a goddamn month-long field trip."

"No kidding," Chase said quietly.

They were two of maybe a half-dozen patrons in the small diner that Chase had led him to after leaving Beckett back at the morgue. She had held her tongue the entire time they had driven here and then had rooted through the stack of newspapers near the front of Patty's Diner. As she had predicted, they had several from earlier in the week, including one from four days ago, which she showed to him now.

Drake's eyes darted around quickly, making sure that no one was within earshot, and then read the first few lines to her.

"Thomas Smith, of the prominent New York Law Firm, Smith, Smith, and Jackson, is well known to the community in which he grew up. A caring and giving philanthropist, Thomas and his family's firm have given more than five million dollars over the past decade. However, this donation to save a library, the land on which it stands aggressively being sought by developers, is Thomas's largest single donation to date, topping 1.2 million."

The waitress suddenly appeared, and Drake stopped speaking and folded the paper over as if he were reading a dirty magazine.

She gave him a look and then turned to Chase.

"Would you like some coffee, dear?"

For a split-second, Drake thought that she was going to order a strange tea, or a non-fat soy latte, hold the sprinkles, and he was going to have to start hating her again.

But she didn't.

Instead, she said, "Please. Black."

The woman nodded and flipped over the porcelain cup and filled it. Then she turned to Drake.

"And you?"

Now it was his turn to hesitate. What he desperately wanted was a coffee with an ounce of whiskey in it and was about to order it too when he remembered what Chase had said to him when they had first met.

Don't ever drink before coming to a crime scene again.

Although Patty's Diner didn't exactly qualify as a crime scene, he wasn't in the mood to test her. But he did need something; his buzz from the Johnny miniatures had long since faded, and he could feel his body start to cry out for more.

"Coffee and a water. And do you have any cheesecake? Pie?"

Chase raised an eyebrow at this, but he ignored her.

The waitress sighed as if his request had tipped the scales of boredom.

"Key Lime? Cherry? Strawberry-rhubarb? What about—"

"Whatever's freshest," he said quickly, making it clear that he wanted to be left alone again. The woman's thin lips pressed together, and she spun on her heels without another word.

Without filling his coffee either, he noticed.

"You just make friends everywhere you go, don't you?"

Drake ignored the comment and instead rolled up the newspaper.

"Mind if I take this?" he asked holding it up.

Chase shrugged.

"It's not mine."

Good point, Drake thought.

The waitress returned with his pie and a glass of water. When he inquired about the coffee, she said that they were making a fresh pot. He considered asking why she hadn't filled his coffee when she had served Chase but was dissuaded by her stern expression.

Instead, he pointed at the pie.

"Strawberry-rhubarb?" he asked.

She shook her head.

"Key Lime," she said and then turned back toward the kitchen.

Drake used his fork to lift the yellowish whipped cream and spied the pink interior filling. He furrowed his brow.

"Your *freshest*, huh."

Chase took a sip of her coffee.

"I'm beat—gonna get some rest. I'll Google Smith when I get home, see what I can find out if he wasn't the perfect citizen he appears to be. You'd be surprised what you can find out just by doing a little Internet digging."

Drake, his concentration fixed on what looked like an artificial strawberry in his pie, said, "What about the family? Want to notify the family?"

Chase shook her head.

"I'll put a call in to missing persons, but I asked them to contact me directly after we found the body if anyone puts in a report in the meantime. Nobody has yet, so I guess it can wait until morning. It is odd, though, that his wife didn't call. I mean, they have a young child."

Chase pulled out the vic's cell phone as she said this.

"A lot of good that'll do," Drake remarked. "I mean, you can't exactly keep going back to Beckett every time you want to open it."

Chase smiled.

"I changed the passcode."

Drake finally put his fork down and lifted an eyebrow.

"To what?"

Chase didn't reply right away. Instead, she stood and stretched her back.

"Ten thousand combinations, Drake. *Ten thousand.*"

And then she smiled and left the diner.

When she was gone, Drake chuckled to himself. Maybe it wasn't going to be so bad working with Chase after all.

He broke off a piece of the pie with his fork, which took considerable pressure, and then grimaced before putting it into his mouth.

It *was* strawberry-rhubarb for fuck's sake.

Drake raised his hand and craned his neck around. The waitress looked over at him, her face pinched so tightly that the thick grooves around her mouth resembled a relief map of the Grand Canyon.

"Hey Broomhilda, bring me a shot of your best whiskey with that coffee, will you?"

Chapter 12

"IT'S NOT HIM," DRAKE said, a hint of frustration creeping into his voice.

"It is, Drake. I don't know why you are being so stubborn about this—it's him; we finally got him," Clay replied, his eyes still trained on the road.

Drake shook his head.

"Seven bodies reduced to bones, a crown made of finger bones from all other victims cemented to the top of their skulls like some sort of demented crown, and you think that this case has been solved by a simple wiretap? You think that the Skeleton King would give himself away that easily?"

Clay scratched at his beard and gave Drake a disapproving look.

"Skeleton King? Really? For someone who detests the media as much as you do, you seem to have really taken to the moniker, haven't you?"

Now it was Drake's turn to look away.

Seven bodies in seven days. People that were never reported missing. Drifters, carefully selected victims that wouldn't raise alarm. And on the last, a single piece of hair with just enough of a follicle to get a DNA profile. Next comes the wiretap, then the all incriminating telephone call placed to... who? His mother of all people?

No, Drake was positive that this man, that Peter Kellington, was not the Skeleton King.

"This is a waste of fucking time," he grumbled.

Clay sighed heavily and the car lurched as they started toward Peter Kellington's home address. They had managed to get a drop on the beat cops, but they couldn't be more than five minutes behind. If it were up to Drake, he would just allow them to bust down the door while he was back at the station following up with some real leads.

Like that hooker, Charlemagne or whatever her name was now that woman knew something. The King had grabbed her, but for some reason had let her go.

If only he could get more time with her…

"What would you rather do then?" Clay shot back.

Drake didn't answer and instead relinquished himself to watching the identical brown townhouses that drifted by and quickly became a blur.

They drove in silence for the next little while, before coming to a stop just as the rain started to fall.

Clay immediately opened the door, flooding the car with the smell of wet smog. Halfway out, he leaned into the cab and said, "Drake, you coming?"

***

Drake awoke with a sour taste in his mouth and the hint of a headache behind his eyes. With a groan, he leaned over, and then caught himself at the last moment before he rolled off the couch.

"Fuck," he swore and then looked down at himself.

He was still wearing the same clothes he had been sporting at Suze's school that morning, including the now incredibly wrinkled sport coat. He shook his head at not having remembered passing out on the couch, and then instantly regretted that choice, too.

His hint of a headache immediately somersaulted to full-fledged.

Swallowing audibly, he looked over at the table next. There was a half-empty bottle of Johnny Red on its side, the cap looking as if it had been placed on instead of screwed.

Drake shut his eyes and took several deep breaths.

His headache receded to a dull throb, persistent but no longer debilitating, and he opened his eyes again before slowly pulling himself into a sitting position. His neck was sore, and he rubbed it absently with one hand, while the other went directly to the bottle. As he righted it, in his mind he imagined flicking the top off and taking a big gulp. A *huge* gulp. A goddamn river bass-type swallow.

But instead, he withdrew his hand quickly as if the bottle had scalded him.

In some ways, he supposed it had.

With another groan, this time accompanied by a grunt, he stood, immediately wincing at the pain in his neck and shoulders. He went straight to the kitchen of his bachelor pad, and his gaze flicked to the glowing green numbers on the stove.

4:14.

He grabbed the bottle of Advil off the counter, withdrew two tabs and put them on his tongue. The sweetness of the coating threatened to curdle his stomach, so he swallowed them quickly, dryly, and then chased them with a glass of lukewarm water.

4:14… I'm not going to sleep again tonight.

And then he thought, *if what I was doing before could even be considered sleep.*

But he couldn't stay here; staying here with the liquor bottle would be like putting a child in a room made of marshmallows and instructing them not to have a taste, a lick, a *smell*.

He had to get out.

And Damien Drake knew exactly where he would go, even at this hour.

Chapter 13

DRAKE ROLLED INTO THE conference room five minutes late, a hot coffee in each hand. He felt like shit and looked even worse.

His fear of not being able to fall asleep again had proved false: he must have drifted off sometime in his parked car, because before he knew it, the sun was blazing down on him, turning his Crown Vic into a cracked leather greenhouse.

If there was one positive thing to glean out of this was that the heat and sweat had managed to smooth out some, but not all, of the wrinkles in his sport coat.

All eyes were on him as he entered, but he kept his focus straight ahead, his eyes locked on Chase, who continued to speak.

For a second, he thought he saw her eyebrows knit when their eyes met, but he might have imagined it. If the detective had an opinion about him, he was certain that he would hear about it soon.

"We have positively identified the victim as Thomas Alexander Smith—a father of an eight-year-old boy named Thomas Jr., husband to a one Clarissa Smith."

Upon mention of the names, the other detectives in the room broke into hushed murmurs.

"Quiet, please," Chase said politely. Drake made it next to her and handed her one of the coffees, which she took without acknowledging him. "And yes, *that* Thomas Smith. He was in the paper this past Tuesday, inaugurating the library in Brooklyn that now bears his name. And to the unenlightened, he is a junior partner at Smith, Smith and Jackson—SSJ. The two Smiths, however, are not Thomas; they are his father, Kenneth, and his older brother, Weston."

A hand shot up, and Drake recognized it as belonging to one of the older detectives; Detective Luke Gainsford.

Chase raised her chin, and Drake was once again struck at how in control she was. Short, slight, attractive, she had all the makings of someone *not* in charge, someone that the others, especially ones like Luke Gainsford, would resent for giving orders. But it was her authoritative, no-nonsense edge that they must have appreciated.

Drake knew he did.

The alternative was that they loathed him so much that she was like a breath of fresh air amidst foul-smelling whiskey halitosis.

"Go ahead Detective Gainsford."

The man cleared his throat.

"I've gotten three calls yesterday from the media, and two more this morning alone. They know that someone has died in the Clinton Hill, and they know that it wasn't just another tweaker. Don't ask me how, but they know it's someone important. Something about Alligator shoes? Anyway, I managed to tell my source to keep things on the DL for now, but I can't promise that he won't go live tomorrow or the next day with the details."

DL? Since when did Luke Gainsford use the term DL?

For as long as he had known the man, he was as square as they came.

Another hand shot up and Chase drew her eyes to him, signifying that he should speak before she answered Detective Gainsford.

"Found three blog sites reporting it; small-time blogs, but still. Luke is right, this thing is primed to blow."

Chase nodded.

"I've seen five blogs myself, one who managed to get a photo of the famed Alligator shoes." Her face changed, softening somewhat. "I know that we can't keep this bottled forever, nor do I intend to. But we still haven't spoken to Thomas's family. Hold your guys off until this afternoon, and I'll release a statement to the press shortly after lunch. That work for you guys?"

There was a murmur of affirmation, but Drake found his mind elsewhere.

When Clay had been murdered, the media had reported him as the Skeleton King's eighth victim and had branded him as the only bearded one, omitting the fact that he was also the only one still in possession of his skin.

Bearded NYPD Homicide Detective is the Skeleton King's final victim.

It made him sick, that a man's life could be parsed down to a fucking beard, or in this case a type of shoe.

"Good. Anything else you guys have come up with? Anything about this butterfly thing?"

Detective Henry Yasiv, who was almost exactly half of Luke Gainsford's age, raised his hand.

"I, uhhh, I know a few things about butterflies," he stammered, his face reddening.

"About the case or about butterflies in general?"

The man's blue eyes went to the floor, offering both Drake and Chase a clear view of his messy blond hair.

"In general," he said softly.

Chase nodded.

"Good. Write a quick summary and get it on my desk as soon as you can." Then to the group she added, "Nothing is out of bounds here, people. Everything can help. And after the press gets a hold of this, it's going to be nearly impossible to weed through the shit."

Drake looked over at her, surprised by the curse. Her hazel eyes were as focused as ever, and in that split second, Drake knew exactly what she was thinking.

Smith, Smith and Jackson were going to make things incredibly difficult for them. If Thomas had any dark secrets, they were going to be like opening a dinosaur oyster with a toothpick; the law firm would lock them out, tie them up with litigation.

What's worse, is they would likely offer a reward for any information leading to an arrest, which would overwhelm their call system to the point of obfuscation.

"Anyone else?"

Detective Frank Simmons, a man with skin so dark that Drake had often joked and called him The Shadow, which Frank had actually taken a liking to, spoke up.

"I met Thomas before at a charity golf event a couple of years back. Seemed like a nice man, polite, even-tempered."

Chase nodded.

"Which is in line with everything that I managed to pull up on him online. I had records look into him as well, and aside from a few parking tickets, all of which he paid promptly, he's as clean as a whistle. Right now, the only thing that stands out is that he has been missing for more than 24 hours, and his wife still hasn't reported it."

"Maybe he was on a business trip?" Frank offered.

Chase mulled this over for a moment.

"Maybe, but he was still local."

"Maybe he *told* his wife he was on a business trip?" Frank said cautiously.

Chase nodded.

"Could be—Detective Simmons, why don't you take Detective Gainsford over to his office at SSJ downtown and ask the secretary about his travel plans. But for God's sake, be discreet. I'm aiming to announce to the press at around one this afternoon. I don't want you to go before that, but if we wait until afterward, I doubt we're going to get anywhere. The law office is likely to be on lockdown once I go live. Aim for getting there at a quarter to and start asking questions at one o'clock."

Frank agreed and Chase clapped her hands, indicating that the meeting was coming to a close.

"One more thing," she said when the chatter picked up. The room quieted. "The official cause of death was an allergic reaction to butterflies."

The chatter instantly increased, and Chase found herself having to speak over the other detectives.

"Thomas was injected with a… a butterfly cocktail, let's say, and the reaction basically caused his lungs and throat to swell to the point of asphyxiation. I want the rest of you to look into where one might get, buy or catch, butterflies in NYC. Also, look into disgruntled entomologists, public garden employees, anyone that might be connected to Thomas or his firm and have access to flocks of butterflies."

Several detectives' hands went up, but Chase shook her head.

"That's all for now. We'll meet again tomorrow morning, same time."

Drake was impressed. Chase had managed to get all her information across before releasing the bombshell—*butterfly slurry*—and had shut the meeting down before she had to waste an hour answering questions that weren't going to help them get any closer to finding the killer.

As the room started to clear out, Chase leaned over to him and whispered, "You smell and look like shit. Go get changed, have a shower, and meet me out front in ten. You're coming with me when I speak to Thomas's wife."

Drake grimaced and he suddenly felt envious of Detectives Simmons and Gainsford who were headed to Smith, Smith, and Jackson.

After what had happened to Clay, the last thing in the world he wanted to do was to tell another family that their father and husband had been murdered.

Chapter 14

TEN MINUTES AND A phone call later, Drake left the police station in a fresh shirt and new khakis. The only thing that remained unchanged was his sport coat, which, upon close inspection, wasn't in too bad a shape. His hair had been brushed, although he had gotten into the habit of keeping so short that it required very little maintenance. His eyes were still red-rimmed, and they stood out on his pale face, but he no longer looked as if he donated plasma for a living.

And he actually felt better, too. The coffee helped, as did two additional Advil, but a quick shower had probably benefited him most.

Another drink would have been ideal, but he didn't want to push it. For whatever reason, Chase was the only one in the damn precinct, shit, maybe even the entire city, that still wanted to be around him. And he had meant what he'd said: he was going to catch the bastard who did this to Thomas.

Chase was waiting out front, her window down, the top half of her face covered in oversized Ray-Ban shades. Drake teased his car keys out of his pocket and wagged them at her.

She shook her head.

"I've seen the way you keep your car. Ride with me."

Maybe Chase was more like Clay than he had first thought, despite their obvious differences. Clay had always insisted on driving, and Drake preferred it that way. It gave him a chance to watch the city go by.

He shrugged.

"Sure," he said, and made his way over to the passenger side of her 5-series BMW. He wasn't much of a car guy, case and point his '94 Crown Vic, but he wasn't so naive that he couldn't recognize a beautiful piece of machinery when he saw one.

Drake got into the car, easing his body into the smooth leather seats. It was like sitting his bare ass on a thick ball of cotton candy.

He whistled as his eyes drifted to the large 8" screen display embedded in the dash. On it was a map, with Thomas Smith's address listed in the top right-hand corner.

"Tell me something, Chase; how does an NYC Detective from Seattle afford a ride such as this?" he teased.

He thought he knew the answer: a rich daddy clinging to guilt from a long-settled divorce.

Yeah, that seemed about right, fit the bill.

Only it *wasn't* right, although at first, he had taken Chase's response as a joke.

"Internet poker," she said as she put the car into drive. Her foot tapped the accelerator and the BMW sprang forward with a smoothness that Drake was unaccustomed to.

When her face remained expressionless, he turned to her.

"Seriously?"

"Seriously," she confirmed.

"Huh," Drake slumped back into his seat. Not only was it at least a thousand times more comfortable than his own car, but it also made his couch seem like a wooden pallet by comparison. He instinctively reached up and rubbed the left side of his neck. It was still sore, but not nearly as bad as it had been this morning. Now it was like his headache; a dull throb that he could almost ignore.

"Isn't that illegal?" he asked.

"Yep," Chase replied.

Drake blinked once, twice, and then fell asleep.

***

"Wake up, Sleeping Beauty." Someone shook Drake's shoulder. "Wakey, Wakey."

Drake startled and opened his eyes, momentarily unsure of where he was. He looked around briefly, then saw Chase's face and it all came back. Using the back of his hand to wipe the drool from the corner of his mouth, he sat up.

"We here?"

"We're here."

Drake peered out the windshield. They were parked on a winding street flanked by large stretches of manicured green lawns. On his left was a wrought iron gate, and in the distance he made out a two-story brick colonial with a detached three-car garage.

Thomas did quite well for himself.

Chase reached for the door but hesitated before opening it. She turned to him, and then lifted her sunglasses.

There was compassion in those eyes, but Drake, for the life of him, couldn't figure out why.

Everyone hated him, blamed him for Clay's death, including himself, but not this woman. Was it because she was from Seattle? Is that it? If it was and her goal was to make new friends and connections, she was going about it the wrong way.

Drake was beginning to think that there was a plague coming, and he was the infamous patient zero.

"You going to be alright in there?" she asked softly.

Drake cleared his throat.

"I'll be fine."

"Good. I'll do the talking, you just observe, okay?"

He held his hands out submissively.

"That's what I do. You know detectives *detect*, am I right?"
Chase chuckled.

"Something like that."

She pulled the door open and stepped out into the morning sun, but before she closed it, she said something else.

"You talk in your sleep, you know that? Jesus, you're like Lady Macbeth."

Drake sat bolt upright just as she closed the door.

He fumbled with the handle, but it was tucked away inside the molding of the door and didn't hang out like a metal lever in his Crown Vic. It took him nearly ten seconds to figure out how to open the damn thing.

"Hey!" Drake shouted as he hurried after her. "Hey, what'd I say? Hey, Chase, wait up!"

Chapter 15

CHASE ADAMS PRESSED THE button on the small gray intercom to the left of the driveway that jutted from the ground like some sort of terrestrial periscope. As they waited for an answer, Drake turned his attention to the wrought iron gate before them. The bars were a half-inch thick, starting close enough to the ground that Drake questioned whether he could slip a piece of paper between them and the asphalt, then twisting twice as they made their way to the arched top ten feet above. The bars ended in dull arrow points that aimed toward the morning sun like pikemen standing at attention.

The voice of a man with a thick Spanish accent coming from the intercom drew him back.

"Jes?"

"This is NYPD Detective Adams with Detective Drake. Is Mrs. Smith home?"

His interest lost, Drake continued to look around, spotting a camera eye tucked into the ferns that flanked the small intercom box. Chase must have seen it, too, as she flipped out her detective shield and held it up. Several seconds later, there was a click and a small section of the fence that was hidden within its greater architecture, roughly the size of a normal door, opened an inch.

Chase led the way, pushing the section completely open. Drake followed her through, making sure to close the gate behind them.

As they made their way up the driveway, he couldn't help but think of that horrible rainy night when he had staggered up the red flagstones to Clay Cuthbert's modest home.

When he had to break the news to Jasmine and Suzan that their husband and father was dead.

"Drake, you alright?"

He looked up.

"Hmm?"

She shook her head.

"Nothing. Just let me do the talking, alright?"

Drake nodded and continued to look around, trying to distract himself.

He guessed the driveway to be twenty meters long, arcing from the front gate and circling around a stone basin in the center that contained a thicket of wildflowers. On either side of the massive red-brick colonial, he could see were more flowers, including an entire section of colorful mums that would make the displays in Central Park bristle.

He wondered briefly if Monarchs were specifically attracted to mums, then shook his head. A blind moth would be infatuated with the radiant display of colors on their teardrop petals.

He nudged Chase and indicated the flowers with his chin. Chase nodded and looked about to say something when the sound of a door opening drew their attention.

The front door to the Smith residence was almost comically large. Like a medieval drawbridge, dark wood planks extended nearly twelve feet high, and Drake guessed nearly as wide. It opened slowly as if by winch, and Drake half expected to see a man sporting an eye patch, muscles rippling from a torn vest, in the entrance, gesturing for them to enter, to *come aboard, Matey* before the marauders take note.

But the man behind the door was so different from this fantasy that Drake nearly laughed out loud. Instead of a muscle-bound doorman, a squat man with deeply tanned skin, short, black hair and a wiry mustache of the same impenetrable shade stood in the opening. He was wearing a plain black t-shirt and a pair of dark denim jeans.

The expression on the man's face, however, was not unlike that of a pirate, Drake surmised: stern, thin lips forced into a frown.

What be your purpose here, landlubbers?

"*Jes*? What is this about?"

Not wanting to shout across the driveway, Chase picked up her pace. She held a hand up politely signifying that she had heard the man but refrained from replying until they had made it up the first of a half-dozen flagstone steps.

"We're here for—" she began, but another female voice from behind the man with the accent caused her to stop short.

"I'll take it from here, Raul, thank you."

The man nodded, bowed his head, and then slid behind a woman who took his place in the entranceway. Drake's eyes followed the former for a moment, noting that he never actually left what he now saw was a grand foyer, but when the woman stepped forward again and was suddenly awash in sunlight, he was otherwise distracted.

Clarissa Smith was tall, blond, and had just about the most amazing body that Drake had ever seen. Thin, but not devoid of muscle tone, she was sporting a white tennis ensemble that was cut in a 'v' just low enough to reveal the tops of her ample breasts and continued downward until it ended in a fringed hem just above her knees. Her hair was pulled back in a tight pony and a plain white headband rested across her forehead.

Her forehead and the tops of her breasts glistened with dewdrops of sweat.

"What can I help you with?" she asked pleasantly as she brought a small towel up and dabbed at her cheeks.

"Mrs. Smith," Chase began. Like Drake, she had also concluded that this could be none other than Thomas's wife.

"Please, call me Clarissa."

Chase nodded respectively.

"Clarissa, may we come in? We have… we have some terrible news."

Clarissa's eyes went from one of something akin to curiosity to concern in a flash.

"Is Thomas Jr okay? Did he get into a fight at school again?"

Chase shook her head.

"We're not here about your son, Clarissa. Now, please, if there was somewhere we can sit?"

Relief washed over the woman's pretty face as she took several steps backward and indicated for them to enter.

As before, Chase went first, and Drake followed.

The foyer was tastefully opulent without being over the top gaudy. The white marble tiles led to a massive winding staircase in the center complete with what looked like hand-carved newel posts and banister. Off to the right, the foyer opened into a large white, country-style kitchen.

Clarissa led them in the opposite direction, taking them into a small, plain sitting room that had two plush couches aimed at each other, with only enough real estate for a glass coffee table between. Drake envisioned this as a space for timeouts, somewhere devoid of distractions where parents could corner a child, get him to spill the beans about cheating on his math test or sneaking a cigarette.

"Would you guys like something to drink? Coffee, maybe?"

Or something stronger, Drake thought, trying again to swallow away the cattail that seemed to have soaked up every single drop of saliva from his mouth and throat.

"No, we'll be fine," Chase said.

"Don't be silly, Raul will fetch you something," she said politely, turning to the man with the wiry black mustache. "If the coffee on the stove is still warm, would you be so kind as to pour a cup for our guests? If it's cold, please prepare a fresh pot."

The man nodded curtly.

"Certainly," he replied before turning and leaving the sitting room.

With Clarissa as their guide, Chase and Drake took a seat on one of the couches, which Drake noted was nearly as comfortable as Chase's car seat, while she smoothed her tennis dress and sat on the opposite couch.

Fearing that he might not be able to tear his eyes away from Clarissa's outfit, Drake's gaze drifted to Raul, whom he could still see despite having already made it to the kitchen.

Something about the man seemed off; Drake had felt this as soon as Raul had opened the massive front doors for them. Unlike some of the more seasoned detectives, he wasn't much for gender roles, case and point him not having an issue taking orders from Chase, and while it wasn't rare for people of Clarissa and Thomas's wealth and stature to have a servant, what struck him as odd was that their servant was a *man.*

Drake filed this away in his mental notes for future reference and contemplation. There was something else unsettling about Raul as well, but Drake couldn't quite put his finger on the source. Before he could consider this further, Chase leaned forward and began to speak in a soft, mild tone.

"Clarissa, there's no easy way to say this…"

Chapter 16

CLARISSA'S FACE CONTORTED AS if someone had sucked the pretty right out of it.

Tears quickly followed.

"I'm so sorry for your loss," Chase said, but the devastated woman didn't appear to hear. Clarissa's head dropped, and for one horrible moment, Drake thought that she had passed out and her face was going to collide with her bare knees. At the last second, however, Clarissa caught her face in her hands. Then the sobbing began.

Drake sat frozen on the couch, gritting his teeth with the awkwardness of the situation.

Should I go to her? Put an arm around?

With Jasmine Cuthbert, things had been different. Drake had known Jasmine well; they had shared more than a couple of bottles of wine together over the years. Even though she had shrugged him off, his initial instinct was to hold her, to comfort her.

But this was different; he had just met Clarissa Smith.

Thankfully, Raul appeared almost immediately, a French press full of coffee and several mugs resting on a tray in his hands. He glared at Drake, then put the tray down on the glass table between the couches.

And then something strange happened. Drake had expected Raul to go to Clarissa as he had to Jasmine six months ago, but the man didn't. Instead, he just looked at her, apparently afflicted with the same uneasy indecision that gripped Drake himself.

Did he hear Chase telling her that Thomas was dead? That his boss was gone?

If Raul had overheard, he sure as hell wasn't showing it on his face. Aside from a mustache twitch, his expression was apathetic at best.

Chase shot Drake a look, and then quickly stood and went to Clarissa. She placed a gentle hand on her shoulder, saving both Raul and Drake from any further embarrassment.

"I'm so—" Chase began, but Clarissa suddenly lifted her head, her eyes red and cheeks glistening.

"How did he die?" she gasped. "Please, tell me how Thomas died?"

Chase was taken aback by the question and only stared. Then she looked as if she were going to say something, but no words came out.

Clarissa reached up and put her hand on top of Chase's. "Please, how—"

"He was murdered," Drake said, breaking his silence.

Clarissa's hand fell away, and she turned to look at him.

"*Murdered?*" she asked, her voice a tight whisper.

Drake cleared his throat.

"I'm so sorry. It's a shock to us, especially given how generous he has been to the city of NYC. I mean, why would anyone want him dead?"

Chase shot him a look, but Drake shrugged it off. He had deliberately let it slip that Thomas's murder hadn't been a random event to judge her reaction.

Clarissa hadn't seemed to notice the hint. Like the uncomfortable feeling Drake got around Raul, he filed this tidbit away as well.

"Clarissa," Chase began, drawing the woman's attention, "can you tell us what your husband might have been doing in Clinton Hill late Tuesday night?"

A look of confusion filled her face.

"Tuesday? In Clinton Hill?" Clarissa shook her head. "No, Thomas is traveling—he's been in Texas on business all week."

Is *instead of* was, Drake thought before he recalled something that Detective Simmons had said during their meeting in the conference room: *the wife hasn't called yet… maybe he told her he was away on business.*

"I'm sorry, but his body was found in a… uh… a warehouse in Clinton Hill."

"Murdered?" Clarissa repeated, not hearing Chase.

Detective Adams pushed a little harder.

"Do you know why he might have been down there at about 3 in the morning? Does he have clients that he visits there? An apartment near there, somewhere he might stay if he works late? "

Clarissa shook her head.

"No—his office is in the main SSJ building. We have another house, but it's in Martha's Vineyard," she shook her head. "He was in Texas…"

"Can you think of anyone that might want to—"

Before Chase could finish her question, the front door burst open and Drake jumped to his feet, his hand snaking toward the holster tucked in his armpit. To his left, he heard Chase stand as well.

Drake never drew his gun.

Instead, his jaw dropped.

Thomas Smith rushed into the room, his face red, his breath coming in bursts.

Drake's eyes bulged and he had to drive his heels into the ground to prevent from stumbling backward.

What the hell?

"What's going on here?" the man demanded. He strode toward them, and Raul bowed his head and slid out of the way. "Clarissa? What's going on?"

Drake expected an outburst from Clarissa, something along the lines of *how dare you come in here and abuse me with your sick jokes,* but instead, her voice hitching, she said, "It's Thomas… he's dead."

As soon as the words were out of her mouth, she started to sob uncontrollably. The man rushed to her then and as he passed Drake, he realized that it wasn't Thomas after all. He sure looked a hell of a lot like Thomas, but he was older, his hair thinner at the temples and on top, and he had a mole on the left side of his jaw.

Chase let out a deep breath, and Drake finally looked over at her, making a face as if to say *what the fuck.*

She returned the expression.

The man who looked like Thomas went to Clarissa and she invited him into her arms. Sobbing, she held him tight. As they embraced, the man turned his now red eyes to look at them, then went back to hug her tight.

Don't shoot the messenger, Drake thought.

This went on for nearly a full minute, all the while Chase and Drake watched on uncomfortably. Eventually, however, they separated, and Clarissa used a tissue that Raul handed her to wipe her nose.

"They say that he was murdered here, in New York… but he was in Texas, wasn't he?"

Drake watched this exchange very closely.

The man swallowed, and his Adam's apple moved up and then down a single time. Unlike Sergeant Rhodes, the Thomas lookalike didn't have a goiter of an apple, just a subtle roundness to his throat. If Drake hadn't been watching closely, he might not have noticed it at all.

But he had.

He just wasn't sure what it meant.

Yet.

"I—I'm not sure. I was away myself," then he turned to face the detectives. "My name is Weston Smith… I'm Thomas's brother."

Drake nodded, putting together the final piece of the puzzle.

"I'm very sorry for your loss," Chase said for what felt like the hundredth time. "We are doing everything we can to find out who did this, and we think that you might be able to help us. I know it seems callous for us to ask, especially now, but the truth is the longer we go without talking, the less likely we are to find Thomas's killer."

Weston's eyes, which were brown as opposed to Thomas's blue, suddenly narrowed.

"How in the world would we be able to help?" he snapped.

Drake, who had not yet sat down since Weston had burst through the door, felt his instincts take over and he tensed slightly.

Chase's reaction, however, was the opposite. She casually lowered herself onto the couch, a flat expression on her face.

"I understand you're upset, and of course you have every right to be," she said. "But we're trying to find out who did this and why. Can either of you tell me why your brother might have been in Clinton Hill in the early morning hours on Wednesday?"

Weston's face contorted in anger.

"Clinton Hill? *Clinton Hill?* Why the hell would Thomas be there? He's a well-respected lawyer, a damn philanthropist, not some junkie!"

Chase held her hands up defensively.

"I don't mean to offend you or Mrs. Smith," she said softly, reverting to a more professional air. "But as I said before, anything that you can tell us might be helpful in finding whoever did this."

Weston suddenly rose. Clarissa reached for him, but he shook her off.

"My brother wouldn't be caught dead in Clinton Hill," he hissed. "That place is full of degenerates and junkies. My brother was a respected member of New York's elite."

Drake cringed at Weston's choice of words. The man must have realized it as well — *caught dead* — or maybe he was just made aware of what he had said when Clarissa exploded into renewed sobs. Weston looked down at her.

"I'm so sorry," he whispered. "But you don't have to answer any more questions. Not now, anyway." Then, to Chase and Drake he said, "as Clarissa's attorney, I'm instructing her not to say anything else at this time. How about a little privacy? Is that too much to ask?"

Drake didn't move. During his tenure as a homicide detective, he had observed the gamut of reactions to the loss of a family member. He had seen cold-blooded killers who had murdered their own kin burst into tears while mourning wives broke into fits of violence and anger. Unlike on TV, Drake had very early on learned that one behavior, or lack thereof in some cases, was no more an indication of guilt than another.

But this — *I'm her attorney, she's not to speak to you* — this was a new one for him.

Chase nodded and stood. Then she teased a business card out of her pocket and laid it gently on the coffee table between them.

"If you think of anything, Clarissa. Please give me a call." Then to Weston, she added, "we'll be in touch. And, again, I'm very sorry for your loss. I'm new to New York City, but what little I know about your brother suggests that he was a kind, caring and giving man."

With that, she turned to Drake and motioned for them to take their leave.

"Raul, please escort our guests out," Weston hissed after them. "And how about a little tact next time?"

Chapter 17

CHASE PULLED HER SUNGLASS from her pocket and slipped them on as they made their way toward the front gate. She opened her mouth to say something, but Drake, remembering the video cameras and unsure of whether or not they captured audio, held up a finger.

She nodded and led the way to her car.

Only once they were safely inside did Chase speak. Before she did, however, she removed a cell phone out of her pocket and chewed the inside of her lip. Then she tapped the large phone against the back of her hand.

"You know what the strangest thing is?" she asked softly. At first, Drake wasn't sure if she was just musing out loud, or if he was supposed to answer the question. But when she turned to him, he realized that it was rhetorical. She tapped the cell phone again. "It didn't ring."

Drake raised an eyebrow.

Her phone didn't ring? Why would Chase's phone ring?

Chase acknowledge the confusion on his face.

"Did you see Raul use a cell phone at all? Go into the kitchen for a long time? I mean, he went to fetch coffee, but I could see him the entire time. He never used a phone."

Drake nodded in agreement. He too had been keeping his eye on the small man and hadn't seen him go anywhere near something that looked like a phone.

"So why was Weston there at the house? I mean, he wasn't there when we arrived… he came in through the front door," she paused for a second before continuing. "The only thing that makes sense is that the minute I pressed the button on the intercom and announced that we were NYPD detectives, Raul must have called Thomas's brother."

Drake's mouth was dry, and he felt his hands start to tremble slightly.

It was going on twelve hours since his last drink.

"So what?"

Chase narrowed her eyes as if to say, *stay with me here, Drake. Pay attention now.*

"So, two detectives show up at Thomas's house to see Clarissa of all people, and the first thing the housekeeper does is call his *brother*? Even before calling Thomas himself?"

And now Drake saw the entire picture.

It wasn't *her* cell phone she had in her hand, but *his; Thomas's.*

"It's almost as if Raul had been instructed what to do in the event detectives came to the estate," Drake said.

Chase smacked the cell phone again.

"Exactly. But the real question is, why? Are they hiding something from Thomas? Clarissa? Or, better still, did Weston and Raul already know that Thomas was dead?"

Drake raised an eyebrow at this last point, thinking that Chase was overreaching. And yet the nagging sensation that something was off about Raul made him wonder.

"Maybe, but if Weston knew that his brother was dead, then hand the man an Oscar, skip the ceremony and the vote. As for Raul... you know what I'm wondering?" Drake asked, turning his attention to the rows of colorful flowers by the gates of the Smith estate. A bumblebee, thick as an infant bat, buzzed into view and then rested its heavy torso on one of the larger white flowers.

"What's that?"

"I'm wondering if our housekeeper Raul also does a little gardening every once in a while."

Chase put the car into drive, and they pulled away from the iron gate.

"Yeah, and whether or not their little garden has butterflies," she said.

***

They were nearly back at the station when something occurred to Drake.

"Why do you still have Thomas's cell phone, anyway?"

Chase smirked.

"I told you that I was suspicious about why Clarissa didn't report her husband as missing. Thought maybe she would try calling and didn't want to miss it. Now, though…" she let her sentence trail off.

Drake was impressed, not only by her caginess but also by her willingness to stretch the rules.

"You going to put it into evidence now?"

The smirk remained on her face.

"No, not quite yet. I'm going to pass it to our tech guys first, see what they can pull off of it. There are a bunch of calls on Monday night, but they are all from blocked numbers. I'm going to see if they can work out who Thomas was reaching out to before his phone went dead. I doubt anything will come of it, but just in case. Here," she said, unlocking the phone and turned towards him. "See this? This is his calendar."

Drake squinted and leaned close to the glowing screen. It showed a monthly view, and most of the days were empty. There was, however, a recurring entry for the first three weeks, all on Tuesday and all denoted by a single letter.

"*V*? What the hell is *V*? Is that some new sort of Internet abbreviation? Like LOL?"

Chase looked legitimately surprised.

"*LOL*? Really? You know what *LOL* means?"

Drake didn't smile.

"Yeah, I've heard it before."

Suzan said it a couple dozen times during dinners at Clay's house.

Sensing a change in mood, Chase let her face go slack.

"No, not that I know of. Typed it into Urban Dictionary, but nothing came up. I mean, some things *did* come up, but nothing that I can associate with *V* in this context."

"Urban Dictionary?"

Chase shook her head.

"Never mind."

She started to pull the phone back, but Drake spotted something else and held it out of her reach.

"What about this? *PSY*?"

Chase shrugged.

"Don't know about that one, either," she said simply.

Drake felt a tingle of pride.

"I do," he said, "After... after what happened, I was required to undergo a psych assessment. PSY was the abbreviation they wrote on my file."

Chase thought about this for a moment.

"Huh," she said, her gaze drifting. "Thomas was seeing a psychiatrist?" she shrugged. "Not surprising, I guess. Lots of money, NYC, even a man with a track record as clean as his is bound to have some demons. I mean, we know he lied to his wife about going to Texas for business."

Drake nodded, as Chase pulled into a parking spot outside 62nd division.

"I'm going to get ready for the press conference," she said. "But I'm going to have to speak to Rhodes first. You want to come along?"

"No thanks," Drake said with a grimace. Chase looked at him as if contemplating talking him into it, but Drake's phone started to ring in his pocket, and she rolled her eyes.

"You should really put that thing on silent."

This time, Drake did smile.

"Yeah, but then how would I know it's ringing?"

Chase chuckled and both of them got out of the car. As his partner headed toward the doors, Drake stayed behind and answered his phone.

"Drake."

"Hey buddy, it's Beckett. Is the rocket with you?"

Drake didn't need Urban Dictionary to know what he meant by that.

"No, she just left."

"Ah, too bad. Because I have something you guys are going to want to hear, and I would rather listen to her pretty voice than your creepy breathing when I tell you."

Chapter 18

DRAKE WATCHED AS CHASE made her way to the podium outside 62nd precinct. Fourteen years on the force, and he was still amazed at how quickly they could erect the damn wooden platform and podium.

What was even more amazing was the number of reporters and TV cameras that arrived nearly as quickly. It was as if they could smell the unease in the air.

At present, Drake, who was standing off to one side with several uniformed officers, counted at least six cameras, and easily twice that number of men and women with cell phones leaning close to either one of the two speakers that had been erected next to the podium, or to the podium itself.

Chase had changed her outfit again. When they had gone to see Clarissa Smith, she had been wearing a dark top with a navy skirt that extended a few inches below her knee, but now she was sporting a white, loose-fitting blouse with pinstriped pants.

Still, even in this conservative dress, Drake was beginning to see what Beckett meant when he had referred to her as a rocket. But any illicit thoughts were ripped from his mind even before they could form when Sergeant Rhodes, who was standing beside Chase, cleared his throat.

Chase stepped forward.

"Good afternoon everyone," she said. Her voice was flat and even, her expression neutral. "I'm sure you are all wondering why we have invited you here today. I have—"

"Is it about the alligator shoes? The murder in Clinton Hill?" someone from the audience shouted.

Chase's expression faltered, but only for a split second. At that moment, Rhodes stepped up to the mic, guiding Chase out of the way.

"Please remain silent until after the detective has finished."

Rhodes waited for silence, almost as if he were tempting whoever had spoken to interrupt again. To his left, Drake sensed the uniforms tense as if ready to remove the offender with a simple nod from the Sergeant.

The situation put Drake in a state of unease. Back before the incident, it had been him up there addressing the media, and while he detested the act nearly as much as he loathed being the bearer of bad news to family members, he knew that forcefully removing a reporter from a media scrum was not the way to start off an investigation.

Especially not one of this magnitude.

Thankfully, however, the reporters remained quiet and no action was necessary.

Chase cleared her throat, and Rhodes stepped aside, allowing her to continue.

"It is with a heavy heart that I inform you of the murder of a man that has called New York City his home his entire life. A man who has dedicated much of his time, influence, and wealth to bettering the city itself. A family man, a father, a husband."

The crowd started murmuring amongst themselves, but a sharp look from Rhodes rendered them silent once again.

"Thomas Alexander Smith was a litigator and a philanthropist, and he was brutally murdered two nights ago."

It was clear from the way that Chase paused that this was the point at which she expected uproar, but it didn't come.

At least not right away.

Shock fell over the reporters like a thin film atop scuzzy water. Most of these same reporters had likely attended the library unveiling event last week, Drake realized. And the man that they had been praising that day was suddenly gone.

Dead.

But this impromptu moment of silence didn't last long. Someone eventually broke through the surface.

"Can you tell us how he died?" he shouted.

"Was he the man in Clinton Hill with the alligator shoes?" another yelled.

And with that, the audience erupted into an incomprehensible cacophony of questions.

Chase waited for most of them to die down before holding her hands up.

"With respect to Mr. Smith's family and the integrity of the ongoing investigation, I will not be taking any questions at this time. We will, however, be keeping you apprised at regular intervals as the investigation proceeds."

"Is there a reason why a rookie detective is heading such a high-profile case?" A man with a tweed hat suddenly shouted above the rest.

Rhodes stepped up to the mic again.

"Mrs. Adams is a well-respected detective with a long list of credentials from her time in Seattle."

"In Seattle, she was a narcotics officer, not homicide. Why—"

"As already stated, we will not be answering any questions at this time," Rhodes said quickly. "We ask any citizens who may have seen Mr. Smith on or around the night of Tuesday or Wednesday the tenth of March to come forward. Working together, I'm confident that we will quickly resolve this case and put this senseless murder behind us."

Rhodes's words and the reporters' questions had worked the reporters into a frenzy, and Drake was suddenly reminded of starving piranhas devouring a piece of meat.

And then, as Rhodes and Chase moved to step off the makeshift stage, another commotion drew his attention. Only this time, it originated within the ranks of the half-dozen police officers to his left.

He turned to the closest man.

"What is it?" he asked under his breath. The man shrugged him off and ignored him. "What's going on?"

Several other officers turned in his direction, but no one offered an answer.

Drake started after the half that made their way to the station, while the rest remained behind as crowd control. He moved quickly, catching up to a young man with short blond hair; an officer who looked even younger than Chase.

"What's going on?" he asked in his most demanding tone.

The man lowered his eyes and mouthed something that Drake couldn't quite make out.

No lip reader was Detective Damien Drake, but the expression on the police officer's boyish face was enough to relay the remainder of the message in stereo.

There's been another murder.

Chapter 19

THE SCENE WAS DIFFERENT—an apartment versus an abandoned warehouse—but the MO was the same: an affluent man murdered, his hands and feet bound behind him, a crude butterfly drawn on his back in blood.

"I see another injection site on his neck," Chase said, leaning close to the victim. Unlike Thomas Smith, it appeared as if this man had been dead for several days. His body had since been released from the grips of rigor mortis, and his eyes had obtained a milky hue like watered-down milk.

Drake observed from several feet, noting that like Thomas, this victim's shirt had been removed and was folded neatly on the couch beside the body.

"Beckett is on his way," he remarked. He looked about the room and saw nothing that seemed out of place. The bachelor pad was neatly arranged, the sheets in the bed still made. The decorations were plain almost to the point of looking staged. In fact, if it weren't for a few photographs in frames nestled on a small table by the front door, Drake might have thought it a poorly conceived movie set.

"There's swelling here, too," Chase said. "Not as much as with Thomas, but you can see that his neck is thicker than it should be."

"Who's the vic?" Drake asked.

"Neil Benjamin Pritchard, local businessman," Chase replied without hesitation.

Another rich man murdered, Drake thought, and was about to say as much when someone else entered the room.

Beckett's face was grim, and he nodded to Drake as he approached the body. He lowered his black bag and studied Neil Pritchard for a moment before saying anything. Then he opened his bag, put on his patented purple gloves, then leaned down and traced the dark brown butterfly stain on his back.

"Ethylenediaminetetraacetic acid," he said softly.

Chase raised her head, acknowledging the man's presence for the first time.

"Say *what?*"

Beckett looked up.

"EDTA—didn't Drake tell you?"

She turned her attention to Drake, shrugging. Beckett looked from Chase to Drake and back again.

"Communication, people. Don't they teach you that in police academy?"

"She was giving a press conference," Drake offered in his defense.

Beckett frowned.

"EDTA is a preservative that prevents blood from clotting. Still no hit on the DNA, but the blood—which is from a woman, in case you need reminding—is not fresh. EDTA is used for blood collection."

Chase stood, shaking her head.

"So, it's not our killer's blood?"

"No idea. All I can tell you is that the blood used to make this macabre art was preserved," Beckett said.

Chase pointed to the man's neck.

"There's swelling here, just like with Thomas."

Beckett walked over and hunched down. He prodded the man's neck gently with his fingers briefly, before tilting his head toward Neil's face.

"Drake? Pass me the probe."

Drake reached into his bag and pulled out the tool that he had seen Beckett use back at the warehouse. Beckett took it, then started rooting around the man's mouth. Without the rigor that gripped Thomas, the man's dead lips flopped around uncomfortably, like a man mumbling in his sleep.

It took several seconds of work before the ME managed to tease something out.

Again, Drake had to look away to steel himself.

It was another caterpillar, only this time the inch and half long insect was stiff as a board.

"Looks like another Monarch," Beckett said, scooping it up and putting it in a specimen container.

A buzzing sound suddenly filled the apartment, and for a brief moment, Drake thought with revulsion that it was the sound of an insect buzzing. But when Chase pulled off one of her gloves and reached into her pocket, he realized that it was just her cell phone.

He took a deep breath and stared at his partner as she answered. Her face, previously a mask of disgust, was suddenly awash with dread. She said a few words, mostly *uh-huhs* and then hung up.

Chase didn't say anything at first, reserving herself to just standing beside Neil Pritchard's body, her silhouette illuminated by the harsh lights that had been erected before they had arrived. Drake saw her take several breaths, before turning to him and staring directly into his eyes.

"That was records. They just informed me of another murder with the same MO in Montreal a month ago," she paused, a far-off look in her eyes. "Drake, I think we have a serial killer on our hands," she said.

Drake shuddered.

It was the Skeleton King all over again. Only this time, he had grown wings.

PART II - Chrysalis

Chapter 20

THE MAN IN BLACK watched as the short, pretty detective got out of her car and looked around briefly. From his vantage point across the street, he could clearly make out her shoulder-length hair framing her face, the prominent frown on her lips. For a second, her seeking eyes seemed to lock on his, and he froze, ready to run if she should make even the slightest movement in his direction.

But after a moment, her gaze continued on.

Like so many others, she had looked right past him, *through* him, seeing only the shadows he shrouded himself with.

The detective turned and started toward the apartment building, the door of which hung open, flanked by two equally distressed uniformed officers.

It had taken longer—*much* longer—for the police to find Neil compared to Thomas, probably because the junkie bitch had opened her mouth with the latter. But despite her presence, things had been easier with Thomas. For one, Thomas had died from the initial injection; he had croaked once, then after seizing briefly, he had fallen unconscious.

Thomas had died an hour or two later.

Neil, on the other hand, hadn't succumbed to the first injection. His eyes had bulged, and at first, the man in black feared that some of the cocktail had formed a bolus that had gone straight to his heart.

A second injection had set things right.

And yet Neil had been easier than Chris. Chris had been a bastard who had fought to the end. Three injections it had taken, and even then, as he lay on the floor of his restaurant with the acrid smell of burning pizza dough in the air, the man in black had thought that he was going to have to strangle him before the light in his eyes finally blinked out.

A second car pulled erratically up to Neil Pritchard's apartment and parked halfway on the curb behind the female detective's fancy BMW.

The man watched from the shadows, his hand sneaking subconsciously into the inside pocket of his dark jacket.

The door to the cream-colored Crown Vic groaned as it was thrust open, and a man with short brown hair that was starting to gray at the temples even though he couldn't have been much older than forty, made a similar sound as he stepped out. Then he spat on the sidewalk and adjusted the collar of his wrinkled sport coat, while at the same time rubbing his neck.

Like the woman, this detective looked around before heading to the apartment. Also like her, his eyes paused when they fell on the park across the street before continuing on.

I know you, the man in black thought suddenly. *I've seen you before.*

It took a few moments, but then it came to him. He recognized the man in the rusted Crown Vic from a newspaper article a few months back.

Detective Damien Drake…

He was the one who had gotten his partner killed in the pursuit of the notorious Skeleton King serial killer.

And now he was back with a new partner and on the case of another killer.

As the detectives started toward the house, together now, the man in the park pulled a small container out of his pocket and held it up to a sliver of light coming from a street lamp that had just clicked on.

"Your time will come," he said softly, observing the caterpillar as it wriggled and crawled over the leaves inside the clear container. "Your time will come. You will have your chance... you will be *reborn*."

Chapter 21

*"**DRAKE, YOU COMING?**"*

Drake reluctantly opened the car door, the rain instantly wetting the sleeve of his sport coat.

"Waste of fucking time," he grumbled.

Clay was already halfway across the road by the time Drake hauled his ass out of the car, and he had to hustle to catch up to him. He was surprised to see that his partner already had his gun drawn. Clay disliked guns so much that it wasn't uncommon for him to leave it back in the office. Not the smartest decision in Drake's estimation, but Clay didn't really need a gun when he had Drake.

The rain was coming down heavily now, and Drake was drenched by the time he dipped under the maroon awning and sidled up to Clay. Somehow, his partner had managed to stay relatively dry.

"Well? What are you waiting for?" Drake asked, not bothering to keep his annoyance from creeping into his voice.

Clay's eyes were wide, his lower lip trembling ever so slightly.

"Door's open," he whispered, using the barrel of his gun to indicate the gap between the door and the frame.

Drake wiped the rain from his eyes and leaned forward, trying to make out the interior of the home.

He could see nothing; it was pitch black inside.

Drake turned to Clay and was surprised that his partner was staring at him in laden expectation. Drake only shrugged.

Door open, door closed, what did it matter? This isn't our guy.

"This is your case now," Drake said harshly. "You lead the way."

Clay took a deep breath, his chest hitching nervously as he prepared to enter Peter Kellington's house. He was uncomfortable, as most people were when thrust into a new situation, NYPD detectives included. Clay was the smooth-talking, deep-thinking yin

*to their yang. Drake, on the other hand, was the muscle; the bad cop
to Clay's good.*

But fuck him, *Drake thought,* he's wasting our time. The
only reason I came along was to see his face when we bust this
guy beating off to cat videos on the Internet.

*Drake had to stifle a chuckle from the visual—Clay's face, not the
act itself.*

*"Should we announce? Tell them that we are NYPD?" Clay
asked, poised an inch from the door.*

Drake shrugged, his meaning clear.

It's your case now.

*Clay nodded and took a reluctant step forward, leading with his
gun. He used his empty hand to push the door wide.*

*"NYPD!" he shouted into the darkness. He waited for a few
seconds before shouting again. "NYPD! We're coming in!"*

*Drake reached into his armpit and pulled out his service revolver.
Then he followed Clay inside.*

***

Drake awoke to the sound of his phone ringing. He
groaned and opened his eyes. He located his phone
immediately—it was on the table beside the bottle of
whiskey—but picking it up proved more difficult. Twice he
knocked it spinning with an uncoordinated hand before he
finally managed to grab it and answer.

"Yeah?" he said groggily.

The man's voice on the other end of the line was the
antithesis of his own: clear, concise, authoritative.

"Drake? Where do you want to meet?"

Drake closed his eyes and massaged his temples.

He felt another headache coming on. For some reason, the diner that Chase had taken him to, the one where she had shown him the article about Thomas Smith, came to mind.

"Patty's Diner on 57th," he said quickly.

"I know it. I'll see you there in twenty," the man replied.

Drake hung up and peeled his sweating body from the couch.

A half-hour later, he found himself the sole patron of Patty's Diner, sitting in a cracked red vinyl booth with a clear view of the door. A young woman came by shortly after he was seated—Broomhilda and her whacked-out Key Lime pie and winning smile apparently had the night off, thank god—and offered him a coffee in a pleasant voice.

"Two creams, three sugars," he replied.

The woman nodded and returned to the bar.

A few seconds later she returned, flipped his porcelain mug over and poured him three-quarters of a cup.

"The cream? Sugar?" Drake asked.

The woman, who had a brown ponytail pulled so tight that it lifted her eyebrows unnaturally high on her forehead, indicated the dish by the window.

"Thanks," he grumbled, realizing that the usual accouterment had been on the table all along.

As he reached for the creamer and sugar, he slowly became aware that the waitress still hadn't left his side.

Drake prepared his coffee the way he liked it, and when he was done and she was still hovering over him, he turned to her expectantly.

She smiled, revealing a large diastema between her two front teeth.

"Going to be a long night? You waiting for someone?" her eyes skipped first to her watch, then to the folder on the table in front of him.

Drake looked up at her, suddenly wishing that Broomhilda hadn't decided to take the night off to feed her dozen cats.

"Thanks for the coffee," he said. "I'll call you if there's anything else."

The woman's smile faltered but didn't quite leave her face. She turned to leave, but before she was gone, Drake addressed her again.

"On second thought, do you have any Key lime pie?"

The woman said they did and then went to retrieve a slice.

"Thanks," he replied.

Drake hadn't even had a chance to sip his coffee when the bell above the door suddenly chimed. A man in a navy k-way jacket, the hood pulled over his head, stepped into the diner. He was tall, over six feet, and walked with a slight limp.

He made his way directly to Drake's booth and slid in across from him without saying a word.

The man was older than Drake remembered, with ash-gray eyes and thick lines around his mouth. He was clean-shaven, and a few strands of long, brown hair, damp from the rain or from sweat, slipped from the hood and framed his round face.

Drake slurped his coffee, then cringed.

It was scalding.

The man reached into his jacket and pulled out a yellow envelope, roughly the size of a videocassette. He placed it on the table beside Drake's manila folder but didn't remove his hand from it.

Drake looked up, and for a moment he thought that the man was going to say something. But he didn't; instead, he let go of the envelope dramatically and reached for the folder. He was in the process of tucking it inside his k-way jacket, putting it in whatever hidden pocket that the envelope had come from when Drake finally spoke. His voice was harsh, his tone deliberate.

"No reference to alligator shoes—you got that?"

The man paused and his thick eyebrows furrowed. Again, he looked like he was going to say something but then decided better.

Instead, he nodded once then left the diner the way he had come.

Drake didn't touch the envelope until after the bell above the door returned to its dormant state. Even then, he first took a sip of coffee. As he reached for it, the young waitress returned with his pie and he pulled his hand back.

She slid the plate in front of him and then smiled widely.

Drake first looked at the pie, then at the waitress, trying to figure out if she was playing a trick on him.

"Key lime?"

The woman nodded.

"Key lime," she confirmed.

Drake used the fork to lift the stale, pale yellow crust, revealing a pinkish-red interior.

"Is everything to your liking?" she asked. Drake couldn't tell if she was deliberately trying to provoke him, if Broomhilda had posted his picture in the kitchen with the caption, *Fuck with this asshole if he comes in,* complete with a cigarette burn in his forehead, but in the end, decided that it didn't matter.

"Fine," he grumbled. "Everything's fine. But get me a shot of Johnny Red to go with my pie, would you?"

It was raining more heavily by the time Drake left Patty's diner, but he barely noticed. He stumbled toward his car, trying to keep the envelope dry while at the same time retrieving his keys from his pocket. He dropped them into a puddle, swore, then almost fell when he bent to pick them up again.

A minute later he was on the road, and ten minutes after that he rolled down a quiet street and parked outside a familiar, plain, brick duplex.

His eyes darted to the glowing numbers on the dash, then cursed himself for not setting the clock. He checked his watch and with one eye closed to avoid double vision, was fairly confident that it was a quarter past one in the morning. On second glance, however, he thought that there was a fifty-fifty chance that it was actually three-oh-five.

But, like the cake, Key lime or strawberry rhubarb or minced meat, this didn't matter, either.

With a heavy sigh, Drake opened his door and stepped back into the rain.

He walked slowly toward the house, careful not to slip in a puddle, and then stopped outside the wooden gate. A black mailbox with a red flag lying flat against its side was just within reach. He opened it, glad that the sound of the rain concealed the creaking of the rusty hinge and slid the envelope inside. Then he raised the flag.

A final glance revealed that the house was dark save a window near the top that was illuminated by a dull yellow glow.

A reading light was on.

Drake felt his breath hitch but fought back the tears that threatened to spill. With a final longing look, he made it back to his car and then passed out behind the wheel.

Chapter 22

THIS TIME IT WAS Detective Chase Adams who was late for their morning briefing. Drake had arrived five minutes early, once again with coffees in hand, and had taken a seat at the head of the table. The pressboard behind them that had been empty the day before now had three photographs on it affixed by a pushpin, each with their names beneath: Thomas Smith, Neil Pritchard, and Chris Papadopoulos.

Chase must have been working late, Drake thought, *which explains her tardiness.*

Detectives Luke Gainsford and Frank Simmons, who had been commissioned to inquire about Thomas's travel schedule at SSJ, walked by the conference room twice, not so subtly looking inside to see if Chase had arrived yet.

Drake held their gazes, but this didn't seem to faze them in the least. There had been a shootout overnight—three dead, two injured, all gangbangers—which had forced Rhodes to redirect some of the resources from Thomas's case. Which left only himself, Detectives Gainsford and Simmons, and Detective Henry Yasiv the budding entomologist, and of course Chase to work on a case that had gone from one murder to three over the course of fewer than six hours.

Knowing Rhodes and his vendetta, Drake considered the prospects of receiving any additional help on the case, irrespective of the influence of the victims' families, was about as close to zero as one could get.

Detective Yasiv suddenly opened the conference room door, a folder in his hand. Upon seeing Drake and only Drake, he lowered his gaze and muttered something about having to go to the bathroom. The man ran his free hand through his short blond hair, apologized ambiguously, and then turned to leave when Chase's voice filtered up the hallway.

"Detective Yasiv? Where are you going? When I say there's a briefing at eight you come at eight? If I'm not here yet, you sit and wait? Got it?"

The man lowered his eyes even further and nodded. He held the door open for her, but she grabbed it from him.

"Detectives Gainsford and Simmons, that goes for you too, alright? Inside."

Hank entered the room, and Luke and Frank hurried in after him.

Drake couldn't help the small smile that formed on his lips. When Chase entered last, however, a scowl on her face, it fell away. She was holding a newspaper like a caveman holding a club. The door behind her hadn't even fully closed before she addressed them in a harsh tone.

"Butterfly Killer?" she nearly shouted as she waved the newspaper in front of her. "*Butterfly killer?* For fuck's sake, I said to keep the press out of this!"

She threw the paper down and it landed on the oblong table with an audible *swack* and unrolled. Even from his vantage point, Drake could see the large, bold type on the front page of the New York Times.

Butterfly Killer stalks New York's rich and famous.

Chase threw herself into a chair and leaned back, her lips pursed.

"It's hard enough with Weston Smith blocking us every time we so much as think of speaking to any members of the Smith family, but now this?" she sighed heavily and closed her eyes. Drake put her coffee on the table in front of her, but either she didn't notice or didn't care.

This was a new side to Chase, one that he hadn't seen before, and Drake was unsure of how to proceed. When he and Clay worked together, Drake was the one to fly off the handle, while Clay was always calm and collected. During these moments, he had appreciated his partner's calculated decision to just leave him alone, to let him work things out on his own and cool down. And now, given his abrupt change in role in Homicide, he afforded Chase the same courtesy.

Eyes still closed, she said, "When I find out who leaked this information, you're going to be pulled from this case and any others I preside over. And you'll be spending your weekends in records alphabetizing petty thefts in Manhattan South."

Silence fell over the five people in the room, which dragged on for nearly a full minute. Drake, for one, appreciated the lack of sound; it served to quiet his headache.

Chase took a deep breath then opened her eyes. When she spoke next, her voice had regained its soft, composed tone.

"Guys, we have three bodies now—this case has officially been upgraded to serial status. With the shootings last night in the Bronx, Rhodes has given us limited resources, despite the status change. And as much pressure as we are going to get to solve this case by members of the affluent community, Rhodes is a bread and butter guy—he is refusing to offer it more than the usual resources, meaning that it's only us. But that doesn't change the facts; there will be enough pressure to turn us lumps of coal into diamonds. This is the sort of case that makes or breaks careers."

Her eyes jumped from one man to the next, skipping over Drake.

Bread and butter guy.

Drake, who had worked under Rhodes for more than a decade, couldn't have said it better himself. Chase continued to impress him with her ability to read people after only brief interactions.

She forgot self-serving ambitious asshole, of course, but that was alright. This revelation would come in due time.

Chase took a sip of her coffee.

"Now, I assume that everyone got my memo last night?"

Drake screwed up his face.

Memo?

Now Chase looked directly at him.

"Check your email next time," she said, but her voice lacked conviction. Then, to everyone, she said, "Three dead, all with the same butterfly on their back." She indicated the board behind her. "Chris Papadopoulos, wealthy Montreal restaurateur, Neil Benjamin Pritchard, a local businessman who owns three print and copy stores and two high rise apartment buildings, and Thomas Smith, who you all know by now. Chris was the first, found dead in one of his restaurants fifteen days ago. Neil was next, six days ago, and Thomas just two nights ago."

Chase let the information sink for a few seconds before picking up a blank square of paper roughly the same size as the photographs of the three men. She plunked it on the corkboard beneath the images of the dead, then drew a circle with a cross beneath it with a black Sharpie: the universal symbol for a female.

"So far the only connection between them is the blood on their back. For the two New York deaths — Neil and Thomas — we know that the blood is female and that it is not fresh, meaning it's unlikely to be our killer's. That being said, this woman holds some sort of…" Chase looked around and then turned to Drake. "Where's Beckett?"

Drake shrugged.

"I told him to come at eight, just as you said."

Chase's face soured, but only for a moment.

"I'm not one for profiles, but the way I see it is that the woman whose blood was used holds incredible importance to our murderer. We find out who she is, and I bet she leads us directly to the killer."

She paused, offering an opportunity for others to contradict her theory.

No one did.

"Frank? Luke? Tell me that you have something from your visit to SSJ yesterday?"

Frank cleared his throat and stepped forward.

"I wish I had good news, Detective Adams, but unfortunately we have little to report. Luke struck up a casual conversation with Thomas's secretary just prior to your press conference, like you said. She had only just told us that she wasn't sure where Thomas was—no mention of traveling to Texas—when we were shut down."

Chase frowned.

"Let me guess: Weston Smith put an end to the conversation."

Luke nodded grimly.

"Not him, but a young attorney who works for him. Pretty much asked us to leave."

"And that's what kind of help we can expect from the Smith's at this point. Drake and I went to see Thomas's wife, but Weston arrived, and we got the same treatment."

"Is she a suspect?" Detective Gainsford asked hesitantly.

Chase turned to Drake for an answer.

"Can't rule her out," Drake said. "I will say that her reaction appeared legitimate, and even Weston, despite his anger, seemed surprised by the news. There was something strange about the housekeeper, and the way that Weston shown up even before Detective Adams had finished breaking the news, but I don't know what it means yet."

Chase nodded.

"If it were only Thomas who was killed, Clarissa Smith would be our number one suspect, and Weston number two. But until we find a connection between them, I'm hesitant to formally refer to anyone in the Smith family as such, especially given their clout in the community." She turned to Henry next. "Detective Yasiv? You have a book report for us?"

Detective Yasiv blushed but stepped forward and held out several sheets of paper stapled together.

"Give it to Drake," she instructed, and the man obliged, keeping his eyes low. "The reason why I was late was because I was meeting a friend in records down at city hall... I asked him discreetly about Thomas Smith, to see if anything came to mind that we might have missed when he ran his name. Turns out, my friend was just talking to a colleague about him, gossiping about the man's death. Apparently, Thomas wasn't always the patron saint he appeared to be when he died; got into some trouble when he was younger, and my friend thinks some of his crimes were pretty serious, too. I'm trying to get more information, but it's gonna take time. Have to get a court order to unseal his juvi records. Anyways, for the last two decades, I can't so much as pin a hangnail on the man."

Drake thought about this for a moment.

"Changed his ways, or just better at committing crimes?" he asked.

"Dunno. Likely the former," Chase answered quickly. "Any idea over the obvious why SSJ and the Smith family are being so unhelpful? Why they are stonewalling us? I mean, Thomas was just murdered, and I bet they know all the stats with respect to how important the first few days are for a murder investigation."

Detective Frank Simmons stepped forward.

"Like I said before, I met Thomas a few times at some of the fundraiser events he held around town. I remember once when we were both a couple of gin and tonics in that he had mentioned something about his father, Ken Smith. At the time, I paid little attention, but thinking back now, when he started running his mouth, it wasn't all daisies and unicorns, if you catch my drift. But what rich boy growing up in Manhattan doesn't have something against their father? The only thing I can remember is that Thomas said something about Ken considering running for public office in the future."

Drake's eyes narrowed.

A dead son would do wonders for swaying public sympathy. And it was all the more reason to keep Thomas's past that Chase was in the process of drudging up a secret. It might also explain Weston's reluctance to cooperate.

Drake voiced his opinion.

"Makes sense," Detectives Simmons and Gainsford responded in unison.

All five then turned their attention to the board. They had set up a similar one when they were investigating the Skeleton King, and Drake suddenly had an eerie case of déjà vu.

Only it was Chase and not Clay leading the investigation.

"Rich boy growing up in Manhattan," Chase repeated quietly. "You know what? There might be something to that. I wonder if Chris, Neil, and Thomas knew each other?"

"I'll get on that," Hank offered enthusiastically, clearly wanting to do something other than writing about butterflies.

Chase was having none of it.

"No, I'll get my tech guy on it—Officer Dunbar. He already managed to pull some things off Thomas's cell phone."

Drake surveyed the others quickly, wondering if they would question how they had gotten it unlocked so quickly.

"What things?" Frank asked, and Drake relaxed.

Chase shrugged.

"We think that Thomas was supposed to meet a psychiatrist the day after he was murdered. There were also several entries for meetings that were only described using the letter '*V*'."

"*V*?" Frank asked.

"The twenty-second letter in the alphabet; that's all we got at this point. Thomas's secretary didn't mention anything about either of these appointments?" Chase said.

Frank shook his head.

"Figures," Chase continued. "Doesn't look like we are going to get any help from the Smith's at all. Unless…" she let her sentence trail off and Drake was about to ask her to elaborate when the door to the conference room opened and Beckett strode in. It looked like he hadn't slept in a week.

"Sorry I'm late," he said. "Damn gangbangers always getting themselves murdered at the worst possible time."

"Everyone, this is Beckett Campbell, Senior Medical Examiner," Chase said.

The introduction was irrelevant; Drake knew Beckett well, and the doctor was already well acquainted with Gainsford and Simmons. A nod between him and Detective Yasiv indicated that they had also met previously.

Beckett scanned the board for a second before continuing.

"As you all know, both Neil and Thomas died from injections of some sort of butterfly cocktail."

Drake cringed at the term but was grateful that the doctor opted against using *butterfly slurry.*

"I found a second injection site on the inner thigh of Neil Pritchard along with traces of thiopental, a powerful sedative. Thomas, on the other hand, seemed to have been killed by the cocktail alone."

"Any progress on a DNA match?" Drake asked.

Beckett shook his head.

"Still nothing. But I can confirm that the blood on both of their backs is from the same female."

Chase thought about this for a moment, then commented on Beckett's previous report.

"Two injections for Neil, with the addition of a sedative, but only one for Thomas, which means that he's getting better at this game. That, combined with the fact that the timing between murders is getting shorter—nine days between Chris and Neil, four between Neil and Thomas—makes me think that we don't have much time before he strikes again. I think, at this point, we can all agree that the murders aren't random, at least. It's on us to figure out how these men are connected, and who's next," Chase said. "Frank and Henry, I want you to keep digging into Thomas's past. Neil's too—he was single, but the location of his murder was a second residence. The media is reporting that he shares his primary residence with his mother, of all things. Go see her and try to find a connection between the two dead men."

"What about the Montreal guy—Chris Popo…?" Detective Gainsford asked.

"Papadopoulos," Chase finished for him. "We are keeping Chris's involvement to ourselves for now. As soon as the FBI gets wind of a cross-border crime, they are going to be all over this. And with SSJ working against us, our only chance of finding the murderer who did this is to work fast."

"And the article?" Gainsford continued.

Chase shot him a look.

"What about it?"

Drake cleared his throat and stepped in.

"Doesn't it mention Chris?"

"It does. But that doesn't mean anything for now. I've dealt with cross-border murders in Seattle and Vancouver, and once the FBI and Canadian Security Intelligence Agency get in the way it becomes a logistical nightmare. And that was in Vancouver. I can't imagine what it will be like dealing with French Canadian cops. The way I figure it, we've got twenty-four hours, maybe two days at best before they take over."

"What about me?" Beckett asked.

"Are you in contact with CSU?"

Beckett nodded.

"Yes, all their findings will go through me."

"Anything on that front?" Chase asked.

"Nothing. They're still combing through the garbage from Luther Street, but Neil's home was pristine—no fingerprints, no DNA, no bodily fluids. I would be surprised if CSU gets anything of value from Luther Street."

Chase appeared to consider this for a moment.

"Do you have someone that can cover you in the morgue for a day or two?"

Beckett nodded.

"Sure, I have a couple of residents with me now."

"Good, then it looks like you are going on a road trip to Montreal. Maybe you can use that charm of yours to see if you can find out more about Chris's death before the FBI storm in.

Just make sure to keep things on the down-low. If anyone asks, you're going for some good ol' R and R."

Beckett smiled.

"Sure thing, boss."

"And me?" Detective Gainsford asked.

"Stay local, I'll have something for you soon when Dunbar gets back to me." Chase said. Luke frowned but nodded in agreement. "That'll be all."

"What about me?" he asked when it was just he and Chase left in the conference room.

"See if you can dig up anything about the psychiatrist; after all, you have some experience with them, don't you?"

Drake narrowed his eyes, unsure of whether Chase was referring to his mention of seeing a shrink after what had happened to Clay, or if this had something to do with the events outside Hockley Middle and High School.

But Detective Adams's face gave away nothing, and Drake was reminded of her sleek BMW outside, the one that she had bought with poker earnings. Internet or not, he was beginning to see why she was so good at it.

"And you?" he asked.

"I'm going to see if I can rejuvenate my tennis game," she replied with something akin to a smirk on her pretty face.

Chapter 23

"PSYCHIATRISTS," DRAKE GRUMBLED AS he made his way to his car. Throughout his entire life, he had only known three psychiatrists, all of whom had left him with a sour taste in his mouth.

The first was an old pervert his mother had visited, leaving him in the waiting room at the ripe age of seven, and who he was now convinced that she must have been having an affair with; the second was the NYPD psychiatrist Stacey Weinager who had interviewed him for a grand total of three hours over two days following Clay's death and subsequently clearing him. And the last had been the man he had bloodied a few days ago outside Suze's school.

Chase's offhand comment about Drake having experience with psychiatrists held no water. Even if any of the three psychiatrists could be of some help in identifying who Thomas was seeing—how this was possible, he had no idea—he couldn't exactly just hop in his car and pay them a visit. For one, the man that his mother had been seeing had been sixty all those years ago, and was more than likely dead. And Stacey? The NYPD psychiatrist? There was zero chance that he would drop by her office. One look at his red-rimmed eyes, pale lips, and a whiff of his whiskey breath and she was apt to rescind her recommendation for reinstatement faster than he could spell her last name. And the third… well, he was just bewildered as to why a uniform hadn't waltzed down into his office and slapped the cuffs on him yet.

For some reason, he had the sneaking suspicion that Suzan had something to do with that. It was the only thing that made sense.

Instead, he found himself hopping into his Crown Vic and pulling out of the parking lot.

Drake rolled down his window, hawked, and spat a glob of yellowish phlegm onto the tarmac out front of 62nd precinct. Then he sped off, heading to the only place in the world that offered him solace that didn't serve any Johnny red.

***

The cemetery was quiet, which was what Drake had hoped for and expected for a Friday before noon. He parked his Vic on the street rather than in the small parking lot, then made his way into the sun, wishing that he had Chase's oversized sunglasses to protect his eyes. He couldn't remember a spring in New York as hot as this one; every day for the past week, it felt like it had hit the mid-eighties.

Before closing the door, he took off his sport coat and tossed it onto the seat. He straightened his back, and the strap around his left arm tightened.

"Shit," he swore. Deserted or not, a passerby might not react kindly to the sight of a man with a gun tucked under his arm perusing gravesites.

After a brief thought, he reached under his armpit and unclicked the fastener. Then he lifted his sport coat on the passenger seat, tucked the gun and holster beneath it, and closed the car door. A quick glance revealed that the street was still deserted, and Drake hurried across the street and toward the cemetery gates.

After passing through the metal archway, Drake made his way down a small, grassy slope then took a sharp left around a small, concrete mausoleum. The tombstones behind the mausoleum started out grand—Drake saw one adorned with a gold-plated angel, which reminded him of a cherub pissing into a fountain—but quickly contracted in both stature and opulence. The only thing that remained consistent through the rows of gravestones was the closely shorn grass, which, by the smell of it, must have been cut that morning.

Clay Cuthbert's tombstone was a plain gray, acid-washed stone with his name and the years *1974-2017* engraved on it.

And that was all in terms of inscription.

There were flowers scattered at the base, but only the tulips were still alive. The orchids had long since wilted and turned brown.

Drake squatted on his haunches and teased the dead orchids from the red ribbon before tossing them aside. Then he ran his fingers over the letters *C-L-A-Y*.

"I miss you, Clay. I miss you, man, and I'm so fucking sorry that I didn't listen. Goddamn it. I would do anything to replay that night over again." He cleared his throat and stood. "It should have been me that was killed, not you, Clay. It was *my* case—I should have gone in first. You're the one with the perfect family, the wife and kid. I'm nothing—just a drunk, a mean…"

Tears spilled down his cheeks and he swiped at them with the back of his hand, trying desperately to collect himself.

"It was—"

A sound to his right caused him to inhale sharply. His ingrained police training kicked in, and he reached for the gun under his armpit… only it wasn't there.

He cursed under his breath, and then crouched low, trying to hide the majority of his frame behind the modest tombstone. His heart racing, the image of a skull with the finger bones cemented to its forehead flashed in his mind.

The Skeleton King has returned.

Drake felt sweat break out on his face and hands as he scanned the cemetery.

At first he saw nothing, but then he spotted a squat figure approaching from the end opposite that Drake himself had entered the cemetery. The man appeared to be holding something close to his chest, but with his back to the sun, his face and body were all shadows. Just when Drake was certain the man—it was a man, he could tell by the way he moved— was going to spot him, he made a hard right and headed up the aisle of tombstones. He walked for another ten or fifteen meters, then stopped in front of a plain stone the way Drake had done just moments ago.

Relief washed over him when he saw the man crouch, make the sign of the cross, and place a small bouquet of flowers on the ground in front of the tombstone.

And yet, even though the adrenaline had flushed from his system and he was certain that the man posed no threat—*it wasn't the Skeleton King, the King is dead*—Drake remained crouched.

It was only when the man turned to leave that Drake realized that like his initial instinct to hide, the reason he remained curled up behind Clay's grave was instinctual, ingrained from his years as a police officer.

The man muttered something in Spanish—something followed by *madre*—and then kissed his hand and touched the stone. When he made his way back down the aisle, Drake's heart skipped a beat.

Unbelievably, he recognized the man. He had only seen him once, but the stark black hair, deeply tanned skin, and the wiry mustache were unmistakable.

It was Raul, and when the Thomas's housekeeper left the cemetery, Detective Damien Drake followed.

Chapter 24

DETECTIVE CHASE ADAMS FELT ridiculous in her white athletic tee and black-trimmed skirt. The sweatbands on her wrists and forehead and the tight ponytail she sported, on the other hand, left her mortified.

Sure, she had done far more degrading things back in Seattle trying to catch mid-level drug dealers in the act. Things that had left her with scars on the inside of her elbows, reminders of how low she had sunk that required cover-up to hide each and every morning.

But that was behind her now; New York was supposed to be a clean slate.

And yet here she was again, posing as something she clearly was not on a half-brained whim of trying to extract information from a grieving widower.

She felt gross, dirty.

Chase slung the bag that contained her tennis racket over her shoulder and pushed these feelings aside.

There were three men dead, three families who deserved closure. And one cold-blooded killer that they needed to get off the streets of New York City.

With a deep breath, Chase strode with purpose over to the intercom outside the gate and pressed the button. She waited for a moment, and then looked up at the camera eye tucked into the shrubs.

"What is it?" a soft female voice asked.

"Clarissa? It's Detective Chase Adams."

"What do you want?" Clarissa's voice was stronger now, almost accusing.

Chase looked away from the camera and stared at the intercom instead.

"Clarissa, I'm sorry about before. I just… I—I want to help, that's all. I've brought my racket," she held the tennis bag up as if to prove her words true.

There was a pause.

"You want to play tennis? *Now?*"

Chase nodded slowly.

"I've been… I have some experience with loss, Clarissa. And what I've found is that exercise is the best way to start, and eventually get through, the grieving process. Look, I know Thomas…" the words were proving more difficult than Chase had expected and she took another deep breath, trying to steady her nerve.

Come on, you can do this. You've talked people off the ledge, worked your way into trap houses full of thugs that should've shot a pretty white girl like you on sight.

"I know you're hurting. And I won't lie to you; the hurt will stay with you for a long time, if not forever. But there are certain things that you still can do to try and extract some pleasure from this world. I know it doesn't make sense to you now—the idea of pleasure and happiness seems impossible—but in time, you will understand. Clarissa, you have to be strong; after all, you still have Thomas Jr. to look after. In order to make sure he can recover from the loss of his father, *you* need to recover first. And exercise can help."

There was a long pause, one that dragged on for so long that Chase had all but given up. She went as far as to turn back toward her car when she heard a metallic click and saw the door size cut-out in the wrought iron fence open an inch. Chase nodded to the camera and then stepped through, making sure to close the gate behind her.

She walked briskly up the long, inclined drive to the front door, and halfway to it, it opened. She had expected the man-servant Raul to be standing there but was surprised to see that it was Clarissa dressed in a tennis outfit. It wasn't sweaty like the other day, suggesting that she had put it on after Chase had pressed the intercom button.

"Clarissa," Chase said softly, unsure of the appropriate greeting given the circumstances. She was reminded of the awkward encounter in the woman's house, sitting across from one another on couches, and hoped that this wouldn't be a repeat of that.

But a teary-eyed Clarissa Smith immediately stepped forward and embraced her. Her grip was so strong, desperate, that Chase nearly stumbled backward off the steps. After regaining her balance, she leaned into the hug and tentatively returned it.

Clarissa broke the embrace and then wiped tears from her eyes. She sniffed.

"Tennis court is out back. Please, follow me."

As Clarissa led Chase through the house, first through the front foyer, and then through a family room, she paid attention to the pictures on the walls or in frames resting on expensive-looking tables.

"Raul's not here?" she asked casually after noting the man's presence in more than a handful of the photographs, smiling behind his dark mustache, his arms wrapped around Thomas's shoulders, or standing behind the three Smith's.

"No. He left about an hour ago. Raul is like family; he lives here, sleeps here, helps look after Thomas Jr. He's either here or he's out running errands for Weston."

Chase raised an eyebrow at this but didn't press. She had seen the way the widow had interacted with Thomas's brother; pressing her further would likely cause her to clam up. Better to just let her talk.

They walked in silence through the family room, and then down two steps to another seating area. The back wall was covered in floor to ceiling windows, but the blinds, the kind between the two panes of glass, were at half-mast sparing them sun's full wrath.

To Chase, they reminded her of sleeping, half-open eyelids. Or sad eyes.

"Court is back here," Clarissa said softly. Her directions weren't necessary. Through the windows, Chase saw a stone patio with several lawn chairs laid out. After about twenty feet of flagstones, the ground transitioned into grass. Just beyond that, she saw the black wire mesh fence and the green artificial turf of a tennis court.

"I usually have a two-hour training session on Fridays, but I canceled my lesson," Clarissa said as she pulled the sliding glass door open and indicated for Chase to exit.

Chase nodded and stepped onto the stone patio, strangely nervous about her game. It had been at least a few years since she had stepped onto the court, and it was all she could do to hope that all those lessons that Gampie had paid for as a child had stuck with her.

Is tennis like riding a bike?

Chase certainly hoped so.

Clarissa must have seen this on her face because she offered a wan smile.

"Don't worry, I'm not very good yet—I've only been learning for the past six months or so," she said as they walked side-by-side toward the court. "I was looking for something to do while Thomas was away on business, and since Thomas Jr started school, I was alone a lot. Thomas suggested that I get a hobby and for some strange reason, tennis popped into my mind. Maybe it was because the US

Open was on the TV at the time, or maybe I just always wanted to learn and didn't know it until that moment. Anyways, two days later, contractors were here, and by the weekend the court was ready to use."

Clarissa recounted this story with a strange mundane quality that made Chase wonder.

Lonely at home, mentions tennis in passing, and husband erects a tennis court the following week?

Clarissa opened the chain-link door to the court, and Chase stepped in, pressing her toes into the strangely spongy ground, trying to get a feel for it.

Keep her close, maybe? Have Raul keep an eye on her?

It was a full-size court, complete with regulation lines. There was even an automatic ball server in the corner, the top overfilled with fluorescent tennis balls. Chase heard the door close behind her and turned to face Clarissa.

The woman lowered her eyes for a moment, before raising them again. There was an incredible sadness in those brown eyes, a sadness so deep that Chase found herself wondering if the loss of her husband was the only thing that had contributed to it, or if there was something else.

An older wound, perhaps, one that had never quite healed.

"You said you knew grief," Clarissa began slowly. "Tell me how you know."

Chase cleared her throat and told her story.

When she was done, they were both in tears and holding each other.

Chapter 25

DRAKE FOLLOWED RAUL OUT of the cemetery. When the man made his way to the cemetery parking lot, Drake whisked across the street and got into his car and waited.

Raul pulled out a few seconds later behind the wheel of a brand-new black Range Rover, and Drake ducked down low, hoping that his rusty Crown Vic wouldn't look out of place on this street.

He didn't think it would; in fact, it was Raul's car that would be noticed.

Nice car for a housekeeper, Drake thought absently. But then considered that it might just be one that he was borrowing from the Smith's.

When the Rover passed, Drake started his car with a throaty roar and pulled a quick 3-point turn and continued after him.

If Raul knew he was being followed, he didn't allude to it. Drake had tailed many a suspect in his day, and he knew not only how to stay out of sight, but also knew what sort of evasive maneuvers people made when they realized they had a tail. In these cases, rare as they were, Drake knew it best to back off, to make the driver rethink whether they were being followed, and to pick up the chase another day.

Raul took the most direct route from the Fallen Heights Cemetery to downtown, driving at or just slightly above the speed limit, signaling every turn. All told, Drake was beginning to think that Raul was perhaps the most courteous driver in New York City.

It was obvious to Drake even before his car was swallowed by skyscraper shadows where Raul was going, but when one of the largest of these monoliths, complete with the emblematic SSJ symbol at the very top, loomed over him, his suspicions were confirmed.

Raul was heading to Smith, Smith, and Jackson Law Offices, Drake was sure of it. Convinced of the man's intentions, he decided not to follow the Smith's housekeeper any longer. Instead, he enacted a risky technique, but one, if completed correctly, would appease even the most cautious driver's fears of being followed.

He sped up and overtook Raul's Range Rover while looking in the opposite direction, and then cut in front of a cab two cars ahead of him. Someone honked, but this was not enough to arise suspicion; after all, it was New York City.

Drake continued toward the impressive skyscraper and then pulled up directly next to a cart selling candied peanuts, half-on and half-off the curb, across the street from SSJ.

He debated getting out but thought it best to see what Raul did first. Chances were that he would enter the underground parking lot, in which case Drake would lose him in any event; there was no point risking being made.

Someone shouted outside his window, drawing his attention. He looked over and saw an Arab man indicating his peanut cart with one hand, and Drake's Crown Vic with the other.

Drake reached over his sport coat on the passenger seat and rolled down the window an inch.

"You can't park here!" the man said, walking forward. "You can't park here!"

Drake scowled and reached into his belt to pull out his detective shield. He flipped the top and tilted it toward the half-open window in order to ensure the bright sun glinted off of it.

"Looks like you made that out of foil! That's not real! You can't park here!" the man continued.

Drake was surprised by the reaction and leaned even closer.

"It's real—I'm a detective."

The man shook his head and then he turned to another Arab man who was also approaching Drake's Crown Vic.

What the hell is this?

Only then did Drake realize that he was parked between the peanut vendor and a yellow cart selling pita gyros. The second man, the proprietor of the gyro cart, was also holding his hands out.

"He can't park here," the first man said.

"No, he can't," the second followed. This man raised a finger and indicated the no parking sign just above Drake's Crown Vic. "Look, you can't park here."

Drake swore, and his eyes darted to the road, confirming that Raul's Rover was still a few cars away from SSJ. He turned back to the vendors and flashed his detective shield once again.

"I'm a detective. I'm here for two seconds, then I'll be gone."

Both men shook their heads.

"Everyone says that. Yesterday a man parked here and ran over to the building," he indicated SSJ with his chin, "said he was the Pope. His car was towed in under five minutes."

"Goddammit," Drake muttered under his breath. "Look, I'm a detective, this is a real fucking badge."

The second man was right up next to the car now.

"Let me see," he demanded. Drake hesitated. A detective shield would go for a pretty penny on the street and there was no way he was passing it through the opening in the window for this man to grab and take off with. "Let me see," he demanded again. Then he smiled, revealing a gold incisor.

Fuck this, Drake thought. *I'll show them proof.*

He yanked his sport coat off the passenger seat and tossed it on the floor.

Drake's eyes bulged.

"What the fuck?" he whispered.

The seat was empty; his gun holster and gun were gone.

Where—?

His heart started to thud in his chest. He had put the gun there when he had gone into the cemetery, to visit Clay's grave, he was sure of it.

Drake remembered unclicking the strap and placing it beneath his coat.

Or did I?

All of a sudden, his memory of the time before he had visited Clay's tombstone, before he saw Raul, grew hazy.

Shit, all of the last six months were like watching an old soap opera on a CRT TV, the screen smeared with Vaseline.

"Let me see the badge." the man demanded again. His hand gripped the top of the open window. "Smells like alcohol in here. What kind of cop drinks on the job?"

And there was that smile again, the gold tooth seeming to glow in the sun.

"Fuck off," Drake said.

The man's smile grew.

"What kind of…"

Drake drowned him out and turned back to the SSJ building. At first, he couldn't see the black Rover anywhere— not behind, beside, or in front of him—and he swore again.

But then he spotted it across the street; Raul must have performed a U-turn and was now parked at the bottom of the main steps leading to the building.

What's he waiting for? What's he doing here?

It was nearing lunchtime now, and there were dozens of people out on the concrete steps, some talking on their cell phones, others sitting in the sun and munching on sandwiches.

"You're taking away from my business! I have a permit!" one of the men shouted.

Drake ignored him and tried to concentrate as he scanned the steps for a familiar face. It was clear that Raul was waiting for someone.

He spotted a man exiting the front doors before hurrying down the steps. Dressed in a fine gray suit, complete with a purple tie and matching pocket square, the man stood out because of the envelope tucked under one arm. It was the kind Drake was intimately familiar with.

In fact, he had received one just the other day.

"Hey officer!" the peanut vendor shouted. "Give this man a ticket! He can't park here! Tow his ass!"

Drake shook his head and leaned over his steering wheel, wishing again that he had Chase's young eyes or at least her large sunglasses.

But as the man neared the Rover, he finally recognized him.

"Shit."

The man in the gray suit was Weston Smith.

"Here! He's here! Give him a ticket!"

"Excuse me, buddy," an authoritative voice addressed him. "You, take your hands off the car, let me deal with this—I know you got a permit. Hey, buddy, you can't park here."

Drake waved a hand at the man without turning to face him.

Weston Smith?

Weston was right up next the passenger window of the Rover now, his lips moving in what appeared to be clipped speech. Then he looked around quickly, before passing the package through the window.

And with that, Weston turned and started sprinting back toward the office building.

A second later, the Rover also started moving again.

"Shit," he swore again.

"Hey buddy, I think you should get out of the car."

Drake put the car into drive, and the officer put his hand on the butt of his gun and raised his voice.

"Buddy! Get out of *the car!*"

"Sorry," Drake muttered as he floored the Crown Vic and yanked the wheel hard, cutting across three lanes of traffic.

As he sped after the black Range Rover, questions flooded his mind.

Why is Weston at work the day after his brother is murdered? What the hell is Raul doing here? And why is Weston paying him off?

And, finally, and perhaps most importantly, *Where the hell is my gun?*

Chapter 26

CHASE WIPED THE SWEAT from her brow and then shook her head.

"Good game," Clarissa said from the other side of the court.

Chase smirked.

It *had* been a good game. The first game Clarissa had wiped the court with her, but the second, once Chase had gotten into a groove, and muscle memory took over, had been more competitive. And this third and final match had been a barn burner, needing a tiebreaker before Clarissa won it with a backhand blast down the line.

It felt good to get out and play tennis, to get the blood flowing through her veins again.

Chase walked over to the net and shook Clarissa's hand. It was sweltering out, and they were both soaked with sweat.

"I've got an extra towel and some water, if you want."

Chase nodded.

"Sure, thanks."

Clarissa led her to a small bench near the door to the court, and they both sat. She handed Chase a towel and bottle of water, and they both wiped the sweat from their faces, their arms.

After catching her breath, Chase cracked her bottle and chugged greedily, then pressed her back into the chain-link fence while at the same time stretching her calves. There was a small awning over the bench, offering them both some much-needed shade.

"You sure you just started?" Chase teased. "I took lessons for nearly ten years. Granted, I was much younger then and didn't have my own court to practice on."

Clarissa smiled, which warmed Chase inside.

"Quick learner, I guess."

Silence fell over them again, and Chase felt bad about breaking it but as much as she liked Clarissa, and she really did like the woman, she still had a job to do.

She decided to take it slow.

"So, Thomas travels a lot with work? That's why he built this for you?"

Clarissa shrugged and stared at the artificial turf.

"Yeah, I mean he used to travel more, but not so much recently. It's hard on Tommy Jr." She looked up unexpectedly. "I haven't told him yet, you know. Just couldn't bring myself to do it."

Chase's heart thumped in her chest.

"Clarissa," she said, trying not to sound patronizing. "You have to tell him—imagine he finds it out at school? From someone else? I mean it was on the front page of the New York Times."

Clarissa wiped a tear from her cheek.

"You're right. You're absolutely right, but I just have no idea how. How do you tell your son that his father is dead, that he's never coming home? Never going to tuck him in at night again? Read him bedtime stories? Sure, Tom traveled a lot, but when he was here, he was a good father."

Chase took another sip of water.

"I don't know if I can say anything that will help you. I mean, I came here just the other day to tell you that your husband was dead. It's… it's never easy, and this was with—pardon my callousness—someone I didn't know. I can't imagine having to break the news to someone close to me, much less a son. Part of me wants to say that it's like a Band-Aid, that it's always best just to tear them off. But everyone must do it their own way, I think," Chase leaned close to the other woman. "But I do know that it is best coming from you, and not from some asshole kids at school."

Clarissa swallowed hard.

"I know, I know. Tommy Jr's not at school today—he's with his Grandma. I know it's terrible, but I couldn't even look at him since you came and broke the news. He just looks so much like his dad, such a miniature version of him, that it was like I was staring at *him*." She paused, took a deep breath, then continued. "How did they tell you when your parents died?"

"My Gampie just sat me down and said that mommy and daddy have moved on."

Clarissa looked surprised.

"Just like that? *Moved on?*"

Chase nodded.

"Yeah. I'm not a fan of the euphemisms, but I was only six at the time. I was smart, and I knew what they meant. I got it."

More silence ensued. Chase checked her watch; it was coming on noon and she felt pressure to move things along.

The killer had waited four days between his last two victims, and it had already been two days since Thomas's murder.

"Clarissa, I like you and I feel for you, I really do. And I think that maybe we can be friends. I feel horrible jeopardizing this, but I also have a crime to solve. A murder. We think the man that killed your husband is still out there, and that he'll kill again. I want to find him and make him pay for what he did."

Clarissa put the towel over her face. When she pulled it away, her expression was tight, pinched.

"I want to help," she said in a quiet voice. "I really do. But you don't understand Thomas's parents. You see this," she indicated the court and the house behind them, "this can all go away just like *that*." She snapped her fingers. "Thomas's parents are all about appearances, about what people think about them. This is the most important thing in the world to them."

"Because Kenneth Smith is going to run for office?" Chase asked.

Clarissa turned to her, surprise on her face.

"How'd you know that?"

Chase shrugged to indicate that she just did.

"Yeah, there's that. But it's more than that," Clarissa continued. "They just have this... this *thing* about how they look, how they are perceived by their peers, the public. That's why they loved Thomas so much because he used his money and influence to rebuild the city. Painted the family in such a positive light, brought a positive connotation to the Smith name. But when Weston showed up yesterday..." Clarissa let her sentence trail off.

"He told you not to speak to the police, didn't he? Or else your house, your car, your money would all be taken away?"

Clarissa's head moved once in a nod so subtle that Chase nearly missed it.

Detective Adams draped an arm around the woman's shoulder. They were both sweaty, and their skin touching was far from a comfortable sensation, but Clarissa leaned into her anyway.

"Clarissa, they can't do that anymore. Even if Thomas has a prenup, you've been with him for what? Five years? Six? All the money he has made since you were married is half yours. And your son... the child support alone would be very substantial to maintain your quality of life. And that says nothing of life insurance. I understand that—"

Clarissa peeled herself away from Chase and stared up at her, fear in her eyes.

"I know what you're saying is true, I know it, but you don't know *them*. They are powerful people, and they're lawyers for Christ's sake. If they wanted to, they could tie me up in court for years before I ever saw a cent, especially after—" her jaw suddenly snapped shut and her eyes went back to the ground.

"What? After what?" Chase asked. She reached out and tried to put her hand on the woman's shoulder again, but Clarissa moved away.

"Nothing," Clarissa said quickly, rising to her feet. "I've… I've already said too much. I think you should leave now. It would be best if Raul didn't see you here."

Chase nodded and stood herself.

"I understand," she said, keeping her voice light. "But please, just tell me one thing. Just one thing, and then I'll be gone."

Clarissa bit the inside of her lip, but her hesitation indicated that she would at least entertain the prospect of one question. Chase jumped at the opportunity.

"Was Thomas seeing a shrink? A psychiatrist?"

A shadow passed over Clarissa's face.

"No, at least not that I know of. A few months back, we—" And as before, her mouth snapped shut again.

"Come on," Chase pleaded. "All I want to do is find the man that murdered your husband. I'm not here to dig up old bones, drag anybody, especially you or the Smith family through the mud, all I—"

"A couple of months back Thomas and I went to see a therapist, to try and work out some personal problems. *Marriage*, problems."

Chase nodded, catching her drift.

"But you stopped seeing him?"

"We just went for a few sessions, then Thomas said he didn't like the guy and that we weren't going to see him anymore."

"What was the doctor's name?"

"Dr. Mark Kruk," Clarissa said with a sigh. "Now please, you should leave. No more questions."

Chase nodded, thanked the woman and quickly rushed back to her car. Once inside, she pumped the air conditioning and grabbed her cell phone.

Chapter 27

DR. BECKETT CAMPBELL'S PLANE touched down roughly at Pierre Elliot Trudeau airport at just before noon, jarring him from a light slumber.

He rubbed his eyes, then turned to the man next to him.

"Sorry," he grumbled, thinking that he must have bumped the man's arm when he had awakened. The man turned to him, gave him a queer look, then turned forward again.

Friendly, Beckett thought.

A recording came on the intercom, and a staticky female voice jibber-jabbered for several minutes in French. Beckett waited for the English version to follow, but when it never did, he raised an eyebrow. He considered asking the friendly fellow with the strange hair beside him for some clarification but decided against it. Instead, he simply waited for others on the small plane to stand, despite the red seatbelt light still being illuminated above, and then did the same. Unlike many of the other travelers, mostly New York natives, he thought, given the way they spoke loudly to each other in English, he only had a small, leather messenger bag that was tucked under his seat beneath him. He fished it out and then waited for the front of the line to start moving forward.

There was a second announcement that Beckett didn't understand, but when it was quickly followed by a pressure change, he quickly skirted down the aisle, offering polite *excuse mes* and *pardonnez-moi*, as he slipped by them.

The stewardess, a not wholly unattractive woman with long blond hair and large, if slightly wide-set, eyes looked at him with a practiced glare of scorn.

Beckett just grinned and shrugged.

There was no way that his grumpy seatmate or this disgruntled airline employee was going to ruin his buzz. The fact was, he was *excited*. Excited in a way that reminded him of the first time he had seen a dead body in medical school nearly a decade prior. Not in any macabre sense, but in appreciation of a mystery.

Beckett's first dead body had been a white male in his late sixties. A sheet covered him up to his nipples, and his eyes were closed, his mouth slightly agape. There was some discoloration around his nostrils and at the corners of his eyes—reddish-blue smudges—but it wasn't immediately clear if they were caused pre- or post-mortem.

Hovering over the dead body, he had tingled with fear and anxiety and… something else. Sure, he was a little grossed out, but while several of his colleagues had to excuse themselves from the room, Beckett had been transfixed.

In his current position as Senior Medical Examiner, he had come to realize that it had all been a ploy, that exposing first-year medical students to a dead body was intentional, and that the intention was to weed out the squeamish. And the doctors leading the course were okay with you if you left, if you needed to purge your stomach of its contents, and none of them held it against you. But you *had* to return.

That was the key.

For Beckett, his anxiety quickly became excitement when the curmudgeonly doctor, who could have been anywhere from sixty to a hundred-and-sixty years of age, had uttered the words that had sent him on the path to become a forensic pathologist more than a decade later.

Just five simple words.

"What did he die from?"

Because with these words, the body had stopped being just a body; it was a mystery, which Beckett had fallen in love with long before he had become a doctor.

Over the past few years, however, the mysteries in his life had all but up and vanished. Most of the time he was resigned to filling out paperwork and performing rudimentary examinations, as he had been doing this morning when the five dead gang bangers had been rolled in.

Filling out the cause of death that a child, should one be so negligent as to allow a child to observe a man with three bullet holes in his chest, another with a hole behind his right ear, and others with various red roses on their faces, limbs and torsos, could have done, no longer held his interest.

But *butterfly slurry* —now that was interesting. That was new. That was exciting.

And now here, in Montreal, a city that he had been only once before when he had been very young, with strict orders to keep things on the DL, Beckett felt like a cross between Dr. Quinn Medicine Woman and James Bond.

With the looks of the latter, and the brains of the former, of course.

Beckett had a certain spring in his step when he approached the custom's officer with his immigration card in hand.

"Bonjour," the man said.

"Bonjour," Beckett repeated in a terrible accent. The man frowned and then addressed him in English.

"What is your business in Canada?" the man asked in an accent that rivaled Beckett's French one.

"Sightseeing. Wanna check out the new hospital."

The man looked up from the sheet of paper.

"What do you do for a living, Mr. Campbell?"

"I'm a doctor—pathologist, actually."

The man seemed less than impressed.

"And you're here to see the new hospital?"

"Yep. Heard great things—you know, want to check out how the other side works."

The man stared at Beckett with hard eyes.

"The other side?"

"Public health care system."

The custom's officer pushed his lips together tightly and handed his immigration card back to him.

"Just be ready to wait in line," he said. His lips transitioned into a smirk, which was difficult to do given his still pursed lips. "Have a good day Dr. Beckett."

"Merci," Beckett replied.

As he headed toward the entrance, his stomach growled angrily at him.

What he had told the officer hadn't been a lie—he was very much interested in visiting the new super hospital—but he had all day to do that.

First, however, it was time to check out the notorious food scene in Montreal. And on the top of his list was Magpie's Pizzeria.

The place where Chris Papadopoulos had been murdered less than a month ago.

Chapter 28

DRAKE SPOTTED RAUL'S ROVER after nearly five minutes of cutting off angry taxi drivers. In all honesty, it wasn't that hard to locate: the large black SUV stood out among the yellow cabs like an albino ant scurrying across asphalt.

Raul was driving with purpose again, much as he had been when he had left the cemetery and had made his way to SSJ. Only now he was heading east, sticking to the major roadways, a clear indication that he still had no idea that he was being tailed.

Drake debated calling Chase but decided against it. If he called her, he would be required to report his missing gun. And that would raise questions, questions that might eventually make their way to Sergeant Rhodes. He trusted Chase, which was strange given that he knew so little about her and could tell from the steely look in her hazel eyes that she was as dedicated to solving this murder as he was. And yet her words, those words that she had uttered that day when he had first crossed the police tape and headed into the alley, echoed in his head.

Don't show up drunk to a crime scene again. I won't go down with your burning ship.

If she thought, even for an instant, that he had lost his weapon while drinking, then she was apt to pull him off the case. And the truth was, this case had done wonders in keeping his mind off what had happened six months ago, visiting his partner's grave notwithstanding. Sure, when he closed his eyes, he still saw Clay's face, but it was gone when they were open now, which was *something*.

Raul took a hard left onto a small side street, and Drake observed his surroundings as he followed.

The concrete jungle that was downtown had slowly yet consistently reduced in stature, and most of the houses in the residential neighborhood he now found himself were of the row variety, constructed of plain brown brick, their windows covered in iron bars. It wasn't until he followed Raul onto the next street that he realized how close he was to where Thomas's body had been found.

What the hell is going on here? Where is Raul headed?

It was starting to look less and less like a payoff that Weston had delivered to Raul, but an errand that he was supposed to run.

Before Drake could contemplate this further, the Rover suddenly signaled and pulled over to the side of the road. The movement was so sudden, or Drake had been so lost in thought, that for the second time that day he passed Raul. He looked away at the last second, but he thought that maybe, just maybe Raul had made eye contact.

Thinking that his cover was blown, Drake sped up and did a quick lap around the block, circling back. When he spotted the Rover again, he was sure to park well enough away, backing his Crown Vic partway into an alley, hiding it from view—thankfully no peanut pushers this far from downtown—and got out of his car.

Even from a distance, he could tell that the Rover was now empty. He scanned the street quickly, his eyes jumping from one plain brick townhouse to another, trying to figure out which one that Raul had entered.

It was a near-impossible task; the street was quiet, and aside from a young black man sitting on the steps outside one building sipping from a brown paper bag, it was empty.

Well, Drake thought, *I've come this far.*

He made the short walk toward the man on the stoop, debating whether to pull out his wallet or his badge.

He decided on his wallet.

"Hey, you see which building the man from the Rover entered?" Drake asked.

The man looked up at him, and Drake realized that he was older than he had first thought. He had coarse black hair thinning at his temples and deep grooves around his mouth.

The man brought the bag to his lips and took a long swig.

Drake waited. When he was done with his drink, he just stared off into the distance acting not only as if Drake hadn't said anything, but like he wasn't even there.

Drake snapped his fingers.

"Hey! Buddy! Where did the guy from the Rover go?"

The man looked at him.

"I didn't see nothin'. And you best not call me *buddy* again."

And with that, the man stared off into space again, occasionally taking a sip from his bottle of liquor.

Drake was starting to regret his decision to choose his wallet over his badge. And yet, he resigned himself to giving it one more chance. He held a twenty-dollar bill out to the man.

"You —"

The man snatched the twenty from his hand with amazing speed, tucking it into his pocket before turning away again.

"The man from the Rover?" Drake asked again, feeling his frustration and impatience growing. It might do both of them some good to throw the man on the hood of his car as he had the psychiatrist.

Still no answer.

Drake took out another twenty, but when the man went to grab it this time, he pulled it back at the last second.

"Which building?" he demanded.

The man looked at him again and sneered, revealing a gold grill.

"12," he said simply. When he went to grab the bill this time, Drake let him have it.

The numbers on the stoop that the man sat read 22, the second 2 having since unfastened and now hung upside down. Drake looked up the street first, then down. The numbers went down away from his car.

Drake started in that direction when the man hollered after him.

"Best you get back in your car, *white boy*. This ain't the place for you."

Drake ignored him and continued up the street. The man with the bottle was nothing but a street punk, and yet Drake wished he had his pistol with him none-the-less. He wondered if Raul had had a similar interaction but decided that he probably hadn't. If he had, then Raul would still be hanging around when Drake had come around the block.

No, Raul knew exactly where he was going.

With a deep breath, Drake headed toward the building marked with the number 12, both digits right-side-up this time, and then made his way to the door. There was an intercom of sorts affixed to the brick wall, nothing at all like the elaborate one outside Clarissa Smith's home, with a half dozen white buttons on it. His heart sunk when he realized that there were no names on the corresponding tags beside the buttons. At first, he thought that they were blank, but upon closer inspection, he realized that there was something on them, only the text was sun-bleached almost to the point of being unrecognizable.

And when his eyes fell on the tag adjacent apartment 6, a smile crept onto his face.

He debated pushing a button, either the one for 6 or maybe even all of them and speaking in a garbled voice with the hopes of someone buzzing him in, but for some reason, he tried the door first.

It was unlocked.

Detective Damien Drake opened the door and stepped inside, moving toward apartment 6, the one that had the uppercase 'V' listed as the tenant.

Chapter 29

CHASE DIALED DRAKE FIRST. On the fifth ring, she hung up and tried again.

"Come on, come on… pick up, Drake. Pick up your damn brick cell phone."

She hung up this time after the sixth or seventh ring, cursing the man not only for not picking up but also for his lack of answering machine.

Chase tried Detective Frank Simmons next, but the result was the same. But at least he had an answering machine.

"Detective Simmons, this is Detective Adams. Meet me back at the station as soon as you get this. I've got a lead on the psychiatrist that Thomas Smith was seeing."

Third on her list of people to call was Detective Henry Yasiv, who she suspected was still with Frank, but she gave it a shot anyway.

The man picked up on the third ring.

"Yasiv," he said, his voice low.

Chase's eyes narrowed behind her sunglasses.

"Henry? Why are you whispering? Where's Detective Simmons?"

"He's in the other room, talking to Neil Pritchard's mother. You were right… they lived together. Not only that, but they were close. Like really close. And Frank, well, Frank… let's just say that the man has a way with the elderly. Shit, she must be at least eighty." Even though he was whispering, there was excitement in his voice.

"And? What's she saying?"

"You aren't going to believe this, but—wait, hold on a second."

"No, don't—" but the man had already lowered the phone from his ear. His words were muffled as if he was covering the mouthpiece with his hand.

"I'm just getting a glass of water; I'll be right with you." There was a short pause. "No, I know it's not polite to keep a nice lady waiting, Frank. I'll be right there." When Henry spoke again, his voice was clear. "See what I mean?"

Chase pushed the start button on her BMW, and it purred to life.

"Get to the point, Henry," she said as she shifted the car into drive and headed away from the Smith estate.

"Yeah, sorry, anyways, Frank asked her about Neil and Thomas Smith and, get this, she says she remembers the man, only when she knew him, he wasn't a man, but a boy. Apparently, Thomas and Neil were best friends back in the day. I mean, *way* back. I thought she was just a little, you know, *old* if you catch my drift. But she isn't... Mrs. Pritchard is sharp as a tack. She said she knew Tommy's—that's what she calls him, Tommy—brother Weston. Even had dinner once or twice with Ken and Samantha Smith."

Chase exhaled audibly.

Neil and Thomas were friends back in the day...

This was the connection she was looking for and had suspected.

"Detective Adams? You still there?"

"Still here, Henry."

"Okay, but that's *still* not all—shit, hold on again, sorry... what? I mean, pardon?" there was a short pause. "Yes, I found a glass and yes, it's clean, not even a water spot. I'll be right there, okay?" And then to Chase, he said, "Yeah, so I just thought that if she—Mrs. Pritchard—knew Thomas maybe she knew Chris Popo-whatever his name is, right? So, I asked her. And you aren't going to believe it. Chris—"

The man was so excited now that he was starting to ramble like someone with ADHD hopped up on a handful of Molly's. Chase couldn't take it anymore. Revelation or not, this was excruciating.

"Chris went to the same high school as Neil and Thomas and they were all pals—chums as she calls them—er, best friends to us, maybe BFFs if you—"

"Henry," Chase said calmly as she took a left onto the highway.

"Do people use BFF still? I've heard—"

"Henry," she repeated. When he just continued to drone on, she shouted his name this time. "*Henry!*"

The man on the other end of the line cleared his throat.

"Yes, Ma'am. Sorry, I'm just a little excited is all. I tend to ramble when I hear—"

"Did either of you happen to tell the woman that her son is dead?"

There was a long pause, and even though she could hear what she thought was Frank's voice in the background, this time Henry didn't answer him.

"No, shit, I guess we forgot."

Chase shook her head and her mouth twisted into a scowl.

"Jesus, you guys have to tell her about her son, about Neil."

"Yes, of course, ma'am. I'm sorry, we—"

"—were just excited? Yeah, I get that. Tell the poor woman, would you? Then get back to the station. I've also got some news to share. But good work, Henry. *Great* work."

She could almost hear the man's cheeks contract in a smile. It was also evident in his voice, which came out just a little squeakier than usual.

"Thank you, ma'am."

"And Henry?"

"Yeah?"

"Let Detective Simmons break the news, okay?"

"Yes, that's fine. I don't li—"

"And don't call me ma'am. Makes me sound as old as Mrs. Pritchard."

Detective Yasiv started to add something else, but Chase had already hung up and was in the process of making her next call before he even uttered a syllable.

Neil and Thomas and Chris were all friends in high school?

Chase did some mental math, considering Thomas's age. The man was thirty-eight when he passed, meaning that they had all been friends twenty-five or so years ago. Did they keep in touch? Were they still friends now? Did they hang out?

Probably not Chris considering that he was in Montreal, but maybe Neil and Thomas. After all, both were wealthy, young, and probably frequented the same types of bars. Maybe—

"Officer Dunbar," a scratchy voice announced.

"Ah, yes, Dunbar, it's Detective Adams."

She paused and Officer Dunbar, the man she had entrusted with Thomas's cell phone, spoke up.

"Adams, I've found something that you might want to see. It's—"

"Bring it to the main conference room in an hour. But I need you to do something for me right away."

"Yep, sure. What do you need?"

"I want you to pull up old high school records from New York in ninety-two or ninety-three. Look at where Thomas went to school first, and then see if you can put both Neil Pritchard and Chris Popolo…"

"Papadopoulos," Dunbar helped her out.

"Yeah, that's it. See if they went to school together, and if not, maybe they went to neighboring schools. I want to know if they played football, baseball, even faced off against each other on the debate team."

Dunbar cleared his throat.

"Can't you just ask Thomas's wife or brother where he went to high school? It would speed things up a bit."

Chase pictured Clarissa's stern face.

No more questions, they can't find out I've been talking to you.

"They aren't cooperating. Anyways, can you do it?"

"Yeah, I can do it."

Chase thought for a moment.

"Is that... is that it, Detective Adams?"

"No, one more thing. Can you check Thomas's phone, cross-reference it for any messages to Neil or Chris? I don't have either of their numbers, but they shouldn't be that hard to find. Any texts, Facebook posts, or Twitter mentions that connect them recently. Can you do that?"

Chase turned onto the off-ramp and continued toward 62nd precinct.

"Dunbar? You still there?"

"Yeeeeah, about the cell phone. Sergeant Rhodes was in here asking about it earlier."

Chase choked and her dashboard lit up, indicating that she was veering out of her lane.

"He what?"

"Yeah, there are some rumors going around in evidence that a lawyer from Smith, Smith and Johnson—"

"Jackson."

"Sorry, Smith, Smith, and Jackson came by the station and wondered why his cell phone, which he apparently never leaves home without, wasn't on the list of evidence collected from the crime scene. He wanted to know if the killer had stolen it. And then Rhodes came down asking about it..."

Chase swore under her breath.

"And what did you tell him?"

"I told him that I hadn't seen it, that sometimes things get delayed when entering into evidence. Could be because they were processing all the gold chains and grills from the gangbangers who died in the Bronx the other night."

Chase exhaled sharply, but still had an uncomfortable feeling in her chest.

"What did he say?"

"He did what Rhodes always does."

Dunbar paused.

"Which is?"

"Oh, sorry. Forgot you haven't been with us for that long. Rhodes turns bright red like a tomato with glasses on and tells us to *get our act together.*"

Chase breathed a little more easily.

"Ok, great. Thank you, Dunbar. We'll get the phone into evidence soon, okay? Just see what you can do about the schools and the messages and meet me in the conference room in one hour. Keep your head low."

"Will do. See you soon."

Chase hung up the phone just as she pulled into 62nd precinct parking lot.

Then, for the first time in what felt like forever, she smiled.

We are going to catch this bastard after all. Whoever he is.

Chapter 30

DRAKE WAS SURPRISED BY the cool air inside the apartment building. This area didn't strike him as a place that would have AC in the individual units, let alone throughout the main lobby.

As his eyes adjusted to the dim lighting, he tried to catch his bearings. To his right was a hallway, and Drake could make out the outline of several doorways along its length. To his left was an old staircase.

He blinked twice and swiped dust motes away from his eyes. Now that his pupils had dilated to the size of olive pits, he could make out a *1* above the door nearest to him. He couldn't see a number over the next in the hallway, but he assumed that this door, and the one after, were *2* and *3*, respectively.

Which meant that apartment *6*—the one belonging to *'V'*—was upstairs.

Drake started in that direction, but the sound of a door closing from somewhere above gave him pause. The sound of footsteps that followed set him to motion.

Thinking fast, Drake spun away from the staircase and pressed his back against it. His eyes whipped back and forth, trying to find a place to hide; an alcove, maybe, or a fire escape.

But there was nothing.

The footsteps were nearing the bottom of the stairs now, and he knew that it would only be seconds before whoever it was—*Raul? Was it Raul?*—spotted him standing there, hands empty.

Drake did the only thing he could think of, grateful for once that he had left his coat in the car and that his shirt, a simple, white t-shirt, had significant, and fresh, sweat stains around the armpits and collar.

He slumped against the stairs, turning his head away from the staircase mouth, and rested his right arm on his crossed legs, palm to the sky. Drake's mouth went slack, and he closed his eyes, trying to force his heart to beat more slowly, to regulate his breathing.

The footsteps continued, and Drake pictured Raul making his way to the front door, perhaps offering a pitiful glance at a junkie who had passed out after shooting too much smack.

Then the person paused, and Drake felt eyes on him.

It took every ounce of his being not to spring to his feet and throttle whoever it was.

And then, just when he thought that his pathetic ruse was going to fail, that Raul was going to come over and tap him on the shoulder, all the while saying, 'nice try, officer,' he heard the footsteps move away from him. A second later, the door opened and closed.

Drake counted to sixty before opening his eyes. And even then, he allowed them to lift only to half-mast. He turned his head with what he hoped was a natural-sounding groan toward the door.

When he saw that Raul's dark face wasn't staring back at him, he leaped to his feet and then took the stairs two at a time.

The upper landing and layout were identical to the lower level down to the cracked floor tiles. And it appeared that his first instinct had been correct: the first door he passed had a number 4 sticker haphazardly glued to it. The next door was blank, but the last had a six drawn in sharpie on the center. There was also something different about this door.

Drake leaned backward, peering over at the door to apartment 5. In passing, they looked nearly identical: both covered in coarse wood veneer with matching gold doorknobs, both of which had bare spots revealing plastic beneath.

Only it wasn't plastic, at least not on the door to apartment 6. This doorknob was too shiny to be plastic.

It was metal.

And door 6 wasn't wood either, Drake thought, inspecting the thick hinges. It had been painted to look like wood, to look just like the others, but it was a facade that didn't stand up to closer inspection.

What is this place? Drake thought, but even before he rapped his knuckles off the steel door, he thought he knew.

And when a light and airy female voice spoke from within, his suspicions were confirmed.

"Raul? That you? Did you forget something?"

Drake said nothing. He heard the woman come to the door, followed by the characteristic sound of locks being turned.

Three of them to be exact.

The door opened a crack and Drake grinned widely. The solitary eye that peered from the opening, green with meticulously applied mascara, widened.

"You're not Raul," she said. Her voice was suspicious, but not alarmed.

"No, I'm not," he said.

The woman opened the door wider and slid one arm up the frame giving him a peak of a black brassiere that fit snugly on her pale, but ample breasts.

"What's your name, sweetie?"

The girl grinned.

"Veronica. What's yours?"

Drake looked her up and down. This was no ordinary call girl, despite the neighborhood. She was pretty, bordering on beautiful, and lacked the loose skin and pallid flesh of some of the other prostitutes that plied their trade in exchange for a quick fix.

This was a high-class hooker hanging out in a neighborhood made to disguise, and perhaps even protect, their very *distinguished* customers.

Drake thought back to what the black man on the stoop had said.

Best you get back in your car, white boy. This ain't the place for you.

No, it wasn't. But maybe it was *a place for Thomas Smith and people like him.*

The woman in the doorway mistook his silence for speechlessness.

"Like what you see?"

He nodded.

"Veronica... is it?"

The woman's eyes narrowed suspiciously at the repetition of her name, and she slid her hand down the back of the door. She also shifted her small frame to one side, clearly getting ready to slam the door if he tried anything.

"I have the police on speed dial," she said, her voice transitioning from sultry to stern without a hint of change in her face or smile.

"That won't be necessary," Drake said, pulling out his badge. "My name's Drake. *Detective* Drake and we're going to have a little chat, you and I."

Chapter 31

SOMETHING OF AN AMATEUR chef himself, Beckett Campbell was in culinary heaven at Magpie's Pizzeria. The atmosphere was comfortable without being grungy, and the service was frequent but not intrusive.

He started with oysters, despite being apprehensive at the idea of oysters and pizza, and they were on point. But it was his main that was simply spectacular.

Wood-fired pizza topped with thick pieces of mozzarella, fresh basil, and handmade meatballs he imagined his Nona would make... had she been Italian, not from Missouri and her favorite meal wasn't 'fancy Mac 'n' Cheese', which meant putting sliced hot dogs in it and throwing a half-melted piece of American cheese on top.

It was, in a word, delicious—the pizza, the Mac 'n' Cheese not so much.

When the waitress came by, a young woman with long brown hair and stenciled eyebrows, to ask him if he needed a refill on his Coke, he nodded and then wiped some liquid gold from his lips.

"I have to say that this is one of the best pizzas I've ever had."

She laughed politely.

"Thank you."

"No, seriously. It's delicious... and I'm from New York."

The woman smiled at him, but the joviality of a moment ago was gone from her face.

"The owners were—are—from New York as well," she said softly.

Beckett feigned surprise at her choice of words.

...*were from New York.*

"Really?"

"Really. But," her voice hitched, and Beckett stood, putting a comforting arm over her shoulder. "I'm sorry, it's just so fresh."

"It's okay," he said, trying his best to comfort a woman that he had only just met.

She wiped a tear from her eye.

"It's just that one of the owners left us unexpectedly."

Beckett nodded.

"I'm very sorry to hear that. Is the other owner in the restaurant? I would like to give my condolences and congratulate him on the fantastic meal."

The woman squinted at him suspiciously.

"You aren't a food critic, are you? Because if you are, this probably isn't the best time. And you have to tell me if you are, you know."

Beckett suppressed a smile.

"No, not a critic. Just here on a quick vacation."

The waitress returned his smile.

"He's here. And he's also the head cook. Let me see if he'll come by."

"Thank you," Beckett said as he took his seat again.

If he had been alone, he might have patted himself on the back for his acting job. Instead, he rewarded himself with another pizza slice, despite his belly's protests.

It was just that good.

Beckett had a mouthful of meatball when a man sat down in front of him, slamming two full beer glasses on the table. His eyes shot up, and then his jaw suddenly went slack.

It was Chris Papadopoulos in the flesh.

Living and breathing.

"I'm sorry if I startled you," he said. "Here, have a beer on the house."

Beckett leaned in close, trying to wrap his mind around what was happening. He had seen images of Chris on the Internet, of his smiling face standing outside the very restaurant he was eating in now.

How is this possible?

But as he concentrated even further, he realized that it wasn't him, not quite. The man sitting across from him was heavier than Chris, with a round face, and a hairline that looked as if it had run scared from his forehead.

"You okay, buddy?"

Beckett swallowed and wondered if somehow the Internet had lied to him.

It wouldn't be the first time, that's for sure.

"Ah," the man said, realization crossing his face, "you must have seen the newspaper article. Chris was my twin brother. My name's Gregor. Here, have a beer."

Beckett finally drew a full breath, and instead of addressing the elephant in the room directly, he turned his attention to the beer instead.

"It's only eleven o'clock," he stated.

"Closer to noon, actually. Anyways, this is Montreal — we drink craft brew for breakfast."

Beckett shrugged and reached for his beer. He took a small sip at first, but then swallowed a large gulp.

Like the pizza, it was delicious. No Heady Topper, but a close second.

"I'm really sorry to hear about your loss," Beckett said.

The man sighed.

"The police say they have leads, but I don't have much faith in them. You know, some people come in here and chastise me, ask me how dare I open the restaurant so soon after his death, but this is what Chris would have wanted. And it's what I want, too; keeps my mind off things, if nothing else."

Beckett nodded.

"I understand. And I must say that I'm glad you did: this pizza is *delectable*."

Gregor's round face brightened a little.

"Thank you. Marissa says that you're from New York? In town for a visit?"

"Yep, just for the day. Read about the restaurant and decided to—"

"It's okay, you can say it: you wanted to see what it was like, after the… after Chris's passing."

Beckett made a face as if to say *I'm sorry* and *You got me*, at the same time.

"It's okay, I get it. Being from New York, though, you should be used to this sort of thing. Here in Montreal on the other hand…" he let his sentence trail off before continuing. "Me and my brother were born in New York, you know."

"That's what… Marissa said. Do you get a chance to go back often?"

Gregor shook his head.

"No, neither myself nor Chris have been back for years. Our restaurants take—*took*," he corrected himself, "up all our time. The restaurant business is tough everywhere, but particularly so in Montreal."

"So I hear. But you keep making pie like this and I see this thing going far. You franchised yet?"

Gregor smirked.

"No, not yet. Have three locations though. Franchising was something that Chris was working on."

"I'm sorry," Beckett said again.

"That's alright. What else you have planned for your visit?" Gregor said, clearly wanting to change the subject.

"Well, truth be told, I'm actually a doctor. Was thinking about checking out the new hospital."

"Ah, the Glen. It's a beautiful place. Slow as shit, but can't fault them on that—you know, public health care and all."

"I hear you."

Gregor drank half his beer in one gulp.

"You know what? I have a buddy that works there… an eye doctor or cancer guy, nerdy bastard, can never understand half the shit he says. Anyways, his name is Lucas Taylor. If you can find him, let him know that I sent you. He'll give you a tour."

Beckett nodded.

"That's awesome. Thanks again."

Gregor finished his beer and stood.

"Enjoy your stay in Montreal. And your meal's on me."

Beckett rose to his feet as well.

"No, I can't—"

The man held up his hand.

"Consider it northern hospitality."

Knowing that Gregor was not going to change his mind, Beckett thanked the man for what felt like the hundredth time and then shook his hand.

With a full stomach and a mind racing with ideas, Beckett left Magpie's and searched for a cab to take him to the Glen hospital.

Chapter 32

DRAKE JAMMED HIS FOOT into the door a split second before Veronica closed it on him. He winced, wishing for once he had been wrong about the construction of the door; it was indeed solid core steel.

"I just want to talk to you!" Drake pleaded.

The woman didn't answer; instead, she gritted her teeth and continued to try to shove the door closed.

Steel or not, there was zero chance of it closing with his foot lodged in it. Veronica must have realized this because without warning, she let go and bolted back into the room.

Drake threw the door wide.

"Oh no, you don't," he said as he stormed into the room. Drake had only taken a handful of steps before he was floored by the interior of apartment 12-6.

Unlike the cracked linoleum and old, worn staircase in the hallway, this room was *exquisite*.

The floor looked like high-grade hardwood, buffed so well that it reflected a mirror image of the bed in the center of the room like a frozen pond. The four corners of the bed itself extended nearly to the ceiling, each adorned with red sheer curtains hanging from them in tied loops.

Off to one side was a series of 'toys', including a black leather mask and something that looked like a cross between a hairbrush and a paddle ball racket.

The sound of a window opening brought Drake back.

He whipped his head to the right and saw only Veronica's pale butt cheeks, black thong, and one ankle still in the apartment; the rest of her was already out the window. If it hadn't been for her Jimmy Choo's—her left heel snagged on the window frame—he would have never made it to her in time. But it was stuck, and while she swore and tried to twist to free it, and then gave up entirely and tried just to shake it off, Drake was on her.

He grabbed her around the waist, which was thin but muscular, and pulled.

Veronica didn't come, at least not right away.

Instead, she shrieked and grabbed the exterior brick wall, her long nails scraping across the surface.

But like at the door moments ago, she realized that this was futile and eventually gave up.

Veronica's body went limp and Drake effortlessly pulled her inside the apartment.

But once inside, she reanimated, her hands whipping about in a whirlwind, her now chipped and torn fingernails clawing at his face, her one heeled foot kicking at him.

"Fuck," Drake swore. He managed to avoid most of her strikes given that he was behind her and squeezing her tightly. But when he lifted her off the ground, she took advantage of her position and thrust the heel of her shoe. It whacked painfully off his shin and he winced.

"Relax!" he shouted.

Veronica didn't hear or didn't care. If anything, her attack became more frantic, and she was soon throwing her head back, trying to smash the back of her skull against his teeth.

Drake had enough. He reared back and launched her onto the bed. Veronica's head banged against one of the bedposts sending a wooden *thonk* throughout the apartment, and she grunted.

"I said relax!" Drake repeated, breathing heavily.

This time, Veronica listened and pulled herself into a seated position while massaging the back of her head.

"I'm not here to bust you for soliciting. I'm a goddamn homicide detective, for Christ's sake."

The woman's eyes widened at the word.

"Come here for a quick fuck, then?" she spat. "I give a reduced rate for men in blue."

Drake scowled.

"I need to know about one of your clients."

She laughed.

"Fat chance of that. My business is based on discretion," she gestured to the room around her. "You think that scuzzy johns paid for all this?" she raised her remaining shoe next. "For these? No, I'm not telling you anything. Not a single word."

Drake stared at her. She was undoubtedly pretty, but she also had a hard streak running through her. For a moment, his detective mind started whirring, putting together a narrative about what had sent her down this path, but he stopped this runaway train by shaking his head.

Who am I to judge? It's her body, her life. Let her do as she wishes.

Drake's tone softened.

"Look, I understand, but I don't want you to open your entire diary for me."

"Diary? I have Quickbooks."

Drake raised an eyebrow.

What the fuck is Quickbooks?

"Anyways, I just need to know about one particular client, to know if he was here Monday or Tuesday. That's it."

Veronica's body slumped a little as if the realization that giving up this little tidbit of information couldn't hurt, and if it did, it would be a lot less painful than the alternative.

"What's his name?"

"Thomas Smith."

Her lips pushed together unconsciously and when she spoke next, Drake knew she was lying.

"Don't know him."

Drake grabbed a chair from behind him and spun it around.

"Look, I know you know him," he said as he sat. "I know that a man came here, Thomas's housekeeper, and gave you a whole whack of cash. Now I'm not sure if it was just to tidy up some unpaid bills, or if it was for you to keep your mouth shut. I'm thinking more the latter. Anyways, I just need to know if he was here that night."

Veronica swallowed visibly.

"He's... he's dead?"

Drake tilted his head to one side, indicating that he was. Her eyes went hard again.

Again, he was struck with the same sensation that he had with Weston and Clarissa Smith: her surprise was genuine.

"I don't know what you're talking about. Nobody has been here today. You, Damien Drake, are my first client."

"You seem pretty cut up about a man you claim not to know, Veronica."

She shook her head.

"Never heard of him."

Drake reached into his waistband and pulled a set of handcuffs loose.

"Okay then, looks like I'm going to have to take you in."

"What for?"

Drake sighed.

"You want to keep your business private? Tell me what I want to know. Because me hauling your ass down to the station will be anything but."

For a second, it looked like she was going to break. Then she scowled.

"I'm not telling you anything."

"Suit yourself," Drake said. He stood and glanced around quickly, spotting something that looked like a nightgown on the table from which he had taken the chair.

"Here," he said, tossing it to her, "put this on. We're going for a ride. And if you try to run again, I'll make sure I parade you around the front of the station wearing nothing but your skivvies."

Chapter 33

THE GLEN HOSPITAL LOOMED large, a hulking, segmented series of squares at the intersection of several major roads and a subway station. The colored blocks—yellow, red, blue, brown and gray—were like the sections of a striped caterpillar.

Beckett Campbell nodded.

"Impressive," he said to himself.

He paid the taxi driver, then walked toward the doors to the front of the blue building.

As he neared, a pleasant-looking woman in her mid-seventies with gray hair sporting a blue apron of sorts opened the door. At first, Beckett thought she was trying to exit, and he hurried to hold it open for her.

She laughed.

"Thank you, but I'm a greeter here."

Beckett cleared his throat.

"Sorry."

She smiled and gestured for him to enter.

"That's alright, it happens all the time. What can I help you with today?"

The AC blasted Beckett as soon as he stepped inside, and the sweat on his face and arms immediately started to dry.

"I'm—" *alright, thank you*, he was about to say, but then he remembered how helpful Gregor had been. "Actually, maybe you can help me. I'm looking for a Doctor…" he racked his brain. "A doctor Lucas Taylor?"

The woman continued to smile, but she tilted her head to one side slightly.

"I'm sorry, but I don't know all of the physicians that work here."

Beckett blushed.

"Yes, of course. My bad."

"That's quite alright. What department is he in?"

"Pathology," he answered immediately.

"Ah, pathology is in block E, which is at the far end of the complex. Floor four."

Beckett turned and was met by a labyrinth of staircases and elevators and narrow hallways.

"Block E?" he asked.

"Just head straight..." the woman began.

***

After figuring out how the color coding inside the hospital worked, Beckett didn't have too much of an issue finding Block E.

Problem was, when he tried the door, it was locked. There was a security desk behind him, but the person manning it was too enthralled in something on their computer screen to pay him any notice.

Besides, Chase had told him to keep a low profile.

A quick peek through the glass window showed a portly woman coming toward him.

She opened the door, and he grabbed it, holding it for her to pass through.

"Thank you," she said.

"*De nada*," Beckett replied, before sliding into Block E. The door led to a bay of elevators, and he took the first one that opened to the fourth floor.

Beckett stepped out of the elevator into a hallway that extended both to the right and left. Before him, however, was a long glass window, through which he saw a man crouching over a low table.

Beckett strode closer to the window, noticing that the man was deep in concentration creating slides from a paraffin block.

"Excuse me, but I'm looking for a Doctor Lucas Taylor?" he asked politely.

The man didn't look up.

"He's not here—giving a tour."

Beckett frowned.

"Expect him back soon? Is there a place I can wait?"

The man sighed and raised his face to look at him, and when their eyes met Beckett broke into a grin.

"Diego? Diego Lopez? What the hell are you doing here?"

The man's eyes instantly widened.

"Beckett! Jesus, it's been so long, how you been? What are *you* doing here?"

Beckett started to answer, but Diego held up a hand.

"Hold on a sec, I'll go around."

The man exited stage left, then a moment later popped his head through a red door. Striding with purpose, he came right up to Beckett and gave him a big hug with his thick arms.

"It's been what, four, five years?" Diego said as he let go of Beckett.

Beckett grinned broadly.

"Almost seven now."

The man clapped him on the back.

"No kidding. Where did the time go? So, what brings you up north?"

"Just a little vacation is all. Wanted to check out the hospital I've heard so much about. You work here?"

Diego offered a mock salute.

"Yep. General pathologist. How about you? Last I heard you were teaching at NYU."

Beckett shook his head.

"I was, but now you're looking at Senior Medical Examiner for the NYPD," he replied with mocking pride.

Diego's eyes went wide.

"Enough work to keep you busy?"

"Shit yeah. Have three residents working under me."

Diego laughed a tight bray that seemed strange for a man of his size.

"Not here, not in Montreal. Rarely get anything interesting like you must get in the Big Apple," he looked skyward briefly in contemplation. "Except this one case…"

"Yeah," Beckett said, still smiling. "About that."

***

"I can't pull the body out right now, but I have some pictures you can see," Diego said, wheeling his chair up to a computer monitor. "Here, take a seat."

Beckett nodded and obliged. Without delay, Diego scrolled through a series of on-screen menus with blazing speed, before a photograph popped up.

Beckett only needed to see one to know that the killer was the same.

The similarities were uncanny: a single length of rope tying the legs and hands together behind his back, a crusty brown butterfly on it. Beckett whistled softly.

"I know, eh?" Diego said. "Pretty messed up. But that's not even the worst part. The worst part is that the cause of death was—get this—allergic reaction to an injection of pureed butterflies."

"A butterfly slurry," Beckett whispered, his eyes still on the screen.

"Pardon?"

Beckett shook his head.

"Nothing—an allergic reaction, huh?"

Diego looked at him suspiciously.

"Yep. But why do I all of a sudden get the feeling that you aren't in Montreal only for vacation?"

Beckett chuckled. He had worked with Diego for over a year during a forensic fellowship in Cleveland. The man was bright, intuitive, and one hell of a doctor. Shit, if it hadn't been for his Mexican descent, he might very well have taken Beckett's job in New York.

"C'mon now, Diego," he teased, "I came for the food, sun, and ladies. But now that you brought it up, I do have a couple of questions for you…"

When he was done asking his questions, Diego let out a deep breath.

"That's messed up."

"No kidding," Beckett replied. "And if—*when*—they ask, I was never here." He waved his hands across his face.

"I'm a ghost."

Diego smiled.

"Sid Vicious's apparition."

A chuckle rose in Beckett's throat and an idea popped into his head.

"You think you can wrap up here anytime soon? My flight's not until ten, and I've been dying to see what the evening night life in Montreal is like."

Now it was Diego's time to titter.

"Oh, I can show you a good time," he said, shutting off the computer monitor. "Up for a little *danse contact*?"

Chapter 34

"KEEP ON WALKING," DRAKE instructed Veronica.

The woman looked ridiculous, her hands were cuffed behind her, forcing her chest forward. The nightgown that he had thrown at her was some sort of blue and teal princess dress with snowflakes on the front.

Veronica spat curses at him every few minutes, some graphic enough to make a sailor blush, but made no attempt to run even after they exited the apartment complex.

Drake squinted in the bright sun and looked around briefly to orient himself.

"Make a right, I'm parked down the alley just up ahead."

Another curse, but the woman did as he ordered.

It was either a bribe, he thought, Weston using Raul to hand over cash to Veronica so she would keep her mouth shut about Thomas's extracurricular activities — which to this point she had done, or it was something even more sinister.

Drake was beginning to entertain the very real possibility that Veronica, along with Raul and Weston Smith, were involved in the three murders.

He pondered this as they made their way toward the alley. It seemed unlikely, and there was the issue of coming up with a shared motive of people from very different walks of life. And yet in Drake's experience, most of the murders that weren't spontaneous were usually committed by someone close to the victim.

Clarissa, then? Could she be involved somehow? Maybe she found out about her husband's infidelity and took a hit out on him?

But that wouldn't explain why Weston was involved in the cover-up. He could understand Raul, but not Thomas's brother.

Love triangle, perhaps? Clarissa was sleeping with Weston and...

Drake shook his head, trying to stem these runaway thoughts.

What about Thomas's parents? Ken Smith? Could they be so ashamed of their son, of him seeing a prostitute, and so concerned that their reputation would be scarred by his actions that they would go as far as to kill him?

This seemed equally unlikely, given that he was the poster boy for their philanthropic side. Even considering Thomas's not-so-perfect juvi record, the Smith's had simply thrown money at people before, so why not now?

And what in God's name was with the butterflies? How did that fit in?

Drake grunted in frustration.

"Here; turn here," he instructed.

Veronica did, but then when she saw his car, instead of cursing, she laughed.

"I know it's old, but—" Drake started, but then realized that she wasn't laughing at his Crown Vic.

She was laughing because there was a man sitting on the hood. The same man who had warned Drake that *this ain't the place for you, white boy.*

Drake reached out and grabbed the handcuffs and pulled Veronica close.

"I think you're a little confused; this isn't your usual stoop," he said. "Too much of that donkey piss, I think. Why don't you just slide off and find another? And, please, be careful not to scratch the paint."

The man smiled and Drake smirked back at him.

He gently guided Veronica off to one side, telling her to stay put. Then he took a step toward his car.

"All right, no more games," Drake said. "Get off the car."

"Or what?" the man asked. As he spoke, two other black men appeared from behind the Crown Vic. While the stoop kid was thin and wiry, these two were heavily muscled, shoulders bulging from identical wife beaters.

The man on the right had a wooden baseball bat slung over his shoulder.

Drake reached into his front pocket, and the thug not holding the baseball bat moved a hand to the butt of a pistol jutting from his belt.

"Easy now," Drake said, holding his other hand in front of him. "Just getting my ID."

The man squatting on his car squinted at the mention of the word ID.

Drake flipped his detective shield and held it out to them, hoping that they could make out the embossed letters NYPD at the top even from more than a dozen feet away.

"I'm a detective," he said. "I don't want any trouble, I just want to take this girl down to the station and ask her a few questions. That's all. You guys turn around and walk away, and I'll forget you were ever here."

The man slid off the hood and Drake thought that maybe his luck was changing. That he might get out of this jam unscathed.

He was in no mood for a fight. What he needed was a drink.

"You? A detective?" the man glanced at the Crown Vic, and then at the man with the baseball bat. Without exchanging a word, the latter reared back and swung the bat, shattering the rear taillight and spraying the concrete alley in red plastic. "I've never seen a detective that drives such a piece of shit car."

Drake shook his head.

What's with people today? First the fucking peanut vendors, and now this... do I look that bad?

"I'm a detective," he repeated, hoping to finally break through to these guys.

"If you 5-0, then I'm Donald Trump," the leader said.

And with that, bringing up the president's name, Drake knew what little luck he might have had, had run out.

Where before he wanted to avoid a fight, Drake found himself wondering if he was going to come out of this alive.

The most surprising thing was that this realization didn't affect him as he expected it to. What did he have to live for, anyway? Everyone at the precinct hated him, maybe all of New York, and his late partner's wife and daughter loathed him.

I should *be dead*, he thought, a grimace forming on his face. *Not Clay—it should have been me lying on the ground, a bullet hole in my chest.*

"I'll tell you what, *cracka*. Let the girl go and get into your car and get the fuck out of here. You have one chance."

Drake couldn't believe his ears. Deathwish or not, there was no way he was going to listen to an ultimatum from a street thug.

"I've got a better idea," he said. "Why don't you and your boyfriends go get another *coupla forties*, get drunk, and feel each other up? How about *that?*"

The second he finished his sentence, the skinny black man sprinted at Drake. He was awkward, and perhaps a little drunk, and Drake easily side-stepped a looping right hook. As he stumbled past, Drake drove his fist into the man's side, hearing him grunt as the air was forced from his lungs.

Drake stepped over his hunched form and reared back, intent on delivering a blow to the side of the man's head next.

Only he never got a chance to throw the punch.

Just as he was about to thrust his fist forward, the baseball bat struck him in the side.

The only thing that saved Drake a collapsed lung, or worse, was the fact that he was leaning backward at the time of impact. The baseball bat landed just above his right hip, and as soon as Drake felt contact, he went with the blow. Propelled by the momentum of the bat, he was sent spinning like a top, dispersing some of the impact.

A flash of searing pain shot up from a spot just above his hip, and he grunted.

Knowing that another strike was imminent, Drake tried to straighten, but found he couldn't; his right side refused to do anything but curl protectively.

The muscular man with the baseball bat stared down at him, smiling with bright, almost florescent teeth.

Drake groaned in agony, then reached for the baseball bat. To his surprise, he managed to grab it. The man yanked it backward, but Drake refused to let it go, knowing that if he did the next blow might be to the back of the head.

"Get the fuck off me," the man grumbled. He pulled his other hand back and in a lightning flash his thick knuckles rapped off the right side of Drake's face in a rabbit punch.

Stars filled his vision and Drake had no choice but to let go of the bat.

Coughing, which caused agony to shoot up his right side, Drake could only just make out the silhouette of the baseball bat as it was hoisted into the air again.

"Do it then," he said, spitting blood onto the ground. "Just fucking end it, put me out of my misery."

Drake closed his eyes in expectation of the finishing blow, thinking about Clay and how he had died.

But it never came.

Instead, he heard the familiar squawk of a police siren, followed by a car screeching to a halt.

"Fuck! Run! *Run!*" Someone yelled, and Drake opened his eyes.

A portly police officer with horseshoe hair leaped from the squad car, gun drawn.

"Freeze!" the officer hollered. "Freeze!"

Predictably, the thugs did not oblige. Instead, they turned and sprinted, bolting past Drake's Crown Vic and deeper into the alley. Even the man whose ribs Drake had cracked seemed to heal and channel his inner Usain Bolt.

With the side of his face pressed against the concrete, Drake watched their feet—a blur of Nike Technicolor—all but disappear. He sighed and closed his eyes. There was no way that Officer Donut was going to be able to catch them, and he couldn't exactly drive after them with Drake's car blocking the alley.

With tremendous effort, Drake somehow managed to push himself to his knees, then to his feet. The agony in his side was still flaring, but the pain in his face had already become a dull throb.

"I said, *Freeze!*" the officer repeated.

"They're gone, dumb ass," Drake muttered.

"This is your last chance! *Freeze!*"

It was only then that Drake realized the officer was talking to him.

What the hell?

Drake turned slowly in his direction, arms raised. As he did, he noticed Veronica, who didn't appear to have moved the entire time he was getting pummeled, slide two steps to her right.

"I'm a detective," Drake said, keeping one eye on her. "Detective Damien Drake, 62nd Precinct, Badge Number 09813. My shield is right there on the ground," he nodded toward the shield that he had dropped when he had broken the stoop man's ribs.

"Damien Drake, I recognize the name," the officer said.

Great, Drake thought, half expecting the man to just shoot him right then and there. But then the officer shrugged.

"Sounds familiar, anyway. Okay, I'm going to grab the shield and check it out. Don't move, okay?" his voice was calmer now.

As he did, Drake saw Veronica start to slide even more quickly along the wall.

"This is my suspect—I'm bringing her in for questioning. For Christ's sake, don't let her run."

"Just a sec," then to Veronica, the officer added. "You stay put, miss."

When the man bent down to pick up the shield, Veronica made a break for it.

Oh, no you don't, Drake thought. Pressing his right arm protectively against his side, he started after her.

"Hey!" the officer shouted, but Drake ignored him.

Shoot me if you want, but I'm not letting her get away after all this.

Despite the pain in his ribs and his throbbing face, he managed to catch the girl in only a few strides.

"Friends of yours?" Drake whispered in her ear as he pulled her roughly toward his car. He opened the door and threw her in the back seat and slammed it closed. Then he turned back to the officer.

"Can I have my shield back?"

The man looked up and swallowed.

"Yes, I'm sorry Detective. I didn't know, I thought—"

"Whatever," Drake grumbled. He swiped it from the man's hand.

"You okay? Your," he waved a finger in a circular motion around his temple, "face is pretty swollen."

"Fine," Drake said, turning his back to the man and making his way to his car. He coughed once and spat a phlegmy wad tinged with red corners.

"Hey, you want me to go after them? Call in some backup?"

Drake shook his head.

Backup? They're long gone by now.

Drake shrugged and got behind the wheel of his car. Then he leaned out the window.

"Are you going to move your car, or are you going to make me reverse all the way back to 62nd?"

The man's eyes bulged, and he quickly hurried to his squad car.

"I'm sorry—sorry."

As the officer started to back out of the alley, Drake spotted a black Range Rover drive by.

Maybe I wasn't as stealthy as I thought.

But when he finally managed to drive out of the alley, the Rover was gone.

As he passed the police officer, the man hollered after him, "Detective Drake! Your tail light's broken!"

Drake looked up to the mirror and saw that a horrible swollen lump was already starting to grow around his right eye and temple.

"Give me a fucking ticket," he grumbled, then sped off.

Chapter 35

DETECTIVE CHASE ADAMS PASSED several uniformed officers on the way to the boardroom, all of whom eyed her strangely.

Chase stared back but bit her tongue.

What the hell is wrong with everyone? Is it Drake? My association with him?

It was obvious that some of the more experienced detectives, especially those who had worked with Clay, were not happy that she treated Drake without disdain or anger. She also knew that they gave her a little leeway because she was new.

Or pretty.

Maybe both.

But now she was wondering if giving Drake another chance had been the right decision. After all, he was teetering on the edge—even she could see that. He was so close that a strong fart might push him over. And yet she meant what she had said to him that first day.

Chase could handle the heat coming off of him, but she wouldn't set herself alight. If push came to shove, and she really, really hoped it didn't—the fact was, she felt for Drake, and what he had been through—then her hands were poised and ready.

She pulled her cell phone from her pocket and dialed Drake's number once again.

Still no answer.

Chase swore and raised her eyes just in time to see a young officer in full uniform walk by and look her up and down.

"What are you looking at?" she snapped.

The man blushed and shook his head.

"Nothing... sorry," he said as he hurried past.

Chase pulled the conference room door open, and breathed in the cool air, thankful for at last having a moment to herself. She placed a folder on the table and opened it, sifting through the photographs she had downloaded from the Internet.

Then she started putting them on the corkboard with Thomas, Neil, and Chris, marking the connections with lengths of thread from one photograph to another. When she was done, she stepped backward and stared at her work.

Too many damn question marks, she thought with dismay.

The door opened and Detectives Yasiv and Simmons stepped into the room.

Henry's eyes went to the board first.

"Jesus, what is this? John Gotti's family tree?"

Chase frowned.

Simmons, however, was only staring at her, his eyes bulging slightly more than usual. Henry followed the man's gaze, and his expression quickly matched that of the much older man beside him.

Chase took a deep breath.

"I get it, you all hate Drake. But you know what? I don't give a shit. Whatever you think of him, whatever you think he did, he is still a detective and a damn good one. All that matters is the case... all that matters is finding the killer before he strikes again. So just fucking deal with it, okay?" she spat, and then immediately regretted her words. She was angry; angry that they were no closer to the killer despite her crochet work on the board, angry that if the killer's pattern stayed true, he was going to strike again in another day or so and they had no clue who his next victim was.

Chase swallowed hard, trying to enact her poker face.

Henry shook his head.

"What? What is it, Detective Yasiv? You couldn't stop running your mouth at Mrs. Pritchard's place, so please don't hold back now."

The man's eyes darted to Frank and then back again.

"It's just..."

"Oh, for Christ sake," Chase cried. "Spit it out!"

To hell with the poker face.

"It's your outfit," he said at last. "You look like a dark-haired Geni Bouchard."

"A *what?*" Chase exclaimed. She glanced down at herself and her heart palpitated. And then it flooded her system with blood, especially her cheeks and ears. Chase wasn't one to embarrass easily, but for the first time since her superior had caught her with a needle still poking out of her arm back in Seattle, she was mortified.

She was still wearing her white tennis outfit, the tops of her breasts still damp from sweat, the hem of her skirt barely covering her upper thighs.

Chase took three deep breaths, scolding herself for being so careless with each one, and then addressed the detectives.

There was nothing to do but own it now.

"Alright, get over it. I was playing tennis with Clarissa Smith and didn't get a chance to change."

The two men continued to gawk.

"You guys okay? You want to go to the bathroom and work the wood out of your peckers? No? Okay, then let's get started."

She turned, trying to will the blood from her cheeks when the door opened again.

"Oh, sorry I thought Detective Adams..." Officer Dunbar's sentence trailed off when Chase spun around again. "Oh, I, uh..."

"You too?" Chase said.

"I'm sorry—"

Chase cut him off by raising a hand.

"Sit down, Dunbar."

The man did as he was told, placing a thin hardcover book that he had in his hand on the table. Detectives Yasiv and Simmons also sat.

Chase turned to the board, her face flushing again when she realized that she had spun too quickly, and her skirt had lifted.

*Well, fuck it. I'm here, I'm wearing this. Let them fill their spank banks. I have a—*three—*murders to solve.*

"Three victims, all of whom grew up in New York City. All have the same MO: butterfly slurries, a butterfly drawn in blood on their backs," she began, pointing to the appropriate photographs as she spoke. "Frank and Henry, you told me that Mrs. Pritchard informed you that the three vics were all friends when they were younger. We also have Clarissa Smith, wife of the deceased and her creepy servant Raul. Above them, Weston Smith, Thomas's brother. And at the very top we have Kenneth Smith of SSJ," she moved her finger laterally now. "We also have the mysterious '*V*' that we found in Thomas's phone, and then this is Dr. Mark Kruk, first the Smith's marital psychiatrist, but now probably just Thomas's."

Chase moved her hand to the very top of the board, where she had placed a photograph of a monarch. Beneath the butterfly were three strings like silk threads leading to each one of the dead.

"And this is our killer. Our *Butterfly Killer* as the press calls him or her," she said sourly before turning back to the others. "Anything else? Am I missing anything?"

Henry opened his mouth to say something, but Frank spoke up first.

"Mrs. Pritchard couldn't say much about the boys, other than that they used to play together."

Chase nodded.

"Beckett called this afternoon. He was in Montreal and confirmed what we all feared. Chris Papadopoulos or whatever his name is was definitely the Butterfly Killer's first victim. Matches the MO. Female blood on his back, no fingerprints, no fibers, no DNA at the scene. Our killer is meticulous, careful, and determined."

Silence fell over the room. Eventually, Officer Dunbar spoke up.

"I've got something, Detective Adams," he said hesitantly.

"Shoot."

He lifted the book off the table and held it for them all to see.

DEER VALLEY ACADEMY, 1992-1993 Annual Yearbook, the cover read.

Chase's eyes lit up. Seeing this reaction, Dunbar was encouraged to continue.

"Mrs. Pritchard was right: all three of our vics went to high school together. In fact," he flipped open to a specific page marked with a sticky note. "I even have a picture of them together."

Chase leaned in close.

"Let me see," she said, and Dunbar handed the yearbook over.

The photograph depicted four boys, their heads thrown back in laughter, their eyes wide. In the background was a fifth boy, half-cut off by the frame. Unlike the others, this boy's head was hung low, his lips curled into a frown. His long arms hung limply at his sides.

Chase recognized the first three, and pointed to them, saying their names out loud as she did. When she came to the fourth boy, she pointed and looked up at Dunbar.

"Who's this?"

The man was smiling proudly.

"*That* is Tim Jenkins."

"Who?" Chase asked.

Dunbar shrugged.

"Still working on it."

Chase pointed at the kid who was cut-off by the border next.

"And this?"

"That I don't know. It's not even clear if he's supposed to be in the photograph or if he just photobombed. I searched through the yearbook and couldn't find anyone that looked like him."

Chase nodded and turned back to the board. She affixed another piece of paper in the same row as the other victims, but off to one side. She wrote the name Tim Jenkins on the paper but didn't run any strings.

Potential victim or suspect?

"Great work. Anything else?"

When Dunbar didn't answer right away, she looked over at him.

The man appeared uncomfortable again, as he had the first time he had seen her outfit.

"What now?" Chase asked.

He mouthed the words, *Cell phone,* his eyes darting to Frank and Henry.

"It's fine, go ahead," Chase encouraged him.

Dunbar cleared his throat before continuing.

"Someone had deleted most of the information in the phone; either that or Thomas was a pretty boring guy. Anyway, I was able to recover some deleted texts from about three months ago. It looks like Thomas contacted Neil out of the blue; as far as I can tell from combing the social media sites, this was the first contact they'd had in years. Anyways, he starts asking some strange questions…"

Chase raised an eyebrow.

"Strange? How?"

"I dunno, it all just seems like idle chat, like they aren't really saying anything. But I get the impression that they *are* saying something. Some sort of bro code, maybe."

Chase tilted her head to one side, trying to get a new perspective on what Dunbar was saying.

"So, is there anything we can use?"

Dunbar started flipping through several sheets of paper on the table in front of him.

"Ah here," he said, referring to a transcript of text messages. "This is from Neil to Thomas, marked Tuesday, December 21st at 2:34 am. There are plenty of typos, but it basically reads: *Tommy boy, when you seeing 'v' again? I think she likes you, hahaha.*"

Chase's breath caught in her throat.

V is a she.

"What—"

"Wait, there's more," Dunbar interrupted, his finger moving to the next line. "Now here's Thomas's return text, nine minutes later: *No more texts.*"

Chase waited.

"That's it?" she said.

"That's it for another two weeks," Dunbar confirmed. "And then we're back to the nonspeak bro code."

Chase pulled a chair from the table and sat down, trying to organize all the new information in her mind. After a few moments, she leaned forward, interlacing her fingers, and tapped them against her chin.

"Okay, so these guys go two decades without speaking to each other, then out of the blue, Thomas texts Neil and they start chatting. It's all idle chitchat, until Neil mentions '*V*', alluding to her as a female, and Thomas essentially puts a stop to the convo. A month later, both are dead. Do I have that about right?"

Dunbar nodded.

"What about Chris Popo-whatever. Has he contacted Neil or Thomas?" Chase asked.

"Not that I know of—not in Thomas's phone and not online," Dunbar replied.

"Okay, so then I can think of two scenarios: one, is that there is somebody out there targeting these boys for something they did a long time ago—we know for one that Thomas Smith wasn't always the ideal NY citizen—or something happened when they got together a few months ago. The former is the only scenario that includes Chris. The key is perhaps this mysterious *V* woman," Chase paused. "Could she be the one whose blood is on the two men's backs?"

A hush fell over the detectives.

"Maybe," Chase said to herself more than anyone else. "Maybe."

She lifted her eyes and turned to Dunbar.

"Find out everything you can about Tim Jenkins and how he fits into this. Also, I'm going to need the names of all the teachers of classes that the kids were in."

"That was twenty years ago," Dunbar complained.

Chase dismissed this with the wave of her hand.

"Retired, still working, doesn't matter, so long as they are still alive."

Dunbar nodded and started to stand.

"Great work," she said, and the man smiled and left the room.

Chase looked to Detective Simmons next.

"Any idea where Drake is? We can use his help right now."

"No idea. Haven't seen or heard from him since the last meeting."

Chase turned to Detective Yasiv.

"You?"

He shook his head.

"Same here. I haven't—"

A commotion from just outside the conference room cut his answer short and drew all of their attention.

"What the fuck?" Chase muttered.

There was a pretty girl in a Frozen-themed nightgown, her hands cuffed behind her, being led through 62nd precinct by none other than the man himself.

Chapter 36

DRAKE'S FACE ACHED, AND a schism of pain shot up his side with every breath. And yet he thought he did a pretty good job of keeping his expression neutral.

He knew how ridiculous the scene must have looked to the other officers and detectives, but he didn't care. After all, he had no reputation to protect, no dignity to uphold.

That had all been lost when Clay had been murdered.

Fuck, I need a drink.

Just as he passed the door to the conference room, it burst open and Chase barged into the hallway.

"Drake? Who the hell is this?"

Drake stared for a moment, his eyes scanning up and down. She was wearing an outfit reminiscent of what Clarissa Smith had been sporting the day they had told her that Thomas was dead.

And he would be damned if it didn't look just as good as on her.

"What the hell are you wearing?" he asked, stifling a chuckle. Veronica continued to walk forward, and he grabbed her cuffs and pulled her back.

"Never mind that," Chase snapped. She leaned in close, and Drake got a strange feeling that she was sniffing him. "What happened to your face? And who the hell is this?"

"This," he said, unable to stop the grin from forming on his face despite the pain, "is *V*."

Chase was floored.

"*V*?"

"Yep, Chase Adams meet Veronica… what'd you say your last name was?"

"I didn't," Veronica growled.

"Ah well, *V* is enough," Drake said.

Realizing that Chase was still staring at him, he turned to one of the officers who had gathered around.

"Tindall, take this woman to booking, please."

The man didn't move.

"Detective Tindall take this woman to booking," Chase repeated.

Detective Tindall, a man with a long nose and painted on beard, stepped forward.

"What's the charge?"

"Nothing for now, just want to talk," Drake replied, handing the woman over. She hissed at him, and he winked. "Just a little chat."

Chase leaned in close to him again.

"Get in the conference room, Drake."

Drake nodded, then turned to the others.

"Can someone get me a nice cold steak for my eye?" When no one moved, didn't so much as crack a smile, he added, "No? Anyone?"

Chase grabbed him by the arm, her grip surprisingly strong, and yanked him in the direction of the conference room.

"Now, Drake."

He let himself be led and once inside, Chase turned to Detectives Yasiv and Simmons.

"Frank, Henry, I'll let you know when I find out about the teachers. Until then, be ready."

The two men stood and left, after offering Drake no more than a cursory glance.

"Teachers?" he asked but was only met by silence.

When they were finally gone, Chase looked at him, her eyes blazing.

"Sit, Drake. Sit and tell me what the fuck is going on."

***

"What was the officer's name? The one who saved you?" Chase demanded when he was done telling his story.

Drake frowned.

"I dunno... didn't get his name. That's what you pick up on? After what I tell you about Raul, Weston... about finding V?"

Chase just stared at him accusingly.

"I wasn't drinking if that's what you're thinking."

For almost a full minute, the two detectives sat in the conference room without saying a word.

Eventually, Chase spoke up.

"I believe you," she said quickly, and then went on to describe the new photographs on the board and the meaning behind the pins and threads.

"But we're still no closer to finding the killer," Drake said, sounding nothing if not forlorn. "You think that this Tim Jenkins might be our guy?"

Chase shrugged.

"If he is, I expect Dunbar to have something for me in an hour or so."

"You want to pay him a visit?"

Chase shook her head.

"No, not quite yet. Let's find out a little more first. If he is the Butterfly Killer, we might be able to catch him by surprise."

Drake chewed the inside of his lip.

"And if he's not the killer? What if he's the next victim... based on the time line the killer is going to strike again soon."

Drake could see that his words had struck a chord with Chase, illuminating something that she had already considered.

"You're right—it's too risky. We need someone on him, tailing him, staying outside his home. I'll get Detective Gainsford on it. In the meantime, I would love to get Raul in here."

Drake balked.

"*Raul*? What about Weston? Or Ken Smith? Now those are two guys that I want to talk to. They're the ones providing the cash, paying people off. Threatening Clarissa."

Chase opened her mouth to reply, but a knock on the conference door interrupted her.

"Yeah?" she asked.

The door opened several inches, and the man who had taken Veronica to booking peeked in.

"Sergeant Rhodes wants to see you in his office."

"Me?" Drake asked out of habit.

"Both of you," Tindall replied and then closed the door.

Drake turned to Chase, who shrugged.

"Let me do the talking," she said. "They're just looking for a reason to let you go."

"No shit."

Chapter 37

SERGEANT RHODES SAT BEHIND his desk, a scowl on his narrow face.

"Sit," he ordered in a brisk tone, one that Drake was all too familiar with.

Both Drake and Chase did as was asked.

Rhodes sighed and leaned forward.

"What in God's name is going on? You think this is a circus act? That you can just…" he let his sentence trail off and then pointed at Chase, "you look like you're dressed for a damn debutante ball, and you," he pointed at Drake next, "you look like you went a few rounds with Conor McGregor. And what's this about some girl dressed in a Disney costume being paraded around the precinct?"

Drake looked over at Chase, but his attention was drawn back when Rhodes slammed his hands down on the desk in front of him.

"Speak goddammit!" he bellowed.

Chase cleared her throat then told of the progress they had made on the Butterfly Killer case, starting with the connection with Chris Papadopoulos in Montreal, to the fact that all three victims went to high school together. Drake expected Rhodes to be pleased, seeing as they were making progress, but as Chase recounted their findings his jowls only seemed to sag lower and lower.

"That's it?" he said when she was done. "CSU has nothing? The ME has nothing? No leads? No suspects?"

"Well, we're still exploring—" Chase started.

"I've got the media breathing down my neck," Rhodes began, his face starting to turn red, "and the Deputy Inspector is chewing me a new asshole at least once a day. I've got so many orifices now that when I go to take a shit, I look like a goddamn sprinkler. And the Mayor... Christ, the Mayor is complaining that every donor with a seven-figure bank account has reached out to him, asking if they are in danger of being next by this... this *Butterfly Killer*."

Drake had seen the man upset before, enraged even to the point that Clay couldn't even calm him down, but this was different. Rhodes, despite all his bluster, seemed scared beneath it all.

And that was something new.

Drake cleared his throat.

"We need to get Kenneth and Weston Smith in here, ask them a few questions—see where the money is going. It would also be good to set up a task force. The killer's cooling-off period between murders has been—"

Rhodes's face turned such a dark shade of red that Drake stopped, concerned for the man's wellbeing.

"Really? *Really?*" the Sergeant shot back sarcastically. "I tell you that the Mayor is all over me and the media is chomping at the bit, and you tell me you want to haul two of the wealthiest lawyers and public figures in New York down here for an interview? Based on what?"

"We have—" Chase started but was once again cut off.

"Nothing, that's what you have," Rhodes finished for her. "You've got some far-fetched theories about bribes and other nonsense. But nothing about who the actual killer is or what the fuck he wants outside of getting his jollies from offing rich bastards. Tim Jenkins, now that sounds like a lead."

"Or maybe our next victim," Drake offered.

Rhodes pursed his lips and waved a hand dismissively.

"We're putting him under twenty-four-hour surveillance, see if we can catch him slip—"

"What about Raul then?" Drake asked, cutting his partner off. Chase shot him a look, the meaning of which was clear: *I told you to let me do the talking.*

"Who?" Rhodes asked now with an air of indifference.

"The Smith's housekeeper. We can bring him on suspicion of solicitation... After all, I saw him heading to the prostitute's apartment with an envelope of cash."

Rhodes shook his head.

"No, no you didn't. What you saw, Drake, was a man in the *vicinity* of the apartment with an envelope you *suspect* was filled with cash," Rhodes corrected. "There is no way you're bringing anyone involved with that family into this precinct."

"What about bringing Raul in just to chat? I mean, informally. It's clear that he knows a lot more than he's letting on. Besides, he might have seen something that he might not think is related to the case," Chase said, taking over for Drake.

Sergeant Rhodes sighed and removed his spectacles before rubbing the red indentations on the sides of his nose with index his finger and thumb. He set his glasses down on the desk and leveled his eyes at Chase.

"Fine. But I want it to be discreet, you got that? And no one is to go near any member of the Smith family. Clear?"

"Got it."

"And get someone on this Tim Jenkins right away; the last thing we need is another murder on our hands. And Chase, get the media off my back. Set up a conference for tomorrow morning."

Chase screwed up her face.

"To tell them what?"

"I don't know, just get them off my back! And if you wear that outfit for the conference, I don't care what HR says, you're done. Now both of you get the hell out of my office!"

Chapter 38

AN HOUR LATER, DRAKE found himself back in the conference room, his eyes fading in and out of focus as he stared at the photographs on the board.

Chase had done a good job piecing things together, but he couldn't help thinking that there was something that they were missing, something big. Something that might break this case.

Three victims, one of whom lived in a different country, two who had just rekindled a two-decade stale friendship, a hooker, an impish housekeeper with envelopes of cash and a fucking butterfly of all things...

Drake was reminded of a similar board that Clay had set up when they were trying to catch the Skeleton King. Only then it had been seven murders, not three, and the victims were castaways rather than New York's most affluent.

Still, there was something similar about them. For one, the Skeleton Killer had a specific MO, as did the Butterfly Killer.

The door to the conference opened and Drake turned to see Chase enter. She was wearing a dark skirt and a cream-colored blouse buttoned nearly to her throat.

"I thought I might find you in here. Did you go interview Veronica yet?"

Drake shook his head.

"No; I'm letting her stew. I told Frank that when he picks up Raul to make sure he sneaks him in through the back way, but to make sure that Veronica sees him. She was pretty tight-lipped back in her apartment; maybe seeing Raul might loosen them up. I considered asking Frank to cuff Raul once he was inside the station, but if Rhodes found out, he'd take a sprinkler shit."

Chase smirked, and he could see in her eye that she thought bringing Raul in and parading him for Veronica might help her remember Thomas Smith.

"Detective Gainsford is stationed outside Tim Jenkins's house on explicit orders not to interact with him if spotted. I said that we would relieve him tonight at ten."

Drake raised an eyebrow but resisted commenting. Watching a man's house was a one-person job. This felt suspiciously like she wanted to babysit him. And it also meant that it wasn't likely that he would be getting any "Key lime" pie tonight.

Or Johnny Red.

"What are we going to do in the meantime? I'm going blind staring at this board here."

Chase smiled.

"What? What is it?" Drake asked.

She threw a pile of papers on the desk and they slid over to Drake. He caught them before they fell to the floor.

"My guy in records came through: Thomas's juvi records. And they are worse than we thought. Much worse."

Drake grabbed the papers and started reading.

"No kidding," he said.

The first line read Thomas Alexander Smith - Juvenile Criminal Record. What followed was several pages of lists of offenses and the penalties.

"Three pages?" he asked with surprise.

Chase nodded eagerly.

"Go on, have a read — it gets better."

Drake turned his attention to the first page again.

The first crime listed was *Grand Theft Auto*.

Drake whistled.

"Wow. Really? This is no kid forgetting to pay for a candy bar."

"Nope," Chase replied with an air of smugness. "Keep going."

Three years in juvenile detention, reduced to six months, released after one month for good behavior.

Thomas was only fourteen at the time.

His eyes drifted to the next indictment.

Theft under $1000; three months' probation, $10,000 dollar fine, 40 hours of community service.

The third crime was Assault in the Third Degree, for which Thomas paid another hefty fine and was given one hundred hours of community service.

Drake looked up and rubbed his eyes. Squinting at the plain black text was making him a little nauseous.

"Yep," Chase said before Drake even asked a question. "They're all like that. Hefty fine, community service. Looks like Daddy had to shell out some cash to keep our angel Thomas Alexander Smith out of prison."

Drake tapped the corner of the page.

"Why didn't any of this come up in our background search? Juvi records are sealed, but there must have been *something* about this in a newspaper article, no? I mean, they can't publish his name, but there are other ways of subtly hinting at it, which would be of interest, especially given Ken Smith's prominence in the community."

Chase shook her head.

"Not one. Not a single article about the crimes, let alone the perpetrators—I had Dunbar double-check after I received the file. I'm beginning to think that Ken Smith's strategic donations might include some very specific editors over at the Times. The way I figure it, if you can pay them to print whatever you want, you can pay them to keep whatever you want *out* of print."

Don't I know it, Drake thought.

"And," Chase continued, "this was more than twenty years ago. No blogs or vlogs back then."

Drake raised an eyebrow.

"I've heard of blogs, but vlogs?"

"Video blogs."

"Ah."

Chase moved around to Drake's side of the desk.

"Take a closer look at the auto theft."

Drake did.

Nothing jumped out at him.

"The co-defendant."

It took Drake a second to find the line, and when he did, he whistled.

"Wow."

Chase's smile grew.

"Yep. Thomas and Neil—both of them stole the car. Looks like the two rich boys liked to get into a little trouble way back yonder."

Drake leaned back in his chair.

"No kidding," he said as he reached over and grabbed the high school yearbook again. He opened it to the page with the photograph of Thomas and Neil and the three other boys, which had been marked with a sticky note. When he had first seen the photo, he had only seen youthful glee in their eyes, their mouths spread wide in laughter. But now, given what he knew about Thomas and his youth, his perspective had changed.

No longer did they look happy, jubilant. Now they looked... *different*. They could be laughing, sure, but it didn't have to be with joy. It could be something else.

"You think that these boys pissed someone off all those years ago, and whoever it was is just getting around to exacting their revenge now? After all this time?"

Chase shrugged.

"I thought about it. I mean, Dunbar can't find a recent connection between Chris and Neil and Thomas—he's still working on Tim. But I doubt they were all chumming about in a ritzy club together. As for someone with a vendetta? I managed to pull up the case files for the most egregious of Thomas's indictments... they are readily available, only the juvi's names are censored. The car they stole belonged to a school teacher, and he was trying to have the charges thrown out. The theft? Macy's. Shit, everyone steals from Macy's. And the assault was from Thomas throwing a punch at a bouncer who wouldn't let him into a club because he was seven years underage. The guy is in his sixties now—and he's a minister."

Drake thought about this for a moment, her previous comment about Ken Smith paying off an editor still at the forefront of his mind.

"You know what? Maybe it's not the crimes that Thomas was arrested for, but for ones he *wasn't*."

Chase clucked her tongue.

"That's what I was thinking, too. But how the hell can we find out about a crime that was never reported? Never filed? No arrest made? Maybe today we can do a computer search for any notes on Thomas or Neil, but twenty years ago? Impossible."

Drake looked up at Chase.

"Not impossible. We just have to ask one of the boys."

Chase looked dubious, and Drake knew what she was thinking.

Thomas was dead, so were Neil and Chris. And they had decided to keep their distance from Tim Jenkins for the time being.

But he wasn't interested in any of them.

He leaned forward suddenly, and his finger landed directly on the face of the lanky boy half cut off by the edge of the photo, his thin lips pulled down into a deep frown.

"*This* boy... I bet he can tell us what we want to know. If we can ever find out who the fuck he is."

One look at her face was enough to tell him that she was skeptical.

"*If* he isn't just some random lurker, which we can't tell. I have Dunbar on it, just in case. Speaking of which," she said as she pulled out another sheet of paper from the folder in front of her.

"More gifts?"

"Dunbar came through again. A list of the teachers that taught the boys in high school. At first, I thought that maybe the teacher whose car they had stolen would be on it, but no such luck. He didn't work in the same district. Anyway, most are dead or long retired. I had Detective Simmons make some calls—apparently, he's good with the elderly—and three of them remember the boys. Him and Detective Yasiv are headed out to speak to them now."

"And Dunbar?"

"He's still working on the Jenkins connection. He's gonna call me as soon as he knows."

Drake spun in his chair and started adding the new information—the teacher, the mystery boy with the long arms and longer face, the bouncer that Thomas had clocked — to the board.

When he was done, he pointed a finger at the psychiatrist Dr. Mark Kruk.

"What about him? Anyone speak to him?"

Chase shook her head.

"You were supposed to, remember? Before you went off visiting hookers and getting punched in the head."

Drake chuckled and then winced as he was reminded of his sore ribs and swollen face.

"It's a waste of time, anyway. He's not going to reveal to you any patient information."

Drake shrugged, remembering how he had loathed the idea of speaking to another psychiatrist when Chase had first suggested it.

But now Dr. Mark Kruk looked like the last person they hadn't interviewed yet.

It might be worth a shot.

For several moments, both of them just stared at the board without speaking.

"Looks like a spider web," Chase finally said.

"More like an immature chrysalis," Drake said.

Chase frowned and was about to say something when her phone buzzed, and she answered it. After a few short sentences, she hung up and turned to Drake.

"That was Detective Gainsford. He's on his way in with Raul now. We should head to the interrogation room, get ready. Make sure Veronica sees him."

Drake nodded.

"Yeah, you head over. I doubt that she'll be too happy to see me first. Might be good if you can smooth things over, make her feel more comfortable. Maybe put that little number you had on before?"

Chase punched him on the shoulder, and he winced when the impact made his side flare again.

"You've got five minutes."

"Five minutes," Drake agreed. When the door closed behind her, he took his cell phone out of his pocket and made a call of his own.

Chapter 39

"RAUL, I'M TRYING HARD here, trying to understand why you were taking money to a hooker in Clinton Hill. Money that you received from Weston Smith," Chase said, leaning over her desk.

Raul said nothing, just stared across at Chase with his small, dark eyes.

Chase sighed.

"I don't understand. You come here on your own volition, without representation even though we both know that all you had to do is whistle and Weston would be here. Why? To just sit here and say nothing?"

Still nothing. Not a flash of anger, sadness, frustration. Nothing. The man's affect was slightly disturbing. Chase decided to push a little harder, try to evoke a reaction in him.

"Why were you paying the prostitute, Raul? Did you rough her up a little last time? Choke her maybe?"

Not even a flicker in the man's dark eyes.

"No? Maybe Clarissa is more your type, with her big—"

"That's enough!" the man shouted suddenly.

The outburst was so sudden that Chase recoiled in surprise.

So, there's the button, she thought. But instead of pushing it, she leaned back in her chair and studied the man. He was small in stature but had a presence that she hadn't truly appreciated when they had first met back at the Smith estate. Back then, she had thought that it would take a large man to open the massive oak doors, and was surprised that instead, it had been Raul.

Now Chase was beginning to think that Raul was "bigger" than she had first thought and made a mental note for Dunbar to look into Raul as well as Tim Jenkins.

Why are you here? Guilt? Duty? Remorse?

Chase massaged her forehead.

"You can leave. At any time, you can leave, Raul. You're not under arrest, you're not being held or detained. This is just a conversation. A conversation between two people who want to find out who killed Thomas Smith. Do you think you can help me with that?"

Raul didn't move; he didn't so much as twitch his coarse mustache. Any anger she had drawn out of him for speaking ill of Clarissa had faded as quickly as it had come. And worse, it seemed to have transferred to her.

Why is everyone involved in this case dead set on making it as difficult as possible to solve? What the hell is everyone hiding?

***

Drake pressed the bag of peas he had stolen from the staff freezer to the side of his head. He inhaled sharply, but the numbing sensation that followed was greatly appreciated.

"This is what I get, trying to do the right thing," he grumbled.

Veronica scoffed.

"I know you were seeing Thomas Alexander Smith. I know because we saw your name in his cell phone," Drake stared intently at the woman as he spoke, seeing if she would give anything away.

Veronica shook her head and rolled her eyes, but kept her lips tightly closed.

"I also think that you were seeing Neil Benjamin Pritchard."

Was that a twitch? Did she cut her breath short?

"It doesn't look good, Veronica. Doesn't look good for you at all. Two of your wealthy clients are dead, and you accepting a bribe from one of their rich families to keep silent. In addition to solicitation, we can book you on obstruction of justice, and maybe accessory after the fact. That's up to 15 years in prison, my dear."

Veronica sneered at this.

"That envelope of cash won't do you much good in prison. You'll still be turning tricks in prison, but it won't be in a giant bed with red drapes, and your clients will have names like Sadie Mae and Squeaky Fromme and not Blake and Finn, let me tell you."

Veronica was unfazed.

"Three murders, Veronica. *Murders.* Thomas, Neil, and Chris. Are their lives worth less than the cash that Raul slipped you?"

Veronica pursed her lips, then crossed her arms over her ridiculous Frozen nightgown.

"Who?"

Drake stared.

He suddenly stood, unable to look at Veronica's smug expression for any longer. Without another word, he stormed out of the room. Then he pressed his back against the wall and closed his eyes.

Just one drink. I'll head to my car and grab the miniature that I stashed in the glovebox and down it. Just one.

Drake opened his eyes and turned, and nearly stumbled when he realized that Chase was standing there, staring at him.

"It's probably thawed by now," she said.

Drake's face twisted in confusion.

"What?"

She nodded at the bag of peas in his hand. Drake growled and threw them into a trash bin by the end of the hall.

It clanged loudly and threatened to topple, but after an obnoxious *whu-whu-whu-whu* rocking sound, it settled.

"You getting anywhere with Indian Oddjob?"

Chase squinted in response to the obscure reference, and the racist nature of the remark, but then shook her head.

"He hasn't said anything. Literally nothing—aside from protecting Clarissa. I mean, why even come down here if you aren't going to speak? What's the point?"

Drake ground his molars so hard that he felt a fine powder rain down on his tongue.

Chase was right. None of this made sense. Drake suddenly found himself in the alley again, nursing his wounds, shouting at the dumb ass beat cop to move his car, when the black Range Rover drove by.

Why was the Rover there? Why would Raul still be hanging around?

Like a flash of lightning, an idea came. Chase must have seen a change in his face because she suddenly became alarmed.

"What? What is it?"

"I want to try something, okay? You said you play poker—"

"—Internet poker."

"Yeah, well can you read people?"

Chase grinned.

"Most definitely," she replied.

"Okay, good. So, here's what I'm going to do," Drake said, and then told her of his plan.

***

"That's it, Raul. You don't want to talk, so there's really no point of either of us wasting our time," Drake said. As expected, the man didn't so much as bat an eye. "No, seriously. I'll walk you out. No more questions. It's not as if you would answer them anyway."

When the man across from him still didn't move, Drake stood and walked over to him. He placed a hand under Raul's arm and helped him to his feet.

This act finally elicited a response. It wasn't so much a recoil from his touch as it was a tremor of surprise.

"Come on now," Drake patronized, "I'm not going to hold your hand."

Raul rose to his feet and turned toward the door.

"Go on! This isn't a trick."

Raul walked slowly into the hallway. He started to turn right, but Drake rushed up beside him and gently guided him the other way.

"This way," he said with a smile. "Head this way; one of the detectives can drive you home."

The man took three or four steps, then finally broke his plea of silence.

"That won't be necessary," he said calmly. "I can take a cab."

"Don't be silly," Drake pressed. "It's no big deal. I'd drive you myself, but I have a sock drawer to rearrange."

As he spoke, Drake encouraged Raul forward. He took several more steps, and they passed the open door to

Interrogation Room 1. Raul peered inside, meeting Veronica and Chase's gazes.

"I'll just take a cab," Raul said, turning back.

"You sure? Because—"

"A cab will be fine."

Drake shrugged and pointed back the way they had come.

"This way then, I'll walk you out," he said with a smirk.

Chapter 40

"TELL ME YOU SAW that," Drake said when he and Chase were once again alone in the conference room.

"As soon as Veronica saw Raul, her jaw clenched, and she glanced away. What do you think it means?"

Drake made a *hmph* sound.

"It means we have been duped, my good partner."

Chase made a face.

"Duped? How so?"

Drake turned back to the board.

"We thought bringing in Raul would make Veronica more likely to talk, make her think that Raul was going to spill the beans, cut a deal. Fucking *stupid*—we played right into their damn hands."

Chase sat and sighed heavily.

"I'm not following you, Drake," she said.

Drake moved the strings on the pegboard around so that a string went from Weston Smith to Raul then to 'V'. He then made one string go from 'V' to Neil and one from 'V' to Thomas. He was about to do the same to Chris but hesitated.

That didn't feel quite right.

"Drake, you wanna clue me in here? Tell me what the hell is going on? I have a press conference in an hour."

Drake cleared his throat.

"We played right into their hands," he said absently.

"Who?" Chase demanded, clearly becoming frustrated. "Whose hands, Drake?"

Drake jabbed Weston Smith's face with the pad of his index finger.

"This man's—or maybe his father, I don't know," he looked at Chase. "When I was following Raul, I was forced to pass him twice and…" Drake suddenly burst out laughing. "Goddammit, these guys are good!"

Chase was at her wit's end.

"For god's sake, Drake! Tell me what the hell is going on?"

Drake took a deep breath.

"I was at the cemetery when I saw Raul. He was putting flowers on a gravestone, which I thought was his mother, maybe—heard him say *madre*. But that row, the row he was standing in, was for fallen servicemen. Does Raul have a family member in the service? His *mother*? I think not."

"What are you saying? That this was all a setup? Why?"

Drake nodded, his grin slipping into a frown.

"That's exactly what I'm saying. Raul knew I would see him at the cemetery and knew that I would follow him. He also knew that if I saw him with Veronica, I would bring her in. You know… when I was being pummeled by those street thugs his car was still there. I bet Raul was the one who had called the cops, to make sure they didn't kill me."

"And bringing him here? What was that all about?" Chase asked when Drake paused to take a breath.

"Shit, he knew we'd do that too. And you saw how Veronica reacted when she saw him. She was terrified—he *wanted* to be here, just to make sure she didn't open her mouth."

Chase's face suddenly brightened with the characteristic glow of understanding.

"What about the envelope, the money?"

"I bet it was all real. I think the money was also part of the deal, a little insurance to make sure Veronica kept her mouth shut. But here's the thing, Veronica said but two words in the interview room, scared shitless that Raul would tell Weston or his father. But when I mentioned *Chris's* name, just once, she said, *who?* She didn't say *'who'* about Thomas, even though back at the apartment she was adamant, and lying, that she didn't know him. Same when I mentioned Neil. But with Chris, she said, *who.*"

Chase thought about this for a moment.

"You think she was seeing Neil and Thomas?"

Drake nodded.

"I do. I think she was seeing both of them, and I think the text messages support that. But I also think that she has no idea who Chris is, let alone sleeping with him."

Chase stood and walked over to the board.

"Weston wants to keep Veronica quiet, presumably about Thomas, but also about Neil, because he doesn't want this business about his son seeing a prostitute to come out. Makes sense. But I still feel we're missing something. What's the connection between Chris and Thomas?" Chase said.

"The high school connection."

Chase shook her head.

"I don't buy it. What happened back then that would take twenty plus years to surface?"

Drake shrugged.

"There's still the psychiatrist and the teacher to interview," he said, his eyes moving across the board. "And the other Smith's."

"Fat chance of that happening."

Drake reluctantly agreed.

"Any word from Detectives Simmons or Yasiv?"

"Not yet. Should be checking in soon," she sighed. "I've got a press conference to get ready for. You going to go talk to Dr. Kruk?"

Drake grimaced.

"No," he said flatly.

"Well too bad, I'm in charge. Go check him out, see if you can get any information about Thomas from him. Make it brief; as I said before, he's likely to jump into the confidentiality speech faster than you can fold rockets with four to a flush on board. But maybe you can startle him with your knowledge of Thomas seeing the high-priced call girl," she shrugged. "I don't know. Just try. If nothing comes out of that or the interview with the teacher, we've got nothing that will satisfy Rhodes."

Drake blew out of his mouth, making his lips vibrate.

Fucking psychiatrists.

"Fine," he said petulantly.

Chase slapped him on the back, and he winced as new pain shot up from his bruised, probably broken ribs.

"Cheer up, we'll have all night to chat, remember? We're relieving Detective Gainsford at ten."

Drake did remember, and he wasn't happy about that either. If he was with Chase, he was going to have to remain relatively sober.

"Yeah, sure, good times."

"What about the girl?" Chase asked.

"Let her go," Drake said. "She's not going to help us here. Maybe the whore will grow a conscience and talk to us later on."

"Sure, and I'm Monica Seles."

Chapter 41

"A LOSS OF ANY loved one — a child, a spouse, a parent, a friend — is always difficult. If you also work with this person, things can be even more difficult. When a parent dies, say, your instincts might be to head back to work, to use work as a vehicle to take your mind off the loss. Clearly, this won't work if your job reminds you of your loved one. When this happens, I think it's best to ask yourself why you want to go back to work. And remember, Drake, everything you say here is confidential. But it's more than that, this place is also a judge free zone. I'm here to help you recover from this terrible loss, nothing more. So please, be honest with me, but most importantly be honest with yourself."

Drake closed his eyes, not bothering to wipe away the tears that started to stream down his cheeks.

"I want to do right by him, by Clay. He deserves as much."

"Can you be more specific, Drake? What do you mean by do right by him? Remember to be honest."

Drake's breathing hitched.

"I want to make sure that his death wasn't in vain."

He heard the psychiatrist scribble something on her ubiquitous pad of paper.

"Can you be more specific? Be honest."

"I mean, he was dedicated to taking murderers off the street."

"More specific, be honest."

"Clay would want me to stay on, to continue in his memory."

"Specific. Be honest, Drake. Be honest."

"He was a — "

"Be honest, Drake. Honest. Be honest."

"I — "

"Honest, Drake, be honest. It's important to be honest… honest. Be honest!"

"It's—"

"HONEST! BE HONEST! BE FUCKING HONEST!"

"I want to catch the fucking bastard that killed Clay! I want to find him, and I want to put a fucking bullet right between his goddamn eyes!"

Drake was overcome by sobs, the word honest repeating over and over in his mind.

"I want to kill him."

More scribbles.

"But you did kill him, Drake. You killed the man who murdered Clay Cuthbert. His name was Peter Kellington and he was the Skeleton King. Clay was his eighth victim."

Drake's eyes snapped open and he caught sight of his reflection in the rearview mirror. His cheeks were soggy with tears, his eyes bloodshot.

"It wasn't him," he sobbed, his hand reaching for the glove box. He popped open and he pulled the miniature of Johnny out. "It couldn't have been him. I saw someone else there."

Drake snapped the top off and finished it in one swallow. Then he wiped the snot from his nose with the back of his hand.

Then he closed his eyes. An image of Clay's face—*Bearded NYPD Homicide Detective is the Skeleton King's final victim*—flashed, and his eyes flew open again.

Startled by the vividness of the image and the messy collaboration of fact and fiction with respect to his interview with the NYPD psychiatrist, Drake ground his teeth and pulled himself out of the car.

The pain that shot up from what he was positive were broken ribs was actually a relief; at least that pain had a tangible source, a physical injury that had caused it.

Something that he could focus his efforts on, distract his mind.

Squinting, he made out a plain white sign amidst many colorful others—Booster Juice, Subway, Audex Accounting of all things—which read: Dr. Mark Kruk, Psychiatry.

Drake made a hard right into the parking lot, and then pulled his Crown Vic close to the white sign out front of the very last unit of the seven or eight-unit strip mall. After another quick look in the mirror—he still looked terrible, the right side of his face turning a sickly gray, punctuated by a smattering of red from burst blood vessels—Drake stepped out into the failing sun.

Dr. Mark Kruk's unit was the only one in the building with the blinds drawn.

Drake walked up to it and grabbed the door handle but hesitated and took several breaths before pulling it wide. For some reason, he felt a strange foreboding sensation wash over him, as if he was going to see the NYPD psychiatrist—Dr. Stacey Weinager—standing in the entrance, her beady eyes wide, her mouth twisted in a scowl as she shouted in his face.

"BE HONEST! BE HONEST! BE HONEST!"

How she had passed him, he would never know.

Maybe it was his indubitable charm. Or maybe it was because he slept with her.

Even though there was zero chance that he was going to do the same with Dr. Mark Kruk, his heart fluttered in his chest nonetheless. He just couldn't seem to shake the feeling that he was a blind mole entering a den of vipers as he pulled the door open and stepped inside.

Chapter 42

"ADAMS," CHASE SAID AS she adjusted the buttons on her blouse. The reply on the other end of the cell phone was muted. "Detective Simmons? That you? I don't have much time to talk now. Going live in five. You got something for me?"

The connection was poor, and she had to concentrate to hear what the man was saying. A uniformed officer popped his head into the dressing room told her that the press was waiting for her.

She waved him away briskly.

"Frank, you're breaking up. Speak clearly."

"…hold on a sec…" Detective Simmons replied.

As Chase waited for him to return, the uniform reappeared.

"Everyone's out there, Detective Adams. Rhodes is —"

Chase covered the mouthpiece of her cell phone.

"Just give me a damn minute!"

The man's face went red and he left the changing room.

One minute… is that too much to ask for?

She brought the phone back to her mouth.

"Frank you really have to —"

"Detective Adams," Frank said, his voice clear now. "I'll be quick. The first two teachers, Mrs. Plouffe and Mr. Swanson barely remember Thomas and Neil. They remember Chris because he was a twin, and only then because they thought it was strange that they never met the brother — he must have gone to a different school. Mr. Urso, on the other hand, he remembers all three of the vics well. Taught 'em math. Says that they got into some trouble, but nothing serious, just 'kid stuff'."

Chase's heart sunk. Another dead end.

"Okay, thanks, Detective Simmons. I have—"

"But there is one thing that you should know about. It's Mr. Urso's car."

Chase perked up.

"Yeah? What about it?"

"I'm not sure if it means anything, and if it weren't for Henry, I probably wouldn't have noticed. I want to—"

"Frank, spit it out. I have to go!"

"Okay, okay, sorry. It's just that Mr. Urso had a new Audi S8 in his driveway."

Chase's eyes widened.

"An S8? You sure?"

"Pretty sure. Henry knows about cars more than I do. Says with the sport package he has on it, it must have cost at least six figures."

Chase thought for a moment.

A retired high school math teacher driving a one hundred-thousand-dollar car?

Her mind turned to the envelope that Drake had seen Weston pass to Raul, which later found its way to Veronica.

"I think that—"

"Gotcha, Frank. I'm thinking the same. I'm going to head to the news conference now, and then Drake and I are relieving Detective Gainsford. Take the rest of the day off, get some rest. We'll meet again tomorrow in the AM."

***

"We appreciate all the help that the public has provided, and we are working diligently to investigate each and every one of the tips that have been made to our call line," Chase squinted into the warm afternoon sun, which cast the reporters outside 62nd Precinct in gold halos. "We would like to extend our deepest condolences to Neil Pritchard's family. Like Thomas Smith, Neil was also a pillar of our community, creating and establishing many jobs for fellow New Yorkers."

Chase paused and as expected, a reporter filled the space with a question.

"Is this Butterfly Killer now considered a serial killer? Why—"

It was a power play, and she held up a hand to silence him. Unfortunately, Sergeant Rhodes, once again standing to her right, felt the need to step in and speak for her.

"Please hold your questions until the end."

Chase shot him a look. So far, her time at the NYPD exceeded every expectation. When she had first transferred from Narcotics in Seattle to Homicide in NYC, she had expected that it would take two to three years before heading a major investigation. From there, she hoped that it would only be a couple more before she could get some eyes in the FBI profiling department to give her a look. But it hadn't taken her years; her first case was the Butterfly Killer, which was starting to garner national news. Chase wasn't naive; she knew that this was mostly Drake's doing, or, more appropriately a result of his *un*doing, but that didn't matter. People had underestimated her before, had put her in positions where she couldn't possibly succeed.

And yet she had.

Her presence on the podium at this very moment proved as much.

"Right now, we are treating Neil Pritchard and Thomas Smith's murders as related. At this juncture, I would like to avoid using buzzwords like 'serial killer'. We ask that the media and the general public be respectful of the privacy of the families and realize that they are mourning the loss of their loved ones."

She cleared her throat.

"I will now answer just a few questions."

Every one of the twenty or so reporters raised a hand. Some even raised two, Chase saw. She felt something like a teacher posing an easy question to her students and having every one of them grunt *"oh, oh, oh,"* and stretch their arms so high that they were dangerously close to dislocating.

Chase pointed at a young man in the front row.

"Did Neil and Thomas know each other?" he asked.

"At this time, we are moving forward with the assumption that they at least knew each other during their childhood. It is unclear whether they have associated since." She pointed at a woman in the middle of the throng next. "Yes?"

"What about Chris Papadopoulos? Is he really the Butterfly Killer's third victim?"

Chase cringed internally at the mention of Chris's name, but when she answered her voice was as even as ever.

"Right now, we are working on solving the two murders here in New York City."

"But is he related? Is the FBI—"

Chase expertly deflected the follow-up question by pointing to a man wearing a k-way jacket off to one side.

"Raul Mendes… the Smith's housekeeper… is he a suspect in the case?"

The question caught Chase completely off guard. Raul had been at 62nd precinct only an hour ago, and they had been discreet about his presence—the cab that had taken him back to the Smith residence had tinted windows and had picked him up from the underground parking lot.

To her left, she could feel Rhodes's angry gaze and heard him start to fidget.

Now would be a good time to step in, Sergeant.

But he didn't, and Chase realized that she had made a near-fatal error by hesitating.

Trying desperately to recover, to not tip her hand, she said quickly, "At this time we do not have any official suspects. We are, however, investigating several persons of interest that may have been with or saw either Neil Pritchard or Thomas Smith around the time of their deaths."

"What about Veronica Wallace? Is there—"

The follow-up question floored her.

Veronica Wallace... how the hell did he even know her last name?

Chase herself hadn't even known it.

"Uh," she stammered, feeling her face flush. The sun, which had been beautiful as it started its celestial descent toward the horizon, now seemed sinister, its orange glow like spears thrown between skyscrapers. "Right now, we only have persons of interest. That will be all the questions for today."

Chase quickly turned, deliberately avoiding looking at Sergeant Rhodes.

"Detective Adams, is the Smith family involved at all? Is Weston Smith..."

Her lips twisted into a sneer, and she felt her heart thud in her chest. She tried to move her legs fluidly, to not let the sheer fury at once again being scooped by the media extend to the way she walked.

And yet she couldn't help but feel as if she was moving like a robot whose joints desperately needed lubrication.

How could they know about Veronica? About Raul?

As Chase and Rhodes passed several uniformed officers standing with their arms crossed over their chests, their faces pinched as if daring the media to rush toward them, she grabbed the one closest to her.

"I want to know who that man is," she seethed. The man startled, but Chase let him go and continued toward the front doors of 62nd precinct before he could get a word in.

The door had barely closed behind her when Sergeant Rhodes started to shout.

"Detective Adams I want you in my office now!"

Chapter 43

DR. MARK KRUK WAS tall and thin with a beak-like nose and light brown eyes that peeked out from behind a set of thick-framed glasses. He smiled warmly at Drake from behind a large desk and politely stood when Drake approached.

"Dr. Kruk, I'm Detective Damien Drake with NYPD Homicide," Drake said, glancing around nervously.

There was no couch in the room as there had been in Dr. Stacey Weinager's office. Instead, in the spot where Drake thought a couch might go were two comfortable looking chairs placed across from one another. The sight of the chairs caused a visceral reaction in him, and he quickly turned back to the doctor. Behind the man was a massive, built-in floor to ceiling bookshelf, which was nearly full of spines from books that were as drab as the content Drake assumed they were filled with.

"I know who you are," the doctor said softly. He reached over the desk and held out his hand. "I'm very sorry to hear about Thomas Smith."

Drake shook his hand, but not without hesitating.

This wasn't the response he had expected; he had anticipated the man feigning ignorance before spewing the party line of not being able to share patient information like some sort of robotic deluge.

"You knew Thomas, Dr. Kruk?" Drake asked, getting right to the point. He noticed several small red marks on the back of the man's hand as he released it.

"Please, call me Mark. If you insist on calling me Dr. Kruk, then I will refer to you as Detective Damien Drake, and this conversation will take much longer than either of us might want," he said with a smile.

"Fine, Mark it is. And just Drake for me, please. As you were saying... you knew Thomas Smith?"

Dr. Kruk nodded.

"Yes, he was a client of mine."

Drake opened his mouth, but Mark tilted his head to one side and continued before he had the chance to speak.

"I can tell by your expression that you expected something different... a different answer, am I right?" Again, he didn't pause long enough to allow for a reply. "Look, Drake, we are both busy men and neither of us has time to waste. The fact is, you wouldn't be here if you didn't know that Thomas was a patient of mine. Truth is, I expected you sooner." Mark squinted, and Drake knew better now than to try and answer. "Ah, yes, and you also know that Clarissa was a patient of mine—I saw them both as a couple."

Drake nodded, his anxiety slowly starting to fade. The man's straightforward nature was unexpected.

Unexpected, but also refreshing.

"Isn't that a conflict of interest? Seeing them as a couple, then Thomas individually?"

The man shook his head.

"No, not at all. If anything, such an approach helped me understand their issues better, speed things up, if you will."

Drake scoffed at this, and Mark smiled.

"We—psychiatrists—are not bad people, Drake. Quite the contrary. In fact, I look at my profession as synonymous to a gardener. A gardener keeps the lawn nicely cropped, disposes of refuse, keeps the garden watered to ensure plants bear the healthiest and heartiest fruits and vegetables. Every now and again, however, they encounter a weed. Any good gardener knows that you can't just yank the top off a weed—you have to get down to the root, make sure you remove every last trace of it, else it might return. And if it does, it often grows larger and bears more spines than the previous iteration. If it regrows a third time, it might be impossible to remove. So, look at me with no less or more scorn than you would a common gardener."

Drake stared curiously at the man, realizing that he might have jumped to conclusions about the man's straightforward nature one jumbled analogy too soon.

If he starts talking about healing stones and incense, I'm out of here, no matter what Chase will say.

As if reading his thoughts, Dr. Kruk chuckled.

"But no, Drake, to answer your question, I never saw them at the same time. I saw Thomas and Clarissa as a couple first, and then Thomas alone after the joint sessions had already run their course."

Drake nodded, his eyes leaving the man's face and continuing around the office. He was hoping that the man might have been so careless as to leave Thomas's file open on his desk, perhaps with a paragraph about someone who was stalking him highlighted.

But Drake had never been very lucky. Amidst the piles of medical and psychiatry journals, there was only a small square notepad with the name Marcus Slasinsky written on the front.

"Your personal experience with psychiatry may not have been pleasant, Drake. And, given the circumstances, I'm not wholly surprised. But have you ever given thought to continuing—"

Drake's eyes whipped back.

"What do you know of my experience?" he demanded harshly. He was starting to think that when Dr. Kruk had told him that he had expected him sooner, he hadn't just been sitting around idly waiting for him.

Mark waved a hand dismissively.

"I remember the newspaper articles about the bearded detective, your partner. The exposé in the Times."

"His name was Clay," Drake snapped. "Clay Cuthbert."

The smile on Dr. Kruk's face faded.

"Yes, of course. I apologize if I offended you in some way, Drake. I only mean to be courteous, but perhaps I've come off as sounding self-serving by espousing the benefits of my own profession." He gestured with his long fingers to the chairs. "Would you like to sit? Not for a session, of course, but to be more comfortable when you ask whatever questions you might have?"

Drake shook his head.

"No, I won't be long. I just have a couple of questions about Thomas."

The smile returned to the doctor's face.

"Of course, but despite my candor, I must remind you that even in death I'm bound to confidentiality."

Ay, there's the rub, Drake thought glumly. "I wondered how long it would take for you to say that."

"Yes, I'm afraid that with respect to these rules I am fairly predictable, unfortunate as that may be for your cause. That being said, I am quite adept at speaking in abstraction. Perhaps you would be interested in some of the more common themes that I might encounter on a daily basis in my practice?"

Drake raised an eyebrow and stared at Dr. Mark Kruk.

He's trying to help, Drake realized after a moment. *He's trying to give me information without breaking confidentiality.*

Drake doubted that this approach would hold up in court, that circumventing the rules in this manner wouldn't be blown apart even by one of the fresh out of NYU slobs in the DAs office, but he wasn't about to question that now.

After all, it wasn't his place. Drake was no gardener. He was the lawnmower that the gardener kept in the shed.

"Okay," Drake began hesitantly. "What would cause Thomas... *err*, why would a couple come to see a psychiatrist in the first place?"

Dr. Kruk answered without hesitation.

"In my practice, I would estimate that ninety percent of my couple client base has issues revolving around infidelity of some sort. Care to guess what the other ten percent is?"

Drake smirked.

"Money?"

Dr. Kruk nodded.

"Love and money rule our lives these days. And haunt us, too, I suppose."

This last part struck a chord with Drake.

His memories had been haunting him ever since he followed Clay into Peter Kellington's house.

Is he still trying to recruit a new client? Drake wondered. This was quickly followed by, *Focus, Drake, focus on Thomas and not your own issues.*

He tried to imagine the scenario that led Clarissa and Thomas to Dr. Kruk's office in the first place.

Did Clarissa find some of Veronica's underwear? There were so many of the damn things draped all over apartment 12-6, that Drake didn't think if Thomas slipped a pair into his pocket that they would be missed. Or maybe Veronica gave it to him. That wasn't out of the question either.

Either way, Clarissa finds out about the affair but based on what Chase told him, the woman is reluctant to file for a divorce, fearing that everything would be taken from her. Maybe big ol' Ken Wannabe-Mayor Smith swoops in and encourages them to stay together, makes sure that divorce court proceedings don't sully the Smith name. After all, it wouldn't be the first time he has meddled in his son's affairs.

So, Clarissa and Thomas arrive here and talk it out... and from all accounts get over it after just a few sessions. And yet Thomas isn't done yet, he's the one who comes back for more.

Thomas has more weeds to pull.

Drake cleared his throat.

"How often do you think these problems get resolved? In your experience, of course."

"Which problems?" Dr. Kruk asked.

"The infidelity."

Dr. Kruk tilted his head to one side and appeared to ponder this for a moment.

"I think that most people can be cured of their addictions, be them infidelity or other," he said with a chuckle. "Money problems, not so much. Drake, have you heard of a trigger event?"

Drake nodded.

"Sure. Like seeing an object or doing something that reminds you of the past. A heroin addict might remain clean while in a ninety-day in-treatment program, but if they happen to pass an alley on the way home, on day ninety-one, and there's a junkie sitting on the ground, thumb on the plunger, I'd reckon it might roll them right back to before treatment."

Dr. Kruk nodded.

"Couldn't have said it better myself. Provided that my patients avoid triggers, impossible as that may be over time, then I peg the success rate at a generous, and also very arbitrary, eighty-percent."

A photograph on the desk caught Drake's eye and he picked it up. In it was a smiling man with his arms around a girl who looked to be about eight and a pretty woman with long blond hair.

Drake's eyes darted up and he scrutinized the doctor, who was now smiling even more broadly.

"This isn't you," he said, holding the photo out to him.

Dr. Kruk shook his head.

"No, it's not."

Drake made a face, and the doctor explained.

"I'm afraid I'm not married, nor do I have any children."

"Then what's with the photograph?" Drake asked as he put it down on the desk again.

"It makes people feel more comfortable. For whatever reason, humans tend to cling to the notion that you can't possibly understand something, or god forbid be an expert in something, if you haven't personally experienced it. That's ridiculous, of course. Can a pathologist understand malaria if they haven't contracted it? If this were a requirement, then I suspect that the hospital might suddenly have a few extra job openings. Silly as the idea is, however, I've found that if I come across as a single man in my late thirties without a wife or kids, my client return rate drops by half. And it doesn't even matter the status of the client. A family man assumes that I can't possibly understand his plight, while a single man is convinced that I can't help them get to where they *think* they want to be. If I put up this photo up, however, nearly everyone comes back."

Drake raised an eyebrow, glancing down at the picture again, then back up at Dr. Kruk's face.

"Seriously? But it doesn't even look like you," he said.

"That's the beauty of it. People know it's there, but they don't *really* look at it," he shrugged, a depressed gesture. "People only see what they want to see. Our minds are wired in this way—an *imago*. After all, what we 'see' is only an interpretation of the world by our brain. Which, as you know, is prone to both error and experience."

Drake looked at the man curiously, and he couldn't help but think that he had a point. But he wasn't here to discuss reality. He was here to find out about Thomas Smith and if the doctor knew anything that might be able to help.

"All right, now you've just jumped from psychiatry to *woo-woo* philosophy."

Again, Dr. Kruk chuckled.

"Not a far leap, I might propose."

"Perhaps. But, back on topic, Thomas and Clarissa come here to discuss marital problems, infidelity—Thomas seeing a prostitute—and then *poof* their problems are solved. Only Thomas has something else he's working out, something that he requires more sessions to… how did you put it? To weed. He doesn't actually stop seeing the prostitute, so I doubt that was his main issue. *That* issue was the wife's issue, which I'm guessing he only came to discuss to appease her. That sound about right?"

Drake was staring at the doctor the entire time he spoke, and the man's expression had remained remarkably neutral throughout.

"This is as specific as one can get," Mark said evenly, "As I mentioned, I am unable to discuss patient's personal issues."

Drake waved a hand casually as if to say, *no big deal*.

"Of course not—I'm just thinking out loud, doc," he said passively before deciding to change tactics. "Hey, let me ask you something? Did you know Neil?"

The man's brow twitched.

"Neil?"

"Neil Pritchard."

Dr. Kruk pressed his lips together.

"Ah, one of the other victims. I can only confirm that I am aware of who he is."

This response struck Drake as odd.

"You told me outright that you were treating Thomas, so why can't you tell me whether you were also treating Neil?"

The man on the other side of the desk sighed.

"You knew Thomas was a patient of mine, elsewise you wouldn't be here. But with Neil, you're fishing. Detective Drake, I am all for being helpful, but I have worked very, very hard to build a career. I won't jeopardize that for a few fishing expeditions, if you follow my meaning. As such, I think that we have come to a natural and fitting end to our discussion, wouldn't you agree?"

Out of habit, Drake checked his watch. It was after five now, which meant that Chase's press conference must either be done, or nearing completion. He looked up and was surprised to see that Dr. Kruk was holding his hand out in front of him again, and the smile was back on his narrow face.

"I think you're right, Mark," Drake said, shaking his hand once more. After two quick pumps, the doctor went to pull his hand away, but Drake held it for a second longer.

"One last question: are psychiatrists good at poker?"

"Well, I suspect they would be; very good, in fact," Dr. Kruk replied, his smile growing to show a set of perfectly white teeth.

Chapter 44

"DAMN IT, ADAMS!" SERGEANT Rhodes shouted across the desk. "What'd I say?"

Chase felt her face grow hot, and she found herself wishing that Drake was here with her.

"*Huh*? What did I say?"

Chase swallowed hard.

"I have no idea how the press found out about Raul... or Veronica. Absolutely no clue. Maybe it was Veronica herself who told them?"

Rhodes scoffed and leaned forward in his chair.

"You're joking, right? You just finished telling me your theory about her being paid off, then she goes to the press about afterward? What the hell for?"

Chase felt her face tingling now and gave up.

"I have no idea."

She had hoped that being vulnerable might make Rhodes go easy on her.

She was wrong.

"Yeah, I know. You have no idea, none at all. Just like you have no idea who killed Neil or Thomas or Chris. And, to make things worse, during your press conference you said, 'serial killer'. Literally, you used those exact words."

There was a sudden tightness in her forehead, and she knew that her brow hadn't so much furrowed as it had folded.

"What do you mean? I said, *I don't want to call him a serial killer.*"

"Right," Rhodes snapped. "But you said the words — what world do you live in, Adams? No one has time to watch a five-minute press conference. Those words coming from your mouth will be made into a sound-bite and will be played over and over again. Shit, I'm surprised that the Deputy Inspector hasn't heard it already. Serial killer, serial killer, *serial fucking killer.*"

Chase swore under her breath. The man was right, but that wasn't what bothered her. What bothered her was that she hadn't even thought of the consequence before opening her mouth. An image of Drake's brick of a cell phone suddenly came to mind.

Maybe he is wearing off on me... maybe his plague stench is clinging to my clothes, my brain.

Sergeant Rhodes sighed and leaned forward even further, his chair creaking like an old woman's death croon.

"Do you know why you are heading this case, Chase Adams?" he asked, his lips parting into a lecherous grin. He looked like a skull with spectacles now.

"No," she said, steeling herself for what came next.

"The reason why I put you on this case, is because no one else would team up with Damien Drake. After what happened with his last partner, after what he did, no one wants to even go near him. But you... you were just so damn *gung-ho,* so eager, that you didn't even stop to ask who Damien Drake was, just like you didn't think about using the words 'serial killer' in front of the nation!"

Chase let Rhodes ramble on, not bothering to correct him.

The fact was, she knew exactly who Damien Drake was before coming to New York.

Chase had done her research.

She also knew that by teaming up with Drake she would be made the lead on their cases. Besides, Drake was a good detective. Despite what happened to Clay, Drake could still do good work and was a valuable asset.

If he kept his drinking under control, that was.

Rhodes finished his diatribe and waited. Chase knew that the man was baiting her but seeing as he hadn't actually posed a question, she didn't feel compelled to say anything.

Keep your ego out of it, her mind warned. And she took heed.

Instead of replying, Detective Chase Adams just sat there and waited. She waited until things transcended uncomfortable and teetered into awkward.

At long last, she said.

"Can I go?"

Rhodes scowled. He had been looking for a fight, that much was clear, and the fact that she hadn't engaged clearly disappointed him.

"Yes," he said curtly. "But this is your last chance. No more slip-ups or I'm making Detective Simmons lead on this one."

Chase nodded, again just avoiding the bait. She stood and exited the man's office.

"Close the door behind you!" he hollered, and it took every ounce of her willpower not to slam it.

Outside the room, she started toward her office, trying to calm her pounding heart, slow the release of adrenaline into her system.

Her hand had just grabbed the door handle to her office, when a male voice from behind said, "Detective Adams?"

She spun, her jaw clenched.

"What?"

The young uniformed officer lowered his gaze. Outside the station he had looked intimidating, his thick arms crossed over his chest in a no-nonsense kind of way. In here, however, he looked like a little boy playing cops and robbers.

"Sorry, I just wanted to let you know that I found out who the reporter was."

Chase squinted at him.

"What?" she repeated, reserving some, but not all, of the venom on her tongue.

"The reporter? The one asking questions about the housekeeper and call girl?"

Chase relaxed.

"Yeah? What's his name?"

"Ivan Meitzer of the New York Times."

Chase racked her brain, trying to remember where she had heard or seen the name before.

The man recognized the concentration on her face and continued.

"He was the one who wrote the article about the Butterfly Killer? Also did a whole series on the Skeleton King about six months ago."

Chase remembered her conversation with the detectives when the Butterfly Killer article had first surfaced. About how she would take whoever was responsible for the leak off the case immediately.

"Thanks," she said. "That will be all."

The man nodded and then left Chase alone with her thoughts.

Chapter 45

DRAKE SAT IN THE booth at Patty's that was starting to feel like his second home.

Broomhilda was back, surly as ever, and it took him nearly ten minutes to get a cup of coffee. He didn't even bother with the Key lime pie.

The place was busier now, which was something that made him uncomfortable. Usually, he preferred to meet later at night, preferably in the early morning hours, but that simply wasn't possible given his impending date with Chase.

Drake wasn't happy about being seen here while the sun was still out, and neither was his contact.

The bell above the door chimed, and a man strode over to him, this time keeping his dark hood on. He slid into the booth across from Drake and then quickly reached into his jacket.

"Wait," Drake said, and the man stayed his hand. "Not this time. This time I need something else."

The man frowned, which accentuated the deep grooves around his mouth.

"Drake, we had an arrangement."

"I know, I know. Did you get the shot of Raul?"

He nodded.

"Good. Now, I know you aren't going to like this—" Drake began but was cut off momentarily by a groan. "—but I need you to do some digging for me."

"What kind of digging?"

"I need you to find an article… a newspaper article," Drake began, trying not to be deliberately obtuse. "One that was never published."

The man leaned back, and pulled his hand out of his jacket, the yellow envelope still tucked somewhere deep inside.

"Like on an Internet site? Drake, I'm—"

Drake shook his head.

"No, this is from a long time ago. Something that may or may not exist."

If his contact could frown further, his lips would have slid right off his face.

"What are you talking about?"

"Before I tell you, you must promise that whatever you find, you won't publish it."

The man shifted uncomfortably.

"Drake, what the hell is this? We had an agreement. After the Skeleton King, you said in exchange for information about specific cases, I would pay you cash. That was it. That was our agreement."

Drake took a sip of his coffee. It tasted like charred tar.

"I know. But this is different. This is something I don't even know exists. But I need you to look in places that I can't. If you do this, I'll promise you the exclusive for the entire Butterfly Killer's case when we catch the bastard." He cringed at his own use of the moniker, but it had been intentional.

And it worked: the man's expression transitioned from disgusted to interested with just those two words. And then, as Drake had predicted, he nodded.

"What do you need?"

"I need you to use your contacts at the Times and any other media outlets that you might have access to. I'm looking for anything from about twenty years ago—anything from, say, nineteen ninety to ninety-six—from New York City that involves the victims Neil, Chris, or Thomas. I'm also interested in newsworthy reports regarding Deer Valley

Academy, the students or their parents, including Kenneth Smith. And butterflies. Seriously, I—"

"Woah," the man interrupted, "anything about *butterflies? Anything?*"

"Yes, anything. But here's the rub: I don't want articles that have been published. I already have a guy on that, and it looks to be a dead end. I want things that *weren't* published. Do you catch my drift?"

"Like articles that have been redacted? Military memos? FBI? Because there's—"

Drake shook his head.

"No, not military or FBI, nothing like that. We're not talking Area 51 shit, just news articles that for some reason an old crusty editor decided at the last minute that, *hey, we're going with something else instead.* Just like that, out of the blue. Maybe he wants the draft copies and the reporter notes, too. And maybe, *just maybe,* this editor starts pulling into the parking lot in a newer model car or is suddenly obsessed with checking the time on his new Rolex, if you catch my drift."

The man was nodding now, and Drake was glad that he didn't have to spell it out for him.

"Twenty years ago? That's going to be all paper. It's going to take time, Drake. Some real grunt work."

Drake sipped his coffee.

"So what? Get someone else to help you out. Two or three people, maybe. Interns. But this has to stay—" what did Simmons say? DL? —"on the DL." The word seemed even stranger coming out of his mouth than *Butterfly Killer.*

The contact considered this and then stood with such suddenness that Drake instinctively pulled back.

"I'll do it," he said as he slid out of the booth. "But only this once, Drake. And it better be worth it."

"It will," Drake promised as the man turned and headed toward the door. "Trust me, it will."

"I'll send you an email when—*if*—I find something."

Then the door chimed, and he was gone.

Less than a second later, as if on cue, Broomhilda arrived at his side.

"Whiskey?" she asked.

Drake thought about this for a moment, before deciding against it.

"No, not this time. Just the bill."

He wanted a drink. My god, did he ever. But he couldn't.

He still had work to do tonight.

PART III - Butterfly

Chapter 46

THE INTERIOR OF THE *house was dark, and the air was thick with the scent of unwashed bodies, the brooding aroma of sweat and urine.*

"NYPD! Peter Kellington, step forward with your hands up!"

There was a staircase extending to their right and a narrow hallway on the left-hand side. Just inside the front entrance, and to Clay's immediate right, was a closed door.

Clay turned to Drake and then indicated the closed door with the barrel of his service revolver.

"Watch my six."

Drake nodded back and moved a handful of steps into the house.

He heard Clay take several deep breaths, then he threw the door open, sweeping the gun from his left to his right. As his partner stepped into the room and started to clear it, Drake turned around, covering Clay's now exposed back.

He pointed his gun halfway between the hallway and the stairs and listened closely. Clay's breathing was still audible despite being well inside the front room now, and Drake thought he heard something like a grandfather clock ticking somewhere deeper in the house. Other than that, he heard nothing.

There's nobody here, *he thought with an air of smugness.* I told Clay this was a waste of time.

Drake was about to say as much to Clay when something clattered across the floor. Roughly the size of a marble, it came from the direction of the front door and rolled awkwardly between his legs and down the hallway.

As he spun toward the front door, he caught sight of something small and white in his periphery, like an over-sized tooth, but he resisted the urge to focus on it.

Drake leveled his gun, lowering to one knee as he did.

"Drake?" Clay called.

He ignored his partner and scanned the doorway, and then the porch.

A flicker of opaque movement among the thinness of night and rain bounded down the porch steps and fled into the street.

"Hey!" Drake shouted, "Stop!"

But the man was quick and lithe, and after he leaped onto the patio stone walk, he seamlessly broke into a run.

"Stop!" Drake shouted again. He rose to his feet and started after him. In a second, he was outside, the rain pounding down on him. It ran down his forehead, blurring his vision. He swiped at it, trying to locate the shadow.

There.

The figure was already forty yards away, heading in the opposite direction of the oncoming sirens.

"Stop!" he screamed. He had taken two steps onto the porch when he heard a sound that would haunt him forever.

The crack of a single gunshot belched from the inside of the house like a thunderclap trapped in a cardboard box.

Drake whipped around, eyes wide, heart racing.

"Clay!" he cried, sprinting back inside.

There was a man standing halfway down the stairs, holding a still smoking pistol out in front of him.

Even in the darkness, Drake could see the man's pale face liquid with shock.

Drake strode forward, aimed, and then fired.

The first bullet missed, the rain in Drake's eyes blurring his vision. There was a dull thunk as the bullet embedded in the cheap plaster wall inches from the man's left shoulder.

The sound of plaster exploding onto the stairs seemed to animate Peter Kellington, and he dropped the gun and swiveled.

He took a single step and then Drake fired again.

And again.

And again.

The seasoned Detective had missed with his first shot, but the next three hit their mark.

The first struck Peter in the torso, just above his left hip. The man grunted and spun in with the impact just as the second bullet shattered his left shoulder blade. The man started to fall backward down the stairs when the third bullet hit.

This final shot tore through the bottom of his skull where it met his spine, severing his brain stem and blowing out the front of his throat.

Peter Kellington's body immediately went slack and he landed on his back and proceeded to slide down the stairs.

Drake didn't need to look at him to know that he was dead. Only a dead body reacted this way.

Instead, he ran to the room, all the while shouting Clay's name over and over again.

He found his partner lying on his back half in, half out of the room that he had been in the process of clearing when Peter had fired his only shot. Clay's eyes were open, but they were vacant, cloudy. His breath was coming in short bursts, and there was a slight hiss and sizzle accompanying each one.

Drake dropped to his knees.

"Clay!" he screamed. "Please, God, no!"

He located a single bullet hole three or four inches below his collarbone on the left-hand side. Blood was bubbling out like some sort of volcanic spring.

"No! Stay with me Clay! Stay with me!"

He put pressure on the wound, but he knew that it was too late. The bullet had clipped one of his arteries, and his life was slowly simmering out of him.

Once again Drake's vision was blurred, only this time it was from tears and not from the rain.

"No," he moaned. "Pleeeease."

He looked up at Clay's face. The man coughed once, the saliva and blood that came forth coating his thick beard, then he went still.

Drake began to sob.

Without thinking about what he was doing, he threw his gun to one side, then reached down and tucked one arm under the man's neck and the other under his legs. With a grunt, he picked his friend up and started toward the open door.

The rain was illuminated in a prism of red and blue, and the sound of police cars screeching to a halt filled the night air.

"No!" Drake screamed. "No!"

And then he fell onto one knee, lowering Clay's dead body as he did, a single thought running through his mind.

It should have been me... it should have been me... it should have been me...

Chapter 47

"WAKE UP," A VOICE said. "Drake, wake up."

Drake grunted and opened his eyes. Startled, he looked at his arms, half expecting to see Clay's bearded face nested in them, a caterpillar wriggling out of his slack mouth. But his arms were empty, his palms upturned as if summoning himself from sleep.

When he recognized the cream-colored seat, he slunk back down and stifled a groan.

"What's with you and sleeping in my car all the time?" Chase asked in an obvious attempt to keep things light.

Drake worked his way deeper into the soft leather.

"It's more comfortable than my couch," he grumbled. He cleared his throat and said, "Was I talking again?"

"No," Chase said. Her voice was even, but Drake got the impression that she was lying anyway.

He decided to leave it alone. No good could come from calling her on it, and it might even lead to her asking questions, and Drake had had enough questions for one lifetime.

Drake turned his attention to the house across the street from where they had parked, which was nestled between seven or eight identical townhouses. It was completely dark. Even the light above the front door—motion sensor, he thought—was off.

Dark like Peter Kellington's house had been.

He shuddered.

"Any movement?"

Chase shook her head.

"No. According to Detective Gainsford, Tim Jenkins arrived home at eight, turned the lights on in the kitchen in what he assumed was the family room to watch TV. At half-past nine all lights went out."

Drake nodded.

He reached onto the dash and grabbed the two stapled pieces of paper. As he scanned the first page, he said, "You really think that this is our guy? That Tim Jenkins is the killer?"

Chase shrugged.

"Don't know. But he's involved somehow, I can just feel it."

Drake cocked his head at this, remembering the certainty by which Clay and the rest of the department had proclaimed that Peter Kellington, a half-wit janitor with three priors for peeking into the high school girl's locker room, had been the Skeleton King.

Drake tried to explain that a pervert doesn't go from peeping tom to serial killer mastermind overnight, the same way that you don't go from fucking around playing street hockey after school to playing in the NHL, but they wouldn't listen.

What had Clay said?

I know it's him; I feel it in my bones.

Drake shook his head and changed the subject. The nightmares had left his waking hours for the time being.

It was best not to encourage a return.

"Hey, why do rich kids always use three names?" he asked.

Chase looked at him.

"What do you mean?"

Drake looked down at the report that Detective Yasiv had made on butterflies and read, even as he spoke about something else entirely.

"Neil Benjamin Pritchard... Thomas Alexander Smith..."
Drake said absently.

"Everyone has a middle name."

Drake looked up.

"Not everyone... but I get it, most people do. Still, only rich kids seem to use it regularly. What's yours, by the way?"

Chase blushed.

"Edith."

Drake chuckled.

"Edith? Jesus, are you an eighty-year-old woman from North Dakota?"

He had expected a laugh but didn't get one.

"It was my grandmother's name," Chase said, turning back to the house.

Drake went silent and returned his attention to the report. He had nearly completed the first page when Chase spoke up.

"What's yours?"

"Hmm?"

"Your middle name? What's yours?" Chase asked.

"Donald."

"Donald?"

"Yep, Donald."

"Damien Donald Drake? Triple D?"

Drake laughed again.

"Yep."

"And you're making fun of my name?"

Drake shrugged and scanned the interior of the BMW dramatically.

"Yeah, but I'm not rich, so I don't use it, Chase Edith Adams."

"Touché, my friend. Touché."

Drake went back to reading.

"Hey, did you know that caterpillars can increase their body weight a thousand times in three months?"

"Really?"

Drake waved the paper.

"So Henry says. It's all here. Our little Detective Yasiv seems to know a shit ton about butterflies—a wee budding entomologist is he."

Her attention peaked, she asked him if there was anything else interesting in the report.

Drake shrugged.

"Define interesting… it's all factoids about the life cycle of butterflies, from caterpillar to chrysalis to butterfly."

Chase looked over at him as he flipped to the last page.

"What's that?" she asked, referring to the final paragraph that was separated by several blank lines.

Drake read the passage.

"Did you know that there's a butterfly conservation just on the outskirts of NYC? Says here that they used to have an annual Monarch festival."

"There are a bunch of butterfly gardens throughout the city, including Central Park. I had a few uniforms check them out, but they didn't come up with anything."

Drake read the passage again to himself.

"Yeah, but like this? Apparently, every year the butterfly conservation releases tens of thousands of Monarchs into the air. Used to be a big thing back in the nineties, not so much anymore."

Chase turned her body sideways to look at him.

"Monarchs? Really? I wonder why this didn't come up."

"Maybe because it shut down six months ago. Lack of funding."

"Shit, I'll get Dunbar to check it out. Might be a trigger of sorts—an ex-employee, maybe. Disgruntled at losing his job, takes it out on rich folk who donate to everything but."

Drake tilted his head. This theory seemed to have some weight to it and warranted further investigation.

Did Thomas snub the conservation, somehow? Neil too? How might Chris be involved?

He was about to pose these questions when Chase's phone started to ring.

"Adams," she said flatly after answering.

Drake watched as her brow progressively furrowed until it nearly buried her eyes.

"Really? You're sure that the lawsuit was SSJ vs Jenkins?"

Drake sat bolt upright, and Chase looked over at him, eyes bulging.

"Shit. And he used to manage the butterfly conservation before it went under six months ago?"

Another short pause and then Chase exhaled loudly. Drake was stupefied.

Chase's theory didn't just hold water, it was a goddamn river of a hypothesis.

"Alright, that's enough for probable cause. We're going to bring him in. Thanks, Dunbar."

Chase hung up and then started to adjust the pistol on her belt without saying anything.

"What?" Drake asked, his breath coming fast, his heart starting to thud. "What about SSJ? Jenkins and the conservation? Jesus, Chase, speak up!"

Chase reached for her door handle and then turned back, smiling smugly.

"Smith, Smith and Jackson were suing Tim Jenkins for some sort of wildlife violation."

"*What?* Why is SSJ suing Jenkins? They do mergers and acquisition, commercial real estate. Now they're vegan rights activists?"

Chase shook her head and shrugged.

"I have no clue. But I think that's probably something that Tim can help us out with," Chase said, unclicking her holster lock. She glanced over at him. "You packing?"

The question took Drake by surprise and he instinctively reached into his sport coat and under his left armpit.

Only then did he remember that his gun had been stolen outside the cemetery.

"Fuck," he grumbled under his breath.

"What?"

"I left it in my car," he lied.

Chase looked at him suspiciously, and he thought for a moment that she was going to challenge him on it.

She didn't.

"Check the glove box—I've got a spare. Grab it and let's go. Let's bring Tim Jenkins in for questioning... see how much he knows about the Monarch life cycle. What do you say?"

Chapter 48

BECKETT CLOSED HIS EYES, swallowed dryly, then lifted the liver in one hand while sliding the scalpel in his other beneath.

With one deft slice, he severed the hepatic artery and the liver came free.

He plopped it roughly into the metal weighing bin where it landed with a sickening plop.

"That, my Gray's Anatomy wannabes, is how you remove the liver."

It wasn't the sight of the blood that made his stomach lurch — Lord knows, he had been doing this job for nearly a decade — but it was the *smell*. And it wasn't the smell of the body, particularly not this one which was fairly fresh, but the smell of the fixative. It was the formalin; the formalin got into his nose, his hair, his pores.

And it wasn't *just* the formalin either.

It was the three beers, seven shots of Jameson, and half a pint of Crown Royal all before ten o'clock at night. Which said nothing of the drinks on the plane on the way back to NYC.

Beckett swallowed hard and gestured toward a resident who he would have normally thought was young enough that his acne scars hadn't healed yet, but this boy — a tall, reedy looking kid with thick glasses — didn't even look old enough to have had acne, let alone be healing from the scars.

Shit, this kid looked so young that his teeth were still rounded from sucking on his mother's teat.

"Reginald, jot down the weight," he said, swallowing several times in a row. "Looks like he had a good time before he went."

"My, uh, my name's Aaron, sir."

Beckett's expression turned smug.

"Yep, sure. Nice name. Now just—"

His phone, which was on the table by the door buzzed and, thankful for the distraction from the very boring conversation that was about to transpire, he strode over to it. As he did, Beckett snapped off his lab gloves and tossed them to the nearest resident. They struck a woman—*girl*—in the chest, splattering her pristine gown with blood from the corpse on the table behind him. She gasped and stumbled backward as if they were a set of eight-pound bowling balls instead of two-ounce lab gloves.

Beckett chuckled to himself as he answered his phone.

"Dr. Beckett Campbell," he said, putting on the most pretentious accent he could muster. "At your service."

There was a short pause, then a rather mechanical voice replied.

"Beckett? It's Seb."

Beckett closed his eyes and squeezed the bridge of his nose with his free hand.

Seb... Aaron... Reginald... who are these people? Really, who *are these people?*

"Look bud, I've got a wicked hangover. Can you give me something more to go on? Hair color maybe? Measurements would be better, but if you don't want to tell, if you're shy, then I guess that says—"

"It's Seb from the lab—CSU. I've been running the DNA of the blood found at the Thomas Smith and Neil Pritchard crime scene? The uh—"

"Shit, yeah, Seb, right. What's up? What did you find?" Beckett asked, pulling his hand away from his face and opening his eyes.

"Well, we got a hit. You see, the reason why it took so long is that first we had to—"

"Just spit it out, Seb. Who's the match?"

"It's from nearly thirty years ago."

The stench of formalin suddenly doubled, or at least Beckett thought it did, and his vision began to swim.

"Thirty years ago? Shit, stay right there—I'm coming down."

Beckett hung up the phone and made his way to the door.

"Dr. Campbell? Sir? What should we do with the body?"

"Just take out all the organs and weigh them," he said, without turning back. "Reginald, you're in charge."

Chapter 49

"**Tim Jenkins, NYPD!**" **Chase** shouted as she banged her fist against the door.

Drake suddenly felt a tightness in his chest. He turned his gaze skyward, wondering with a precursor of anxiety, that it might start to rain.

And then it really would be he and Clay at Peter Kellington's place again.

"Tim! We just want to talk!" Chase pounded again. "Tim! Open the door!"

A thump, followed by what sounded like breaking glass, came from somewhere inside the house. Chase whipped her head around to look at Drake.

"I'm going in," she said, reaching for the doorknob.

Drake went to grab her arm, but he was too slow.

"You can't," he said. "Rhodes—"

There was another thump, then a choked cry.

"Fuck Rhodes," Chase whispered as she grabbed the doorknob and threw it wide. "Tim! *Tim Jenkins!*"

Chase was standing in the doorway when they heard heavy footsteps upstairs, which sounded as if they ended somehow *outside*.

"Drake, go around back," Chase said, her voice high and tight.

Drake shook his head.

"No fucking way, I'm coming in."

Another thud.

Chase waved her arm.

"Go 'round back! Fuck, I'll be fine! He's making a run for it! *Go!*"

Drake bolted. He sprang from the porch and first ran east, but then quickly realized that there were at least a half dozen attached houses on that side.

He swore, then ran the other way. Three houses after Tim Jenkins's, there was a break between the townhouses, blocked by a short wooden fence.

Breathing hard, Chase's gun held out in front of him, Drake reached over, lifted the lock and then burst through.

There were cheap chain link fence partitions between the narrow yards of the individual units, and Drake catapulted over the first one without incident.

Two more, he thought as he neared the next fence.

His heart suddenly skipped a beat, and all those nights — every night for his six months on leave and, truthfully, for a considerable time before that — of drinking caught up to him.

He gasped, stumbled, but still somehow managed to get over the second fence. When he made it to the third, he was wincing, grabbing his injured ribs with one hand, the gun gripped tightly in the other.

Drake was forced to stop. Eyes wide, he tried to find Tim's house in the darkness but spotted something out of the corner of his eye. The rear fence, also chain link, shook, and his eyes instantly darted in that direction. For a split second, he thought he saw a shadowy figure vault over the rear fence before disappearing into the night.

"Hey —" Drake started, but then stopped himself and shook his head.

It's like the Skeleton King all over again, he thought. *Your mind playing tricks on you. There's no one there — you never saw anything.*

A heavy scratching sound from his left, high up, drew his eyes back. Tim Jenkins's porch light switched on and reflected off the flagstones, casting the small slanted roof in a grayish-yellow glow.

A man stood halfway out the window, a pale leg and barefoot sliding across the roof shingles.

"Hey!" Drake shouted. "Don't even think about it!"

Despite being in the next yard, Drake was still close enough that he figured even with the poor lighting that he could hit the man clean.

The man on the roof turned in the direction of Drake's voice, and then he did the strangest thing.

He pointed.

A pale white arm extended in the direction that Drake had seen the shadowy figure catapult over the fence. He was tempted to follow the finger, to confirm what he thought he had seen, but he had learned his lesson.

Fool me once…

He wouldn't fall for the misdirection. Not this time.

"You take one more step and I'll shoot," he said calmly. There was a commotion from inside the house, and then Chase's voice drifted down to him.

"Step back inside the house, Tim."

"Chase," Drake yelled to his partner, "he's unarmed."

Tim Jenkins slowly lifted his leg and then ducked back into the house. The moment he was out of sight, Drake was off again, this time without a hint of tightness in his chest.

***

"I got it, I got," Chase said as she led Tim Jenkins out of the house with his hands cuffed behind him. The man was wearing only his boxers and didn't look that much different than the photograph from the high school yearbook: medium length brown hair, a round face, strong nose, and large eyes.

"Did you see him?" Tim asked as Drake stepped aside to allow them to pass. "Did you see him?"

Drake shook his head, trying to clear his thoughts of the Skeleton King, of Peter Kellington.

"Did you see him?" He screamed into the rain. "Did you see the man running?"

Detective Frank Simmons hurled his body up the porch steps, crouching down to inspect Clay's unmoving body.

"See who? See who Drake? There's no one else here!"

Drake started to sob.

"There was someone else…"

"Drake, you alright?" Chase asked.

Drake nodded briskly.

"Fine."

"Did you see someone back there? He keeps talking about someone breaking into his house, that someone was in his bedroom trying to choke him."

Drake swallowed. It felt like he had a potato lodged in his esophagus.

"No—didn't see anybody," he croaked.

Chase leaned in close to Tim and whispered just loud enough for Drake to hear.

"You hear that, Tim? Nobody in the house except you and your buddy here."

Buddy?

It was only then that Drake realized that Chase was smiling; no, she wasn't smiling.

She was *beaming*.

And she was also holding something in one hand: a specimen container. Inside, there was a live caterpillar.

Drake simply gaped.

"It was in his bedroom. There's a syringe on the floor as well," Chase said.

Jenkins stopped walking, and Chase shoved him forward.

"It's not mine," Tim snapped over his shoulder. "I told you, there was someone in my house, standing over me. When you knocked, I woke up and he ran out the window," he hooked a chin at Drake. "I was going after him when you saw me."

Drake ignored the man and reached out to take the container from Chase's hand.

The caterpillar inside reared back, pulling its sticky legs from the inner surface like plucked guitar strings, then seemed to pause as if waiting for something.

"You heard Detective Drake, there was no one back there. But don't worry, you can keep up this charade back at the station."

Chapter 50

TIM JENKINS WAS BROUGHT into the station the same way that Veronica and Raul had been: in Chase's BMW with tinted windows driven underground and brought up through the rear elevator. Only with Tim, there was no commotion within the precinct itself. Part of it was the hour—it was nearing midnight—but Drake surmised that there was more to it than that. While Tim was only wearing his boxers and a white t-shirt that they had retrieved from his house, he didn't have the same allure as a pretty woman in an Elsa gown.

Yet his presence did raise several eyebrows.

"I'll take him to Room 1," Chase told Drake. "You—"

"I've told you already, you're making a mistake," Tim interrupted. "I haven't done anything... you should be out there looking for the person who broke into my house!"

"You'll have plenty of time to talk, Tim. Just wait for the cameras to be rolling before you make your confession," Chase said. Then to Drake, she added, "Take our furry friend and the syringe to Beckett in the lab. Get him to confirm that it was the same cocktail that was injected into Thomas and Neil—if he's still around. If not, wake his ass up."

Drake held the specimen bag up and grimaced at the sight of the caterpillar, still leaning away from the interior of the container like a miniature cobra readying to strike.

"He'll be here."

"Wait!" Tim interrupted, his tone changing from annoyed to distressed. "You think I killed Tom and Neil?"

"As I said, you'll—"

"This is crazy," Tim gasped, his eyes widened. "I thought... are you guys nuts? I had nothing to do with their deaths! There was someone in my house! *He* left those things.

Shit, I think he was going to use them on me! I didn't do anything! I didn't—"

Chase tried to guide the man forward and into the interrogation room, but he dug his heels in.

"This can't be happening! I—"

Drake shoved Tim from behind and he stumbled forward.

"Get moving. Don't give her a hard time, Tim," Drake said calmly. "You'll have your chance."

Chase started after the suspect but turned back to Drake before she entered the interrogation room.

"Get those to Beckett, then hurry back."

Drake nodded.

"Don't start without me."

***

Drake was surprised to discover that while he was looking for Beckett, Beckett was also looking for him. They ran into each other just outside the elevator.

"Jesus, you look like you've seen a ghost," Drake said as the elevator doors opened.

"Must be the hair," Beckett replied, then quickly added, "got a hit on the DNA from the vics' backs."

Drake gawked.

"*What?* Who?"

He hadn't expected that they would ever find a match to the bloody butterfly.

Beckett shook his head, and grabbed Drake by the arm and led him toward the conference room that they held their daily updates in.

"More like *when*," Beckett said. When the door clicked closed, he held a stack of paper out to Drake. "Trade."

Beckett snatched the evidence bag and handed over the DNA report. Caterpillar and syringe in hand, his eyes drifted to the corkboard with all of the new photographs with strings attaching.

"Jeez, you guys ever hear of an interactive board? This looks like it belongs in the seventies," Beckett gave Drake a quick once-over. "Sorry. Forgot you were forty going on fucking ninety-five."

Drake shook his head, trying to remain focused.

"What do you mean *when*? Who is the blood from?"

Beckett smiled.

"Oh, yeah. Sorry, battling a wicked hangover. Anyways, you have the case file in your hand. The blood on Thomas and Neil's back is from a woman who died nearly thirty years ago," he put on a British accent when he said the name, "A Martha Slasinsky."

Drake raised an eyebrow.

"Who?"

"Exactly. *Who?* A woman who died in her apartment from an apparent suicide. But here's the kicker, she was dead for nearly a month before anyone found her."

Drake stared at Beckett, his mind whirring, trying to fit this new piece of evidence, this big pile of steaming evidence, into the appropriate slot in the pegboard.

A woman dies thirty years ago, and her blood resurfaces in the murders of three wealthy New York City businessmen? What's the connection?

"But here's the kicker—yeah, yeah, we already had a kicker, I know, but here's the *real* kicker," Beckett continued, his pale blue eyes glowing now. "Martha, who was a nurse, by the way, had a son."

Drake leaned in closer.

"Yep, a son. And he lived with her."

Drake screwed up his face, failing to see the significance.

"He lived with her? So what? What does—"

Beckett shook his head.

"No, big fella, you don't get it. The boy was only eight when his mother died, but he turned nine before she was found."

Drake couldn't believe what he was hearing.

"What?"

Beckett nodded.

"Martha's son lived with her body for nearly an entire month after she died. Eventually, the neighbors complained of the horrible smell coming from the apartment, and New York's finest came 'aknocking. But it doesn't end there. The boy managed to convince the two uniforms that there was nothing wrong, that they were just defrosting their freezer—can you believe that? A nine-year-old boy… anyways, two days later, the officers came back and this time they went inside the apartment. The boy was enraged, and struck the officers, telling them that the crying had finally stopped, that they were finally living in silence, in peace. He told them not to take her, that she was all he had."

"Jesus," Drake whispered, picturing the scene in his mind. A shudder ran through him.

"It gets worse, my good friend."

How? How could it get worse?

"After the cops came the first time," Beckett continued, "the boy opened the window to try and get rid of the smell. But as smart as he was, he didn't anticipate the bugs."

Drake swallowed hard, an image of the nightmare he had of Clay's dead face, a giant caterpillar crawling out of his mouth flashing in his mind.

"Yep, you guessed it. The apartment was full of Monarchs."

Drake suddenly had to sit down. He reached for a chair and collapsed into it.

"Drake, you okay?"

He winced and held his side.

"The fuck happened to your face, anyway? You say I look like I've seen a ghost, but you look as if you've been beat up by one."

Drake didn't answer... he was too lost in his own world to offer anything. He was imagining how horrible it must have been for that boy, to have his mother first commit suicide, then be alone with her rotting body for a month.

"What happened to him?" he asked, his voice barely a whisper.

Beckett shrugged and pressed his lips together.

"He spent a number of months in a state psychiatric institution, and then was released. No record of him after that, except that he received a hefty life insurance policy from his mother, being a nurse 'n all."

"How can a nine-year-old boy just go missing?"

"As far as I can tell, he didn't 'go missing', the police report just ends."

Drake mulled this over for a moment, before standing and adding several more pieces of paper to what Detective Henry Yasiv had called Gotti's family tree.

"It's all in the report," Beckett offered, but Drake was barely listening. "What's this, by the way? Another butterfly slurry?"

"Yeah, I'm pretty sure it's the same stuff, but let me know as soon as you can."

"Well, it's definitely a Monarch caterpillar that's for sure."

Drake ignored him and continued adding squares of paper to the board.

He wrote *Martha Slasinsky* on one piece of paper, then poised his pen over the other.

"What was the boy's name?" he asked absently.

"Lemme check," Beckett said, and Drake heard him flipping pages from the police report. "Marcus—Marcus Slasinsky."

Drake dropped the pen.

He had seen that name before. He had seen it just that afternoon, in fact.

Chapter 51

DRAKE KNOCKED ONCE THEN barged into the interrogation room without waiting for a reply.

Tim startled and looked up at him as he entered, his eyes wide.

"I didn't kill anyone. I don't know what you guys—"

"What happened to your mother, Tim? Or should I call you Marcus?"

Tim visibly recoiled.

"My mother? What does this have to do with my mother? What does *any* of this have to do with my *mother*? And who the hell is Marcus?"

Drake pressed his hands against the table and leaned forward.

"Marcus Slasinsky—that's your name, isn't it?"

Tim recoiled again, but this time it was different from when Drake had mentioned the man's mother. There was something else there, something that might have passed for recognition if under other circumstances.

Drake didn't know for certain.

"What are you—" Tim started, but the door to the interrogation room was suddenly flung opened.

Drake turned to see Chase barge in.

"Detective Drake, can I speak to you outside for a moment?" she asked, ice in her voice.

"Just a sec—"

"Now, Drake."

Drake swore and pounded his fist against the table before straightening and heading toward the door. Chase held it for him as he stepped through.

"What the hell are you doing?" he asked when the door was finally closed. He tried not to let his frustration leak into his voice, but it was a losing battle.

"Me?" Chase shot back incredulously. "What the fuck are *you* doing? I was waiting for you, just like you asked!"

Drake shook his head.

"It's not him," he stated simply, shaking his head. "Tim's not the butterfly killer."

"What? What are you talking about?"

Drake quickly recounted what Beckett had told him. Chase listened with earnest, but by the time he finished, she was the one shaking her head.

"I don't know what the connection is yet, or if it has anything at all to do with our case, but Tim's our guy."

Drake balked.

"You don't know what this has to do with our case? Are you listening to me? The blood from Thomas and Neil and probably Chris's back is from a woman who died thirty years ago! A woman who was infested with Monarchs! *You don't know what this has to do with our case?*" he mocked. "What's wrong with you?"

Drake realized that his blood pressure was rising, and with this, every one of the wounds suffered at the hands of the thugs outside Veronica's lair started to throb and ache.

Chase tilted her head to one side and narrowed her eyes at him.

"What's wrong with *me*? You're not seeing the facts, Drake. Just calm down… I don't want to have to remind you that I'm the lead here, that you're on thin fucking ice as it is without these outbursts."

Drake ground his teeth, wishing that he hadn't opted out of the whiskey at Patty's Diner.

He saw red.

Who the fuck does she think she is? She's now a replacement for Clay? Well, I'll tell you what, sister, Clay is fucking irreplaceable. You're not him; you're just a two-bit narc from Seattle.

"Who got to you? Rhodes? Was it Rhodes?" he hissed. "Yeah, I bet it was Rhodes. Well fuck him and fuck you too."

Chase's furious glare suddenly turned to mush and the pain on her face instantly made him regret his words. After all, Chase had been nice to him, the only person that had given a shit about him.

"I'm sorry," he said, lowering his eyes. "I didn't mean that."

Chase took a deep breath before answering.

"No one got to me," she said calmly. "And there's nothing wrong with me—there's something wrong with *you*. You're losing it, unraveling at the seams. This is just like the Skeleton King. Did you see someone there, at Tim's house? Huh? A black shadow, maybe?" Her words stung him like arrows.

The truth was, he remembered the rear fence shaking and someone—some*thing*—disappearing into the darkness.

Or did he?

Did I see someone?

"No," he said softly. "Maybe... I don't know."

"Yeah, and that's the problem: *you don't know*. What happened to your gun, Drake? I know sure as hell it isn't in your car. Did you get drunk and leave it somewhere? Hmm? Let me guess, *you don't know* where it is."

Drake sighed heavily.

"It was stolen from my car," he replied, all conviction gone from his voice.

"Yeah, I'm sure it was. Go home, Drake. Go home and sleep it off. Get your shit together. I told you once, and I'll tell you again: you can burn with your fucking sailboat, but I'm not going down with you."

Drake swallowed dryly. After a moment, he raised his eyes and leveled them at Chase.

"Can I just ask him one question?" he said, desperation clinging to his tongue. "Please—just one? You can give me that much, can't you?"

Chase grimaced.

"Fine. But I'm coming with you. And I swear to God if you try anything, I will arrest you for obstruction. Do you understand?"

Drake nodded and turned back to the interrogation room. He moved to the door, but Chase stepped in front of him at the last moment and pulled it open. Inside, Tim looked up again, startled like a fish hoisted from water.

"I didn't do it! I didn't—"

"Shut up," Drake spat. "I just want to know one thing: do you have a passport?"

"A passport?" the man repeated, his face contorting.

"Yes, a passport. Small book about *yea* big? Let's you leave this country?"

Tim considered this for a moment, not so much racking his brain to determine if he indeed owned a passport, but more likely trying to figure out the meaning behind the query.

"No," he replied at last. "I've never left the US. Why?"

Drake said nothing but couldn't help the hint of a smile that formed on his lips. Without another word to Tim Jenkins, he turned toward Chase and the still open interrogation room door.

As he passed her, he whispered, "Hard to murder a man in Montreal with no passport, isn't it?"

Chase scowled but bit her tongue.

Chapter 52

DETECTIVE DAMIEN DRAKE WAS furious as he stormed out of 62nd precinct.

Furious at Chase, at Sergeant Rhodes, at Tim Jenkins.

But most of all he was furious at Clay Cuthbert.

Why weren't you wearing your vest, Clay? Why the fuck *weren't you wearing your vest that night?*

Less than ten minutes later, he found himself pulling his Crown Vic into Patty's 24-hour diner.

It wasn't adding up; if Tim was their guy, if he was pissed at Thomas Smith and his family for shutting down the Butterfly Gardens, taking his job away from him, then why did he murder Chris and Neil? How did they fit into the picture? And while in some twisted way the butterflies in the victims' mouths made sense, what Drake couldn't understand was the blood. *Martha Slasinsky's* blood. What the hell was that all about?

Drake shook his head. Tim Jenkins wasn't the Butterfly Killer; he was sure of it. But he also knew that it would be next to impossible to convince Chase otherwise. After all, it was her case, and she knew all about the Skeleton King, about Drake's reluctance to accept the fact that the man responsible for terrorizing New York City was Peter Kellington—a fucking perverted janitor.

In a daze, Drake entered the cafe and took his usual seat in the booth opposite the door.

Broomhilda came by, her patented sneer plastered on her lined face.

"Key lime?" she asked with something akin to disdain.

"Fuck the pie," Drake spat. "Johnny Red, double, neat."

The weathered woman nodded and then left to retrieve his drink. Drake was the diner's only patron until the door chimed and a man in a k-way jacket stormed in. His hood was down, his long brown hair a mess. He strode over with purpose and tossed a piece of paper onto the table between them.

"You should answer your damn phone," the man said, frowning.

Drake looked at him for a moment, before pulling his phone out of his pocket. He must have switched it off after speaking to Beckett. He turned it back on and set it on the table before picking up the paper.

"What's this?" he asked absently.

"It's what you asked for. And the Butterfly Killer exclusive better be good, Drake. I went to great lengths and pulled in a lot of favors for this."

Drake ignored him and turned his attention to the note. It looked like a draft written on a typewriter, and the date confirmed that this was likely the case: *SEPTEMBER 12, 1994.*

The headline read: *Boy, 14, bullied into a coma at the Butterfly Gardens.*

"What the hell?" Drake muttered. He looked up at the man across from him, but he only shrugged.

Drake kept reading.

It started out as a routine class trip, one that the grade nine students of Deer Valley Academy take every year. A field trip to witness one of the most awe-inspiring and beautiful scenes that nature provides, one that videos simply cannot do justice: the start of the Monarch butterfly migration.

Except this time, when the tens of thousands of butterflies took flight, they left a grisly scene on the ground below. The circumstances that left a boy in a coma and four others—sons of prominent New York businessmen—under investigation are unclear, but teachers and fellow students report that the victim, whose name has not been released, was the constant target of bullies.

Drake looked up and he waved the paper.

"That's it?"

The man across from him shrugged again.

"It was an incomplete article. As soon as the editor—Leeds, editor Gentry Leeds back then—saw the draft, he shut it down."

"Fuck," Drake swore.

"But I did manage to find out the affluent kids' names."

The man was smiling now, and at that moment, Drake knew who they were.

"Chris, Neil, Tim, and Thomas," Drake said, no smile on his face.

"Hmph. I guess you heard this story already. But did you know this one? The name of the boy that was in the coma?"

Drake shook his head and the man with the long hair threw a second piece of paper on the table.

There were only two words on this one: *Marcus Slasinsky.*

The breath was suddenly sucked out of Drake's lungs.

Marcus Slasinsky...

"Where's Marcus now?" Drake asked, folding the piece of paper with the name on it and tucking it into his pocket.

"No idea. You're the detective, I'm just a reporter."

Drake went to grab the other piece of paper, the one with the opening paragraphs of a news story that was never published when the other man grabbed it first.

"Naw, I'll keep this one. Like I said, I pulled in a lot—and I mean *a lot*—of favors for this. For one tiny nothing article that so far as I can tell never led to anything, somebody spent a shit ton of loot keeping it sealed. The only reason I found it was because Gentry got sick and hasn't gotten around to clean out his office yet, even though he retired more than six months ago. He's not coming back anytime soon, and guess who has squatter's rights?"

Drake eyed the man's pocket. He didn't need the typed page, not really. All he needed was the information in the article. And now he had it. What it all meant, however, he wasn't completely sure. Not yet, anyway.

Drake nodded.

"Thanks. Appreciate it," he said curtly.

The man tilted his head to one side, hair falling over his left eye.

"It wasn't a gift, Drake. It was a trade. And remember, you owe me now."

And with that, the man stood and slid out of the booth.

"Go home Drake, get some rest. You look like shit."

That's the second time tonight someone's told me that.

Drake watched him go and pounded the last of his drink. No sooner had the bell above the door stopped chiming did another sound fill the Diner.

The sound of Drake's cell phone ringing. He picked it up.

"Drake," he said, hoping that his voice didn't come off half as tired as he felt.

It's Chase, telling me to come back, that Tim isn't their guy. That she needs my help again.

But it was a male voice that answered.

"Detective Drake? I think it's about time you come see me."

"What? Who is this?"

"It's Kenneth Smith… and I think we should have a drink tonight. What do you say?"

Chapter 53

WHEN CHASE OPENED THE door to the interrogation room, she felt oddly calm, as if a weight had been lifted off her shoulders.

She hadn't meant to snap at Drake the way she had, but the pressure from Sergeant Rhodes and Drake... well, Drake being Drake, had pushed her over the edge.

But none of that mattered, she realized. What mattered is that she had a suspect to interrogate. And armed with the additional information that Officer Dunbar had provided her right before Drake had burst into the interrogation room, and the high school yearbook, she felt more than confident that Tim Jenkins was involved in both NYC murders.

So what if he "said" he didn't have a passport.

Everything else pointed at him.

And he very much fit the profile.

"Tim, I'm—"

"I didn't do it!" Tim yelled.

"Relax, Tim. You aren't under arrest. I just want to ask you a few questions. I apologize for my partner's outburst earlier; it was uncalled for. And, as I mentioned to you in the car on the way over here, you are entitled to a lawyer, and you can ask for one at any point during this interview. Do you understand?"

Tim nodded.

"I just want to go home," he pleaded. "This is just a fucked up misunderstanding. There was someone in my house, and he was standing over me, his hands..." he shuddered and for a split second, she almost believed him. "And *he* brought the container and syringe with him. I swear, on my mother's grave."

Chase found the word choice curious considering what Drake had been shouting when he had burst into the room.

"Is she... alive?" she asked.

Tim shook his head.

"No, she died last year. Wh—what does that have to do with anything?"

Chase shrugged.

"Doesn't matter. I want to ask you a few questions about your relationship with Neil Pritchard and Thomas Smith. Let's start small. Did you know them?"

Tim crossed his arms over his chest.

"Yeah, I knew them both," his eyes flicked to the high school yearbook that Chase had set down on the table. "I went to school with them."

Chase nodded.

"And what happened? They went on to illustrious careers while you went on to what... work at a minimum wage job at the Gardens?"

"No, not minimum wage. And I don't really know what they went on to do."

This wasn't true, and they both knew it.

"Tim, if you're going to lie about something as small as this, then we are going to have a problem here."

Tim pressed his lips together petulantly for a moment, then slumped in his chair.

"Fine. I know what they did for a living—shit, everyone does. It was all over the papers. The *Butterfly Killer* and all that. Do I feel bad? No. Maybe for Neil, but not for Thomas."

"Why? Because he ended up with your high school sweetheart? With Clarissa?"

Tim glared daggers at her, and Chase responded by opening the yearbook. She spun it around so that he could see.

"What? You thought I didn't know?" she pointed at the photograph of a much younger version of Tim and a Clarissa who looked nearly identical, wrapped in a tight embrace, both wearing formal attire. "It's all in here, Tim. You loved her, and she got away. Maybe she didn't like the fact that you were working minimum wage, while Thomas was a junior partner in one of the most powerful law firms in the city. Huh, one that his dad and brother *own*. Was that it? Was that why she left?"

Tim scowled at her, his face turning a deep crimson.

"It's not minimum wage," he spat, and Chase knew that she had touched a nerve. "And that's not why she left me."

"Is it because you live in a townhouse in the Bronx? Is that why? Because I've been to Clarissa's home. It's ridiculous — a mansion. Seriously, you should see it."

Tim leered.

"Oh, I know, I've seen it."

Chase made a *hmph* sound.

"Really? That's interesting because you told me a minute ago that you haven't seen Thomas in years."

"I haven't."

Okay, okay, I see where this is going.

"C'mon now, Tim. You want me to believe that you — *you*, working as a common gardener — could get with Clarissa? Could make her cheat on Thomas? Gimme a break."

Tim turned red again and he leaned forward. His breath was coming out of his nostrils in short bursts.

"You wanna know what happened? Well, maybe you should talk to Thomas' bastard of a brother Wes, or maybe the godfather, Ken. Did you know he was planning to run for mayor?"

Chase nodded.

"Yeah, I knew that."

Tim seemed surprised by this, but then continued as if she hadn't offered a reply.

"Well, then you must know that he has been going around town spreading his money around, trying to clean up the filth that Thomas had piled on top of the Smith name. I bet you didn't know that, did you?"

Chase recalled what Detective Simmons had told her about the teacher with the brand-new Audi. She had her suspicions that Ken Smith was doing exactly as Tim suggested, but decided to keep this information close to her chest.

"Go on."

"Well I hadn't spoken to Neil for years, but he contacted me a few months ago. Told me he had a hookup with a high-priced call girl. Wanted me to get in on the action, said it would be like old times. I wasn't interested but went along with it—the Butterfly Gardens were strapped, and I thought maybe I could ask him to make a donation. But when I found out that Thomas was seeing this call girl, too? I—I couldn't believe it. I mean, he had Clarissa, what more does a man need?"

"So, you killed him for cheating on her? Your first love?"

Tim laughed, a high and tight sound.

"I didn't kill anyone. But I followed Thomas, just to make sure that Neil wasn't just talking out of his ass like he used to do as a kid. And I saw him. Thomas was seeing that call girl—Veronica, I think her name was—once a week. Sometimes more. I did some more digging and found out that he would tell Clarissa that he was going away for business and stay with Veronica for days at a time. I mean, *days*. Can you believe that?"

Chase nodded.

"I understand why you would be pissed."

"She didn't deserve that. Shit, she deserved better than Thomas. Sure, he would go to all of these events, give money to these causes, but it was all a show. Thomas wasn't a saint, far from it. He was just a spoiled rich kid with too much money. Thought he could do whatever he wanted and get away with it, that daddy would just pay everyone off, make them forget. But obviously not everybody..."

A strange expression crossed Tim's face as his sentence trailed off.

"But not you, right Tim? They can't buy you off. And when they tried... well, that was the final straw, wasn't it? Did you ask for money? Blackmail the Smiths to make a donation to the Gardens? What, they turn you down?"

Tim scoffed.

"I don't want their money."

"Then what did you do about it? About Thomas cheating on Clarissa?"

"I went to *her*, I went to see Clarissa. She didn't believe me at first, but I had evidence. Photographs that even she couldn't deny."

Chase mulled this over for a few seconds, wondering if he was telling the truth. If he was, then Clarissa was a much better liar than she had ever thought.

And I'm supposed to be good at reading people...

"So, you tried to, what? Get her to seek revenge on Thomas by propositioning her? And she rejected you? But you couldn't hurt her, right? Because you still love her."

Tim frowned deeply.

There was that raw nerve again. He *did* love her.

"You went after him instead. Threatened him. Eventually, things went wrong, and you ended up killing him."

Tim shook his head emphatically.

"I told you already, I didn't kill him. I didn't kill anyone. I left after Clarissa told me that she was leaving him. She was going to pick Thomas Jr. up from school and just leave."

"But she didn't, did she?"

Tim growled.

"No, she didn't. I got a text from her the next day saying she had changed her mind, that they were going to work things out. That wasn't her; that wasn't Clarissa."

"So, what happened?"

Tim leaned back in his chair.

"I'll tell you what happened. That creepy housekeeper showed up at my doorstep the next day with an envelope full of cash—twenty grand, can you believe it? He said I just had to keep my mouth shut, and I could keep it. No strings attached."

"But you refused."

Tim nodded.

"Damn right I refused; as I said, Clarissa deserved better."

"She deserved you?"

He shrugged.

"It doesn't matter. Anyways, I didn't take the money and a week later I get a letter from the court. The Butterfly Gardens were being sued by SSJ, and I was being held personally liable for some bullshit charge about breaking some law about exotic plants. Gimme a fucking break. It was Ken Smith again, waving his fucking wallet around, trying to keep his son's infidelity a secret, trying once again to clean up his mess. The impish maid came by, said that it could all go away if I just took the money." He clenched his jaw. "I refused."

The room fell silent, and Chase took the time to process everything that Tim had said. It sounded reasonable, even seemed to make sense based on everything that she knew about this case. And yet it wasn't the entire truth, she knew that too.

What else is he hiding?

"Can I go now?" Tim asked.

"No, you can't."

Tim threw his hands up.

"I've told you everything. You should be out there, searching for whoever broke into my house. That's your killer, not me!"

"You know what, Tim? I don't think you've told me everything."

Tim raised an eyebrow, silently urging Chase to continue.

"You haven't told me about the butterflies."

Something dark flashed across his face. Chase opened the yearbook and flipped through the pages, stopping when she reached the photograph of Tim, Neil, Chris and Thomas, their mouths wide in either joy or fury. Then she lowered her finger to the only boy that they had yet to identify, the one with the long arms hanging at his sides, the one with the frown.

"Who's this, Tim? Who's this boy?"

Tim's face went completely dark.

"I've said enough."

"Tim, tell me who this is."

"I've said enough!" he bellowed. "And now I want my lawyer."

Chapter 54

UNLIKE HIS LATE SON, Ken Smith didn't live on an estate in the outskirts of the city. Instead, he lived in a high-rise in downtown Manhattan. As Drake entered the building, a security guard approached, confirmed his name, and then asked him to put his gun in the box along with any other weapons.

Drake reluctantly put Chase's gun in the bin and then made his way with escort to the elevator. Inside, the man pushed the 'P' at the top, then flashed his keycard to make the elevator ascend.

Drake, tired, slightly drunk, looked around until his eyes fell on the camera located in the upper left-hand corner of the chrome elevator. For some reason, he winked at it.

When the elevator came to a stop on the top floor, the security guard held the door for him and then the man, a portly fellow with eyebrows that exactly matched his mustache both in color and size, followed him out.

Not much could startle Drake after what he had seen during his tenure as an NYPD detective, but Ken Smith's apartment rendered him speechless.

It was like nothing he had ever seen; from the elevator, the entire floor opened up, open concept to a new extreme. He could see a sitting room off to one side, complete with wall to ceiling bookshelves, a fireplace, and furniture that looked as if it might have been on loan from the *Louvre*. There was a kitchen with stainless steel appliances, high gloss white cabinets, and a fridge that looked large enough to contain Drake's entire apartment.

The soft sound of a waterfall came from a backlit fountain to his right, which was flanked by glass cabinets that seemed to contain relics of some sort: an antique gun, a yellowed parchment of paper, an ancient-looking clock.

"That'll be all, Stewart," a voice called from the sitting room. "Thank you."

The man with the mustache replied, "Are you sure, Mr. Smith?"

The reply was calm and relaxed. Mellow, even.

"I'm sure. I have Raul to help serve my guest."

Raul? Raul's here?

Drake's eyes whipped around, trying to find the source of the voice. It took him a while, but he eventually spotted a thin trail of smoke drifting upward from one of the chairs in the sitting room, with the back to him.

"Have a nice night, Mr. Smith," the security guard said as the elevator doors closed.

When the whirr of the metal box faded, Ken Smith stood and turned to face Drake.

He was tall, with a shock of white hair and matching stubble that stood out on his tanned skin. Drake thought he looked to be in his late-fifties, but based on the age of his late son, he expected that the man's actual age might be closer to seventy. Despite the hour, he was wearing a neatly pressed white shirt, sans tie, and navy-blue slacks that ended in coffee-colored loafers.

"Welcome, Detective Drake," Ken Smith said, opening his arms in a friendly gesture. "I'm glad that you could make it."

Drake grumbled something of a hello as Ken brought a cigar to his lips and puffed.

"I promised you a drink? What would you like?" he asked, turning his attention to the kitchen. "Raul? Please get our guest a…" he looked expectantly at Drake.

"Johnny Red," he said.

Ken chuckled.

"I'm sorry, but my bar is not fully stocked. I do, however, have a supply of Johnny Walker Blue. Would this suit you just as well?"

Drake said it would do.

"Then as Raul prepares your drink—neat, I presume?"

"Yes."

"Good, then we shall *palaver*."

Drake made a face, realizing that he had entered another world.

Palaver?

"Please, take a seat," Ken said, indicating the chair opposite the one he had been sitting.

Drake did, and as soon as his ass hit the plush, olive-colored material, he let out an audible sigh.

It was like sitting on a marshmallow.

Ken laughed briefly, a pleasant, friendly sound.

"There's nothing quite like it after a long day of work. Believe me, I make the same noise every single night."

Raul suddenly appeared, wearing a white shirt with a black bow-tie, a rock glass with three fingers of golden liquid at the bottom in hand.

Drake squinted up at the man, trying to get a read on him. Raul gave away nothing; he was as stone-faced as he had been while driving the Rover and as quiet as he had been at the station.

"Raul has been with our family for a long time," Ken said, puffing on his cigar again. "He is more than our servant; he is part of our family."

Raul nodded, and then placed the glass on the table beside Drake.

"Your errand boy? Bringing cash to people all over the city?" Drake said.

Ken smiled.

"Maybe. Sometimes. He does what we ask of him and is compensated accordingly."

Drake stared at the man across from him. He had seen photographs of Ken Smith, and while he looked pretty much the same in real life, his attitude and demeanor were different.

In the photographs, he had given off an air of authority, in a utilitarian way, which was almost to be expected as the lead 'Smith' in SSJ. But *this* version of Ken Smith was different. He was calm, relaxed, unfazed. Friendly, even.

And it was off-putting to Drake. He was a New York City detective investigating the death of his son in the presence of the mustachioed servant who he had questioned less than twenty-four hours ago.

No one should be this calm.

Especially not Ken Smith.

"Cohiba Behike 56," Ken said suddenly.

"Excuse me?"

Ken smiled again and held up the cigar.

"I'm sorry, please excuse my lack of manners. It has, after all, been a long week. Would you like a cigar? So long as you don't tell, of course—they are Cuban."

Drake shook his head and frowned.

No, this man really wasn't afraid of anything.

"Suit yourself, but before we get started, I suggest you try your beverage."

Unlike the cigar, this was not an offer that Drake declined. He reached over and picked up the glass.

It was like liquid oak.

Smooth, clean, *perfect.*

He tried to remain ambivalent but knew that his eyes gave him away. Drake gulped and swished the liquid around his mouth unconsciously for a second before swallowing.

"Delicious, isn't it?"

Drake drank the rest and held it up.

"Raul?" Ken said, "why don't you fill up our guest again, but leave the bottle this time."

Raul returned and did as he was asked.

"Now," Ken began. "I have a proposition for you, one that you would do well to consider carefully."

Chapter 55

CHASE BREATHED DEEPLY, PUSHING her back against the interrogation room door.

"Hey, Detective Adams, you okay?" a uniform asked.

She looked up.

"Yeah, fine. Look, officer…"

"Hale, Trevor Hale."

"Alright Officer Hale, can you do me a favor?"

The man shifted on his heels.

"Sure, I'm here all night."

"Good. The man in room 1 wants his lawyer. Make sure he gets a phone, okay?"

Officer Hale nodded.

"Sure thing, Adams. Should I book him, too?"

Chase looked down at her shoes, grateful that she had worn her flats today. It had been a long, *long* day.

"No. Just hold him. No charges. Let the clock start now on his eight-hour break. I'll be back in the morning. Whatever you do, don't let him go, okay Hale? And don't let anyone speak to him, except for his lawyer."

Trevor Hale said that this wouldn't be a problem, then started shifting uncomfortably again.

"Is there anything else?"

He looked down, and for a moment Chase thought that he was blushing.

"Yeah, I mean if, you know, you're—"

"No, Trevor. The answer is no—before you even ask and embarrass both of us."

The tops of the man's ears went a deep crimson. He was cute, in a boyish sort of way. Cute and innocent.

Chase started toward him.

"Just make sure he contacts his lawyer, okay?"

***

Chase parked in her driveway and sat in her car for a few moments to collect herself.

It was past midnight now, and she was beyond exhausted. And yet, she knew that she wouldn't be getting much sleep tonight. Not with people out there like Tim Jenkins.

With a heavy sigh, Chase opened the door to her BMW and stepped out into the night. She was fishing the keys out of her pockets when the door to her house suddenly opened and her heart leaped into her throat.

"Jesus!" she gasped, but then relaxed when she saw her husband's handsome face. He looked tired as well, his puffy eyes an indication that he hadn't slept yet tonight, either.

"Hey hon," he said, as he wrapped his arms around her. Chase leaned in, breathing in his smell, and squeezed back.

After several full breaths, Chase pulled away.

"You okay?" Brad Adams asked as he surveyed his wife.

Chase nodded, and together they went into the house, making sure to lock the door after them. Once inside, Chase flipped off her shoes and immediately went to the sofa, sinking into the soft cushions.

No matter what Drake said, the couch was always more comfortable than her car seats.

The television was on, but it was muted. Sports highlights ran, which was fine by her.

A necessary distraction.

"You want something to eat?" Brad asked from the kitchen. The question was rhetorical; she could already hear him fussing with the cutlery, putting together a plate for her.

"Sure," she said as she transitioned to lying down.

"Saw you on the news today," Brad said as he came over to her. In one hand was a warm bowl of pasta with several shrimp piled on top, in the other was a beer.

Chase sat up and took both.

She hadn't thought that she was particularly hungry, but the smell changed her mind.

She devoured her pasta in record time.

"How'd I look?"

"You looked great," Brad answered. "The man with the glasses and the beady eyes... him not so much."

Chase nodded and took a gulp of her beer.

"Sergeant Rhodes. He's on my ass, second-guessing everything that I do."

Brad tapped her legs, and she moved over to give him space to sit.

"And your partner? Damien? How's he doing?"

Chase tilted her head to one side.

"I'm not sure."

Brad took her beer and had a sip before handing it back.

"You want to elaborate?" he asked.

Chase shook her head.

"No, not really," but then she did anyway. "He's a good man, Detective Drake. I know he is. It's just... he's... he's..." *he's haunted by demons,* she wanted to say, but instead, she went with, "he just makes some mistakes. A good cop, a good man, but troubled."

Brad nodded, but it wasn't a patronizing nod. Looking over at him, staring at his blue eyes, his flat expression, Chase knew that he understood.

After all, he had spent the better part of his adult life defending criminals; like Chase, he had seen and experienced the gamut of the human condition.

Brad put a hand on her thigh.

"You going to be alright?" he asked.

Chase nodded.

"Nothing I can't handle."

He leaned over and kissed her on the forehead.

"I'm heading to bed, then."

Chase rose with him, taking her dishes to the sink.

"I'll be there soon," she said, but while Brad went down the hallway and turned into their bedroom on the left, Chase went the other way.

She carefully opened the door on the right and slid inside.

There were glowing stars on the ceiling and a Disney poster on the wall. At one end of the room, there was a toy chest, the lid not completely closing based on the sheer volume of toys within.

She chuckled to herself, imagining Felix's face as he tried desperately to close the lid.

Chase walked over to the bed and stared down at her son, watching his chest slowly rise and fall with every breath.

The boy's comforter was pulled right up under his chin, only his smooth, eight-year-old face and stark white hair visible.

Chase suddenly felt emotion threatening to overwhelm her, but she fought the sensation by leaning down and kissing Felix gently on the cheek. She rose, watched him take several more breaths, and then left the room as silently as she had entered.

Chase *almost* went into her bedroom, *almost* laid down for some desperately needed rest. But at the last moment, she withdrew her hand from the doorknob and went to her office instead.

There was little if any sleep to be had tonight; Drake wasn't the only one haunted by demons.

She slumped into her chair, rubbed her eyes, then started up her laptop.

When Windows loaded, she double-clicked on the poker client.

Chapter 56

DRAKE BALKED AT THE man across from him.

One hundred and twenty thousand dollars plus bonuses? For what? To do some research for him?

"I can see that you are incredulous, and I don't blame you. But I've been watching you for a long while, Detective Drake."

"Just Drake," he grumbled, taking another sip of Johnny Blue. "Why do you want me? After all, you have Raul."

Ken Smith gave him the same wan smile.

"Raul is a man of many talents, but you have... *skills*... that might come in handy."

Drake leaned forward.

"Handy for what? For your quest for office? For mayor?" He had hoped that his inside information would shock the man, crack the fake veneer he wore like a satin robe, but was sorely disappointed.

"Yes, that's correct. I need to surround myself with individuals, individuals such as yourself, who can stem problems even before they raise their ugly heads."

Drake frowned and leaned back in his chair.

"You know what gets me about this whole thing?" he waved his arms about, indicating their *palaver* and the massive penthouse apartment in which they sat.

"Indulge me," Ken said, puffing on his cigar.

"I've been here for nearly a half-hour now, and you haven't once mentioned your son. I'm investigating his murder, for Christ's sake, and you haven't asked me how things are going."

Ken was again unfazed, and this continued to annoy Drake. He was going to make it his purpose to fluster the man.

"I'm aware of the situation," he replied simply.

Drake nodded.

"You have someone on the inside. Is it Simmons? The young detective, Yasiv?"

Ken said nothing but this was telling enough.

"I bet it's even higher up. I bet it's Rhodes."

"It doesn't matter who it is," Ken replied calmly. "Suffice it to say that I am aware of your progress on the case."

"And? How does it make you feel?"

Ken shrugged and brought the cigar to his lips.

"What the hell is wrong with you? Your son is dead and yet you sit here puffing on a cigar, sipping expensive scotch? Do you not give a shit about him?"

"Oh, I do care," Ken said. "But the facts are that Thomas is dead. You know as well as I do that death is a one-way street—nothing I can do can change that. I learned long ago that fretting over the past is a fool's errand. Sure, I'll put out a reward for anyone with information leading to an arrest, but that's one debt I doubt I'll have to pay out."

Drake shook his head, incredulous. He remembered telling Rhodes to let him bring the man in, expressing his desire to grill Ken Smith. But now that he had him here in front of him, it was Ken who seemed to be guiding the interrogation.

"How can you be so calm? Complacent?"

"That's what New York City needs, a mayor who is calm, calculated. A man with ties to the community. A *real* local, someone who has suffered just like all the rest."

Drake's eyes narrowed, and he finally understood. He just couldn't believe it, the utter callousness of the idea.

"You're going to use your dead son to sway the sympathy vote."

Ken shrugged.

"We use what we can in this world, Drake, you know that. We use the tools and skills and connections to get to where we want to be. To *become* who we want to be."

Drake shook his head in disbelief.

"Your own son—fuck, that's low."

Ken sighed, and for the first time since he had arrived in the man's penthouse apartment, Drake felt that he was seeing the real Ken Smith.

"Is it? I call it happenstance."

Drake scoffed.

"Happenstance? *Happenstance?* Really? Your son's death is happenstance?"

"Yes, it is. Like how your partner was murdered and six months later you already have a new partner—a pretty little thing, I might add."

Drake pressed his lips together tightly, trying to fight his emotions. It might have been his goal to break Ken, but he was acutely aware that the exact opposite was happening.

"You leave her out of this."

Ken ignored the threat.

"She's cutting corners, Drake. Cutting corners to keep your head above water. That's a dangerous game for a rookie detective in New York City. You know that. But the question is, are you just going to stand by while another partner goes down?"

Drake lost it. He jumped to his feet and pointed a finger at Ken.

"Leave both of them out of this!" he roared. He heard a sound from behind him and turned to see Raul approaching.

"And you stay the fuck away from me."

"It's fine, Raul, everything's fine. Go back to the kitchen."

The man nodded and without a glance in Drake's direction, receded to his post.

"Please, Drake, calm down."

Drake whipped around to face the pompous prick who was pushing his buttons.

"Don't tell me to calm down. You should be the one who's upset. *You* should be the one yelling."

Ken raised an eyebrow.

"Really? And what does that accomplish? How far has that gotten you, Drake?"

Drake was furious, and it was all he could do to resist reaching over and throttling the man.

"Please, sit."

"No," Drake spat. "I'm done here."

Ken held his hands out, palms up.

"I'm sorry that I've upset you, Drake. But please, consider my offer carefully. The people who go places in this world are the ones who align with those already on the rise. I'm offering you an opportunity—an opportunity to make sure that your current partner, Mrs. Chase Adams, is on the fast track to first-grade detective, maybe even Chief, *and* enough cash to fill Mrs. Cuthbert's mailbox ten times over. Think about it, Drake."

The comment about the money in the mailbox floored him. Was Raul there? Watching him from his black Range Rover?

"I—I—" he stammered, suddenly feeling his head start to swim. He regretted drinking so much.

"I have to go," he said at last.

"Very well," Ken replied, rising to his feet. "Please allow Raul to walk you out."

Drake shook his head.

"I can manage on my own."

He turned and started toward the elevator, aware that Ken was still staring at him as he went. He passed a small table with a glass bowl on top, overflowing with sets of keys and crisp white business cards.

"Oh, and Drake?" Ken asked after him. "Along with the money, I can also provide resources."

Drake concentrated on the business card on top, trying to read the letters that seemed to drift in and out of focus.

"Resources for what?"

There was a short pause, and Drake managed to make out the name on the card.

It was a business card for Dr. Mark Kruk.

Why the hell —

But Ken's next comment stripped away all thoughts of the strange psychiatrist with the spectacles.

"To find the real Skeleton king, Drake. To find the man who was really responsible for Clay's death."

Chapter 57

CHASE ARRIVED EARLY, WORKING on only a handful of hours of sleep, and yet she still wasn't the first one at the station.

Rhodes's car was parked in his usual spot. The man worked late but wasn't known as an early riser, and the sight of his car made Chase's heart thump in her chest.

Why is he here?

She parked, and then hurried into 62nd precinct, grumbling a hello at several of the uniforms who had just clocked out after the night shift.

No sooner had she reached her office, did she notice that the door to interrogation room 1 was ajar.

What the hell?

She strode toward it when she spotted Officer Hale, who she had instructed to make sure that Tim Jenkins got his eight hours of rest, standing by the water cooler.

"Hey, Hale," she snapped. The man turned, and when their eyes met, his face immediately turned a sickly shade of gray. "Where's Jenkins? Did you move him?"

Hale dropped his gaze and Chase reached for one of his arms.

"Hale? Where's Jenkins?"

The officer took a deep breath.

"I tried, Detective Adams. I tried—"

Chase felt her brow furrow.

"You tried what? Where the hell is he?"

The man looked nearly on the verge of tears.

"I had no—"

A stern voice from Chase's left drew her attention. Sergeant Rhodes was leaning out of his office, his face red.

"Adams, in here, *now!*"

Chase gave Hale a glare, then let him go.

No sooner had the door to Rhodes's office closed did he throw a newspaper on the desk.

"Where's my suspect?" Chase asked.

Rhodes ignored her, and stood, back to her, hands on his narrow hips.

"Did you read the paper this morning, Adams?"

"No, I haven't. I came straight here to resume the interview with my suspect."

Careful now.

"Well, you and your *Butterfly Killer* made the front page, again."

"What?"

Chase looked down at the front page of the Times, and she felt her face go slack.

Housekeeper or call girl… could either of these be the Butterfly Killer?

"Fuck," she said under her breath.

"Yes, that's right, Detective Adams; *fuck*." He turned, and she was taken aback by the calm expression on his hairless face. "I told you yesterday that I didn't want any more leaks! Yesterday, I said that."

Chase felt her lips move, but no words came out.

"So, please, explain to me how the *fuck* this happened?"

She shook her head.

"Detective Adams, are you going to just sit there and move your lips like a puppet, or are you going to say something?"

Chase remained silent as she flipped to page two. There was a composite photo of Raul exiting the station, and Veronica in her ridiculous Frozen costume entering it. Beside each was a photo of Raul that must have been taken at some fundraiser or another at the Smith home, and a mug shot of Veronica that looked a few years old. "I don't know who—"

"Damn right you don't," Rhodes snapped. "But you're going to find out who the leak is and bring them to me. Do you understand?"

"Yes," Chase replied, lowering her eyes.

"You've said that before, so let me just make myself crystal clear. You find out who is tipping off this Ivan Meitzer and let me know or I'll have IA all of your investigation."

"I'll find out who," she said sheepishly. "I'll plug this leak."

"You better. This is your last chance. *Last* chance."

Chase nodded then changed the subject.

"What happened to my suspect? To Tim Jenkins?"

Rhodes sighed.

"I let him walk."

Chase popped to her feet.

"You *what*?"

"I said, I let him walk," Rhodes barked back. "I had no choice!"

"He's the prime suspect in three murders! He—"

Rhodes suddenly exploded at her.

"This is your fault!" he yelled. "The minute you left to get your beauty sleep, I get a call from Weston Smith, Jenkins's counsel. He threatened to sue the department for harassment! Wanted to go after you directly, said you violated Tim's rights and refused him access to counsel. We can't have this now! Not now! Not with an election looming."

Denied him counsel? What the—

But then something else occurred to her.

"Wait," Chase said, incredulous. "*Wes Smith* called?"

"Yeah, he's Jenkins's lawyer."

Chase felt her mind working double-time. She shook her head.

"No, no. That can't be. Tim *hates* Weston, hates the Smith family. There's no way he would seek counsel from Weston."

Rhodes looked at her suspiciously.

"It's in the transcript from my interview last night," Chase continued. "He was being sued by SSJ."

Rhodes raised an eyebrow, urging her to continue.

"He... he knew about Thomas's infidelity, was urging Clarissa to leave him. He claims that they tried to pay him off, keep the Smith name untarnished. But he refused."

"You're sure?"

"We found court documents outlining the case of SSJ versus Tim Jenkins and the Butterfly Gardens. They shut the gardens down."

Rhodes took a seat.

"And the infidelity?"

Chase nodded.

"We know that both Neil Pritchard and Thomas Smith were seeing the call girl... Veronica Wallace. Jesus, Rhodes, you let him go?"

The man pursed his lips. When he spoke again, all anger had left him. Instead, he was working hard to save face.

"I had no choice. But I put Simmons on him, watching his every move. Any update on the syringe or the sample found in his residence?"

Chase shook her head.

"I only just arrived; I have no idea yet. But he has motive and means to have pulled this off, Sergeant Rhodes."

Without saying a word, Rhodes picked up his cell phone and dialed a number.

"Detective Simmons? It's Sergeant Rhodes. Status update."

Chase waited while Rhodes listened.

"Stay on him. Don't let him out of your sight at any time. Detective Adams will replace you this evening," Rhodes said then hung up his phone.

"Tim was dropped off at home by Weston Smith and hasn't left his house since. No activity since early this morning. Adams, find his prints on either the syringe or the specimen container and I'll sign the arrest warrant myself."

Chase stood, still shaking her head. She couldn't believe it. They *had* him. They had the Butterfly Killer in their custody and now he was free.

She stood.

"And find out whoever is leaking to the public, Adams! Find the leak and plug it!"

Chapter 58

"TIM JENKINS IS OUR number one suspect," Chase said, indicating the man's photograph tacked to the board. "He was in possession of a syringe and a container with a caterpillar inside. I think we busted him when he was on his way to kill again."

Detectives Yasiv and Gainsford stared at her like she had three heads.

"Who was the intended victim?" Gainsford asked at last.

Chase hesitated.

"At this point, the victim is unknown. Maybe this man," she said, pointing to the image of the surly boy from the yearbook that she had blown up and pinned to the board. "Marcus Slasinsky, but I'm not sure. I don't know how he fits in. But Jenkins…" she let her sentence trail off, still incredulous at the fact that Rhodes had let him go.

And that he was being represented by Weston Smith.

Her head was starting to ache.

"So, we're working on the theory that Tim Jenkins is still obsessed with Clarissa Smith and he lost it when he found out that Thomas was sleeping with a prostitute? That he also sought revenge on Neil Pritchard because he set the two of them up? Is that it?"

Chase nodded. She knew what was coming next and tried to come up with a satisfying answer in her head before replying.

"And what about Chris Papadopoulos? Why was he targeted? Officer Dunbar said that he hasn't left Montreal for several years, and even then, it was to vacation in Mexico. How does he fit in?" Detective Yasiv asked.

Nothing came to Chase.

"I don't know. Maybe... maybe he was taking out all of the boys from high school?"

An uncomfortable silence came over the conference room. It wasn't a perfect fit, but it was all they had to go on.

"Where's this Slasinsky kid now?"

Chase shook her head.

"We don't know. Can't find him anywhere; no record of any kind — he's not in the system. I have Dunbar searching for him, but so far no luck."

"And the blood on the victims' backs?" Detective Gainsford turned to the paper on the table in front of him. "This Martha Slasinsky? How does she play into all this?"

Chase swore.

"I don't know," she threw up her hands. "I have no fucking idea."

More silence, which was eventually broken by Detective Yasiv again.

"Maybe she was a prostitute back then? Back when they were kids? Seduced them? And now Tim's using her blood as a sort of calling card?"

It was far-fetched, but at least it was *something*.

"Maybe. Let's get some eyes on Veronica. She might be involved, or she could be our next victim." Chase rubbed her eyes. "Fuck."

"What next?" Detective Gainsford asked. "Interview Raul again? Talk to Weston Smith?"

Chase shook her head.

"No, we can't go after them right now. They're too hot... Rhodes..." she didn't finish the thought.

There was something about the way Rhodes seemed more interested in stemming the leak than solving the murders that was bugging her.

Drake's words suddenly reverberated in her mind.

Weston and Ken are using Raul to pay off everyone involved in this case.

"Detective Adams? You okay?" Detective Gainsford asked.

"Fine," she snapped. "Yasiv, you were with Simmons when he interviewed the teacher, correct?"

The detective said he was.

"Go speak to him again—put some pressure on him. I want to know if the boy in the photo is Marcus Slasinsky. I want to know why he wasn't in the yearbook outside of that one photo. Gimme something, anything to go on."

Before the young detective could answer, the door to the conference room suddenly opened and a disheveled looking Damien Drake strode in.

His eyes were red, and he was wearing the same clothes as the night before, only today it looked as if he had slept in them.

"I think I've got something," he said without offering so much as a hello. "A source told me that something happened in high school... something at the Butterfly Gardens. And whatever it was, it was bad. Marcus Slasinsky ended up in the hospital, in a coma."

"*What?*"

Drake swallowed visibly.

"I don't know *what*, but I know that Tim, Neil, Chris, and Thomas were involved somehow."

Chase stared at the man for a good minute before answering. She could smell the reek of alcohol on him from even fifteen feet away.

"Clear the conference room," she said softly.

"Adams?" Detective Gainsford asked, an eyebrow raised.

"I said get out!"

All three men stood and moved toward the door.

"Drake, you stay," she spat.

When the door closed and she and Drake were alone, she instructed him to take a seat.

"My source is credible," Drake said quickly. "Whatever happened in the garden all those years ago is the key to breaking this thing open."

Chase took a deep breath and an impending sense of dread overcame her.

"Who's your source, Drake?"

Drake frowned at her.

"It's legit."

Chase slammed her palms down on the desk. The sound was so loud that it startled them both.

"Goddammit Drake, who is your source?"

"I can't—"

"It's Ivan fucking Meitzer, isn't it?"

Drake didn't say a word, but he didn't need to answer. She could see it in his face.

"Jesus Christ, Drake! You've poisoned this case! Rhodes wants your head, and you're selling information to a New York Times reporter? Have you completely lost your mind?"

Drake looked down at his hands.

"I was with Ken Smith last night."

"You were *what?*"

Chase couldn't believe what she was hearing. She was beginning to feel like she was living a Twilight Zone episode.

"He called me, wanted to talk. He—"

"I don't care," Chase seethed. "You're off the case. I have no choice but to report you to Rhodes."

Drake stood.

"This is the key, Chase. Marcus—"

"I don't care!" she shouted. "Get out!"

" —it's Rhodes, he's—"

"Get out!" she screamed.

Drake looked at her for a moment, and she thought that he was going to keep talking.

Only he didn't.

Without a word, he spun on his heels and left the room, leaving Chase alone with her own thoughts.

She massaged her temples, instantly regretting not getting more sleep the night before.

All this time, Drake was sabotaging the case... for what? To get back at Rhodes for what happened to Clay? For not believing that Peter Kellington wasn't the Skeleton King? Was that it?

She swore several times then reached for her phone.

"Officer Dunbar? It's Detective Adams. I need you to look for a report from twenty-odd years ago." She paused. "No, forget about that for now. Look for something on a boy, Marcus Slasinsky. It was a serious event, landed him in a coma. Let me know as soon as you have something."

Detective Chase Adams hung up and stared up at the board.

Where are you hiding Marcus? What is your story and how in the hell do you fit into all of this?

Chapter 59

CHASE NEVER HAD ANY inclination to follow Sergeant Rhodes; in fact, when she left the station, she was heading to the lab to follow-up on the fingerprints on the syringe and container found at Tim Jenkins's house. But when she saw her boss leave in a hurry, she naturally watched him go.

Then she got into her car and followed. She told herself that this was stupid, career-ending, and potentially dangerous, but couldn't help herself.

It *was* strange the way that Rhodes had let Jenkins loose, SSJ backing him or not. They had forty-eight hours with the man before they had to let him walk or arrest him. And the nonsense about denying him counsel? That was bullshit, and all Rhodes had to do was watch the recording of the interview to know as much.

None of this was sitting right with her, and she had learned long ago to follow her instincts.

They had gotten her this far, after all.

Rhodes took a circuitous route around the city, and Chase was beginning to think that this was intentional, an attempt to lose any potential tails.

Or maybe that was just her own paranoia projecting.

Eventually, however, when he pulled up to SSJ and parked in the underground garage, Chase could follow no further.

And her suspicions were confirmed.

She parked across the street and waited.

Her phone suddenly buzzed and with her eyes still locked on the garage exit she picked it up.

"Adams," she said quickly.

"It's Officer Dunbar. I found something that you might be interested in."

"Go ahead."

"I really think you should come in and see this."

"No, can't come in now. Just tell me what you've found."

There was a pause.

"I don't know if it's what you're looking for, but there was an accident report filed in September 1994. The location was the Butterfly Gardens, just as you suspected."

Chase turned all of her attention to the phone call.

"What happened?" she demanded.

"The report is thin, something about a juvenile having an episode that resulted in hospitalization."

Shit. Maybe Drake was right. Maybe...

"Anything else?"

"No, that's pretty much it, except..."

"What? What is it?"

"The report was filed two days after the incident, which is strange. Even stranger was the fact that it was immediately closed with no further investigation."

Chase took a deep breath, knowing the answer even before she asked the question.

"Who was the reporting officer at the time, Dunbar?"

"See that's the thing, that's what makes this a, uh, a little *sensitive.*"

"Just spit it out, Dunbar."

"Well, according to this, the reporting officer was Heath Rhodes."

Chase's breath caught in her throat.

Chapter 60

THE MAN DRESSED IN all black waited outside Jenkins's house for several hours, expecting CSU to come and tear the place apart.

When they didn't arrive after the first hour, he grew curious. And when the sun started to rise, he grew convinced that they weren't coming at all.

Slinking in the early dawn, he retraced his steps, using the table out back to hoist himself onto the awning. From there, he simply slid into the house via the window he had exited only hours before.

It was pitch black inside, which suited him just fine. He tapped the containers in his pocket, and the syringes in the other, silently commending himself for having brought several sets instead of just the one.

Last time had been sloppy, this time it wouldn't be. This time he wouldn't hesitate.

The man slid under the bed and crossed his arms over his chest and closed his eyes.

They would pay for what they did.

All of them would pay.

The man in black waited with bated anticipation. After all, he had waited all these years, what was a few more hours?

Chapter 61

DRAKE LEFT THE POLICE station in a fog, the Johnny Blue still coursing through his system.

He had known that he couldn't keep this up forever, that eventually he would be ousted for selling information to the press. He just hadn't thought that it would happen this soon.

But he should have known.

He should have known that Rhodes would do everything in his power to find the leak and that Chase would be his proxy to do so.

The Sergeant hadn't just put Chase on the Butterfly Killer case because she was the only one who would work with him. Rhodes had also chosen her because she was an outsider, someone who would do anything to gain his favor, to stem any leaks that could potentially soil the Smith name.

Drake hopped in his car and sped off, wondering how long it would be before uniforms came after him. He figured that he might have an hour, maybe more if Chase gave him a chance to get away.

This is it, he thought with something akin to satisfaction. *Rhodes got his way and I'm going down.*

There was just something he wanted to do first.

Two people he had to talk to, to express how sorry he was for what had happened.

It was with these thoughts rattling around in his head that he arrived outside Mrs. Cuthbert's house.

He parked across the street and waited.

The seats in his Crown Vic were worn, cracked, and uncomfortable, but he fell asleep never-the-less.

For the first time in the better part of a year, Drake nodded off without the fear of the nightmares returning.

Chapter 62

CHASE DIDN'T FEEL COMFORTABLE meeting Beckett at the station and instead instructed him to meet at Patty's Diner.

Part of her hoped that Drake might be there too, but she didn't hold her breath.

She was also grateful that she hadn't gone immediately to Rhodes and reported Drake. She had a feeling that she might need him before the day was out.

Beckett strode through the door with his hair spiked, a smile on his face.

"Not the type of place I would have chosen for a first date, but hey, I'll take it," he said as he slid into the booth across from her.

"Thanks for meeting me," Chase said, ignoring the man's comment.

Beckett nodded.

"And the reason we are meeting here is…?"

Chase looked down.

"I just needed to get away," she said quickly.

"Okay… and what do you need me for?"

Chase mulled this over for a second. She needed to know about the syringe and caterpillar, but she also needed to know something else as well.

"You're friends with Drake, right?"

Beckett smiled.

"What's this? You looking for dating advice? Need to know if Drake has a thing on the side?"

She shook her head.

"No, it's not like that."

Beckett winked at her, and she rolled her eyes.

"Just asking for a friend, huh? Well, go ahead. Ask away."

Chase leaned in close and lowered her voice an octave. She was positive that the handful of patrons wouldn't pay her much mind—the place struck her as somewhere people went to be anonymous—but she couldn't be too careful.

"I need to know about his relationship with Rhodes."

"Ah, the big chief, huh?"

Chase nodded.

"Yeah."

Beckett shrugged.

"Never saw eye to eye, not really. Back before... back when we used to go out for a few drinks, he usually spouted off on the man, talked about how he always got the impression that Rhodes was out for his own advancement, didn't give a shit about solving any crimes, if you catch my drift."

Chase caught it alright; it was no smoking gun but served to solidify her own opinions.

"You ever get the idea that Drake was jealous of him? That he wanted the man's job? Maybe pissed because Rhodes got the promotion to Sergeant while Drake toiled as a detective?"

Beckett's face turned serious.

"What's this about, Chase?"

"Just humor a lady, if you would. Was he jealous?"

Beckett chuckled.

"Fuck no. Drake is exactly where he wants to be—in the field, getting his hands dirty. Shit, it would torture him to be behind a desk all day. You've seen him, you know what I'm talking about. Drake is... complicated, but he's a good detective and a better man. The six months off nearly killed him."

Chase nodded slowly.

"That's what I thought."

The waitress came over, but Beckett waved her away.

"Is that it? May I be excused, Madame?"

"Just one more thing: did you hear from the labs? Were Jenkins's fingerprints on the syringe? The container?"

Beckett crossed his arms over his chest and pouted.

"And why would I know that? I mean, I only deal with bodies, not with insects."

Chase continued to stare at him.

"Alright, you got me. I *may* have called in a favor to a buddy in the lab. Asked about the evidence."

Chase offered a weak smile.

"I thought you might. And?"

"And there were no fingerprints. Not a single one on either the container or syringe."

Chase swore under her breath.

"Well now, that's not very ladylike."

Chase got to her feet.

"That's cuz I'm not one. I'm a detective." She held out her hand. "Thanks, Beckett. I owe you one."

"And you can repay me by going on a date perhaps? A real date, not this shithole."

"Maybe another time, Beckett. Thanks again for your help."

Beckett held up his hands defensively.

"Can't knock a guy for trying, can you?"

"Nope. Definitely can't knock you for trying."

Chapter 63

DRAKE AWOKE WITH HIS mouth so dry that it felt as if he had fallen asleep gorging on a bag of cotton balls. He clucked his tongue, tasted the familiar flavor of sour whiskey, and then his head started to ache.

For several seconds, Drake was disoriented, unsure of where he was. He was in his car, that much was clear, but the street seemed unfamiliar to him.

Am I at Tim Jenkins's house? Am I watching for movement?

His eyes eventually fell on a familiar black mailbox, this time with the flag down, and everything came flooding back.

Sorry, no more cash infusions now and probably for a while, he thought.

As Drake shifted his hips trying to work out the stiffness that had built up as he slept, a car pulled onto the quiet street. He had misplaced his Timex and the dashboard clock blinked 12:00 but judging by the way the sun had already started its descent, he thought that it might be early afternoon.

Just around the time that Jasmine Cuthbert might be arriving home from work.

When the car slowed as it neared the house, his heart rate quickened. When it pulled into the driveway, he was on the verge of hyperventilating.

He hadn't spoken to Jasmine since that night in the rain, the night he had knocked on her door weeping.

Jasmine Cuthbert stepped out of her car and Drake was momentarily frozen. She was pretty, if tired-looking, with dark brown hair pulled into a loose ponytail, pale features, and striking eyes. Sporting a tartan skirt that ran to mid-calf and a white blouse tucked in, she went directly to the trunk.

Before looking inside, she glanced around, her eyes scanning the dusk for something.

She never noticed Drake sitting in his car across the street.

With a deep breath, a failed attempt to slow his adrenaline, Drake reached into the glovebox and cracked his final miniature and swallowed it in three gulps.

He grimaced with the accompanying searing sensation in his throat, then tossed the bottle onto the floor of the passenger seat with the others and stepped out of his car.

With hesitant steps, Drake started across the street, his eyes fixated on the woman's back.

It had been six months since he had seen Jasmine, and he wasn't sure how she would react to his presence. If the woman was anything like her daughter, then things were destined to go very, very poorly.

But he *had* to speak to her one more time. He just *had* to.

"Jasmine," Drake whispered. The woman was rooting in her trunk, struggling to hoist several brown paper bags out at once.

"Jasmine," he repeated. When she still didn't hear him, he reached out and gently put a hand on her shoulder.

Jasmine Cuthbert whipped around so quickly that she almost fell into her open trunk in the process.

"Who—" she started, but then her gaze fell on his face.

This is it, Drake thought. She's going to scream and yell and hit me and I'm just going to sit here and take it. When she's exhausted and collapses, I'll hold her and then she'll curse me, and I'll get back into my car.

Then I'll grab Chase's gun from the glovebox, check that it's loaded and stick—

"Damien?" she said softly. "Oh, Damien, what happened to your face?"

When she reached out and ran her soft fingers across his puffy cheek, Drake lost it.

He burst into tears and collapsed into her arms.

***

"It's been… incredibly difficult," Jasmine said, her eyes focusing on the glass of tea cupped in both hands. "Particularly for Suze."

Drake looked down at his own steaming cup and wished that Jasmine had put something stronger than Orange Pekoe in it.

He thought back to the morning he had waited outside Hockley Middle and High School, to how visceral Suze's reaction to his presence had been.

How obvious her hatred for him was.

No, Suzan hadn't taken her father's death well, not that any child should. But Clay had been particularly close with her.

"How are you holding up?" Drake asked softly, trying to steer the conversation.

Jasmine didn't raise her gaze.

"I get up every day," was all she offered, and Drake felt himself nodding. Sometimes, getting up was the hardest part.

For others, for those like himself, it was closing his eyes that proved most difficult.

Jasmine finally looked up, and he noticed that her eyes were red.

"Suzan's applying for college this year," she said, pulling the conversation back to her daughter. "Wants to do pre-med."

This surprised Drake; he had known that Suzan was interested in medicine—Clay had talked about it *ad nauseam*—

and in becoming a doctor, but going from high school directly to medical school?

It felt odd knowing that the world continued on even when your existence seemed to cease.

"Good for her," Drake managed after a short pause. "I'm glad that she's continuing to..." he scrounged his mind for the right words, eventually settling on Jasmine's own. "...get up every day."

Jasmine nodded and then took a sip of tea.

"I want to thank you, Damien," she said without warning.

Drake frowned.

"Thank me? For what?"

Jasmine seemed to consider this for a moment. Then she sighed and said, "I know that you were the one behind the article in the Times. While you were on leave and before it was published, I asked around the precinct, trying to get more information about Clay's death. Everyone I asked said the same thing: the *report is sealed; it's for internal affairs only. If there is an arrest, you will be notified.* I mean, Clay had many, many friends in the precinct, across the city even. But when he died... when he was murdered, everyone handled me with kid gloves, if they would handle me at all. I could see it in their eyes—they were terrified of me. Scared and sad. They wouldn't even tell me where you were, if you were okay, if you still worked there."

Drake felt himself nodding.

The time immediately after Clay's murder had been and still was, hazy to him, but he remembered picking up his cell phone, hearing Jasmine's voice and being unable to do anything but listen. He couldn't speak—no words would be sufficient to express his sorrow.

It had taken six months and basically his career to be over for him to muster the courage to come here.

"And then the article came out," she continued. "It was you who leaked the information about what happened, wasn't it?"

Drake swallowed hard and closed his eyes.

While he had been unable to formulate words to express his condolences to Jasmine, he had reached out in the only other way he knew how.

He had picked up the phone and called the Times, knowing full well that if he spoke to a reporter, his career would effectively be ruined. More than that, he was breaking a cardinal rule in the NYPD world, and was going to alienate himself from every other police officer in New York City.

But Drake was compelled to tell what really happened that night; he just couldn't live under the guise, the collective narrative that Rhodes and the press liaisons were spouting.

The lies about how he and Clay had been ambushed, and that Drake himself was a hero, taking out the Skeleton King after he had shot Clay.

Drake knew better.

After all, he had carried Clay's bloody body into the rain and collapsed on the porch.

He swallowed again. His throat suddenly felt incredibly dry and he reached for his tea.

Before he could answer, before he could confirm Jasmine's suspicions, the front door opened.

"Mom?" Suzan's voice drifted to them in the kitchen. "I'm home, mom," there was a short pause. "Whose shoes are these?"

Chapter 64

CHASE LEFT PATTY'S DINER shortly after Beckett and found
herself driving aimlessly while she thought about the
Butterfly Killer. She had done this often as a Narc in Seattle;
driving around, watching the wet city sluice by while her
mind struggled to silence distractions.

It was clear that Rhodes was in Ken Smith's pocket,
something Chase had known even before seeing the man
drive to SSJ. It was the reason why he was so reluctant to link
Chris's case to the others, knowing that the FBI would show
up and start poking their noses into places that he didn't want
them looking.

But Rhodes wasn't the only one who had taken bribes to
keep his mouth shut: the high school teacher, Veronica, Raul,
even Clarissa in a backward sort of way were not talking
because of the man's influence.

It dawned on her that Drake might also be taking bribes
from the man but quickly dismissed this thought. After all,
everything he was doing was in direct opposition to what Ken
wanted: he was going to the press and dragging people
involved with links to the Smith family down to the station.

As for their meeting? Chase probably should have seen that
coming. After all, the two men were on a collision course, a
concentric circle that pitted both of them in the center.

No, Drake's destruction was self-inflicted.

And when the dust settled, Chase foresaw only one
possible outcome, no matter the results of the case.

By week's end, or perhaps even sooner, Damien Drake was
no longer going to be an NYPD detective. This served
everyone's interests, including Rhodes and the rest of the
detectives who loathed him as much for what he let happen to

Clay as his exposé in the Times following his murder, and the Smith family.

The only one that would come to harm was Drake himself. And she had seen it in his eyes; he would go down without a fight. The man was broken, so shattered by his own guilt that he believed that everything that came his way was deserved.

Chase had told him soon after they had met that she wouldn't go down with his burning ship, but she also couldn't imagine letting him die with it. She might abandon ship, but Chase was not so career-driven that she wouldn't throw him a lifeline.

How to do that, however, and not drown in the undertow was still something that she was trying to work out.

Her first instinct had been to accompany Detective Yasiv to the teacher's house, to see if she could extract more information about what happened all those years ago but decided against it. She wasn't in the frame of mind to interview anyone, let alone an elderly school teacher who had been paid off already.

Her second inclination was to go to see Officer Dunbar, to put pressure on him to find out what happened to Marcus Slasinsky after the accident. But that wouldn't accomplish anything; the man already had enough on his plate, and her presence would likely only slow him down.

Instead, Chase eventually found herself on the outskirts of the city, turning down the winding, arbor-embraced street that led to the Smith Estate.

It's for the case, she thought, but then immediately dismissed the lie.

It wasn't for the case—it was for her. She needed a friend to talk to, something that never came easily to her.

And Clarissa Smith was the closest thing to a friend that she had.

Chase parked across from the iron gates and took a deep breath before getting out of her car. She had only just pushed the intercom button when the door to the estate blew open.

Clarissa Smith rushed out, dressed in pajamas, her hair a mess.

"You promised!" she yelled as she rushed toward Chase.

Chase, so surprised by this outburst, took a step backward. "Wh—what? Clarissa, I—"

"You promised!" Clarissa shouted again. She was pointing her manicured finger at Chase with such anger that at that moment it looked as dangerous as a loaded gun.

Chase shook her head, confusion washing over her.

"I don't—I don't know what—"

Clarissa grabbed the fence now, and Chase saw pure fury in her wide eyes.

She took another step back.

"I thought you were my friend! You come here, sweet talk me, play tennis, pretend to be a friend, and then you leave here and go right to the papers, didn't you? They printed the prostitute's name on the first goddamn page!" Clarissa shouted.

"N—n—no, I didn't. It was—"

"You promised me that you would keep this quiet! My son—my eight-year-old son—was bullied at school, the other kids telling him that his dead father was cheating with a whore!"

Chase felt her heart thudding away in her chest.

"And do you know what that bastard Ken Smith did? Hmm? Do you know what he did to get back at me?"

Chase was nearing tears now. It had been a horrible, horrible mistake to come here.

"I don't—"

"He froze everything! Every last dime I have, he froze. I have nothing now! *Absolutely nothing!*"

Chase licked her lips.

"He can't—he can't do that," she stammered.

Clarissa's eyes went so wide that they almost bulged.

"Oh yes he can, and he *did!*"

"I'm sorry," Chase said. "I'm so sorry, I never meant for any of this to happen."

"You stupid bitch," Clarissa spat. "You came here, and you tricked me. I thought you wanted to help, but the only thing you wanted to do is further your career."

Chase was shaking her head so hard now that she could no longer focus on Clarissa's angry face anymore.

"No, it's not true!" she exclaimed. "It's not true! I just—"

"You're only out for yourself," Clarissa said quietly.

Tears started to streak down Chase's face.

"It's not true, I—"

"*Get out!*" Clarissa suddenly screamed. Chase took a step back, tripped, and fell hard on her ass. "*Get off my property! Get off my property now, you stupid bitch!*"

Chase picked herself off the pavement and sprinted for her car, yanking the door open.

Once inside, she buried her face in her hands and started to sob.

Chapter 65

"**WHAT... WHAT ARE** *YOU* doing here?" Suzan gasped, her eyes locking in on Drake's.

Drake lowered his gaze and started to stand.

"I was just leaving," he said softly. "I didn't mean to upset anyone."

"Upset anyone?" Suzan said, stepping forward. "*Upset anyone?*"

"Suzan, please," Jasmine said, also rising to her feet. "Drake was—"

Suzan's eyes darted from Drake's to her mother's.

"He was what, mom? He was here to say sorry for what he did? Or maybe he was here to take out you, too, mom? Did you ever think of that?"

Drake reached for the young girl, but she recoiled.

"Don't touch me! *Don't you fucking touch me!*" she screamed.

Jasmine strode forward, but her daughter pulled away from her mother as well.

"You don't touch me either!"

"Suze, I'm so sorry—"

She turned to Drake, hatred in her eyes.

"Fuck you and your 'sorries'. We were a happy family! A perfect family and you took that all away from us!"

"You still have your mother—you still have each other," Drake said softly. He wasn't trying to make excuses but was at a loss for what else to say. Suzan had been incensed outside her school, but Drake saw that even then she had been reserved.

Now, her true feelings were coming to the fore.

"We have nothing! This—" Suzan motioned to herself and Jasmine, "—this is just an empty shell... a husk of a family. A fake. A phony."

In his periphery, Drake saw Jasmine break down and begin to sob.

It was a mistake coming here. I've just made things worse.

"I'm going to leave now," Drake said softly. He took a step toward the door, and Suzan slid out of the way, going to her mother. "I didn't want to upset anyone."

"Get the *fuck* out!" Suzan called after him. "You ruined everything! We had the perfect family and now we're... we're..." her voice broke as she started to cry too. "Now we're just an empty shell."

Drake stumbled out the front door, tears streaming down his face.

And yet despite the anguish that crushed his soul, his detective mind hadn't shut off. Not quite.

Something Suzan had said struck a chord with him, and it wasn't until he had peeled away from the modest Cuthbert home that he realized why.

Empty shell...

He had heard someone say something like that before.

It had been Dr. Mark Kruk.

This picture? It's much like everything else in the image we portray to others: just an empty shell.

There was a click deep within Detective Damien Drake's brain, and he yanked the steering wheel to the left and pressed the accelerator.

He remembered what the psychiatrist had said, and he also remembered one of the files he had seen on the man's desk when he had spoken to him.

MARCUS SLASINSKY.

Chapter 66

CHASE'S PHONE BUZZED AND she used the heel of her hand to wipe her eyes and nose before answering.

"Adams," she said softly.

"It's Simmons. I interviewed the teacher again... Mr. Urso?"

She cleared her throat.

"Yes? And?"

"Yeah, you were right—just a little pressure and he broke. Said that Chris, Tim, Neil, and Thomas used to bully the Slasinsky boy to no end. Somehow, they found out about his mother, about how she had committed suicide and the whole butterfly in the mouth thing. When it came time for the class trip to the Butterfly Gardens, Slasinsky had been granted an exemption, but the other boys tricked him into coming along. They goaded him into the center of the garden, just before the butterflies were released. He started to cry, and they mocked him. When the butterflies came, he lost it. Started screaming and thrashing on the ground before eventually going silent. Fell into a coma. Mr. Urso said he called the police, but when they arrived the Smith clan was already there. They gave him twenty grand to keep his mouth shut, and he thinks that the officer might have been paid off as well. Urso says he took the money because there wasn't much to do anyway. What with the kids just bullying Slasinsky, it's not like they could press charges or anything. I mean, back then bullying was just a part of life..."

Chase chewed the inside of her lip. At the time, nothing legally could be done to *random* boys, but to these kids in particular, especially Thomas Smith, their reputation was everything. And considering his past—with the auto theft and assault charges—maybe there was a lot that could be done.

"Did he say what happened to Marcus Slasinsky after he came out of the coma?" Chase asked.

There was a short pause.

"No—says he isn't sure. He went to visit the boy in the hospital but wasn't allowed to see him. There were rumors that Slasinsky had hit his head and couldn't remember much about what happened. Last Mr. Urso heard was that he changed his name and then left New York."

Only to come back again, she thought with a chill. *Who are you now, Marcus?*

She was beginning to consider that Tim Jenkins wasn't so much a suspect as a potential victim.

Just as Drake had suggested.

"So we know that the abusive father was out of the picture and that Marcus's mother committed suicide. Dunbar said that he got a hefty insurance settlement from his mother's death, but that was... what? Eight years before he fell into the coma? Seven? Ken Smith must have set him up as well."

"Right, that's what the teacher thinks, too. But how are we going to trace that money?"

"We can't," Chase responded quickly. Even if they could break into the fortress that was SSJ and find out where the money that Ken Smith had given Marcus Slasinsky went, which was unlikely, she was going to have to go through Rhodes first. And that wasn't going to happen, even if it led to them figuring who Marcus was today.

Because they paid Rhodes off then, and they continue to pay him off now.

"I think I've gotten as much out of Mr. Urso as I can— there's not much more to know. He actually seems genuinely sorry for the boy, and remorseful for not doing more to help him when he could. Do you think that this Marcus kid is the Butterfly Killer? Or should we still focus on Jenkins?"

Chase paused.

"Let's stay on Jenkins. Either way, he'll help us break this open, I'm sure of it."

"Sounds good," Detective Simmons replied.

"Good work, by the way. Now go home, get some rest. We'll reconvene in the morning. Same time."

Chase was met with only dead air.

"Simmons?"

"Are you sleeping at all, Detective Adams? Perhaps—" Simmons said cautiously.

"I'm fine. Go home, Simmons," Chase replied quickly, then hung up the phone.

A quick glance at the clock showed that it was coming up to seven PM, and although she wasn't supposed to relieve Detective Yasiv until ten, she thought that maybe she would let him go home early, too.

***

Twenty minutes later, she pulled up behind Detective Yasiv's Blue Toyota and then got out of her car.

The crescent sun was bright as it dipped below the horizon, and she was forced to lower her over-sized sunglasses to deflect most of the glare. As she neared the vehicle, she made out the outline of a person leaning against the door.

Fearing the worst, she rushed to the door and tried to pull it open.

It was locked.

Inside, Henry Yasiv's forehead pressed against the glass. His eyes were closed, and his mouth hung agape.

He was motionless.

"No!" she cried and tried the door again. There was a flicker of movement in the corner of Henry's mouth. "No!" she shouted, convinced that at any moment the head of a caterpillar would poke out from between his pale lips.

Chase rapped her knuckles hard on the glass and Henry suddenly started.

He peeled his head away from the glass and rolled down the window.

Chase put a hand on her chest, and gaped, still trying to catch her breath.

"Chase?" Henry asked, wiping the drool from the corner of his mouth. "You okay? What's wrong?"

Chase's eyes narrowed behind her sunglasses.

I thought you were dead, she wanted to say. *I thought that you were the Butterfly Killer's fourth victim.*

"I'm here to relieve you," Chase said flatly. She was pissed that he had fallen asleep, but her relief at him being still alive forced her anger away for the time being.

Detective Yasiv nodded nervously.

"It's *ughh*—it's a little early, isn't it?"

Chase flipped up her sunglasses and glared at him.

"I think it's plenty late for you, don't you?"

If his face had been red with embarrassment before, it was bordering on crimson now.

"Yeah, I just, ugh, I have a newborn and, uh, the—"

"Go home, Hank. Go home and get some sleep," Chase ordered.

"Yeah, I just—"

"Go home," Chase repeated more sternly as she made her way back to her car.

No sooner had she slipped into the cream leather seats of her BMW, the tail lights of Hank's Toyota flicked on. A second later, he was gone, and Chase was alone.

Chapter 67

DRAKE HUNG UP HIS phone and tossed it onto the passenger seat.

No answer.

He had called Dr. Kruk three times, and all three times it had gone to voicemail.

He sped toward the strip mall that housed his psychiatry office with purpose. If anyone knew who or where Marcus Slasinsky was, it would be him. Drake was sure of it.

After all, he had a notepad with the boy's name on it on his desk when he had arrived.

Drake pulled into the parking lot and his heart sunk when he saw that the lights to the office at the end were off. In fact, the entire lot was empty. He took the empty parking spot directly in front of the office and jumped out a split second after jamming his car into park.

He tried the door first but found it locked. Without much hope, he made a fist and banged on the door.

"Dr. Kruk? Dr. Kruk, I need to speak to you," he said loudly.

Come on, come on. Please be here, please be here...

He knocked again and again.

The way Drake saw it was that he had two options: to call in for a warrant or to wait until Dr. Kruk arrived to work next.

Getting a warrant was a laughable prospect; even if he hadn't been booted off the case, and if for some reason Rhodes hadn't sent out a patrol to arrest him for obstruction, there was no way a judge would facilitate a warrant.

As for waiting for the doctor to arrive? It was Friday evening—the doctor wouldn't be in until Monday at the earliest.

No, Drake couldn't wait, either.

There was of, course, a third option, Drake thought as his eyes drifted to the trunk of his car where he kept a crowbar. Just as he made a move toward his Crown Vic, he heard a lock disengaging, and the door opened a crack.

It was the secretary he had met a few days ago.

"Is Dr. Kruk here?" Drake asked, trying to keep his voice neutral.

The woman, who was in her mid-sixties with a shock of pitch-black hair, eyed him suspiciously.

"Who are you?" she asked.

Drake flipped out his detective shield.

"Detective Damien Drake, I was here yesterday, remember?"

Drake was growing impatient. If Dr. Kruk was in his office, then he had to speak to him immediately. The man could use as many abstract analogies as he could muster, but Drake would get him to reveal who and where Marcus was.

He had to; he had to before someone else was murdered.

The woman's eyes suddenly widened.

"Ah, yes, I remember now. I'm sorry, Detective, but Dr. Kruk hasn't been in today."

Drake swore under his breath.

"I—I need to come in," he said.

The woman's brow furrowed.

"I'm not sure that's such a good idea," she said hesitantly. "Dr. Kruk is—"

Drake shook his head.

"It's important. I left something here," Drake said, thinking quickly. He knew that in this instance, his red eyes and disheveled appearance might come in handy.

And he also knew that what he was about to do would not only put the nail in his proverbial coffin but would also toss the first few shovelfuls of dirt on his career.

Fuck, they might even forgo the coffin altogether and bury him alive.

But that didn't matter.

"I left something about a very important case... forgot it in his office. I'm sure you know which one I'm talking about?"

The woman looked confused and then suddenly extended a finger at him. As she did, the door opened a little more and Drake leaned in to make sure she couldn't close it again.

"The Butter—"

"Shh, don't say it. I mean, I'm in so much trouble, I just need to get the file back."

She shrugged.

"Tell me what it looks like and I'll see if I can find it for you."

Drake shook his head emphatically.

"I can't... it's about the case and if..." he let his sentence trail off, grimacing the whole time.

The woman offered him a wan smile in return.

"Okay, come on in. But please, be quick. Dr. Kruk is fairly particular about people being in his office without him being present."

Drake suppressed a smile. When the secretary opened the door, he quickly pushed by her and went straight to Dr. Kruk's office door. He tried the knob.

It was locked. He jiggled the knob, confirming that it was a flimsy, brass-coated piece of plastic.

Worst case scenario he could break it off.

"Do you have the key?"

The woman looked a little apprehensive now.

"Yes," she answered.

"Then please, do you mind? I mean, you can watch me in there if you would feel more comfortable. I'm just looking for my file, that's all."

This seemed to calm her nerves, as she nodded and then fetched a single key from the top drawer of her desk.

Some security system, Drake thought.

When she came over to him, he quickly took it from her hand.

"Allow me," he said with a smile. As Drake fiddled with the lock, he added, "I can't thank you enough for this. Seriously, without—" the door unlocked, and he opened it.

He turned back and looked at the secretary for a moment.

"You've really helped with the investigation," he said. And then, before she could get a word in edgewise, Drake entered the room, slamming the door and locking it behind him.

"Hey! Hey Detective!" the woman shouted from the other side of the door. Drake ignored her and took a deep breath.

Then he looked down at the single key still clutched in his hand.

What's done is done, he thought as a strange sense of calm fell over him. *Now it's time to find a killer.*

Chapter 68

CHASE PRESSED HER FOREHEAD against the driver's side window, her breath fogging the glass with every breath.

She had been staring at Tim Jenkins's house for an hour now, but it felt as if it was twice or three times as long.

Mostly because nothing happened. Not so much as a light had flicked on within his residence. In fact, it was so quiet that Chase was beginning to doubt what Detective Yasiv had told her; that Tim had been dropped off by Wes Smith and had remained inside ever since.

Had he snuck out the window, as Drake had caught him doing yesterday?

Chase supposed it was possible, but why would he leave? He must know, Butterfly Killer or not, that the police would be watching him.

Did Weston Smith give him instructions to lay low? To stay out of sight?

It made sense. Anything that linked back to them, to the Smith reputation and family name, had been silenced to this point. Despite the deep-seated anger toward the Smith clan, Tim had secrets in his past that he wanted to keep buried as well.

Like being part of a group of bullies that put a young, troubled man in a coma.

Tim had been so distressed by what he had done, so affected by it, that he had foregone a prosperous career like the ones held by Thomas and Neil to work at the very place that they had nearly killed Marcus.

A sort of penance for his crime.

It was in his face when Chase had spoken to him back at the station, further corroborated by him clamming up as soon as he mentioned Neil.

Chase had been getting close, and Tim couldn't deal with it. No matter how much Tim loathed Wesley Smith *et al*, his guilt over what he had done to Marcus far outweighed his anger.

So, yeah, if Wes told him to stay low, maybe threatened to reveal Tim's involvement back then, he might just listen.

But was he a killer?

She was beginning to severely doubt it.

Chase sighed and closed her eyes. But any concept of peace and quiet from her thrumming mind was shattered when she saw Clarissa staring at her from behind her lids, her mouth twisted into a snarl.

He froze everything! Every last dime I have, he froze. I have nothing now! Absolutely nothing!

"Fuck," she whispered.

After all, she had put the woman through, she was no closer to finding her husband's killer.

Chase took another deep breath and tried to force the images from her mind.

To force everything from her thoughts.

Chapter 69

DRAKE IGNORED THE WOMAN'S pleas from the other side of the door and set to work immediately, scanning the man's desk where he had first seen the notepad with Marcus Slasinsky's name on it.

Only it wasn't there.

There were other folders emblazoned with names he didn't recognize, but not one with Marcus written on it.

"It was here," he mumbled to himself, as he continued to scan the desk.

There was a folder with Tim Jenkins's name on it, which he thought odd. But when he opened it, it was empty, and he tossed it aside.

"C'mon," he nearly moaned.

He pulled open the top drawer of the desk and a dozen pens rolled to the front. There was a pad of yellow lined paper in the drawer as well, but after flipping through it quickly, Drake realized that it was completely blank. He checked the second drawer next, but there weren't any patient notes in there either.

And definitely no notepad.

Where would he keep patient notes? He wondered, hoping that Dr. Kruk didn't keep them at an off-site location.

His eyes drifted to the bookshelf next, but there were only books on the dark wooden shelves. There was no sign of the dark green notepad he had seen.

Dr. Kruk's secretary knocked on the door again.

"Detective? Did you find the file? I really think that you should go. I think—"

"Still looking!" he shouted. "I'll only be a minute. I'm so sorry about this, but it's confidential, as you can probably understand."

And he figured that he only had a few minutes before the woman got fed up and called the police. Desperate now, Drake dropped to his knees, looking first under the desk, then under the two chairs facing each other on the other side of the room.

Still nothing.

Shaking his head in frustration, he looked around again, trying to quiet the swirling thoughts in his head, the ones that suggested that maybe the doctor took the notebook home with him for the weekend.

"Nowhere! There's nowhere—"

But then he fell silent.

There was nothing *beneath* the two blue chairs, but there was something slightly off about the one on the right. He dropped to the floor again and took another look.

The bottom of this chair sagged lower than the other one. It made sense that this chair was the doctor's, and the other the patient's, given the proximity of the former to the desk, but Dr. Kruk had been a slight man.

There's no way he made this chair sag.

Still on his knees, he scrambled over to the chair, and then turned on his back and slid beneath it like a mechanic checking a leak.

He prodded the material and found that it was indeed loose. And there was something inside; something rectangular, something that moved when he pushed.

Grasping the corner of the fabric with thumb and forefinger, he was prepared to tear it away from the chair frame. But his efforts weren't necessary. The material was fastened with Velcro and pulled away easily.

He grunted as two objects fell out, one of which hit him in the face—a book—and the other on his shoulder—some sort of three or four-inch plastic cube.

Swearing, he grabbed both items and pulled himself out from beneath the chair.

In his right hand was a book, a plain notebook with the name 'MARCUS Slasinsky' on the cover in black text—the one he had seen yesterday. In his right was a cube of either plastic or some sort of wax. Inside was a preserved Monarch butterfly.

He swallowed hard.

"Did you find it in there?" the secretary hollered.

"Yeah, I uh, I found it," Drake said, staring at the butterfly as he turned it over in his hand. "It's just, ugh, missing some pages is all, I'm going—"

He shook his head and closed his eyes.

"Fuck it," he said to himself, then to the woman on the other side of the door, he added, "I'm going to be five minutes. That's it. Five minutes and then I'll be out of here, okay?"

He didn't wait for an answer. Instead, he placed the encased butterfly on the table and then sat on one of the chairs, the one that hadn't housed the notebook, and opened it.

A grainy photograph slid out, and Drake grabbed it before it floated to the floor.

"Jesus."

It depicted a dead woman slumped on a wooden chair. Her forearms were resting on her distended belly, her palms face up. There were ragged, hunks of torn flesh hanging from her wrists. The woman's eyes were open, the corneas so opaque that they almost seemed to glow in the black and white image. Her mouth was slack, her teeth bared as the gums and lips already started to recede in death.

It's Marcus's mother, Drake thought with a shudder. He placed the photo on the table beside the butterfly, then turned his attention to the book.

He was looking for anything that would help him find Marcus Slasinsky—an address, a phone number, even a social insurance number—*anything* at all that might help locate the murderer.

To locate the Butterfly Killer.

Drake's initial elation at finding the book didn't last. Any hopes of an introductory page, a description of Marcus, perhaps, or maybe even an address, were immediately dashed.

The handwritten notepad jumped right into it in a familiar interview-style format: a single line with the name Kruk, followed by a question, and then a line with the name Marcus, followed by an answer.

Figuring that the details he sought might be buried in the doctor's interview, Drake started to read, skipping over the initial preamble.

Chapter 70

WHEN CHASE OPENED HER eyes again, the only light in the sky was from yellow incandescent street lights.

She sat bolt upright.

I fell asleep! She realized in horror. *After admonishing Detective Yasiv, I fell asleep.*

Groaning, she stretched her legs, which immediately started to cramp. Expecting the painful tensing to subside, Chase waited, but when she couldn't get her muscles to relax, she opened the door to her BMW and stepped into the street.

After rolling her neck, she reached down and touched her toes, trying to force the stiffness away. It dawned on her that part of her pain must have been from playing tennis the other day—she couldn't remember the last time she had done any strenuous exercise.

Just as she was making a mental note to pick up running again, or maybe yoga, her eyes drifted toward Tim Jenkins's house.

"What the hell?" she whispered.

The door was open. From inside her car, it hadn't been noticeable, but now that she was outside, she could clearly see that it wasn't completely closed—the door didn't quite meet the jam.

Chase continued to stare at the door for a few seconds, debating what course of action to take.

I should call Rhodes, the rational part of her brain suggested. But she knew how that conversation would go; Rhodes would tell her to wait it out.

Conflicted, Chase shut her eyes for a moment, hoping that when she opened them again, she would realize that it had all been an optical illusion and that Tim's door was really closed.

Only when she opened her eyes again, the door was still ajar.

Making up her mind, Chase unholstered her gun and strode toward the house.

Clarissa was right; fuck her career. There were lives on the line.

Chase moved swiftly across the street, crouching low, keeping her gun even lower. She didn't think that there would be anyone out at this hour—which she estimated to be around midnight—but it wouldn't do anyone any good for a nosy neighbor to call the cops.

When she reached the door, she put her hand on it, standing off to one side and away from the opening. Just a gentle push caused it to swing open two feet.

"Tim? Tim Jenkins?" she said into the dark interior of the house.

There was no answer.

Struck by a sudden sense of déjà vu, minus, of course, Drake's presence, she opened the door even further.

"Tim? It's Detective Adams," she said, announcing her presence louder this time. "I'm coming inside."

When there was still no answer, Detective Chase Adams stepped through the doorway.

Chapter 71

Excerpt from Dr. Mark Kruk's notes, dated March 1st, 2017.

Kruk: Now, I want you to tell me about your childhood, Marcus. About your parents.

Marcus: Well, it wasn't always so good. Daddy was mean a lot. He would get angry all the time—like real angry.

Kruk: Did he yell at you?

Marcus: Oh, yes, all the time. And when he got really angry, he would hit me and mommy.

Kruk: He would physically strike you?

Marcus: Yes. And sometimes…

Kruk: You can tell me, Marcus. This is a safe place.

Marcus: Sometimes he would put cigarettes out on me. On my back, and on my hands.

Kruk: And what would your mother do when your father put out cigarettes on you?

Marcus: She would only cry. She would just sit there and cry. This would only make Daddy madder. He would punch her until she stopped.

Kruk: Did your mother ever call the police or tell anyone about what your father did to you?

Marcus: I don't know. I don't think so.

Kruk: Did you tell anyone?

Marcus: No.

Kruk: And why not? Why didn't you tell a teacher or a friend at school?

Marcus: I didn't.

Kruk: But why not, Marcus? Why didn't you tell?

Marcus: The kids... the kids at school made fun of me. Called me names when I came with bruises.

Kruk: That's okay, Marcus. You're doing a good thing by speaking to me today. Please, take your time and if you need a break, just let me know.

Marcus: I'm fine.

Kruk: Okay, then we'll continue. When did your father stop hitting you?

Marcus: One day he went to work, and just never came home.

Kruk: And then it was just you and your mother?

Marcus: Yes.

Kruk: Did things get better after your dad was gone?

Marcus: No—a little.

Kruk: Can you explain what you mean?

Marcus: Mommy never hit me or yelled at me. But she was always crying. Always, always crying. The only time she would stop crying is when she would sleep.

Kruk: How old are you, Marcus?

Marcus: Eight—almost nine.

Kruk: And after your Daddy left, did your mommy make you food? Breakfast? Dinner? Did she help you get ready for school?

Marcus: No. She only cried. I had to do everything for myself. But I was so, so tired. Only I couldn't sleep because every time I tried, I could hear her crying. And I was scared.

Kruk: Why were you scared? Were you scared that your father would come home?

Marcus: Yes; I was scared that he would come home and get angry because Mommy was crying.

Kruk: Did the crying ever stop, Marcus?

Marcus: I don't want to say.

Kruk: It's okay, Marcus, you won't get in trouble. Remember, this is a safe place, and I'm here to help you.

Marcus: You promise?

Kruk: I promise.

Marcus: Mommy fell asleep in her chair one day after Daddy left, and I was just so tired. Only I knew that as soon as *I* tried to go to sleep that she would wake up and start crying again. I was so, so tired.

Kruk: What happened next, Marcus?

Marcus: I went to the kitchen and opened the drawer with the adult knives. I wasn't supposed to go in there, but I couldn't ask her, because all she did was sleep and cry. I had been in there before when I needed to cut open a bag of chips—there wasn't much food in the house. And then I walked over to Mommy and tried to wake her up, to ask her not to cry anymore.

Kruk: And then what happened?

Marcus: She wouldn't wake up, so I cut her. I cut her arms, her wrists. There was... there was so much blood and I thought that she was going to wake up and get mad at me for getting her dress dirty. It was her favorite dress, she used to say that. It was the one that daddy liked best.

Chapter 72

THE NOTEBOOK TREMBLED IN Drake's hands and his eyes darted to the photograph of Marcus's mother dead in her chair.

Beckett and Dunbar had been wrong.

Martha Slasinsky didn't commit suicide, she was murdered.

She was murdered by her son.

"Jesus," Drake whispered.

Who are you, Marcus Slasinsky?

He shuddered, then started reading again, the air in the office suddenly feeling very, very cold.

Chapter 73

Excerpt from Dr. Mark Kruk's notes, dated March 1st, 2017.

Kruk: What did you do after your mother stopped bleeding?

Marcus: I tried to wake her up again, but she just kept sleeping.

Kruk: And then what did you do?

Marcus: I made dinner and went to sleep. It was… it was the best sleep I ever had. Mommy didn't wake me up crying at all.

Kruk: And the next morning?

Marcus: I made breakfast, kissed mommy on the lips and went to school.

Kruk: Alright. Now I want you to move ahead a little bit. I want you to tell me about the butterfly.

Marcus: Okay—it came around the time that the neighbor lady asked me if everything was okay. She said that there was a smell in the hallway and wanted to know if we had a problem with the toilet. I told her everything was fine and when she asked to talk to Mommy, I said she was sleeping. I told the woman that Mommy was very happy now, that she had stopped crying. The lady went away, and I opened the window just in case.

Kruk: And then what happened? Where did the butterfly come from?

Marcus: Every morning before I went to school, I kissed Mommy on the lips and told her I loved her. Then, one day, when I kissed her, I felt her lips move. At first, I thought she was waking up, and I was very happy—only she didn't open her eyes. I watched as her lips moved and I thought she was trying to tell me something. I leaned in close and then the most beautiful thing I have ever seen came out of her mouth.

Kruk: A Monarch butterfly?

Marcus: Not just any butterfly—the most beautiful butterfly that ever lived! It had bright orange wings and black spots on them that looked like tiger eyes. I let it walk onto my finger and when it stretched its wings, I kissed it; it was like kissing Mommy, but instead, I was giving the butterfly kisses.

Chapter 74

DRAKE WAS AWARE THAT he was clenching his jaw and that his stomach muscles were so tight that they were making it difficult to breathe, but there was nothing he could do to make them relax.

What had happened to the boy was horrible, unimaginable.

But there was also something very strange about the transcript.

Dr. Kruk himself didn't look a day over forty, and yet Martha Slasinsky was murdered something like thirty years ago. He couldn't possibly be the psychiatrist who had seen the boy back then.

What about after the coma?

That didn't make much sense either; even if he overlooked the fact that in the notes Marcus claimed to be eight, and very much spoke like an eight-year-old might, Dr. Kruk had to be less than twenty at the time of the incident at the Butterfly Gardens.

And the notes themselves were dated from earlier in the month.

It doesn't make sense.

Drake scanned forward in the notebook. It was filled with pages and pages of the same format: Kruk with the question, Marcus with his answer.

It went on and on and on, with seemingly no end.

Frustration began to mount inside him, and his thoughts suddenly flicked to Suzan, and the way that she had screamed at him, told him that he had ruined their lives.

Drake placed the notebook on the table, and then picked up the butterfly encased in the plastic and stared at it as he turned it slowly in his hand.

It was bright orange, just like the one that Marcus had described. Even the dark spots on the majestic wings appeared to look like cat's eyes, vertical slits that ran their length.

Where are you, Marcus? Where the hell are you now?

Drake closed his eyes, and he was instantly bombarded with an image of Clay's face, blood and spit clinging to his bearded chin. In his mind, Drake leaned in close to his friend's lips as they parted, half expecting to hear his final words.

Only they weren't words. They were the wings of a butterfly as it emerged from his dead mouth.

Drake shot to his feet.

"Where are you Marcus!" he yelled and flung the crystal butterfly with all of his might.

The cube flew across the small office and struck the end panel of the bookcase.

Drake expected one of two things to happen: either the cube would shatter, or it would *thonk* off the wood and leave a dent.

Only neither happened. Instead, the butterfly made a scraping sound and embedded itself in the wood.

"What the hell?" he muttered.

"Is everything okay in there, Detective?"

Drake ignored the secretary on the other side of the door and quickly made his way over to the bookcase. The entire structure looked to be made of solid wood, except for the section at the very end where the cube had struck and was now embedded in. This section appeared to be made of veneer. Drake grabbed the cube and pulled it free and his suspicions were confirmed.

Without thinking, he put his hand in the hole and pulled. The veneer, which he realized ran floor to ceiling, bowed outward but didn't come free.

Drake pulled again, and although this time he heard splintering wood, it still held fast.

"Detective!" the woman shouted, her voice shrill now. "*Detective!*"

Drake forced the first two fingers of both hands in the hole now.

"Oh, shut the fuck up," he muttered and then yanked with all his might.

The veneer came free in one long sheet, and Drake stumbled backward. He tripped on his heels and went down, pulling the veneer on top of himself.

He swore and thrust it aside before turning his attention back to the bookcase.

Despite all the air being sucked out of him, he was still somehow able to utter three words.

"Oh my god," he whispered as suddenly everything became clear.

Chapter 75

"NYPD! I'M INSIDE YOUR home, Tim!" Chase shouted. "I'm inside!"

There was still no answer, and Chase felt adrenaline flood her system. She quickly scanned the rooms near the entrance, then made her way upstairs.

Her heart was beating rapidly in her chest when she made it to the top landing. She gave a cursory glance around but went straight for the bedroom that she had found Tim in when he had tried to escape out the window.

The window was still open, which she found odd, but she was grateful for the moonlight that flooded in.

Chase found Tim lying on his stomach in his bed, the covers pulled up to the back of his neck.

"Tim?" she whispered. Chase stared closely at his still frame for a few seconds, a feeling of dread starting to wash over her.

He wasn't breathing.

"Tim!" she said more loudly this time. Gun still at the ready in case this was some sort of ploy, she reached down and grabbed the bedsheet.

Chase took a deep breath and then yanked it down.

"No," she moaned as the moonlight reflected off the bloody butterfly drawn on Tim Jenkins's back, giving it a strange blueish hue.

How is this possible?

The sound of a car backfiring drifted up to her from the open window and she rushed over to it. Leading with the gun, she scanned the street, wondering how she had let this happen.

How *any* of this had happened.

Chapter 76

THE SCARS ON DR. Kruk's hand that he had seen when they had first met, the reason why Marcus was only eight in a journal dated less than a month ago, and his cryptic comments—*People only see what they want to see. Our minds are wired in this way—an imago. This picture? It's much like everything else in the image we portray to others: just an empty shell*—it all added up to one thing: Dr. Mark Kruk *was* Marcus Slasinsky.

He swallowed hard and stared up at the glass aquariums with a mixture of awe and horror. Drake counted seven of them in total, each roughly a foot and a half tall, and if he were to assume that they were the same width as the bookcase, about a foot wide.

The bottom three were filled with dirt, upon which lay scattered leaves. There were dozens of caterpillars milling about the soil, either eating or resting atop the leaves. The sight made his stomach lurch.

The other aquariums were filled with the most beautiful array of butterflies he had ever seen. Most were monarchs, their orange and yellow wings making a fiery rainbow as they fluttered. But there were others, too, other types of butterflies with names that Drake didn't know, including bright blue ones, green ones, ones with shimmering wings like miniature peacock feathers.

It was only then that Drake was aware of the meaty smell of old earth filling his nostrils. And it was this smell that snapped him from the mixture of horror and beauty of what he saw.

Drake scrambled to his feet and reached for his phone. It snagged in his pocket, and for the first time in his life, he wished that it wasn't a thick brick but something slim and sleek like Chase's.

Chase!

The name ripped through his brain like a skewer through an overripe avocado.

"Detective!" the woman veritably screamed. "I called the police!"

Drake finally got his phone free.

"Good!" he yelled back. "Tell them to hurry!"

Then with a final, shuddering breath, Drake dialed Chase's number, hoping that he reached her in time.

Chapter 77

THE MAN IN BLACK watched as the detective with the dark hair came into the room, waving her gun about like a road flare. He watched as she slowly crept toward the body in the bed, her steps slowing as she neared Tim Jenkins.

His lips parted in a grin when she pulled the sheet back and gasped when his artwork was revealed.

A car backfired, and the detective bolted to the window. As she did, the man slipped his gloved fingers through the crack between the closet door and the frame and slowly eased it open. Sliding silently into the room, he froze when a phone started ringing. She almost turned then, and he knew he had to act quickly. When the detective lowered her gun to pull a cell phone from her pocket, he moved even closer.

"Yeah?" she said breathlessly, her brow furrowing. "What, slow down! I… *what?* It's *who?* Drake, what are you saying?"

The man was close enough now that he could smell her perfume, a gentle vanilla aroma, mixed with her sweet, adrenaline-laden sweat.

"Tim's dead," she whispered. "I—"

He snaked an arm over her mouth while slapping her gun from her hand with his other.

She screamed and dropped the phone, but he slid the syringe into her neck before she could squirm away from him.

As her body started to go limp, shouting from the phone on the floor drifted up to him.

"Chase! Chase, are you alright? What's happening! Answer me—"

The man drove his heel onto the phone, cracking the screen. He continued to grind his boot into it until it eventually went silent.

Chapter 78

"—CHASE! STAY AWAY FROM—"

But the line suddenly sounded stifled, and Drake pulled the phone away from his face.

"Chase? You still there?"

There was only dead air.

He turned his head to the sky and shouted. Then he hung up and dialed Chase's number again.

It went immediately to voicemail.

Drake swore, dialed again, then swore again.

The woman on the other side of the door was screaming at him now, hollering that the cops were on the way, but Drake ignored her.

His mind flicked to the empty folder he had found on the desk.

The one with Tim Jenkins's name on it.

If she was out at Jenkins's place...

They were supposed to go there together, to relieve Detective Yasiv around ten. Could it be ten already? He glanced at his wrist, but he had forgotten to put his watch on last night or this morning or whenever the last time was that he had gotten changed.

He supposed it could be. There were no windows in the office, but it had been getting late when he had arrived, and there was no telling how much time he had wasted reading the damn notebook.

I have to get to her. I have to save her.

Even though every fiber of his being was telling him to run, to get in his car and drive across the city to Tim Jenkins's house, he didn't.

At least not right away.

Instead, he glanced over at the butterflies. The cases weren't all the same size, he realized. The one on top, the one just at arm's reach was smaller and there appeared to have a handle.

It was portable.

Drake ran over to the bookcase and then stood on his tiptoes, trying to block out the smell as he reached up. His fingertips grazed the bottom of the portable aquarium and teased it out. With a grunt, he lifted it and it fell off the shelf and into his waiting arms.

And then he tucked it beneath his right arm and bolted toward the door, unlocking it and throwing it wide.

Dr. Kruk's secretary backed away as he leaped through the opening, her face going slack.

"Wh—what is that?" she gasped, pointing at the case under his arm filled with a cornucopia of butterflies.

"When the police come, tell them to head to Tim Jenkins's house. Do you have that—"

The woman gaped, but that wasn't why Drake paused. He paused because what he was saying didn't make sense. If Dr. Kruk—if Marcus Slasinsky—was at Tim's house, then he either already had Chase or she had him in custody. Either way, it would do him no good to go there.

And if they *weren't* there, then they would be somewhere else. He thought back to when he had been sitting in the car with Chase before they had brought Tim in the first time.

He had been reading the report that Detective Yasiv had put together, the line about—

And then it clicked.

"No!" he shouted at the secretary, who recoiled as if she had been struck. "Not Jenkins's house! Tell them to get to the Butterfly Gardens! Can you remember that?"

Drake was running toward the front door as he spoke.

"Can you remember that? Can you *remember?*" he cried as he jammed his palm into the door and thrust it open.

He thought he saw the woman nod but couldn't be sure. It didn't matter, anyway.

By the time the cops got there, it would be too late.

It was up to him now. It was up to him to save his partner.

Drake sprinted through the night, threw the container of butterflies on the passenger seat, and then sped out of the parking lot.

Chapter 79

WITH THE POLICE CHERRY on his dash illuminating the night in blue and red hues, Drake's rusty Crown Vic sped across the city. He didn't know exactly where the Butterfly Gardens were, but he had a vague idea based on Detective Yasiv's notes. And less than half an hour later, he located the first road sign directing him to the Gardens. Scheduled for destruction or not, the wheels of Road Bureaucracy turned slowly in NYC, and the signs gave no impression that the Gardens were closed.

When he got close, Drake switched the cherry off and slowed to a crawl. The front gate leading to the parking lot was bent backward just far enough for him to weave his car through all the while staring at the looming geodesic dome in front of him. The moon was full and bright, and its blue rays reflected off the gray surface of the Butterfly Gardens with such intensity that it almost seemed to glow.

Drake shut off his headlights next and then cut the engine entirely. One of the perks of such an old car was that he could coast in neutral even with the engine off.

And that's what he did now. The large parking lot was mostly empty, save a series of bulldozers haphazardly parked and a small corrugated storage container off to one side. But as he neared the front doors to the Gardens, he spotted a car tucked within the shadow of the dome.

It was a black, or maybe navy blue, BMW.

Drake's heart sunk.

She was here. And the only reason she would be here was because *he* had brought her here.

An image of Chase Adams on her stomach, hands and feet bound behind her, her throat swollen closed, that awful butterfly scrawl on her back flashed in his mind.

No, he thought with such veracity that his teeth snapped closed with an audible *snap. I won't lose another partner.*

He grabbed the gun that Chase had given him from the glove box, then hooked his other hand through the handle on the butterfly box.

As quietly as possible, Drake left his car and made his way toward the entrance to the Butterfly Gardens.

Like the gate by the front of the parking lot, this door was partly open; someone had pried the flimsy lock off and it lay broken on the sidewalk.

Drake silently slipped inside, moving quickly away from the entrance, pressing his back against a wall bathed in shadows.

And then he waited; waited and listened.

The layout to the Butterfly Gardens appeared simple enough, the nature of which Drake had even guessed from the images on the signs leading up to it: a narrow hallway flanked on either side by washrooms, a cafeteria, and gift shops extending away from the entrance before it blossomed into a giant geodesic dome.

And that's where they'll be, he thought. Marcus would take Chase to the location that he had been brought by those damn kids all those years ago.

The spot where he had collapsed into a coma.

Drake waited until he caught his breath, then started to strafe along the wall toward the dome.

He had only taken half a dozen steps when something brushed against his foot and he kicked at it instinctively. A rat hissed and then skittered away, and Drake cursed himself for being so careless. The only thing he had going for him now was surprise. And if Dr. Kruk's secretary did as bid, then the night would soon be alive with sirens.

Moonlight couldn't penetrate the dark hallway, but ahead, where it opened to the dome, Drake could see shards of light illuminating the area in swashes of gray and blue.

He took ten steps, then twenty.

Thirty.

And then he stopped, trying to calm his breathing.

He heard a voice.

It was a man's voice, or maybe a child's; it was difficult to tell as the sound funneled down the hallway to him.

"You are going to give me a kiss, just like Mommy did."

A chill shot up Drake's spine as the image of Martha Slasinsky, propped on her chair, wrists ragged flashed in his mind.

"You are going to give me a kiss, pretty lady."

Drake picked up the pace, moving quickly now, sacrificing silence for speed. He paused only when he got to the mouth of the hallway.

The dome opened before him as he expected, but what Drake wasn't prepared for was the vegetation. It appeared gray in the moonlight, but he thought that it might very well be the same color by the noonday sun. Leaves of massive plants in various states of decay nearly blocked his passage.

Drake slunk low, using the decomposing foliage to hide his form as he moved toward the voice.

It didn't take long before he saw them. For a moment, he simply stood there, ramrod straight, not believing his eyes.

Chase was in the center of the dome, standing on some sort of platform, her arms pulled behind her and tied around a pole that ascended all the way to the metal triangles that made up the dome high above.

There was a rag in her mouth, and her eyes were wide.

A man stood beside her, his back to Drake. It was Dr. Kruk as he remembered him from the day in his office: tall, lean, with a thin neck and spindly arms.

Only it wasn't.

The man's posture was different. No longer was he adroit, giving off a sense of professionalism, of authority. Now, his arms hung low at his sides, dangling almost.

He looked as he had in the yearbook photograph, which had captured him half in and half out of the frame.

The single photograph that Ken Smith had missed.

Chase blinked once, twice, and then her eyes seemed to focus on him. When recognition washed over her features, Drake realized that he was still standing in the open. Without thinking, he dove to his left, landing softly on several broad leaves that turned to dust as he fell.

It was almost a perfect landing—a perfectly *silent* landing. And it would have been, too, if not for the butterfly case.

One of the corners clinked off an area of exposed ground and instantly filled the air with the sound of cracking glass.

Drake ducked his head beneath some half-dead shrubs just as Dr. Kruk whipped around.

"Who's there?" the man cried.

Drake cursed, trying to figure out the best course of action.

In the end, it was Dr. Kruk who pressed his hand.

"I've got a gun, and I will kill this woman," he said flatly.

And there it was, the cool air of professionalism that had been missing in his stature.

Drake swallowed hard before tucking Chase's spare gun into his rear waistband and slowly pushing himself to his feet.

Chapter 80

"**Marcus, it's me,**" **Drake** said holding his hands out to his sides to show that he was unarmed. "It's Detective Drake."

Marcus Slasinsky had slipped behind Chase and peered over her shoulder at him, a gun aimed at her temple. He didn't think that his partner's eyes could possibly grow any wider, but it seemed that they did until the whites on either side of her hazel irises glistened in the moonlight.

"Ah, Detective Drake. I thought I might be seeing you again," he shrugged. "Actually, I thought that I might meet up with you sooner. Did you come for your gun or the girl?"

Drake squinted hard, trying to focus on the gun. It was hard to tell from his distance, but it could very well have been his.

"You stole it from my car?"

"It seemed I overestimated you. At the time, I thought you were getting close, and I couldn't risk being caught. I still had work to do. I had to make them pay."

Drake shook his head.

"You made them pay. All of them—they're all dead now. You killed them all: Chris, Thomas, Neil, and Tim. It was… it was terrible what they did to you. But Chase—Detective Adams—she hasn't done anything. She doesn't deserve this."

The man shook his head, and he seemed to get younger as he did. He moved away from Chase and grabbed the sides of his head with both hands, including the one clutching what Drake now recognized as his service pistol.

"You don't understand… they brought me here and the… and the butterflies… they were *everywhere*—all around. And then they started crying—mocking me. I can't *stand* the crying."

And then Drake saw that the man—a boy now, eight years old again living with his rotting mother's corpse—was the one with tears on his cheeks.

"It's over, Marcus. It's all over."

Marcus sniffed and then laughed.

"I forgot all about it… years in psychiatric care made me forget. First about Mommy, then about what those bastards did to me. But… but when Thomas and his wife…" his sentence trailed off and he stared upward, gazing at the moon.

"It was a ploy, Marcus. Don't you see that? You were set up—it was no accident that Thomas came to you. New York City is a fucked up place, with a lot of fucked up people. There must be a thousand psychiatrists… what are the odds that they came to *you*?"

Drake let his words sink in for a moment, watching as Marcus's face contorted, flicking from the rational mind of the psychiatrist to that of an abused and confused young boy.

"It was no accident," he continued, more softly this time. "It was Ken Smith, the man who gave you the money to go away after his son put you in a coma, the man who gave you the means to change your name, to get psychiatric help not only to change who you are, but who you *were*. And when it suited him, he brought Marcus back, didn't he? Ken Smith is responsible for the death of his son, for the deaths of the other boys, not you."

The man growled and he leveled the gun at Chase again.

"Woah, easy Marcus. Chase hasn't done anything to you."

The man shook his head, and his face twisted into a grimace.

"No, no, she didn't. But she kind of looks like mommy, doesn't she?" He smiled at her when he said this, and Chase moved as far away from him as she could given the way she was tied. "Yes, I kind of think she does. And I want mommy to give me a kiss again, to give me—"

"Butterfly kisses?" Drake finished for him.

Marcus pulled away from Chase, his brow furrowing in confusion.

"You—how?" His face relaxed. "You found my notes, didn't you?"

Drake nodded. A flash of color danced in his periphery, reminding him of the butterfly container that he had dropped and nearly smashed. He inched his foot closer to it.

"It doesn't matter," Marcus said, shaking his head again. He slid a container from his pocket, something clear that the moonlight shot through—save a thick, wriggling black shape. "There is only one thing left to do."

Marcus reached over and pulled the rag from Chase's mouth. She gasped, sucking in a huge lungful of air. And then he started unscrewing the cap with one hand.

Drake suddenly realized what the man was going to do, and it made him sick to his stomach. It wasn't just the caterpillar—it was the fact that Martha Slasinsky had been dead when she had given her son the Butterfly Kiss, the one that had made what he had done all okay.

The one act that proved to Marcus that his mother loved him after all.

As if on cue, Marcus popped the top of the container off. Chase's eyes locked on the wriggling caterpillar, her lips mumbling *no, no, no, no* repeatedly. She didn't see Marcus's other hand, the one with the gun that slowly rose toward the back of her head.

Drake didn't think, he just acted. His right foot shot out, colliding with the flat side of the butterfly case. The sound of cracking and then shattering glass drew Marcus's attention and he spun in his direction.

Drake remained completely still, arms still out, hoping that he had smashed the case this time. When no butterflies fluttered in front of him, however, his heart sunk.

"Please, Marcus. She's done nothing to you. Let—"

And then, just as he was about to give up hope, a flutter of movement caught his eye.

A butterfly lazily took flight, its wings unfurling as if they had been damp and only now started to dry.

"Wha—" Marcus started, but as he noticed the butterfly, he gasped and stumbled backward.

And then, in an instant, two dozen butterflies were suddenly airborne, the moonlight changing their orange wings into shimmering shades of blue.

Marcus screamed, and when that sound faded, Drake heard something else.

The sound of Chase crying.

Drake didn't hesitate, he reached behind him, pulled the pistol from his belt and then strode forward, firing two shots in rapid succession.

The first bullet missed, tearing through the foliage behind both Marcus and Chase.

The second, however, struck Marcus in the side, just above his left hip. The force of the impact sent him reeling, the pistol— Drake's pistol—flying from his hand.

He went down, hard, a cry of his own on his lips.

Drake sprinted forward, ignoring Chase's moans. In a matter of seconds, he was hovering over Marcus's fallen body.

The man's mouth was open, his eyes rolled back in his head. The caterpillar and the gun were gone, and he was holding his side. Blood leaked through his thin fingers.

"Just make the crying stop," Marcus sobbed, in a high-pitched voice. "Please, just make it stop forever."

For a brief moment, Drake felt sorry for him.

Beaten by his father, forced to live with his dead mother's corpse for nearly a month. And if that wasn't enough, tormented by bullies to such a degree that he had fallen into a coma.

But then Drake remembered his partner, Clay, and the way he had been murdered.

That was someone who deserved pity. Not this man. This man was a cold-blooded killer.

Drake straddled Marcus Slasinsky.

"You killed my partner," he hissed.

Marcus's eyes flipped forward, and they were boy's eyes again, eyes that had seen torment and horror well beyond their eight years.

"You killed my partner," Drake said again, this time more forcefully. "You killed my *fucking* partner!"

He raised the gun and aimed it directly at Marcus's face.

"You—"

"I'm not dead!" Chase screamed from somewhere behind him. "I'm not dead, Drake! I'm right here! I'm right here! *Please!*"

Drake ground his teeth and drowned her out.

"You killed my partner," Drake said again, only this time his voice was low, almost a whisper. "You killed Clay."

And then he pulled the trigger.

Chapter 81

DRAKE WATCHED FROM THE audience as Detective Chase Adams slid in behind the array of microphones sporting the same white blouse that she had been wearing when she had addressed the media a few days prior.

"Good morning," Chase began. Drake thought that she looked pretty good, given what she had been through and how little sleep—next to zero—she had gotten. "It is with a heavy heart that we mourn the loss of another one of our own: last night, Tim Jenkins, thirty-eight years of age, was murdered by the same man who took Thomas Smith, Neil Pritchard, and now we are fairly certain a Montreal restaurateur Chris Papadopoulos from us."

Drake had to smile; after all this time, Chase finally got his name right. His smile faded when a reporter in the audience, a man standing directly beside Drake called out.

"Is the Butterfly Killer dead?"

Chase held up a hand as if to say, one moment please, and then continued.

"Although we continue to mourn the loss of good men, of true New Yorkers, we will also sleep a little easier tonight knowing that their murderer has been apprehended."

A small cheer, demure, but audible, rippled through the crowd.

Chase held up a hand again, and this time Drake thought he could make out red marks on her wrist from where Marcus Slasinsky had bound her.

"Is he dead? There are rumors that he was shot," someone yelled.

This was followed quickly by more shouts.

"Who was he? What's his name? What link does he have with the victims?"

Chase shook her head.

"During the apprehension of the suspect, the suspect, Dr. Mark Kruk, nee Marcus Slasinsky, was shot and is now being treated in critical care. He is, however, expected to survive."

"Was Dr. Kruk Thomas Smith's psychiatrist?" someone yelled, and this seemed to stun Chase for a moment. But she quickly regained her composure.

"That will be all for now," the crowd groaned, but Chase pressed on. "I want to thank the city of New York, its proud citizens, and NYPD's finest for all their hard work in putting an end to the short but violent bout of terror inflicted on our beautiful City. Thank you all."

With that, she turned and left the podium, Sergeant Rhodes at her heels.

Drake started to disperse with the crowd, to head toward the entrance of 62nd precinct, when his eyes met those of a man with dark brown hair and thick grooves around his mouth.

Ivan Meitzer nodded at him, and Drake bowed his head and hurried toward the station.

***

Drake rubbed his fingers over the relief pattern on his detective badge, feeling solace in the texture, the familiar pattern of the shield, of the letters.

He would miss it, of that he was certain. But it was also his only choice.

A chance to start over.

The door opened behind him, and he slipped the badge into his pocket.

"Detective Drake," Sergeant Rhodes said flatly as he crossed behind him and then took a seat at his desk.

Neither man said anything for several moments, both eying each other up, as if waiting for the other to crack.

"Is this over?" Rhodes asked at last.

Drake was smart enough to know that he wasn't referring to the Butterfly Killer.

"I'm not sure," he replied flatly.

Rhodes leaned back in his chair.

"Your partner doesn't seem to think so. She keeps asking questions, prodding areas that shouldn't be prodded."

Drake scowled.

"You mean Ken Smith—his relationship to Marcus Slasinsky and certain members of this department. About his upcoming mayoral run."

Rhodes held his hands out to his sides and his face acquired a smug expression.

"I'm curious about that, too," Drake said, his hand slipping off the badge in his pocket. "I might just go ahead and do some prodding of my own, maybe speak to a friend or two at the Times, see what they can dig up."

Rhodes offered a wan smile and pulled a folder out of the top drawer of his desk. He opened it, then spun two photographs around for Drake to see. The first was of him winking at the camera in the chrome elevator. The second was also of him, only now he was sitting across from Ken, a drink in his hand, a smile on the latter's face.

"Looks like you're the one with a connection to the man in question. But nobody needs to know about what we do in our personal lives, do they, Drake?" he paused only long enough to let his words sink in. "Look, your partner has a bright future as a Detective. She's good—smart, dedicated. She'll go far, and maybe she'll be sitting in this seat someday."

Drake squinted at Rhodes as he waited for the man to get to the point.

"But," he held a hand up, "but she's made some mistakes. Some very serious errors that could jeopardize everything."

"What are you talking about?" Drake snapped.

Rhodes's eyes shot up.

"Well, taking evidence, for one, destroying the chain of custody. This won't go over well with the DA if Marcus or Dr. Kruk or whatever the fuck his name ever makes it to trial."

Drake could feel anger building inside him.

"What evidence? What are you talking about?"

Rhodes had the gall to smile at Drake, his face so dripping with contempt that it looked like a melting candle.

"The cell phone for one. Thomas Smith's cell phone."

Drake leaned backward.

"What? *I* took the cell phone, not Chase."

Rhodes shrugged.

"Who's to say?"

"*I'm* saying, that's who. I took the damn cell phone."

"Someone also broke into Dr. Kruk's office without a warrant. Now, the secretary—a nice woman, but old and forgetful—says that a detective tricked her to gain access to his office. She says that it was a man with an athletic build, closely cropped hair that's getting a little gray at the temples. But I'm not so sure about her memory. I mean, I'm positive it was a detective who broke in, but it doesn't have to be someone tall, does it? It could have just as easily been someone shorter—*much* shorter. Someone with brown hair and hazel eyes, maybe. What do you think, Drake?"

Drake shook his head, realizing what the man was trying to do.

"You bastard—it was me who broke into the office, you know that. I even told her my name."

"What I *know* is irrelevant. It's not for me to *know* things, Drake; my job is just to present the evidence and for the DA to decide. Now, if a senior detective were to admit to some of these more benign transgressions, while at the same time handing in his badge, well that might carry some clout, don't you think? That might take the guesswork and memory problems out of the equation. Speaking in hypotheticals, of course."

Drake felt like leaping over the table and punching the pompous prick in the face. But he restrained himself.

"And it would go over even better if said detective had a little chat with the newcomer, just a friendly conversation to let her know that the Butterfly Killer has been captured and that the case is closed."

Drake chewed the inside of his lip.

With a deep breath, he reached into his pocket and took out his badge. He stroked the ridges again as he stared down at the brass shield.

"I'd ask you for your gun, but that's in evidence, isn't it?"

Drake tossed the detective shield onto Rhodes's desk. It bounced once, twice, and then landed in the man's lap.

Then he stood and started toward the door.

"I'd say you're going to be missed, Drake, but then again, I'm not a liar."

Drake's hand hesitated above the doorknob. Then he grabbed it, a smile firmly etched on his face.

Epilogue

TWO WEEKS AFTER SHOOTING the Butterfly Killer, Damien Drake found himself back at Patty's Diner. Only this time he was clean-shaven, his hair neatly coiffed, and he was wearing a fresh shirt.

All in all, he felt pretty good—he felt alive again. The NYPD had sucked a lot out of him, and the idea that the pieces of his soul that had eked away with every case could never be replaced had proven wrong.

Off the drink, Drake could see things more clearly now. He had even almost come to terms with hovering over Marcus Slasinsky, moving the gun a foot to one side before pulling the trigger.

With how close he had come to murdering a man in cold blood.

Broomhilda strode over to him, a scowl on her face.

"The usual?" she asked in a bored tone.

Drake smiled and shook his head.

"No, just black coffee and some of that spectacular Key lime pie."

The waitress grunted, then turned back to the kitchen.

As he waited, Drake's eyes drifted toward the door. The smile fell off his face when it opened and a man in a dark k-way jacket stepped through.

And he didn't look at all pleased.

"I'm still waiting for my exclusive, Drake," Ivan Meitzer said even before he had taken a seat.

Drake had been dreading this encounter. Chase's words started to echo in his head, the ones she had pleaded with him after he had told her that he was done with being a detective and that she should close the Butterfly Killer case.

Please, I made a promise... to Clarissa Smith. Please keep her family out of this, Drake. I'm begging you.

Drake smiled again, only this time it wasn't quite genuine.

"I'm sorry, Ivan. As you probably know, I'm not with the NYPD anymore."

The man scowled.

"So?"

"So, as far as I'm concerned my business with you ended when I left the force."

Ivan pressed his lips together and shook his head. Although clearly disappointed, Drake could tell that the man must have seen this coming.

"I figured as much. You know Drake, you've burnt so many bridges over the past few months that you're pretty much stuck on an island."

Drake shrugged.

"I think I'm going to enjoy island life."

Still scowling, Ivan stood and as he did, he withdrew a yellow envelope and threw it on the table. There was something hard inside and it cracked loudly off the cheap plastic top.

"I wouldn't be so sure," Ivan said, and then turned and left the diner.

Drake stared at the envelope for a long time. It lay untouched even after Broomhilda had brought him the suspicious Key lime pie and had filled his mug with steaming tar.

Don't open it. Drake, don't open it.

And for a while, he thought he might be able to leave it — to just get up, exit the diner and never touch the envelope. But he couldn't do that. After all, associated with the NYPD or not, Drake was still his *imago*.

He slid a finger between the seal and the envelope and flicked it open. Then he reached inside.

In addition to the hard object, there was also a sheet of paper inside. He pulled the paper out first, then grabbed the hard object, roughly the size of a dice, and squeezed it tightly in his palm without looking at it.

On the paper was a single word: *RESOURCES*.

Drake swore and he turned his head skyward. As he did, his eyes passed the television above the bar.

Ken Smith's face filled the screen, and although the TV was muted, the banner across the bottom told him everything he needed to know.

Kenneth Smith, father of victim Thomas Smith, formally announces his bid for New York City Mayor.

Drake closed his eyes and shook his head. When he opened them again, he found himself staring at the object in his palm.

It was a single phalanx, a gleaming bone from the end of a human finger.

The Skeleton King's calling card.

Drake felt wetness on his cheeks, but did nothing to wipe the tears away.

Broomhilda appeared at his side almost instantly.

"Everything alright, mister?" she asked, her tone surprisingly compassionate.

"Fine," Drake said. "Just get me a Johnny Red. And make it a double, neat."

END

Author's note

Special thanks go to *Pizzeria Magpie*, which is a real restaurant in Montreal… and one of my favorites. If you're ever in town, hit up *Magpies* and let Boris know that you read about the place in *Butterfly Kisses*—I'm sure he'll hook you up with something. And no, there have been no murders in the restaurant (as of yet), but the meatball pizza is amazing. Trust me.

Butterfly Kisses is a bit of a departure from what I normally write—namely horror—and while it has horror elements, it fits squarely in the thriller genre. As a reader, I like to genre hop, and as I progress through this adventure that is writing, it seems to be following along this path as well. If you're a hardcore horror fan of mine, don't fret; plenty more horror novels on the docket. Up first, however, is the second book in the Detective Damien Drake Series—*Cause of* Death—which is already on pre-order at your favorite ebook retailer. There will be another Drake book to follow this one, as well. I've grown attached to the supporting cast of *Butterfly Kisses* the way a wart clings to a toe, so I'm excited to announce that both Chase and Beckett will be getting their own series this year. The latter focusing on Chase's quest to become an FBI profiler, and the former of Beckett… well, being Beckett. That should be enough, shouldn't it?

I can't always pinpoint where I get my inspiration from, but for *Butterfly Kisses,* I have been influenced by several TV shows, mainly The Fall and The Killing. Another massive influence for this book, and I suspect many to come, has been the podcast *Casefile.* The first few episodes sound as if they were recorded using a potato, but the stories… *yeesh,* the true crime stories truly are more sadistic and twisted than (almost) anything I can come up with. It's on regular rotation on my podcast stream, sandwiched between Sam Harris and Joe Rogan.

If you want to sign up to my newsletter to keep apprised of sales and new releases, please visit my Facebook page: www.facebook.com/authorpatricklogan. Comments? Suggestions? Did I miss a damn typo? Just drop me a line at patrick@ptlbooks.com. I reply personally to all emails, even if it is only to inform you of an impending restraining order.

Keep reading and I'll keep writing.

Best,
Patrick
Montreal, 2017

Made in United States
North Haven, CT
11 May 2024

52323636R10232